Jonathan Myerson was born in Cardiff and educated in London and Oxford. He has written plays for the stage, radio and television, and has worked as a theatre director in rep, on the fringe and at the National Theatre. His most recent work includes an animated adaptation of the *Canterbury Tales* for S4C. He now lives and works in London. This is his first novel.

noise

JONATHAN MYERSON

review

First published in 1998
by REVIEW

An imprint of Headline Book Publishing

First published in paperback in 1998

10 9 8 7 6 5 4 3 2 1

ISBN 0 7472 5904 6

Printed and bound in Great Britain by
Clays Ltd, St Ives plc

Headline Book Publishing
A division of Hodder Headline PLC
338 Euston Road
London NW1 3BH

To my father, Aubrey Myerson, 1926-1986

With thanks to Dr Richard Bull, Howard Morris and Mike Laddie, for all their advice.

They create a wasteland and call it peace.

Tacitus
Life of Agricola

'Vicki stood up and put the revolver on the table – it had been hanging on a nail by the doorframe. It was Czechoslovakian, years old. It dragged your hand down, constantly reminding you of what you'd decided to do.

'I allowed it to hang by my side, its grease smearing my thigh, and went towards the room where your father was waiting. I think I was still wearing my coat – the air was thin. I was hot, sweating, and then I was trembling with the cold.

'I tried to think about your brother and everything that had happened to him. I tried to think about South and Jem and what had been done to them. But it wouldn't come.

'Instead, all I could remember was an article I'd read about an executioner. It was in one of those weekend magazines and really it was just another chance for grainy photographs of the gates of Holloway and women in washed silk dresses, hugging brilliantined men. But at that moment, what I clearly remembered from the piece was that the hangman was proud of how fast he could rush a condemned man from cell to noose to open trap. Less than a minute, or something like that.

'So that's all I was thinking when I went into the room. There just wasn't the space to think anything else.'

part one

CHAPTER ONE

Hal's mind had emptied and, for a moment, she didn't know where she was or why.

Then she was walking back from the canteen – she saw the crater of missing plaster round the Sluice Room door, terracotta powder crumbling like sponge cake and an odour of damp. Each time the door was shut, more fell onto the lino below. She had finally rung Estates Management herself: they'd said a pipe was leaking up above, said they had it scheduled.

'He's in there waiting for you.' Kitty was rushing out of the ward towards her, a sheaf of X-rays flapping in her hands.

'I'm not late.' Hal was reaching for her watch.

'Everyone else thinks you are.' Already past her, Kitty's whisper echoed back down the corridor.

Hal remembered her watch had stopped while she was on call the night before last and she hadn't bothered to reset it properly. 'Shit. Thanks.'

Kitty stopped by the double doors at the far end of the corridor: 'Been there at least five minutes. Tapping his foot. Looking for something to look at.' Then she swung round into the stairwell and out of sight.

Shoulder first, Hal pushed through the slapping, rubber-edged doors into the ward and immediately saw his striped shirt, navy tie with coat of arms, red and black pentels in the shirt pocket, grey-flecked hair.

'Good morning, Doctor. I hope.' Everything he said he said for effect, everything he did. The students around him – mostly bright, undamaged faces – responded accordingly.

'But then hope springs eternal, doesn't it? Especially in these dark halls, eh?'

Hal, sliding her folders off the central desk, knew a breezy, open smile would serve best. Any kind of explanation for her lateness would only provoke another witticism.

But he was determined to force a way into Hal's silence: 'Got everything now, have you?'

'Thank you, Doctor Ridgeway.' And Hal smiled again, refusing him more. His courtiers looked away, distancing themselves, flattered by his preference.

They swarmed round the first bed and Hal watched the Consultant earning their loyalty by a combination of certainty and rhetoric. He felled demons with cortisone and crossed gorges on steroid bridges; he offered them simple paths to follow. Hal stood near the back, taking notes, allowing Sister to do the facts.

When they reached the newest patient – an acute systemic lupus with possible East African connections – Ridgeway looked at Sister's notes and asked why she'd been admitted.

'It was diagnosed on General Medical last night, sir.' Sister said in her deliberately clearest voice.

'Who admitted her to my ward, please?'

'Doctor Dowson.'

Ridgeway turned towards Hal. He didn't have to say anything, he just looked at her, hinted at a raised eyebrow. 'I thought I had asked for personal approval on all departmental handovers, Doctor Dowson?'

'Did you, sir? That's the first I've heard of it.' Had she missed a memo or had Sister deliberately kept it back from her?

'Don't play innocent with me, Doctor.' Ridgeway's eyes were narrowing.

'It was about seven last night when I was called down to this patient.' Hal tried to recall the sequence of events.

'Would you want me to ring you at that sort of time?'

'Everything can be delayed. Surely you've learned that much?'

'I didn't think it could. She had severe cutaneous involvement with marked skin necrosis. I felt she wanted immediate medication.' Hal deliberately gestured down at the woman, still barely conscious, covered in plaques. 'As you can see.'

'Administer whatever you choose to prescribe and then wait till I arrive. At the bedside if you must.'

'Medical Reg wanted the bed, was threatening to send her home. You know how they are down there. And I saw no point in risking the patient's condition by not—'

'You're back in the real world now, Doctor Dowson. You told us you were fit to return to work. Either you can handle it or you can't.' Ridgeway's eyes had become solid points of anger. 'There's no room for any sort of special consideration on my firm.'

'I wasn't asking for any, thank you, sir.'

'Good. Nothing we can do about this I suppose, so let's see what you've prescribed the poor woman.' He turned on one of the students: 'You, what should Doctor Dowson have prescribed for Acute SLE?'

Hal savoured the peace that followed, the quiet ordinariness of life continuing on the ward.

Ridgeway and his students were gone and Hal wanted to clear her mind, use what was left of the day. She needed just thirty minutes to properly reconsider two of her patients, try to get their regimes right. They weren't responding to the current therapies and Hal was certain they could and should.

But first she had three bleeps to deal with and the Formulary Manager waiting for a meeting.

Kitty came and sat on the edge of her desk. 'Did he give you mild or severe roasting?'

'Slow chargrilling over an open flame. Each time I thought he'd forgotten me, he turned up the burners again.'

'I heard he wasn't pleased about the lupus you admitted.'

'What is all this, no handovers without his personal say-so?'

'Sister reckons they're about to audit this year's stats and he's been tipped off that his death rates are higher than last year.'

'You mean he's going to refuse to admit just because someone might die on him?'

'If he can just weed out some near-fatals, then his strike rate's bound to get better. It only takes a few to make a difference.' Kitty almost laughed at this, hardened to the new, ruthless logic. 'And your lupus has got complications, Ridgeway doesn't fancy her chances.'

'Then I'll prove him wrong.' Hal felt a surge of the old determination. 'You can't run a ward like that.'

'This place changed while you were, when you were on—' Hal heard Kitty – even Kitty – stumble. 'While you were away. Management's leaning on everyone really hard.'

'Christ, what am I doing here?' Hal had only been back at the hospital about two weeks and already she felt dislocated, unable to find a way back into its labyrinth. Before, she had taken its workings for granted, now everything seemed fogged with paperwork and hostility. 'It seems so hard just to—'

Sister Ursula interrupted her: 'They need you down in A&E, Doctor. Some sort of burns case, apparently.'

'Thanks.'

'Here's a copy of Doctor Ridgeway's memo about hand-overs in case you've mislaid your original.' Sister Ursula, a compacted woman with a faint Ulster accent, enjoyed her authority – she didn't hide the fact that she thought Hal had come back to work too soon. 'It doesn't apply to A&E, of course.'

'Thank you, Sister.'

As Sister hovered away across the ward floor, Kitty said 'Maybe I should come down there with you.'

'I'm fine. Really.'

'All the same.'

They had been treating him for burns down in A&E for at least two hours before anyone thought to ask Dermatology's opinion.

As soon as Hal entered Resus she saw the boy's skin was dying from within, a toxic reaction not a fire. He was lying on the trolley, unconscious or sedated, and looked no older than seventeen, with dark, washed-out eyes, conical shoulders, orange curly hair, his harsh ribs under-fed. He was running a fever of over a hundred and two and his skin was peeling off in sheets, separating from his chest in red waves. His legs seemed to be fidgeting, the toes flexing in spasms.

At the foot of the trolley lay a heap of ragged clothes – threadbare jumpers and bootsocks, grey with grime, an olive-green puffa jacket, a once-yellow baseball cap providing the only memory of colour. While Hal scrubbed down, the nurse told her the boy was sleeping rough – an outreach worker from one of the shelters had found him down on Kingsway. The boy, still without a name, had rolled himself in his sleeping bag into the gutter. There were tyre marks across the bottom edge of the sleeping bag and they needed to X-ray the ankles just in case. The social worker now stood half-willing, half-aloof in the corner of the room, swivelling his earring, his filofax stretching the pocket of his denim jacket. His pager went off while Hal was looking at him. He asked a nurse where he could find a phone.

Hal moved across to the trolley. Down the sides of the

boy's rib cage, abdomen, neck were the blisters, violent red circles, sometimes building to purple in intensity. The unaffected skin was yellowgrey and listless.

On the boy's chest – thin and weak and fragile and hairless – the blisters had merged into a single crimson mass. The skin was lifting off where he had been handled. What was left of the epidermis seemed so thin that his chest might at any moment be laid entirely bare.

Hal was immediately furious: it was so typical of the mechanics of A&E, they only ever looked for superficial symptoms which they could hose down – they had labelled him a burns victim, sent for the Plastic Surgeons, and left him lying there, not even resuscitating him properly. It was the trainee nurse who sent for Dermatology.

Hal turned to the Casualty Officer, little more than an overgrown schoolboy: 'You really couldn't see this was toxic epidermal necrolysis?' She didn't want to think about where this anger was coming from; she'd known far worse blunders; she'd known patients killed by inefficiency, by ignorance and by doctors. 'TEN is an emergency, can you really not see that?' Hal could feel Kitty standing in the corner, keeping watch over her.

The Casualty Officer was unmoved, the practised sangfroid of the future consultant: 'He came round for a minute, mumbled something about burning.' This boy-doctor was even wearing a striped shirt in readiness.

'Of course it feels like it's burning. Look at him. Turn your head and look at him. Go on.' Hal almost reached across the trolley and took the Casualty Officer's chin, twisted his head, forcing him to look down. 'Imagine how that feels. He's not a photo in a book. Think about what that feels like.' Hal stared at him, dared him to find a way of tucking it away behind words.

Instead, he braced his shoulders and pointed to the heap of possessions on the floor: 'Look, his sleeping bag's singed, all round the top. These are the dog-ends we tipped out of it.' He flicked at an aluminium kidney bowl.

Hal pushed it away. 'Why didn't you look at these blisters on the soles of his feet, look at the size of them?' Hal decided to be matter-of-fact, textbook efficient. 'On his palms, Christ even in his mouth. These are standard mucosal lesions. How could you possibly think it was burns?' Hal found herself leaning across the boy to grip the Casualty Officer's shoulders, steering him to look at the boy's feet.

He shrugged her hands off his white coat. 'Just lay off, will you? We all know about your thing with A&E.'

In a rush, Hal heard the room quieten around her. The nurses fitting a drip at the other bed silenced their movements, pretended not to look across. Hal looked squarely back: 'What do you mean by that?'

The Casualty Officer didn't want this, didn't expect to be faced down. 'You know, your "thing". The . . . tragedy thing that . . . happened.'

Hal realised everyone in the hospital knew about it. Of course they had all heard and they all told each other about it. As she walked past, they said What A Tragedy and Incredible and Terrible and all the other words that flattered the true awfulness. But nobody had ever said it out loud before, not to her face. Hal heard the blood in her temples. Then Kitty's voice at her shoulder: 'We've all got more than enough work to do, surely?'

'I'm waiting for a porter.' Hal didn't move. 'I'm admitting this patient to my ward.'

Kitty moved forward, separated them, gently, silently, nodding to the Casualty Officer – 'Thank you, Doctor.' She asked Hal to steady the drip while she herself started to steer the trolley out through the swing doors and towards the lifts. 'I gave our porter a tea-break,' she said too loudly.

Hal said nothing, concentrating on keeping the boy as still as possible. But once in the lift, over the boy's purple torso, Hal had to release her fury: 'A simple biopsy, that's all they had to do. Basic resuscitation. It's not asking much, is it?'

'Don't let it get to you.'

'You heard him – he knows all the facts; he spotted all the symptoms. But still treats it as a burns case!'

'I don't think you should be doing A&E takes.'

'It isn't that. It really isn't.'

'Sure, OK.' Hal saw that Kitty had decided not to argue. 'Do you want to start taking me through the therapy?'

Hal didn't want to let go of her anger. Someone had to pay for this boy's pain, someone had to answer why. This time, if not before. If he had been treated correctly from the moment he was found, he would already be stabilising. As it was, he was going to suffer much more before things got better – if they ever did. At best he'd be carrying scars all over his body for the rest of his life.

'Doctor?' Kitty was gently touching her on the shoulder. Thinking about the boy, about her own intolerance, she hadn't noticed the lift stop, the doors open.

They manoeuvred the trolley out of the lift and along to the ward: 'I'm worried about renal failure. He'd better have fluids intravenously – crystalloids and colloids – six litres pd. Check his Us and Es; tell me as soon as you can. And we can get started on methyl pred, pulsed intravenous, twenty mil per hour.'

'If he's already suffering from a toxic reaction?'

'We don't know that yet. And Ridgeway always wants steroids. But get his clothes; we'll see if he was taking anything. And a diamorphine pump for the pain. Get his name if you can.'

Two hours later – his blood pressure was up and his electrolytes stable – he came round. Hal was standing by the bed, adjusting the IV line when she heard a low growling. At first, she thought there was air in the tube. He hadn't opened his eyes but there was a weak bubbling of spittle in the corner of his mouth.

'Can you hear me?' She bent down until her face was alongside his. She could smell the dirt on his neck, the traffic in his hair. 'Are you awake? Can you make out what I'm saying?'

The low growl rose in pitch. Knowing he was heard, a desperation entered the noise, almost a keening.

'We've put a dressing across your eyes, so you won't be able to see anything. Don't worry about that.' Hal was trying to reach out to him where he was crouching in a corner of his dark cave. 'And I know it probably hurts to move. Don't try.'

His noise started to come in whimpering pulses – they would be cries if he could use his tongue, if he could just let the sound rip out of him. His breath was short and jerking, there was sweat forming on his forehead.

'You're in a hospital. We're doing everything we can, alright?' Hal knew the words were inadequate. 'Keep calm, it'll help. Do you need more help with the pain?' She had wanted to get him into an ITU bed but, as usual, Cardiac had taken the last vacancy.

Then the boy's bleating broke into 'Help.' At least, Hal thought it was that, not just a noise. Then it came again. Yes, it was 'Help'. Then 'Help. Me.'

'We're trying. I'm a doctor. You're going to be alright now.' What ridiculous clichés, she thought.

His body was totally still – he didn't need to be told not to move. He was trying to get his breathing under control, prepare for the effort. Then, each word coming with what would have been a sob, the sounds blunted by his swollen lips: 'I. Don't. Want. To. Die.'

'You're not. You're going to be alright. You're getting better already.'

'Prom. Ise. I. Won't. Die.'

'You're getting better already.'

'Prom. Ise. Me.' He was vomiting these words out of his chest.

'You're going to be well looked after here. We know just what's wrong with you, what to do to make you better.'

'Prom. Ise. Me.'

The boy's condition was critical. How could he ask her to make promises?

'Prom. Ise. Me.'

'I promise you—' but she had to force it out of herself. 'I promise you won't die.' And she touched a clear patch of skin on his cheek, felt his tension soften, felt him leaning back on her words. She said it again, 'I promise you won't die.' And she wanted him to know she meant it.

But the last time she had made that promise it had been a lie.

Hal walked through narrow, unused streets up to Camden Town and caught the tube from there.

It was the end of the rush hour and the platforms were clearing, there would be seats for nearly everyone. But the men around her still seemed anxious, warily watching the horizon for the next challenge. In the morning Hal watched their eyes check each skirt-length, check calves, ankles, buttocks, then breasts, face, hair. Any skirt above the knee left a wake of attention as it walked down the platform. Now the men stared distantly, rolled *Evening Standard*s under their arms, dropped hard metal briefcases down by their feet, read the text of posters advertising TM courses.

Hal tried to think about getting home to Nicky, about what he would be doing – he'd be in bed, reading or being read to. She tried to remember what book he was on – it was one of the Famous Five, which one? She wasn't sure, she couldn't remember for sure. For a moment she was horrified: how could she forget? Then her attention was distracted by three new men bursting onto the platform, a sudden gust of noise and movement. They had been in a wine bar – one carried the unfinished bottle – and they were morning men again. Everyone else drew back against the tunnel wall, giving them room to pass, avoiding their enlivened eyes.

One of them pointed exaggeratedly at the information panel: 'Fucking eight minutes. And then it's only a fucking Kennington.'

'It's the fucking misery line.' They were trumpeting. 'What do you expect?'

'Want'a wait?'

'Fuck it, let's get a minicab.'

And they left the platform as instantly as they had arrived on it. A draught seemed to run along the platform in their wake and muscles relaxed.

In the silence that followed their departure, Hal watched a mouse moving below the tracks, trembling by every crisp packet, every ball of newsprint, oblivious to the approaching thunder as the train entered the platform.

Hal thought some more about Nicky.

Dimitri was home before Hal. There had been a time when this was a rarity; now it was usual.

He was sitting on the L-shaped sofa, diagonally opposite Gareth, right ankle on left knee, his wide fist clenched, banging the knee up and down, beating a rhythm only he could hear. They were talking business, vodka bottle and tumbler on the glass table in front of them, papers spread around, Gareth's laptop open, the electric blue haze dyeing the cushions.

'You're back late, darling.' Dimitri stood, unsteadily. He moved over towards her, leaned forwards, pecked her on the cheek, started to work his thick fingers inside the vent at the back of her coat.

'This is normal for me. You're home early.' Hal moved away, out of his hand's reach, unbuttoning the coat. 'I'm only late if I'm on call.' From the dazed look on his face, she could tell it was a long time since his first vodka of the day. She thought she could smell whisky as well. She stood in front of the fireplace, the gas flames warming her tights.

Dimitri looked histrionically at his watch: 'Christ, no, look at the time. Just decided to have a drink. We've been talking over some figures, you see.' He momentarily lost his footing, collapsed back onto the sofa. 'I didn't realise.' He was half-sitting, half-lying, looking up with a slumped smile, an inane smile. He reached forward for the bottle, poured more into his tumbler: 'Get yourself a glass. Gar, you sure you won't?' he remained slouched forwards, propped on one elbow, his short arms almost hidden by his barrel chest. 'Are you sure?'

Hal looked across at Gareth intently scribbling something on a yellow pad. Did he realise about Dimitri's drinking or was he inured to it – the slurring and the stumbling and the far-away look? Had they both forgotten there had once been a different man behind that face?

Gareth finished and looked up: 'Hi, Hal, sorry, didn't want to lose the wording, we'd just got something sorted.'

Gareth was tall, blond-haired, healthy and fit, bred from money. Only the spectacles perched in front of his blue eyes spoke of imperfection, and even they added to his air of easy authority.

He flipped the covering page over, spun the pad into his open briefcase on the floor. 'Good day at the factory?' Gareth always insisted on this reduction, that they were all engaged in the same basic pursuit.

'So-so, only one major foul-up on the line. And not in my department anyway.' Why did she give in to him like this?

'Toxic reaction of some sort. He'll probably live. Might lose a few bits along the way.' She didn't mention her stupid undertaking to the boy, her promise of certainty.

Hal put her coat on the peg and heard the quarter-bottle in Dimitri's coat clink against the wall. It sounded empty. She decided Nicky wouldn't be asleep yet, she could still pop up.

But halfway up the stairs she was finding it hard to lift the weight of her feet. The carpet felt spongy under her, too soft. She stopped on the landing, stared at her muted half-reflection in the clip-frame – dark brown straight hair, always trying to fall over one eye, flicking up in the faintest curl round her neck. Green eyes, though the right seemed to be growing browner these days – or was she imagining it? And lines round her eyes, cutting a path into her hairline, more every night, especially since. She tried a smile but it just seemed too false to be worth bothering with. She knew she wasn't smiling enough – certainly not at home. Practise more, they said at the counselling – but how?

She reminded herself of what she was doing: Nicky's hair, Nicky's shoulders, Nicky's breath. She wanted to stop thinking.

As she climbed the second flight, she started to find more energy, felt her heart beating faster. From outside Nicky's room she heard him reading out loud, forcing his way through the page of words.

She entered and there was Nicky sitting up in bed, eyes wide, a red baseball cap on his head, peak to one side.

'Dad bought me a Street Sharks cap!' No hello, no surprise, just pride in his new trophy.

Sitting down beside him on the bed: 'He spoils you, you know that?'

'I've got the blue trousers. From my old Thunderbirds suit. I only need a T-shirt with a red S on it. This big.' He held his hands apart, twice as wide as his chest.

'Well, we'll have to see. Let's see at the weekend.'

'But the party's tomorrow.' Nicky's voice went up an octave, started to whine. 'I've got to go as a Street Shark. Everyone is. Can we do it tomorrow? Please? After lunch? And I need white trainers.' He was pulling her jumper. 'I need these kind of white trainers with a red stripe down the side.'

'We'll see.'

'That's what you always say. They're not that much. How much are they?'

'Do you want me to read the rest of the chapter to you or shall we just talk? What did you do at school today?'

'Chapter. Chapter.' And he was already throwing the book at her over the bedcover.

'Budge over then, lie down.' He shifted over and Hal lay down beside him, on her side, tucking him into the curve of her body, the crown of his head under her chin, her elbow pivoted on his hip, holding the book. *Five Go Down to the Sea* – of course it was. Of course.

When the chapter was finished, he begged for more – the cliffhanger was delicately poised – but she pulled the duvet up to his shoulders, kissed him, put the baseball cap back up on the shelf, and left the room, switching off the light.

Gareth was on the landing right outside. He seemed embarrassed to find her coming out of Nicky's room. He quickly said 'Just going to the loo. Sorry.'

Hal felt she had to explain, somehow make it easier for both of them: 'I was just seeing if everything was alright. Thought I heard a noise. It was the radiator probably. They're not properly balanced, always banging and creaking.'

Gareth nodded 'Sure' and went.

In her bathroom, she splashed water on her face, tried to clear the grey hammering confusion from her mind. But the

noise continued, the grind, the false importance of everything around her. Nothing would bring Nicky back; nothing
would replace the warmth and simplicity of his six years.

She dried her face on the towel. The towel was soft,
giving, moulding to her outline. She renewed her eye-liner,
lipstick, made a brave face.

And going back into the sitting room: 'Sounds to me like a
takeaway night.' She practised her smile.

'Is the Pope fucking Jewish?' Dimitri thought he was
being particularly funny, rocked back, giggled, leaned forward, picked up his glass. 'I want ghosh, I want biryani.' He
emptied his glass, even the ice cube, which he started to
chew as he shouted. 'And more wine, Innkeeper.' He
laughed again. For reassurance he looked across at Gareth
who was busy over his laptop again. Dimitri was on an up
cycle. Tomorrow would probably be a down, drink even
more.

'I'll get the menu.' Hal went into the kitchen and
unpinned the Tandoori menu. They always ordered the same
things anyway; she could do the numbers from memory.

When she had first met him, Dimitri never swore. It was
partly an affectation but he had also been brought up to
think it was ungodly, ungentlemanly and unworthy of him.
Until only a couple of years ago, he had kept it up. But now
the drink sucked it out of him: he was building a barricade of
ugly words round himself, protecting himself from their life,
their home, Nicky's life.

CHAPTER TWO

By the time Hal's shift started the next morning, the boy from A&E was no better. There was blistering round the nail beds and the nails themselves were starting to lift. With so little skin left covering his chest, his temperature was falling rapidly.

He had regained consciousness again in the night and someone had increased his analgesia. Blisters now covered most of the top half of his body – his chest, his thighs, his back, his shoulders, his face – and it was impossible for him to move without immediate pain. He lay on his back, a thin line, motionless, his hands on top of the sheet, bandaged like a boxer's.

When Hal arrived, he was groaning rhythmically, his mouth held open in an insane grin, long guttural moans emerging from the darkness of his throat, cracking on the edge of fear.

'Can you hear me?' she whispered into his ear.

The reply was just another moan.

'Jem, can you hear me?' During the night, he'd managed to give a nurse his name. 'It's the doctor, Jem.' Hal wanted to touch him but there seemed to be nowhere that would not agonise him. 'I'll keep my promise.'

In the course of the day, as he slept, layers of his hair started to fall out, cross-hatching the pillow, cloaking his head in a transparent orange halo. When he woke in the late afternoon, he lay looking up at the ceiling, quietly whimpering, a nurse almost constantly beside the bed, willing him to relax. When Hal went over, bent over him, she saw a face trying to understand its pain, his jawbones pulling at the skin. His eyes stared upwards, looking for a purpose.

Or was he just an unthinking ridge of pain and it was she who was looking for some purpose behind it all? Hal looked down at the body, minutely writhing, almost vibrating. There must be some reason.

Kitty came and stood alongside her: 'Why doesn't he just lose consciousness?'

'It's almost like he's afraid to. Last time he went to sleep he woke up like this.'

'Can you tell if he's losing his eyesight?'

'Not until he can speak to us, but the corneas have almost certainly been scarred. The only question is, how much?'

'Do you want to increase the diamorphine?'

'I said I'd save him.' Hal could hear the desperation in her own voice.

'Don't be ridiculous. You're a doctor not a lifeguard.' It was what they always said if someone started to get too involved.

'I'm serious, I promised him. He made me promise him last night.'

'Come on now.' Kitty put an arm round Hal's shoulder. 'This sort of thing is bound to happen. Go and sit in your office. I'll make sure no one hassles you.'

Hal was determined to hold it inside. 'A promise is a promise, Kit.'

'You know what this is all about, go and sit down.' And Kitty led her to the office, dropped the blinds.

She had arranged to go into work late and walk Nicky to school herself – usually the childminder arrived before she left at eight and the last she would see of him was pyjamas and a bowl of weetabix. But he had desperately wanted to show her his new secret route – one of the side-streets off

Queenstown Road; he was sure there were clues and strange things on it that might lead to treasure or spies up to no good. He had been begging her to take him for days.

They had walked down the garden path, immediately crossed the road and walked under the row of plane trees. Hal remembered the thick wet mist clinging to the pavements and a heaviness that filled the middle of the road, only to be pushed aside each time a car came through. Hal had felt the droplets prickling against her face and pulled her scarf tighter. Nicky had seemed totally unaware of the cold, pulling along ahead of her, his school shoes cracking the pavement frost, running to where there was a secret covering leading into a tunnel in the wall of the old factory. Hal said she thought it seemed very strange and Nicky held his chin between thumb and index finger in the thinking pose he'd seen in illustrations.

'What do you think we should do about it?' he had asked. Or maybe he had said 'This could be important.'

'Better keep an eye on it,' Hal had probably replied. 'There's plenty of time.'

'Don't you think we should open it up, see where it goes? There might be a cave down there. You could get out into the river from here and then out to sea really easily.' He had looked up at her, determined to believe it, a hurried smile breaking at the edge of his face. 'They might escape before we know what they're doing.'

'Let's just keep watching it, see if anyone goes in or out. Then we'll know.'

'OK. I'll make a list of who watches when. You can do tonight.' And he ran on ahead – he didn't need to get more than thirty feet away before he started to disappear. The fog was lowering and his navy blue anorak merged into the background.

'Nicky, come back.' Hal had shouted. 'I think you ought to hold my hand.'

He had stood and waited for her to catch up by the traffic lights at Cedars Road. His shirt was already sliding out from under his jumper. He was trying to read the name of an ice cream advertised in the window of the corner shop, his breath white around his face. 'Maga— mang— What's this?'

'Magnum. And it's far too cold for ice creams.'

'I wanted to know what it was called for next year. How long till summer? Then it's my birthday.'

'Christmas first, then my birthday, then yours. A long time yet.'

'I know. I know.'

They had crossed to the other side of the junction and started to walk along the main road. Hal hated this bit – there was no other way through except to walk alongside the grumble of this traffic dieseling down to the South Circular. She felt as though she was walking on the edge of the world. Two steps to the side and they would be in the abyss. It was about three hundred yards before they could turn off onto the road beside the Common – she held Nicky's gloved hand tight and marched them as fast as she could through the brittle air.

Once they had turned off, they could look down on the school at the bottom of the slope. But not today: even the banner up outside for the Bonfire Party was obscured by the mist. The Common, off to their right, was immersed in the whiteness, only the highest branches of the oak copse emerging through the blanket.

Nicky was talking about pyramids and how they built them – the night before she had let him watch a documentary about American archaeologists trying to rebuild one. Hal's mind had drifted to a difficult case on the ward. Relieved to be past the main road, she hadn't thought about the rumbling coming from behind, the slowly approaching grind down the hill behind her. She was still holding Nicky's hand – she was on the Common side; he was on the road side – when the lorry's noise started to register at the back of her brain, started to make it harder to hear what Nicky was saying. She was thinking that lorries weren't supposed to come down this road, though she knew they sometimes did, pretending to be lost and looking for a short cut.

And then there wasn't enough time. The noise was louder and closer and there wasn't even a chance to see why. She squeezed Nicky's hand tighter as she turned her head and then suddenly his hand was no longer in hers and there was a lorry going past instead. It was a blue parcel van – she noticed that the cab section was painted blue. She couldn't read the words on the side; she only felt the rush of air. She thought she remembered Nicky's hand being ripped out of hers, the sudden sliding away, her own arm jerked forward. It was important to remember this. And then the lorry was swerving back into the middle of the road, swivelling wildly on the frost. It shifted across to the other side and stopped against a tree. The branches jerked and then waved slowly.

Nicky had made no noise. He had just flown away, leaped across the pavement in front of her, landing up against the chain-link fence. He was lying on his back and there was blood coming out of the back of his head, seeping through his hair. Hal's eyes read the symptoms but she could not move. Nicky was lying on his back and his left leg was twisted impossibly beneath him and he was bleeding and broken and still Hal could not move. The pavement was changing colour and the air was turning blue, but what had happened? Not enough for anything to have genuinely changed. If everything was going to change, something big should have happened. Instead they had been walking so easily, walking to school and talking about pyramids and the Famous Five and then he had been plucked from beside her. Hal hadn't even been scratched.

Then she moved. There was a pulse, she checked the

pupils. She pulled off her scarf and laid it under his head to pressurise the bleeding. By now she could hear mothers' voices coming up behind her, running up from the school. She remembered now the howl of the lorry's tyres after Nicky was hit. She took off her coat and put it over him. There was nothing else to do but wait. She looked over her shoulder and saw the lorry driver now standing by his cab – he was looking over at them but not daring to come any closer. She looked back along the pavement and saw the tyre marks where he'd gone up onto the kerb. She took Nicky's hand in hers and realised he'd lost his glove and only then realised she was still holding it in her left hand. She had never lost hold of it, Nicky had been swept out of it.

The van driver had come over and said 'Is he going to be alright?'

Hal had said 'You ought to sit down. You're in shock. Just sit down.'

The driver had said: 'I didn't see him. I just didn't see him at all. I saw you. I didn't see him at all.'

Someone else had said 'They've called an ambulance.'

And someone else had said 'Is he going to be alright?'

Lots of people were saying things like 'Oh God'.

And Hal had said 'Get back. He needs air. Please don't crowd him.'

And they all pulled back. And they all waited while the sirens approached.

In the ambulance, Hal sat and watched. They drained his lung and got his neck into a brace; they monitored his heart and gave him oxygen. Then they were at the hospital. It was the one where Hal had done her own clinical training but it had all been rebuilt since. She followed the trolley through grey hessian doors, past crisp grey desks. Someone had rung Dimitri.

She stood in the corner of the Resus Room and watched them cut the school uniform from around her son's body.

The blue woollen coat and the pilled blue jumper with the red shield emblem she had sewn onto the breast and the white nylon shirt with cuffs green-brown from painting sessions and the vest striped blue and white. His body was pitifully broken, there were bloodbruises breaking out all over him. A nurse suggested she go and sit in the waiting room, they could bring her a cup of tea. She insisted on staying. The nurse looked dissatisfied but someone whispered in the nurse's ear and then she was left alone.

The three men worked their way methodically over the body. But this was Nicky's body. They said they were trying to find what was broken and the little that wasn't. Couldn't they go any faster? A fourth started to examine Nicky's skull, a nurse shaving back the hair. There was talk of haemorrhaging and maybe they should drill immediately. Yes, immediately, yes. The heart-beat was erratic and there was definite blood loss into the chest. These men were moving so slowly – there was so much to do, so much to start healing – they must know they didn't have long, why didn't they hurry up?

When Dimitri had arrived – for once she was glad to see his hip flask – they both went into the Waiting Room. The nurse came about twenty minutes later and told them Nicky had died in Resus before they had a chance to operate. Hal said they could have moved faster, could have done things. She said it again when she and Dimitri went back into Resus to see his body. There was some shouting and a nurse tried to stop her. They all stood mute and she screamed. She had questions to ask and no one seemed willing to face her and answer.

The next day Jem's condition was approaching critical. The prednisolone was having some effect on the blistering, but it was becoming difficult to control his temperature. He was liable to freeze to death for want of skin, overheat if they protected him too carefully. And anyway his skin couldn't stand even the slightest pressure – too much weight on it and a patch would crack open and bleed.

He rose and fell in and out of consciousness throughout the day. When awake, he gave out a droning, rhythmic groan, begging them for relief, his probably unseeing eyes staring through anyone who approached.

Ridgeway wanted the boy's dressings changed every eight hours, but as soon as he had gone back to Sloane Street, Hal told the nurses to leave it – there was already too much pain.

Each time the nurses drew the sheet back off the metal hoops, Hal looked down at his angular, ignored skeleton. The disease had reduced him to a geometrical shape but he had never been strong. He was a wiry boy, dodging, eyes always wide, waiting for the next crisis. He would stand on a street corner looking both ways, his back to the bricks, rubbing his chin on the shoulder of his jacket, knotting and unknotting the waistcord of his jogging pants. If someone spoke to him, he would look away, mumble downwards, walk away as soon as he could. Everything was a danger and he had learned loneliness was the safest path.

Now, like a snake moving over the desert sand, his body was shedding its first layer and he was moving forward into a new disguise.

Hal leaned over the bed, whispered in his ear: 'Just get through today, tomorrow, you'll be OK.'

His eyes shot open. She didn't know if he could see her at all, but she knew he'd heard her voice, the voice that had made the promise. And she knew he was waiting for her to make it good.

Hadn't she promised Nicky the same?

Hal walked away and tried to write up her notes leaning on the flat of the deep windowsill. Looking out at the railway depot, at the traffic on Goods Way, she watched the lorries grinding in and out of the station, the men in cars, the suited bodies in the cars, tight and trapped in their uniform skin. She looked down at the file and saw the salt-water drop of a tear smudging her handwriting.

Sister Ursula came up beside Hal, leaned against the wall, side on to her. 'He's through the worst, I'm sure.'

She wasn't going to let Ursula know how this boy's loneliness was taking hold in her mind, that this was her life she was watching change as much as his. Something had ended with Nicky and now she and Jem were both shedding their skins and they would both emerge somehow different.

It was hardly an affair. They had been meeting for about six months. One of the days after Nicky died, she had rung and said she wouldn't be seeing him again. He had clearly heard and didn't try to argue with her. She had meant it as a kind of penance, the first of many mortifications she deserved, but after she'd put the phone down she started to wonder if the affair itself hadn't been the penance.

He was a House Officer on a Renal firm and whenever he was on overnight take and she was on call, they would go to his allocated room. If they were lucky, they would get an hour together, usually less, so the sex was immediate. They would move quickly into the cold sheets, the other's instant nakedness even more of a shock, and then their joint heat would carry them. His body was ribby and white, his actions nervous but determined. For Hal, the pleasure – both taking and giving – was uncomplicated. For as long as it lasted, it seemed to be a solution.

And afterwards they would talk, usually about other people in the hospital. He was young, much younger than her, and still looking for the light at the end of the tunnel. Hal lay on the sagging foam pillows and luxuriated in his carelessness. The room was minuscule, hardly bigger than the single bed itself. She imagined that the tight, bare walls genuinely confined her life and this concise act of sex was all that was being demanded of her. She always suggested another meeting as soon as their schedules coincided. He always agreed, and smiled as he did so.

About a month after the funeral, he had sent her a postcard ("Hope you're doing OK. We miss you here. Keep well.") And Hal had agreed to meet him. 'I would have liked to come – to the funeral, I mean,' he said. 'I thought it was too risky but I'd heard so much about him, after all.'

'Did I talk about Nicky that much? I didn't mean to.'

'No, it was fine. I liked hearing about him. I really did. If you want to talk about him now, I mean, don't feel . . .'

'No. I don't want to. Thanks anyway.'

'You just say what you want. What do I know about what you're going through after all?'

The accident stood between them: they had become alien to each other. They used to make fun of their age difference, for instance – now it would have only emphasised their estrangement. And they had made the mistake of meeting in a restaurant – just a basic Italian place – but they sat staring at the tablecloth, waiting for the food to be brought, looking across at the waitresses standing idly by the bar. One of them was pregnant. Hal slid the condensation off her glass of mineral water.

And Hal had realised what his silence meant. It meant that what they had been doing – affair, sex, whatever – was as empty for him as it had been for her. She had no right to feel disappointed.

He looked at her: 'Is your husband . . . how's he coping?'

'He has his ways. We shouldn't talk about him either really. It isn't fair, is it?' Hal knew it was up to her to brighten things: 'Tell me about the hospital. What's all the gossip then?'

And he had told her about who had split up, who had got

together, who had got promoted, who had been moved sideways, whose department budget was under threat, who had landed a research grant – all the simple things it was easy for her to hear. She sat back and listened easily, wanted to know more, wanted him to keep telling her more. She remembered what she had enjoyed about those short hours spent lying in his bed.

But as he had walked away from her afterwards – he had given her a simple dry kiss on the cheek and squeezed her arm – she realised how good it felt to be free of him and how she needed to be free of the rest.

Hal knew Kitty was watching her whenever she went to check on Jem, could feel her eyes flicking over from whatever she was doing. And she knew Kitty meant well, but she wasn't going to let her get in the way.

In 1978 she had travelled for six months on her own to the Far East and Australia and she remembered it now as the last time she had felt unimpeded. Before that she had been straightened by school, asked to conform; afterwards she had returned to England, started her medical training and never again found the time to choose.

She had first noticed the Greek boy on the Greyhound bus during the drive up from Port Augusta, heard him struggling to make himself understood to the driver. As the boy made his way back to his seat, the driver leaned back to find a pure white face he could trust. He found Hal's: 'I don't mind them coming over here, but least they could do is learn the bloody language. Is that too much to ask?'

'Actually I think he's a tourist, I saw some airline stickers on his knapsack.' Hal heard her Home Counties vowels, their ostentatious roundness.

'Too right. They treat the whole country like they're tourists and piss off back to Greece as soon as they've ripped us off. They don't pay taxes, not one lousy cent.' He turned his attention back to the dirt-track that led to Alice Springs. 'You're not supposed to speak to the driver anyways, he must know that much.'

Hal twisted and looked back down the aisle. The Greek boy was crammed foetally into a seat at the back, his head thrown to one side, watching the passing landscape. He was thick-set like a rugby player, wide nose, rounded lips, hard forehead, black curling hair, solid neck, his legs just as stocky. He was probably fractionally taller than her, but seemed shorter – Hal had noticed how he carried himself anxiously, almost scared, hunched, ready.

Hal turned to look back at the land: the flatness, flat as far as the horizon, on all sides the rubbed flatness of it.

The afternoon of the next day she and the Greek boy had been in the same group climbing the Rock and still they had not spoken. This time it was Hal's decision: she wanted to be alone on the rock and resented the restrictions that sent them up in batches. Once at the summit, she sat, determined not to speak to anyone, hiding behind a boulder. Then all the others began to make their way down again. She heard the chainlink rattle as they steadied themselves, skidding down smoothed slopes, giggling, shoes scuffing. Then it was silent.

It was only just gone noon and the surface of the rock was almost untouchable, powdery dry, reflecting the sun's heat without a thought.

The silence was absolute.

Hal squatted down, licked her fingers and wiped them across the pitted stone. Her fingertips yelled with the heat as the dust stuck to her, defining the swirls in red grains, fine as talc but not without a sharpness, like ground glass. She unhooked her water-bottle from her belt, poured some into her mouth and the rest on her hands, allowing it to splash down onto the ground, to form mercury bubbles in the hostile dust.

She started rubbing her wet palms on the ground, then intertwining them, soaping them in the red dirt. Wiping her hands across the rock again, gathering up more dust, working the redness along her forearms, and onto her shoulders, her neck, her collarbones.

She knew they'd be waiting for her on the ground, tut-tutting, drumming white fingers, and instead she stood and looked across the plain, grinding the redness into her skin, into her jawline, onto her thighs and calves. If only she could slip, now, down into the body of this rock, into this single, defiant mark on this sea-flat desert.

When she got back down they all wanted to know if she had tripped and fallen, was she alright?, did she want to get an X-ray? They so badly needed to explain away her red-streaked body, her matted hair. All of them except the Greek boy, who didn't have the language, and anyway remained at a distance, watching her, arms folded, hands clenched in fists.

In the bar that evening, the redness showered off if not her stigma, she and he had found themselves standing together at the zinc counter, waiting for the barman to notice either of them.

Hal felt she should try to entice him into conversation – he seemed to have practically no English, she had absolutely no Greek. She unravelled that he was doing much the same as her – travelling round on a one-month Greyhound bus pass, seeing as much of the country as you could take.

They sipped and smiled at each other, signalled that the beer was very cold. But good. They had waited a long time to be served. But at least they had it now. Even the glass was cold. They kept them in ice. Yes, you could see the frost round the rim.

With every desperate, staccato communication, Hal felt

herself more observed, but more determined to persevere. The bar belonged to the locals, not the tourists: the wet metal counter, everything else cream-tiled or green enamel-painted. Three Aboriginals stood in a cluster at one end of the counter, not even looking at the whites, occasionally jerking their chins up for emphasis, their eyes drawn back.

This was not a place for comfort or women. It didn't help that she and this Greek boy had to communicate so openly. They spent the evening together, watching the locals peel back to their homes, their wives, their dry meals. The Aboriginals remained in the corner, drinking slowly, proving their point.

When they left the bar at the end of the evening, she knew everyone was watching her and that's probably why she did it. She had come to this country for a chance of solitude and begun to find it and now she was about to puncture it with this Greek boy. But she felt angry at the insinuating glances she had absorbed all night and proving them right seemed to be the easiest way.

She hadn't had many boyfriends before, only two she had slept with. The first had been a shy, melancholy boy she had met at some school dance. She was seventeen and felt weighed down by her virginity; she got herself drunk. After him came the one who wanted to be a poet. They went out for about six months until he decided she was too shallow.

So she led the Greek boy to her motel chalet, looking forward to the absence of words and their foreignness to each other. He had seemed muscled and stocky in the bar. But now his hands were shaking and it gave his fingers a tentativeness when he touched her breasts – it was like the shock of static, a sting of surprise for both of them. She could feel him already hard against her thigh, the wiry hair of his legs rasping against her sunburn. He had wanted to turn the light off but Hal stopped him – in darkness they would turn into any two lovers. Instead she held his head firmly in her hands and forced him to look at her, her breasts, her belly, her sex; she forced herself to see him looking at her. She watched his fingers tangling in her hair and then she watched the shaft of his penis as he came into her. For the first time, she found herself unashamed and willing to see and be seen. He fell asleep and she remained awake.

At about five-thirty, he returned to his room, saying he would see her on the bus.

At nine, when she got on the bus, she went right to the back but he had already gone – thumbed a lift on up to Darwin apparently.

Dimitri flopped into bed when Hal was already asleep. Another takeaway night and again Gareth in the sitting room working at his laptop, Dimitri sitting, standing, flexing, apparently working, usually drinking.

Hal woke to feel Dimitri's thick fingers fumbling round her hips, ploughing his thumb down between her buttocks. 'Sweetie?' She had woken immediately, tensed, ready, not moving, undecided.

His hands jerked from one part of her body to another with a suddenness that Hal knew well. 'Shall I get ready for bed or what?' His words were thick as well, bumping into her ear with phlegm and alcohol and onion.

'I'm asleep. And you're drunk.' Why didn't she accuse him of this when he was sober in the morning, when he might listen and realise?

She twisted her arm round behind her back, removed his hand from her thighs, discovered he was still fully dressed. His fingers were sticky with chocolate.

'I'm fighting fit. Come on.' And he pulled on her shoulder, forced her round onto her back, loomed over her. 'I want to. Please.'

'Seemed to me you wanted to spend the evening with Gareth again.' Why was she avoiding the real question?

'It's about the business, it's important, we're doing something big. I'm making a big decision. About something big. We do work together, Gareth and me, you know.' His words tumbled out, repetitive, slurred, barely connected. 'Now I want some time with you. Some of that stuff we do together. We need to do things together.'

Hal knew that if she delayed long enough, he would simply fall asleep where he was, not for the first time spending the night in his clothes. She got out of bed. 'I'm just going to get some water from the fridge.'

'Gareth – he's on the sofa.'

'Again?' Hal couldn't believe it. 'Aren't there taxis in this city?'

'Too late. Not worth it. Doesn't matter, does it?' Dimitri was already sliding towards sleep, lying face down on the bed, his cheek turned to one side, his braces rucking his shirt.

She went downstairs in her dressing gown, stepped onto the cold tile floor of the kitchen, opened the fridge door, turned the tap on the cold water box, filled a glass.

'Can't sleep?' Gareth was standing behind her, in just his shirt and boxer shorts, leaning against the archway, his legs bluewhite in the electric light.

Hal closed the fridge door and they were both safe in the near-darkness. 'Haven't you got a home to go to?'

'What's the point? Back in the saddle in six hours.'

'We're a cowboy now, are we?' Hal sipped the water, clearing the weight from her throat. Gareth allowed the silence to extend, Hal terminated it: 'Want some water?'

'Thanks.' Hal was reaching for another glass, but Gareth leaned forward, took hers. She watched him empty it. He handed it back to her, saying 'Why don't you like me any more?'

'I don't know.' Hal felt a surge of freedom. 'I want to blame you, but it isn't your fault.'

'What isn't?'

'We both know.'

'I'm helping Dimitri actually.'

'You're ignoring him. Carrying on like he's actually doing something.'

'And you're not?'

It was true. They were both allowing him to sink – both of them equally aware of the bottle in the coat, the three doubles at lunchtime, the bottle on the desk through the afternoon, the evening that ended in near oblivion, and the lies that allowed all three of them to ignore it.

'I'm going back to bed,' Hal said and started to squeeze past Gareth.

'Let's talk about it then. Come on.'

'Not now, Gareth. Not now.'

'We can do things if you want.'

'Dimitri's waiting for me upstairs.'

'Come on.' Gareth's voice sounded almost hurt. 'It's so obvious what you should be doing, what we should be doing.'

Hal tried to get back to the stairs. The corridor was narrow and he didn't move.

She manoeuvred past him, stepping over his bony feet, her breasts brushing his folded arms. He remained leaning, only his head swivelling to watch her go.

'See you in the morning,' he threw after her. 'Full cooked breakfast, seven o'clock, no shirkers.' But she was already up the stairs.

Lying sideways across the bed, his lips flabby on the pillow, Dimitri was asleep. She rolled him onto his side, turned off the light, listened to the silence left by Nicky, listened to the street.

CHAPTER THREE

'Four, five, six.'

'Where the hell's the defibrillator?' Hal looked up at the ward doors, determined to see it burst through.

'Seven, eight, nine, ten.'

Hal started pumping the boy's chest again. 'We called at least five minutes ago. Where is it?'

'Two and a half minutes actually.' Sister Ursula's tone was clipped, bent over the boy's face and preparing to breathe more air into his mouth. 'And there was a Crash call six minutes before ours. Over on Gynae.' And she added before Hal could ask: 'The other box is bust.'

Hal looked at her unworried face: how could she be so calm? This was everything they stood for, everything Hal stood for. She had promised this boy. She had failed Nicky and now this. If she couldn't manage this, what use was she? 'What are we supposed to do? Plug him into the fucking mains?'

Hal saw the nurses stiffen. You weren't supposed to care and you weren't supposed to make commitments. Hal forced her voice back to the mechanical tone: 'Half a milligram of atropine, please.' The nurse was already passing it to her. Hal injected it, listened for a change on the monitor. Nothing. Hal had to make something happen – she had perhaps another two minutes.

She had been in the ward office when she heard the Crash call. She ran in to see them crowding Jem's body, drawing the curtains round the bed, someone else pulling aside the sheets, starting CPR. She knew immediately his fluids had dropped too low. She had run the length of the ward, feeling it recede from her, pushed through the circle of nurses, wanting to use her hands, wanting to make sure she was the one touching him.

'Two, three, four.'

Hal looked across at the doors again – motionless – turned to Sister Ursula. 'Eight minutes already we've waited for Crash. It's a disgrace.'

'Not quite that long. But I'll ring again.'

'Please. Please do that.'

'Eight, nine, ten.'

'What about the box down in Paeds?'

'Ten, Doctor.'

Hal wanted to hit someone. Wanted to push someone up against the wall and hit the side of his head with her open hand, watch him bend at the waist, squeal out his shock. Instead she continued to massage.

'I'm going to bleep Crash again, alright?' Sister Ursula seemed to float across the floor to the desk, unhurried. 'They're probably already on their way here anyway. Kitty, you take over here, please?'

Kitty took Sister's place and Hal went on pumping, counting, pumping the boy. Kitty leaned towards her. 'Take it easy, it'll be OK.'

Hal whispered back: 'I know I'm over the top. But I don't want to . . . I can't lose him, Kitty.' By now Hal's hands were too greased by the cream from Jem's chest – her hands slipped down beside the ribcage each time she had mustered the force to jolt some life into him. 'Can someone wipe him again? I can't get a hold. Do it gently. Please, really carefully.'

Another nurse grabbed the end of the bedsheet and, during Hal's count of three, tried to clear some of the grease from Jem's chest, revealing the raw blister craters and the baked-paper thinness around them.

'Anything?' Hal asked the nurse standing by his head,

fingers on the boy's slack neck.

'Asystole.'

'Adrenaline, please, twenty mil.'

'Eight, nine, ten.'

Hal returned to pumping, feeling ribs crack, feeling the boy's whole body giving under her weight each time. She wasn't going to let him go. She listened to the count, pumped, counted.

'Nothing.'

Hal, working almost mechanically, concentrated her eyes on the boy's face – for the first time he looked serene. Would it be fairer to let him slip, in spite of everything? No, she couldn't, it was too late for that. She had to make this promise stick.

'Still no pulse.'

'Adrenaline's ready, Doctor.'

Sister Ursula came back. 'Crash are still in Gynae. I've called Fourth Floor, see if they've got a spare box.'

'They'd better get a result in Gynae.' Hal felt bitter, felt the black gall filling her throat. This was her patient – she'd rescued him once from the hamfists in A&E: was she going to have to revive him again now, using only her hands?

'Don't worry about that now,' said Sister.

'Don't tell me how to behave.' Hal said it sharply, more sharply than she knew she intended.

A moment of silence as the nurses stilled – shocked to see their leader rebuked so publicly. Some of the women turned to look at Hal, some continued with what they were doing, fiddled with kidney bowls. Hal wanted them to notice. Hal didn't want them to notice. She knew they were thinking about her and Nicky, blaming it all on Nicky.

She picked up the hypodermic. 'Is this ready?'

A nurse said 'Adrenaline. Twenty mil. What you asked for.'

'Thanks,' and Hal placed the tip of the long needle

between Jem's fourth and fifth ribs and then started to work it in. When she felt it drawing in blood, she touched her thumb against the plunger and slowly forced the liquid into his heart. She eased the needle back out again, felt it scraping through the ribcage, pulling against the muscle walls, and then the sudden release as it left the body. She let it clatter back into the metal tray.

'Could someone else massage it in, please?'

Sister Ursula moved forward.

Hal waited for the monitor to register a change. She watched Ursula knead at the chest around the heart. Ten seconds, fifteen, twenty.

The nurse standing by Jem's head said 'I think I've got a pulse. Hang on. Yes.'

Hal moved up to his neck, rested her fingers against the artery. Alerted by the shock of adrenaline, his body had jerked back into motion. He was breathing again. She watched his chest rise and fall. 'Well done, everyone.' She allowed herself to take a deep breath.

'Right, let's get this dressing back on; he'll have lost a lot of heat. Sister, immediate Us and Es. We need to get the heating turned up in here.' Hal reached for the cream, started painting it across his chest. Kitty took the tub out of her hands:

'I'll do it. You're rushing it.'

'We'll need to get his ribs X-rayed.'

'I don't think we should move him until he's stabilised, do you?' Sister Ursula was flexing her muscles again.

'We'll get it done in here with the portable.'

'Bust.'

'Forget his ribs then, it won't kill him.'

'I'll see if I can borrow one from the basement.'

'Forget it. We couldn't strap him up anyway.'

Hal stood back, allowed the nurses to go about their routine: the cream, the drips back into the line, then the shining metal hoops over his chest, the sheet and blankets over that. The boy remained apparently dead, as they lifted and bent his arms, rolled his torso, raised his legs, adjusted his head on the pillows. They smoothed his thin, tufted hair, now just orange islands floating on a nearly bald, raw skull.

'Fifteen-minute checks, please. Until further notice.' Hal slipped through the gap in the curtains and walked into the openness of the ward. The light flooded her eyes and the other patients all turned their heads to her.

She smiled a reassuring smile to let them know, to let herself know she'd won.

Hal met Dimitri soon after she returned to London to be a Junior Registrar at the Royal Cross.

The shortlist had consisted of five men and her. She sat in the waiting room listening to the trains outside and the men inside discussing the prospects of an England Grand Slam – apparently the captain would be retiring this year and it was all he had ever wanted to achieve in life. Most of them reckoned he'd earned his crack at it.

Doctor Ridgeway, Consultant Dermatologist, later told her he wanted a woman's touch on his team, said he was 'Sick of all those heavy-handed oafs. Dermatology requires finesse, tact and a touch like Tinkerbell.' The nurses standing round looked as though they had heard this too many times before, waited for the ward round to start, tested their biros on the corner of temperature charts.

That first week, Hal wondered if Ridgeway was gay, he seemed so pompously camp, so unaware of his own pretensions. In the second week, over what Hal thought was a working dinner in the Thai on Eversholt Street, he slid his hand up her thigh, the dry skin on the tips of his fingers momentarily catching threads in her tights. He left his hand there, stared at her eyes, asked 'Are you lonely?'

Hal was determined not to be. There had been no one for the last year, but that had been her Senior House Officer year, at Wolverhampton General. She was permanently exhausted and fractious – but they all were. Was that why the nurses got all the offers? What was it about women doctors? Was it just her? She knew she was liable to turn aggressive, to stand on her dignity. But when the men did it, everyone looked up to them, marked them for promotion. When a woman did it, she was a bitch – Hal knew that's what the nurses called her behind her back. On the train down from Wolverhampton, Hal had decided to change her life. She knew she was lonely.

But an affair with her consultant was not the answer. She paid her share of the bill and pleaded a six o'clock take the next day. Ridgeway made no further attempt.

So by the time she sat on Gareth's sofa a couple of months later, a plate of salads and cold pasta balanced on her lap, she knew she wanted someone to emerge from the mass, to stand next to her, to protect and understand her angers.

She had done a month at the Royal Cross by then and was sick to her heart of the struggle. The out-patient clinics had been the worst shock. London's walking wounded, bringing with them their vague acquiescence, their willing-ness to suffer and endure a grinding quality of life, to carry their load. They drifted into the clinics, with their cigarettes or chewing gum, with eczema, with impetigo, with chemical burns – all curable or avoidable but still festering. Hal examined them, encouraged them, prescribed for them, sent them back out into the damp and darkness.

The work sapped all of her daytime emotions, never giving her a chance to recharge or reconsider. Each return journey back to what she called home – whether in the evening or the early morning after a night on take – prom-ised only more dislocation. She would open the plywood door into her automatic, rented flat off the Kennington Road and go from room to room wondering if she really lived there and what it meant if she did.

And now, on that Friday night, she sat on the sofa in Gareth's Cromwell Road basement and forked a mouthful of butterfly pasta salad and looked around at Gareth's friends. Bankers and stockbrokers and management consultants – 'friends from work' – even some 'media types'. Gareth made sure he kept in touch with people; he'd made sure he kept in touch with her. At university he had been the type who organised people, got everyone out on a picnic or put plays on – they had met when he found her repairing a hem in the laundry and insisted she make the costumes for *The Crucible*. Gareth was tall and blond and self-assured and naively good-looking and people at university wanted to know him. Gareth's father was 'a businessman', he said. In fact, Hal later discovered he was one of those who were always being appointed to directorships or turning up in the Birthday Honours. Gareth had grown up in a world of duty and dutiful socialising and he made it part of his own life without ever asking why. His parties were a well-oiled necessity, not a celebration – but that suited Gareth.

Even now Hal didn't know why she'd come to this one. Getting ready an hour earlier she had wanted nothing more than to cut herself clean off from this world of straight backs, swivelling eyes, handkerchiefs in breast pockets. She had wanted to silence all the talk of houses bought and sold, men and women married and unmarried, share deals closed and open. She had continued dressing, done her eyes, chosen a lipstick and rung for a taxi.

She sat on the sofa, waiting, anxious. Was there something wrong with her? Did so much life involve being alone?

Gareth came towards her, trailing another man in a suit. He introduced them, hurried back to his food table. At first this man was just another banker – this time a banker with plans to start his own business.

He sat down next to her, his weight on the sofa cushion encouraging her to slide down towards him. She pulled herself forward, put her plate down on the table in front of them, flicked her hair back, looked sideways at him: dark-skinned, curly hair, solidly built.

He talked about the chain of shops he wanted to start – apparently everyone thought his idea was crazy, it was an invitation to bankruptcy. But he was sick of moving other people's paper money round the world, he wanted to do something of his own, he said. And he mentioned he was Greek; his parents were from one of the islands. Hal saw Gareth watching them, turning from the salad bowl to scan their faces.

He was telling her about his family – his father worked in shipping and as a result he'd been brought up in New York and then Marseilles and then London, and when his parents had moved back to the US he had opted to stay in England. But Hal was thinking about Australia. Over the eight intervening years – medical school, clinical training, Tommy's and then Wolverhampton – she had not forgotten that night. She had never told anyone else about it – not because she was embarrassed or hurt, but because it had revealed to her some possibility of transformation. And that was something she hadn't experienced since.

'My name's Dimitri,' he looked at her, light smile, thick lips. 'Tell me yours, I'm sorry, I missed it when Gareth said.'

For a moment, she didn't know it herself. Her cheeks were still hot with memory. She drained her glass – warm, sharp wine. 'Hal.'

'Like the Prince?'

'Kind of.'

'It's not your real name, is it?'

Hal hated this: 'Henrietta. Dreadful, prissy thing.'

'It's pretty.'

'No, it isn't.'

He leaned forward, slid the glass out of her grip: 'Can I get you another drink? Let me, please.'

'Only if you're —'

But he was already standing, his wide body blacking out half the room. 'White wine, yeah?'

Hal knew she could just stand up and leave now, slip out the door like the first Greek boy had slipped away to Darwin years ago. She saw Gareth move across the room, say something to Dimitri, look across at her — was he being protective or possessive?

Dimitri sat down beside her again, handed her the glass, crossed his arms, his jacket straining across his shoulders.

'Thanks. Aren't you having anything?'

'I didn't fancy anything. Gareth doesn't drink so he always lays on total gutrot.'

Already sipping her white wine: 'Thanks.'

'No, I didn't mean, it's just . . .' Hal saw his composure slipping for the first time.

'Forget it. I can't tell the difference. How do you know Gareth?'

He rang and asked her out a few times. To begin with she had been unwilling, but he hadn't let her go and at least he made her laugh. As she started to know him better, Hal discovered the fear hidden by his confident front, the eager need to prove himself that underlay his sometimes arrogant personality. Every few months they argued: she said he had to control everything; he told her she should take more control. The row always fizzled out and they stayed together and neither of them changed and Hal's interior walls grew thicker. Being with Dimitri meant that she wasn't lonely and months together rolled into years without either of them really noticing. It was the same with his drinking — growing until it became his only way of marking through the day.

They each still had their own flats when Hal discovered her pregnancy: twenty-nine and a Junior Registrar, Dimitri by then in partnership with Gareth and the chain of shops starting to be properly established. Twenty-nine and still unsettled and a man who was offering her marriage and partnership and a child. Kitty said it might be just what she needed and Hal believed it.

Until then, Hal had never thought in terms of staying with Dimitri forever. Or rather she had simply never thought. She presumed it was love; she could not return to the daily loneliness she had known before.

By the end of the day Jem's heart rate was almost normal. Hal decided it was safe to go home.

Coming down the escalator from the mezzanine, she didn't expect to see Gareth standing in the foyer. He was looking down the list of departments.

'Gareth, is everything alright?'

He spun to face her. 'Why shouldn't it be?'

'Why are you here?'

'To see you. Of course.'

She felt him taking her hand and holding it. 'Me? What about? What's happened?'

'Not about anything. About now. How about now? Is now alright?' He seemed unnaturally alert.

'Gareth, what's going on?'

'You look good.' Gareth was staring at her with too much intensity. 'I don't often see you like this.'

'Like what?'

'You look really happy.'

'Do I?' But Hal wasn't surprised to hear it. 'I've saved a life today.' She was happy, she was as happy as she could remember since Nicky. Was that why she felt she ought to apologise for it?

'I thought you did that every day. I thought that'd be boring old routine by now.'

'No, usually I just prolong lives a little. Fight the struggle a bit longer. Then consign them to the darkness.'

'Very philosophical.'

'Too much for you, I know.'

Gareth stood there in front of her, his eyes shining. He was still holding her hand. Hal pushed it back, smoothed her hair by way of excuse.

'I like seeing you like this, you know, kind of in a different place.' Gareth had moved closer. 'Can I buy you a drink? A coffee. How about a coffee?'

There were always hidden agendas with Gareth – but it might be fun finding out what it was this time. 'Alright. Over there. What they call the Bar Venezia. We can get a cappuccino.'

'Here?' Now it was Gareth's turn to look nonplussed. 'Here in the hospital, you mean?'

'There's nowhere out there, you've seen what it's like round here.'

'It's all a bit public, isn't it? I mean, right here, where you work. I'll drive us somewhere.'

'Fine, drive me home.'

'OK. Sure.'

He had left his car on the double yellow line opposite. He pulled out into the traffic, accelerating to get ahead of an oncoming van. Hal remembered what agony it was being driven by Gareth.

'I don't believe you came all the way out here just to see me, Gareth.'

'Well, yes and no. I had a meeting over at the old TV-AM place. I thought I'd just . . . you know.' But he still seemed to be too awake, his eyes slightly too wide.

They drove through Bloomsbury in silence. Then:

'It's not the first time.'

'First what?'

'First time I've called in to see you. Sort of unannounced like this.'

'Yes, it is.'

'No, there was an evening a few months ago, you know before the . . . sorry, anyway, you were apparently busy.'

'I do work there. Saving the nation's health.'

'Except you weren't on the ward.'

'There are other places I have to go.'

'They went and looked for you but you weren't any-where else.'

Hal felt like she was playing twenty questions. 'Gareth, I'm lost.'

'It's nothing important.' Gareth shrugged and concen-trated on the traffic. 'Forget it.'

They drove for a few minutes. Hal tried to watch the streets go past, shop fronts and bus stops. They had just crossed the river when Gareth swerved into the kerb and stopped the car. She looked around and realised that she was checking to see how busy the street was. He leaned towards her, she could smell his anxiety. His hand was suddenly on the lapel of her coat. 'Nice, with the fur collar round your face. All Russian – sleighs and wolves and things.'

'It's fake fur.' Hal felt her own stillness.

'It's still gorgeous.' He reached up, ran the back of his fingers down the side of her cheek. His fingers were damp.

'What are you doing?'

'I wanted to feel the difference. The fur, your skin. Which is softer. I had to know. Sorry.'

'Your hands are clammy, Gareth.'

Gareth quickly rubbed his palms down his trouser legs. Hal reached for the door handle and Gareth immediately flicked down the central locking, left his elbow pushing down on the button.

Hal's blood was beating. 'Just hear me out.'

'Gareth, I'd like you to let me out of this car.'

'I just want to say something else. Just a little something.'

'Let me out or I start making a scene.' Was this really happening, like this, in a car? 'People are bound to see, let's not get into that.'

Gareth pulled up the lock and all the doors clicked open. 'We'll talk later, OK?'

'I've no idea. I doubt it.'

Hal stepped out of the car and walked straight into the first shop she could see that was open. It was an all-night store. She stood flicking through tired and greasy magazines until she could see that Gareth's car had pulled away.

'What about this light – I'm shining my torch into your eyes?'

'Yeah, yeah,' course.' Jem moved his head, searching for the source of the light. 'It's bright.'

The cardiac arrest – purely because his fluid level had dropped too low – marked a turning point and from then on Jem's condition improved steadily. Nothing was going to mend the long-term effects of the toxic abreaction, but after two days he was sitting up and on the third he was eating. By the fourth, Hal was able to start testing the extent of the damage.

'What about colour, what colour's this file? Hal held her notes a few inches above his eyes.

'Yeah, yeah. It's sort of green, isn't it?'

The file was green. 'Now tell me what's written on it.'

'I . . . I don't know. What's it matter?'

It would be as though he was looking through frosted glass – shapes, colour, movement, no detail. His fingertips were still bandaged so he hadn't yet reached up and sensed the bare patches on his scalp.

'Tell us where you're from, Jem.' They still only had his first name. He refused to tell them more. He looked about seventeen.

'I don't want no one coming here.' An edge of fear and anger slid into his voice. 'I don't want any of them here.'

'It's alright, we won't tell anyone if you don't want us to.'

'So why do you want to know?'

'It helps. For our records.' But Hal knew, above all, they needed his trust. 'It helps us to see your medical notes, find out why this happened to you.'

'I don't want people knowing about me. People are always reading things about me.'

'I'm not going to tell anybody anything. I'm not interested in the rest of your life, I just want to get you better.'

'Fucking right.' His speech was slurred, disturbed, his tongue forced to move carefully round the ulcers, the broken membranes inside his cheeks. But the anger remained clear.

'Are you the one that did me when my heart stopped?'

'I was involved, yes.'

'The other nurse, the Sister said I was dead for five minutes.'

'Not really. It's just your heart stopped. We had to start it again. It's just an engine.'

'What would've happened if you hadn't done it?'

'You would now be dead.'

'So all that time my heart wasn't going, I was dead?'

Too often, Hal had known depression follow heart failure, a flow of sadness growing out of the momentary step into otherness. 'No, one of your organs ceased functioning briefly. It doesn't mean you were dead. When you turn off a car's engine, it doesn't mean it's dead, doesn't mean you can't start it again.'

'Shows you don't know nothing about motors then.'

'You're right there.' Since Jem's fever had dropped, the blisters had also subsided, but the skin on his chest was still dangerously thin, any body movement causing rifts to crack open and another layer to peel back.

'So who started the engine up again? Who was it?'

'All of us. We all played a part.'

'It was you, wasn't it?'

'I made sure it happened, yes.'

'See? I knew it was you. I knew you wouldn't let me down.'

'It really isn't like that. It's just my job.'

'I knew you would. I knew it.'

Hal busied herself checking the drips. When she looked back at Jem, she saw the tear tracks down his cheeks: 'I'm in the dark, Doc. It's so fucking dark in here.'

Until the funeral everything was forgiven – Dimitri's vagueness, Hal's anger – but afterwards everything had become visible.

The Royal Cross had insisted on three months' leave. How could she tell them that was the last thing she wanted – three months with nothing to distract her? But they sent a man from Human Resources who said they'd have a hard time defending an action if she went back sooner; the insurance wouldn't cover it.

Gareth had said the business could survive without Dimitri for as long as he wanted – Dimitri should take whatever it took. Dimitri said Gareth was being really understanding.

So the two of them sat in the sitting room, lay in the bedroom, sat in the garden, stood by the kettle in the kitchen. They stared across at each other, they stared at the ceiling. Sometimes the radio was on. She would pick up a book, turn on the television, read the paper and her mind would absorb nothing. It wasn't as though she was thinking anything either – it was just that her mind was blanked. It wasn't fogged, it wasn't swirling, it was more of a white-out, a solid barrier round her. If she couldn't think about Nicky then she couldn't think about anything – it was like a deal she'd made with her subconscious.

She and Dimitri had nothing that had to be talked about and so nothing was said. In the hall, in the kitchen, they walked past each other in silence. Even the accident itself required no effort from them – the lorry driver had not seen Nicky, he said, hadn't even known he had mounted the kerb. The first he had known was the impact on the bonnet, the loss of control, then Hal's face past his side window, skidding to a halt in front of the tree. He wasn't trying to pretend it wasn't his fault and so they didn't even have the satisfaction of a battle to fight.

She spent days watching the people on the Common. She would sit on the bandstand and watch boys playing football on the tennis court, watch a whole game through from beginning to end. She would go into the Co-op on Lavender Hill and end up buying a tin of pasta and a Mars bar; then she would put them in the fridge; two days later she would throw them away. She refused to tidy the house; if she put on make-up, she was liable to wipe it off immediately; if she dressed properly, she soon reverted to leggings and a T-shirt. Anything else seemed to restore a normality to her life which was undeserved. She did not dare enter Nicky's room, leaving it exactly as it had been that morning.

Occasionally friends – from the hospital, parents from the school – called in. All she saw was the new emptiness of her life mirrored in their eyes. They soon left. For the first couple of weeks even Kitty could not find a way to talk to her – Kitty was her oldest friend, they had known each other since they'd met during Hal's clinical and Kitty's pre-nursing – but now Hal looked across the table at Kitty and knew she had been cast adrift. The undertow was pulling her away from the secure shore where Kitty was standing and she didn't have the strength to swim against it. They couldn't even start to talk about it.

Until one day Kitty had arrived at the door with a roll of binbags and a stack of cardboard boxes. She had taken Hal firmly by the hand and marched her up to Nicky's bedroom. She walked straight in and said 'Let's start'.

Hal stood in the doorway. She saw a faint greying of dust on the book jackets, on the plastic stacking boxes. All at once, she saw the ordinariness of Nicky's life and the specialness. Her belly felt hollow and she couldn't find the strength to step inside. Kitty took both her hands and, walking backwards herself, sleepwalked Hal into the room. 'Of course you don't want to. But we have to start.' She shut the door.

Now Hal was standing in the middle of the room: one foot on one of his discarded school vests, the other by a Saturday-made space station, a box with holes cut through and lollipop stick on the side. A normal, fretful, pasta for lunch, what-can-I-do Saturday, except that it was his last Saturday. She looked down at the floor and tried to see these possessions as just objects. She stared and stared and eventually, through clouded eyes, they turned into cardboard and sellotape and dirty clothes. She bent over and picked them up, dropped one into a binbag, the other into a cardboard box.

Together they started tidying it, deciding together. 'Would they want this lego in Paediatric?'

'They've got more than they know what to do with,' said Kitty.

'What about this game for Ortho, for the kids forced to lie still?'

'Good idea, in here.' She held out another binbag.

'I'm not giving anything to A&E.'

'I wasn't going to suggest it.' Kitty gave her a long-suffering look. Hal had wanted an enquiry into what had happened in A&E, convinced they had been too slow, too unwilling to operate: Nicky could have lived, she was sure. She had watched; she was convinced. Eventually Ridgeway had been sent to talk her out of it. It was the day before the funeral and she was too tired to argue.

Kitty said 'Let's just get things sorted into separate boxes, then everything's a whole lot easier.'

But Hal refused to strip the room. She could see it tidied and organised but it had to remain Nicky's.

'You'll regret it,' Kitty had warned.

'I need it. It's simple. I'm over it but I need it. No, I'm not over it. I'm over a part of it.'

'And what's the next part?'

'Deciding what the next part is, I suppose. Deciding what I have to do about everything. And then the part after that is doing it.'

'I think I understand. How's Dimitri?'

'It's hard to tell.'

'Is that the next part then, the bit you've still got to decide about?'

'It's a lot more complicated than just that.'

CHAPTER FOUR

She had always hated the way Gareth looked at her in the morning (after sleeping the night on their sofa), staring at her for too long and then smiling when he caught her eye. Even with Nicky sitting between them, eating his cereal. She'd known what it meant but refused to believe it. Now, after what happened in the car, she couldn't avoid it any longer.

But she hadn't told Dimitri. He wouldn't've believed her anyway, wouldn't've wanted to believe her. But it meant that now she and Gareth shared a secret and when Gareth had come to the house the day before, his eyes had told her he knew she hadn't and wouldn't ever tell Dimitri.

Hal stayed upstairs until Gareth left and then rang for a minicab.

She sat by Jem's bed, waiting.

'You still there, Doc?'

'I'm writing up my notes. This is as good a place as any.'

'What do I look like then?'

'That accent sounds like Yorkshire to me.'

'Fucking shithole of a place.'

'Been in London long?'

'Anything's better than Sheffield.'

'I've never been there.'

'Keep it that way. I'm never going back neither.' Jem's face, even through the creams, was rigid. 'Haven't been there for years anyway.'

'Where did you live before you came to London?'

'A home, charity place. Near Preston. Another fucking shithole. You going to leave me alone now?'

'If you want.' Hal started to collect her notes, put the lid on her pen, pushed back the chair.

When he heard that: 'How long's this going to last?'

'Quite a few weeks I should think.'

'Then I'll be able to see again?'

Occasionally in Epidermal Necrolysis patients, the loss of sight was psychological, just a shock reaction to the sight of the body shedding itself. But usually it was an irreparable scarring of the cornea.

'Why aren't you saying nothing?' In just his three days of blindness, he had already developed a raw-nerve awareness of silence.

'It varies.'

'What you saying? What you fucking saying? I'm not going to be fucking blind forever, am I?'

'We'll do everything we can.'

'Shit, I don't believe this. I don't fucking believe this.'

'It'd help if we knew what had brought this on.'

'You're the fucking doctor.'

'Did you take anything, Jem? Drugs, drink? Before you started to feel bad?'

'I took whatever I could get. You share things.'

'Do you know what you took? The night you started to get sick?'

'Some kind of downer. Tranquilliser or something. Might've been tazzy.'

'Because that may be what made you ill, Jem. A reaction to that.'

'Fuck. Shit. Shit. Two shitty tabs?'

'Are you sure you wouldn't like us to get in touch with someone?'

'Piss off, will you? Alright? Just piss off.'

★

The note on the door said "Frisbee By The Pond On The Common, Join Us". It was in Gareth's handwriting. It was a taunt. She was unwilling to let it pass.

The Common was a stark Winter plain, bleached of colour, the wind snagging on the bare branches. She found the two of them near the bandstand, Gareth still wearing his suit, his hands on his hips, Dimitri in the distance, lurching off to collect the frisbee. She wandered up alongside Gareth, her hands firmly in her pockets, her shoulders hunched against the cold.

'You going to join in?' he asked her, not even saying hello, barely turning to face her.

'Not really my sort of thing.' Hal didn't look at him either. She was determined to be there and not be there. 'I didn't think it was your sort of thing either?'

'I told Dimitri he needed some exercise.'

They both stood watching him in the distance bending to pick up the frisbee, leaning against a tree to catch his breath.

Again, without turning to face her: 'I don't know why you're fighting me like this.'

'Don't start that again. Please.'

'Look, OK, let's just talk, alright, nothing can happen here. You can walk away if you want to.'

'I will if you start.'

'We could be really something together. I know it.'

'You can't be serious.'

'You're wasted on Dimitri.'

'That's . . . look, that's none of your business. I'm not interested in having this kind of conversation with you.'

'I'm . . . I don't think I can take much more of this.' Gareth's voice started to thin out. 'I'm really breaking up here.'

Was that genuine desolation or was he faking it again? 'You're his business partner. He's your best friend.'

'Kind of.'

'What's that mean?'

But the frisbee was coming towards Gareth, resting on a current, curving away to the left. He ran across, caught it, threw it immediately back. Again it shot past Dimitri, into the space beyond. Dimitri threw up his arms; Gareth was doing it on purpose.

'That time I came to see you at the hospital. The first time, when I couldn't find you.'

'Christ, not that again.'

'They looked for you everywhere they said.'

'Why didn't they page me?'

'They didn't need to. They could've just rung you. They knew where you were.'

Hal needed a chance to think. She said: 'Take me through this again.'

'The nurses knew exactly where you were.' The frisbee came towards them, Gareth caught it, threw it.

'There you are then. Why didn't they come and get me?'

'That was the problem, you see. They said they didn't know. That's the game they were playing. Except I found out, found it all out.'

'I can see you're dying to tell me. Go on, tell me everything you found out.'

'Well . . . that time, one of the nurses was clocking off. So I took her for a drink.' Catch, throw. 'Nice girl – Irish, of course. She said everyone knew about it.'

'Knew about what, for God's sake, Gareth?'

'You and the young House Officer. I don't remember his name. She did tell me. We got quite drunk, you see. Well, she did.'

'What young House Officer?' She was trying to sound baffled and innocent and knew she wasn't succeeding.

'Now, that would be silly, Hal, to make me go through it all, all the sordid details. You don't want all that, do you?' He ran and caught and threw.

Hal thought about what could happen. She thought about anger and mess but nothing seemed impossible any more, nothing seemed indestructible.

She and Gareth stood side by side in silence.

Catch, throw.

Then he said: 'Did you really think they didn't know about it?'

Yes, she said. She always thought they were careful. 'It's over now anyway. I ended it.'

'I thought as much.'

'So you can just keep it to yourself now. It was completely unimportant.'

'My lips are sealed, Hal, you don't need to worry one jot.'

It had been a simple, passionless affair, but it had been hers. Now it was his as well.

Suddenly his voice was much calmer: 'I mean . . . I wouldn't want to have to tell Dimitri.'

'What the hell are you talking about now?'

'I mean, don't force me to tell Dimitri.' Catch, throw.

'Why would I do that?'

'By being stupid.'

'And what do I have to do to be clever?'

'Just take me seriously.'

'I do.'

'My proposal. Just take my proposal seriously.'

'You're barking, Gareth. You're saying we should . . . we should what? Have some sort of relationship otherwise you'll tell Dimitri about some silly thing I got into at work? That's really going to get us off to flying start.'

'I'm saying there are two ways to end your marriage – and that's long overdue. Either you end it nicely, or it can be nasty, that's if Dimitri finds out.' Catch, throw. 'So I'm giving you a chance to do it your way.'

'Jesus Christ, you're conniving. No, it's beyond conniving.'

'I'm trying to be honest here. And I'm trying to give you a real opportunity to end this ridiculous marriage of yours honestly. Once you're free of it, you and I can see what happens. I'm sorry if I was little too forward the other day, in the car.'

'Are you drunk, Gareth?'

'Dimitri and I have been celebrating actually.' He jogged his shoulders, showed it wasn't that important. 'Shared a drop of Moët.'

'What have you got to celebrate?'

'Big things. Big, big things. Dimitri's taken a big step. That's why you've got to sort out everything else.'

'Nice of him to tell me all about it. What is it?'

'I think he should tell you himself.'

'You love secrets, don't you, Gareth? Pretending things are far more difficult than they are. More to find out than there really is.'

'Your skin's a secret.' And he was stretching forward again to touch her face. Hal pulled her hand out of her coat pocket, slapped his fingers away. After half a second of looking offended, his face hardened into a wet-eyed smile. Hal's eyes flicked across to see if Dimitri had seen. He hadn't. Then Gareth said:

'What are you so scared of?'

'Please, don't, Gareth. It's silly.'

Gareth's smile remained determined: 'There's nothing silly about—' Suddenly the frisbee was accelerating sharply up into the air in front of them. Dimitri had thrown it straight upwards and was now running towards them to catch it himself. Gareth turned sharply from Hal and sprinted across to intercept it. The two men ran towards each other as the frisbee started to curve back downwards and then both leaped into the air. Gareth, taller anyway, snapped the frisbee out of the air and as he landed, brought his heel down, scraping along the skin of Dimitri's calf.

With an instant yelp, Dimitri collapsed into the wet grass. 'Fucking hell, fucking hell.' Lying on his side, he clutched at his leg, pulled up his trousers and looked at the reddened skin. 'Shit. What was that for?'

Gareth spun the frisbee round on a finger. 'Bad, is it?'

'You did that on purpose.'

'Stretcher bearers! Is there a doctor on the common?' Gareth was enjoying it. He looked across at Hal, making sure she'd seen.

'Help me up, you bastard.' Dimitri waved a hand towards Gareth. 'You bloody did that on purpose.'

But Gareth just stood looking down at Dimitri: 'You're exaggerating. As usual.'

Hal took Dimitri's arm, hoisted him up. Dimitri pulled out the hipflask, threw back his head, drained it.

When he'd finished, Hal asked 'Any for us?'

'Sorry, didn't realise. Let's go home. Plenty more there.'

'You people go. My car's parked by Clapham South tube,' said Gareth. 'I'll see you tomorrow.'

'See you tomorrow.'

Hal and Dimitri walked in silence until they reached the road. Then Hal asked 'So what's the big decision you've taken?'

'Gar told you, did he?'

'He just said you'd been celebrating something big.'

'Yes, we have.' Dimitri pursed his lips in a half-smile. 'I've sold him my half of the business. I'm getting out. It's brilliant, isn't it?'

CHAPTER FIVE

'It's a brilliant deal. I don't have to do anything, I get a monthly cheque. Gareth has to handle all the day-to-day boring stuff – God, am I sick to my teeth of all that – I just take the money.' Dimitri took a large gulp from his tumbler, leaned forward, poured in more vodka. His hand wavered above the tonic bottle, decided against. 'He's bought me out in staggered payments, you see. I just have to agree not to go into a similar business. Dream on.' He levered his leg back up onto the chair and groaned histrionically.

Hal, standing by the hob, aimlessly stirring tepid, congealing soup, watched his jerking, uncoordinated movements: 'How much is this monthly cheque then?'

'Enough. More than enough. Of course, it depends on how the business does, of course. There are other variables built in as well, it's only fair.'

'I thought the business was important to you? Something you had created.'

'I couldn't care less. I'm sick of it. It's all a sickening waste of time.'

Hal knew that everything had turned into a waste of time – for both of them – and she knew they should be talking about it. But even talking it out was a waste of time.

'So what are you going to do with your time?'

'It doesn't matter. Isn't that wonderful? We can do what we want. Isn't that brilliant?'

'Maybe I don't want to.'

'Then you can do what you want. It's a free country.' Dimitri looked away. 'We could think about another . . .' But he didn't finish the sentence. He didn't have to.

'And Gareth just walks away with everything? Everything you've build up. Suddenly the whole business belongs to him?'

'He's done me a favour. Frankly, between you and me, the shops are on their last legs – the High Street recession's hit us bad and the chain needs refloating.'

He was sitting at the round pine table, rotating his glass through its condensation ring, picking at the varnish. He didn't look up when he said: 'I thought you'd be pleased.' He was whining now. 'I really thought . . . you've always said I needed a change. Now I've got a real chance.'

Hal picked up her teacup, cradled it in two hands, turned to look out the back window, the garden fighting back into life – the daffodils already browning, everything else shooting pure green. With her back still to him: 'Why didn't you tell me you were doing this?'

'It's business, Hal – do you ask me what to do with your patients?'

'It wasn't my fucking fault. I was in the pub, just playing pool, with my mates. We were playing this bloke, he thought he were the right fucking bollocks except I'd hustled him for a ton already.' Jem lies perfectly still on the bed, only his mouth moving. 'We was playing a second frame double up. He was about to bollock the eight ball and I was going to be two hundred quid up before I'd finished my pint.

'Then suddenly the landlord's yelling at me, saying Mum's on the phone. She's got to speak to me urgent like. I tell him she can wait. He says it's that urgent. Except the bloke said I was chucking it in. I fucking threw away two hundred quid just to speak to her. But it's your Mum, right? You've got to do what she asks.

'She's going crazy on the phone. Shouting and screaming and crying, saying he's coming to get her; he's outside, trying to break in, smashing the front garden up, saying he'll kill her. Says he's got the dustbin; says he's going to throw it through the front window.

'She were talking about my Dad. When there's trouble, it's always my Dad. They don't live together or nothing. Not since he went to the Falklands – he was at Goose Green – and came back with this metal plate in his head. Says it helps him think. Never thought nothing in his whole fucking life before he went and he never thinks nothing now. He's a moron. Before he went to the Falklands he just, like, hit my Mum, broke her jaw once. Now he's back he wants to kill her. Says she's a whore and no one says that without getting a pasting from me. No one, right? Last person said that ended up in hospital, eating through a tube.

'I get round to her flat and he's broken in through her front door, straight through the wood, a bloody great hole shaped like him, you know, like in Tom and Jerry, it was brilliant. I go in, up the stairs and there he is hammering on my Mum's bedroom door.

'I can hear her screaming inside, fucking terrified and he's standing there in his camouflage jacket, pissing against the door. He's just standing there with his wood in his hand pissing into the lock, running down the door, steam and everything.

'He turns round and sees me and says something clever like Fuck Off. He's still holding his dick, piss still pissing out of it. I tell him to fuck off and leave my mother alone. He says it's his business and I can shut up. I walk up to him, we're standing like this, and tell him to leave her alone. That's when he tries to head-butt me, but he's too fucking pissed and he just sort of staggers forward, falls down onto his knees. He sort of coughs and I think he's going to chuck up on my boots, but he just stops there, on all fours. That's when I kicked him, under the chin, not hard, and he rolled over onto his back. He was saying he was my father, I wasn't supposed to go hitting him. He'd fucking laid into me enough times. It was his turn now.

'I told him to stand up. Try and hit me if he wanted. Each time he swung at me I just laid another one into him. In his guts, on his face, I put my elbows into his kidneys and he went down again, like he was praying. I pushed him down the stairs. He went down there like some great hairy rolling thing, banging against the rail. Ended up at the bottom, this ball of hair and jacket and piss.

'That's when the police got there. They said Did I do that? I said Yeah. On my own? I said Yeah. They couldn't believe it. My Dad's like huge, about twice the size of me. They said I should be doing their job, I'd be good. I said I might one day.

'Banged me up for assault for that, they did. Said my Dad was too drunk to fight. Out of order that was. I was only trying to protect my own fucking Mum.'

He finished.

'I thought you said your Dad was a steel worker?'

'Did I?'

'What about your Mum?'

'What about her?'

Gareth's car was parked by the 7-11, Gareth sitting in the open passenger door doing up his shoes. He knew she walked this way to work.

'How dare you?'

'Sorry?' Gareth was all amazed innocence. 'Dimitri's leg isn't that bad, is it?'

'You said the other night you wanted to help him. This buyout isn't going to help him one bit.'

'I told him he should have discussed it with you earlier.' Gareth looked up at her with little boy eyes. She couldn't help noticing how blue they were. 'He insisted on secrecy until it was all done and dusted.'

'You should be ashamed.'

'I'm not ashamed in the least. It's a mutually beneficial arrangement that rewards both parties for their commitment to date,' Gareth slipped so easily into this dead language. 'And it's incremented for any future turns in the market.'

'He'll go to pieces without a job.'

Gareth turned back to the laces of his brown brogues. Hal looked down at where his pale hair was starting to thin on top. Then, he said, without looking up: 'I've been changing these shoes for the last fifteen minutes waiting for you to turn up. God knows what people thought I was doing. Probably thought I was some congenital idiot. Or just plastered, I suppose.' And with that he looked back up, half-smiling.

'You're a complete bastard.'

'Maybe, but I'm the complete bastard you should be with, not that drunk.' Did he really believe this would win her over? 'You've always played so hard to get with me, Hal. Now's the time to let it all go and admit your mistakes. I won't hold them against you.'

'You've ripped him off. What's this monthly payment crap?'

'It's what he's worth. We haven't got the capital to buy him out outright – that's thanks to his cock-ups, in fact – but this way he'll keep getting share-related payments, it's pretty equitable.'

'Till you get bored. Till you make him sign another agreement he can barely even read.' Then Hal realised: 'You've fired him, haven't you?'

'Face it, Hal, he's worse than useless these days – no one in the office listens to him, they have to come to me to get everything checked. Every time he picks up the phone we all hold our breath, wonder what balls-up we're going to have to sort out afterwards.'

'You told him the company wasn't making a profit any more.'

'With him in charge, we wouldn't be. Look, Hal, you don't understand, I've got big money wrapped up in the shops. I can't let a drunk blow it all. We can't watch him all the time. Do you know what he ordered last week? He faxed this supplier, and—'

'Spare me, Gareth. You've sacked him from his own company.'

'But he doesn't know it, does he? He doesn't have to say it.'

'What about his shares? He could vote you out.'

'His shares are valueless. If he insisted on full voting rights, the company'd go under overnight. I've been very generous when all's said and done.' Gareth stretched his cheeks out, ran his tongue round the inside of his square teeth.

'What about my shares?' Hal asked, though she knew the answer.

'Dimitri has signing rights on those; he sold them to me as well. If you don't want that, I'm quite happy to sell them back to you.'

'Yes, please.'

'It will reduce the payments we make to Dimitri. Do you want to think about it?'

Why was she doing this? What battle did she feel she was fighting? 'Forget it. Keep the stupid shares.' And instead of going to work, she turned around and went back home. She heard Gareth calling for her to come back but he didn't follow her.

In the sitting room, Dimitri was asleep on the sofa, on his back, his cheeks vibrating. Hal walked upstairs.

She felt as though she was breaking up into islands, becoming separate parts of herself.

She was lying on Nicky's bed. His sheets, his duvet but they no longer smelled of him. She imagined his head on the pillow or down beside the pillow where he usually ended up, his limbs twisted left and right.

She'd rung the ward and told them she had a migraine. She almost wished she did – something to end this fractured feeling, something to justify the panic that was rising through her. No, it wasn't panic: it was need, desperate need.

She remembered the night Nicky had sleepwalked downstairs, telling them about the kittens who had been attacking him in his room, in his bed, a swarm of kittens all over his face. She had led him back up to his bed and he had gripped his koala and settled immediately. He didn't remember it in the morning; recently Dimitri couldn't remember it happening either.

She had tried to save Dimitri from himself. He would slide away fast now, without at least the pretence of the office to visit. Maybe it all needed to come to a crisis and he would start his climb back up all the sooner.

But what about her?

And every other day, when they had to change the dressing on Jem's fingers, he would yell, his white anger filling the ward, a furious, endangered noise spilling out of the curtained cubicle. Ridgeway had reduced the level of his oromorph – Jem was already classed as an outlyer; he had exceeded his Expected Bed Stay and Ridgeway was determined to limit the cost.

Under the dressing, in their lightless existence, his finger ends were almost green. Without nails, they seemed somehow inhuman, shining, wrinkled probes.

'Careful now, Jem, you'll make it worse. We've got to do this.' The nurses were ever sensible. But he was beyond logic, beyond sedatives, beyond safety, in his own world of pain, asking for his mother or his father.

'But I thought you and your Dad, you said you had a big fight?' Hal asked.

Jem turned and looked towards Hal, patiently.

Kitty took Hal downstairs for a coffee. 'You're too focused on the TEN boy. You seem to spend all the spare time you've got talking to him.'

'I'm trying to find out who he is, where he's come from. We still don't even know his second name.'

'It'll happen. You can't force it.'

'What am I doing wrong? Am I neglecting the other patients?'

'Not quite. But one or two have noticed you're always talking to Jem not them.'

'They've said that?'

'Yes. To me, to other nurses.'

'So what?'

'I don't care about what they think, Hal. It's you I'm worried about.'

'I'm OK.'

'You don't look it. And what's this migraine, you've never had them before, have you?'

'I didn't. I just couldn't face the ward yesterday.'

'You see. That's even worse.'

'I needed a day off. You're making it sound like the sinking of the Titanic.'

'And Dimitri, how's his new life?'

'Nothing to it.'

Most mornings, Gareth rang at about half past seven. Hal told him she wasn't ready to talk and hung up on him. This morning he rang straight back, she told him to Fuck Off and left the phone off the hook.

Then she made herself a cup of tea, sat alone at the kitchen table and waited for the morning to begin.

Opposite Sainsbury's, a gangling, grey-bearded man was selling *The Big Issue*. He was wearing a thin, stained, porkpie hat, a patchy once-blue windcheater. Hal bought a copy and as she looked for the coins, found she was asking him if he'd ever come across a boy called Jem.

'That's right, I've got a son called Jem,' he replied, staring straight back at Hal with clear, hazel eyes. 'I've got a boy called Jem.'

'How old is he?'

'About sixteen.'

'Is he sleeping rough?' The walls of her heart were shuddering.

And suddenly the man was looking down at his plimsolls, mumbling, biting the wisps of his beard. Hal reached out a hand, wanting only to reassure him. He swung away.

'Please tell me.' Hal had to know. 'Your son, Jem, is he sleeping on the streets?'

The man looked up again, looked at the pictures moving and changing on the front of the supermarket: 'My son's called Africa.' Again, the man was gazing at her, down into her. This time, Hal started to notice the red rings, like ripples from a stone in a pond, expanding round his eyes. Hal waited patiently while he sold another copy of the magazine, then: 'Is your son called Jem or Africa? Please tell me. Which is it?'

'I wish I'd had a son. I wish it. I always wanted a son. Never got the chance. But hostels are disgusting places; you couldn't take a baby in there. Not fit for a dog.'

★

73

Hal remembered leaving Nicky at the school gates – he didn't want her to come in with him – watching him race across the tarmac, leaping into the air, and as he landed, grasp his best friend round the neck and pull him to the ground.

When Hal arrived on the ward she found that Jem's chest was no longer protected by dressings, but instead the papery, purple skin was open to the air, the sheets drawn back. His skin was cool to the touch.

'Who's that?'

Hal's hand jumped; she had thought Jem was asleep; he had been so still, his breathing so shallow.

'It's the doctor. Sorry if I woke you.'

''Bout time. What's happening? I'm fucking freezing.'

'Why are you uncovered?'

'Don't ask me. Can't I have one of them baths like I always do?'

'I'll find out. Hold on.'

Hal walked across the ward to the nurses' station. 'What's happened?' she asked Sister Ursula.

Leaning on the counter, continuing with her paperwork, not looking up, Sister Ursula: 'Doctor Ridgeway changed the boy's therapy.'

'When was this?'

'He came in last night, thought the lad was coming on well. No more creams, no more soaks. Said his skin was too damp. It needs to start breathing.'

'Why wasn't I consulted, he's my patient?'

Only now did Sister Ursula look up. 'This is Doctor Ridgeway's ward.' Her voice was flat, administrative, vengeful.

The two women looked at each other. Hal knew that Sister Ursula's ability to use the system was far more acute than her own. She was going to have to do this herself.

She walked down the corridor to the dispensing cupboard, took out a cardboard box of emollient. Then she
walked into the bathroom, opened the taps, emptied the
sachet into the turning water. She walked back into the ward
and up to Jem's bed: 'Time for a soak, Jem.'

'Thank God.'

And Hal eased her hand under his back, gently lifted his
thin torso up off the mattress. His shoulders caved backwards and his hands dropped onto the mattress beside him.
'Come on, you can support yourself if you try. Please, Jem,
for me.'

Reluctantly Jem started to use what was left of his
strength, bending his arms, taking some of the strain into his
elbows. His toes were searching for the floor as Sister
Ursula swept across.

'Can I do anything to help, Doctor?'

'It's time for Jem's emollients.'

'Doctor Ridgeway doesn't think that's necessary any
more. I'm sorry, I thought I'd made that clear?'

'I want him to have it.' She was standing behind Jem,
talking to Sister Ursula over the boy's shoulder. 'I'm going to
help you stand now, Jem.' She bent forward, slid her hands
under Jem's arms and slowly, gently started to take the
weight. He groaned as her sleeves rubbed against the
exposed skin of his back. 'The more you take your own
weight, the less friction there'll be, Jem.'

'It hurts like fuck.'

'You can't hope to get him into the bath on your own.'
Sister Ursula was still standing there behind Hal, waiting for
a disaster only she could relieve.

'Are you going to help me or just get in the way?' Hal
was now walking backwards as he slid his feet across the
lino like a skier.

'That's a table there, isn't it?' Jem's voice was both proud
and fearful.

'Just here, that's right.'

'I caught my toe on it last time. Total agony.'

Hal steered him round the island of filing cabinets and into the open area of the ward aisle. She was sweating. All the other nurses had stopped to watch their halting progress.

'Hold the doors open, will you?' asked Hal.

But Sister Ursula just crossed her arms in cliché refusal.

'Hold still a moment, Jem.' Hal lined herself up against the swing doors and then pushed them open while slowly guiding Jem through. Sister Ursula dodged ahead of them.

Hal, moving backwards, facing Jem, didn't know Sister Ursula had stationed herself in the bathroom doorway until she bumped into her. The voice came over Hal's shoulder: 'I can't let you do this, Doctor.'

'It's just a soak, for Christ's sake. We'll discuss it with Doctor Ridgeway when he comes in.'

'He specifically said no more of this.' Her voice was tinged with panic.

'Can you get out of my way? Please?'

A cluster of nurses had now gathered round the ward doors watching them through the wired glass.

'What's going on, Doc?' Jem's voice was thin, emerging from the darkness in which he stood, barely balancing.

'Don't worry, Jem, nearly there.' To Sister Ursula: 'This patient is going to fall or something worse, unless we get him into the bathroom.'

'I'll take him back to his bed then.' Sister Ursula tried to squeeze her hand between Hal's hand and Jem's elbow. Hal clenched tighter.

'Just hold on here, Jem,' and she guided his mitten-bandaged hands to the towel rail. 'Support yourself there. Just for a few seconds.' Then Hal took Sister Ursula by the shoulders and forcibly started to move her sideways out of the doorway.

'Will you let go of me, please, Doctor?' She was rooted to the ground, though doing nothing else, knowing that if she struck out she would be diminished. 'Will you please stop that, Doctor?'

'No, Sister, I won't and I can't. I've got work to do.' And with a final lurch, Sister Ursula stumbled sideways into the corridor, regaining her balance after a few drunken-looking hops. 'Sorry,' Hal said and locked the door.

When Hal turned off the taps, she could hear Sister Ursula in the nurses' office next door, on the phone to Ridgeway in Sloane Street.

'Sometimes on the Bridge you can get a couple of quid in just half an hour – especially if you get there for the commuters, early morning, when people still think they're rich, when they still want to feel holy, feel they're getting something out of their shitty lives, not just grinding and grudging and tramping out of a train into a fucking office back out into a train. You don't use a sign, that's what I say, they think that's too organised, you've got to look them in the eyes, ask for the money. That's what they can't take. But when it's raining, it's the worst, you can forget it, they don't want to stop, don't even see you with their umbrellas, and all the time you get pissed on. Fucking awful.'

Jem was lying on his back, reciting from his manual of street survival.

Hal asked 'So what do you do when it's raining? I mean, what do you do to eat, things like that?'

He didn't answer immediately, and then he said: 'What am I going to do if I can't see them proper?'

'Don't worry. You'll never have to go back to that.'

'Why not? What else is there?'

'Tell us your name, Jem, the rest of your name, where you're from.' Hal knew she mustn't sound as though she was

77

begging. 'We'll get in touch with someone. Get you sorted out.'

'I'm never going back to them people.' But his voice betrayed the doubt, the fear that meant he might soon start to tell them.

Hal decided to push harder: 'You're going to need help, Jem, you're—'

'Could I possibly have a word, Doctor?' Ridgeway was suddenly at her shoulder.

'Who's there?'

'Just the Consultant, you remember.' Hal stood up. 'I'm going to go and have a word with him.'

'What's wrong? What's happening to me?'

'It's nothing to do with you, son.' But Ridgeway's attempt to mollify merely added to Jem's fears.

'You going to come back, Doc?'

'Sure. Soon.'

Noiselessly Ridgeway led Hal away to the office. With his customary excessive manners, he opened and closed the door for her, easing the knob back into place. It was as though he imposed himself on objects by reducing them to silence.

She stood by the desk, reminded of school, of talkings-to from teachers who claimed to be disappointed. Why was she letting this man do this to her?

Ridgeway had taken up a position standing framed by the shelves of olive green files. He interlocked his fingers: 'I've had complaints from the nursing staff. Several over the last few weeks. This morning, as I am sure you are well aware, merely brought things to a head.'

Hal said nothing.

Ridgeway waited for her to speak. Then: 'Tell me, Doctor, are you surprised?'

'What was it about this time?' Hal did her best to sound bored.

'Come, come, you are well aware of your actions.'

'I'm never surprised by what they can dig up. You know they never like women. It's a harem thing.'

'Is it them or you who doesn't like women?' Ridgeway stared at her, prepared to wait.

But Hal refused: 'Can I be told what this is about?'

'That boy, the Necrolysis boy. Fundamentally, they think you're too involved. Apparently you were offensive to Sister, during the occasion of his cardiac arrest.'

'We wanted a defibrillator, we had to have one—'

'I'd say history proves you wrong there,' he said nonchalantly.

'We were lucky. She didn't seem to care that there weren't any available. All but one are broken, did you know that?'

'You were blaming Sister for this state of affairs?'

'We've got to blame someone. Otherwise . . .' Hal had to look away, out over the hospital car park. She watched a man battling with the ticket machine.

'Otherwise what?' said Ridgeway. He had moved round, was sitting on the desk just in front of her. He had accomplished the move silently.

Hal knew he was drawing her out, forcing her to say what doctors were supposed never to say. She stood and looked back at him. He laced and unlaced his fingers, ran an index finger along the spine of a book on the desk. 'I appreciate you have problems, but I'm not sure this anger is the right solution.'

'I've got a lot of work to do. I'm behind on my list. Can we continue this later?'

'Then there's the business of the soak this morning.'

'He was freezing. And his skin was far too dry.'

'I adjusted his regimen yesterday evening. And I believe Sister Ursula made that plain to you.'

'There wasn't time to wait until you were next in.'

'I believe the telephone has been invented.'

'I know. I heard Sister making extensive use of it.'

Ridgeway finally exploded, his face flushing, his voice full: 'Of course. I had given express instructions which you were deliberately flouting. She was doing her job. You were not.' He wasn't shouting, but his voice was coloured by how much he despised her, by how little respect he had for her view of the patients' needs. 'If you can't handle being back at work, don't show it by disrupting the work of this ward. We're all very sorry for you and further compassionate leave is unlikely to be a problem.'

She stood silent, watched the cars move round and round the car park, queuing for spaces. Ridgeway continued: 'I've looked at his notes: it is my opinion that he is due to be discharged pretty soon.'

'He can barely move! The blistering's subsided but he's got no new skin on most of his torso.'

'He's ready for home care. He doesn't need a hospital bed any more. He's already an outlyer.'

'He's got social problems. He's been living on the street.'

'That's my fault?' Hal was momentarily winded: Ridgeway said this with such calm, such casualness. He continued: 'We make decisions on medical grounds – the sociology is someone else's problem, I believe.'

'It's ours if he's going to come straight back here.'

'That's what Social Services are for, Henrietta.' Now Ridgeway smiled: he had moved beyond derision. 'You're no longer the dispassionate healer you once were. We need to treat the patient as is medically best – that's not always hospitalisation.'

And he walked out of the room.

Leaving Hal staring down at the mêlée of papers on the desk. She swung her hand across the desk top, watched them cascade up and then slowly slide across left, right, left and down. And then the room was again still but for the grinding of engines outside, trolleys in the corridor, the plaster easing itself off the wall.

For the next week, Hal moved silently past Jem's bed, exploiting his sightlessness. From the far end of the ward, she watched him shiver, watched his clumsy hands exploring his nakedness, asking the nurses for something to soothe him, asking them for her.

She stood in the corner, concentrating on other cases, waiting for Ridgeway to fail, waiting until they needed her to rescue the boy.

CHAPTER SIX

Hal arrived home early, just before four. She saw from the street that the curtains were still drawn.

She walked up the stairs, hearing noise from the bedroom. She pushed the door open. It was the hiss of an untuned television and the room was lit only by the crackling greyblue of the screen. She stood for a few seconds, her eyes readjusting to this hazy, moving light.

Dimitri was asleep on his back, his legs stretched out, the duvet in a heap at the foot of the bed. His shoes were still on and his trousers had been pulled down, a frustrated knot round his ankles. His shirt was open and in his right hand he held the trunk of his prick, the purple head skewing sideways out of his fist. Across his torso was the morse code line of congealing semen, most of it collected around over his fingers, some of it in droplets in the hairs of his chest, some sliding yellowhite into his navel.

There was an unopened box of tissues beside him on the bed. Next to the tissues was the remote control for the video recorder. He had carried the machine up to the bedroom and finding the cable barely reached, had been forced to leave it propped on its side against the chest of drawers. There was a bottle of brandy next to it.

Hal looked at this man who had shared her life and who had fathered their dead child. She found it hard to be surprised.

She didn't wake him. Instead she picked up the remote; rewound the tape for a few seconds; pressed Play.

She was looking at two women, wearing G-strings which seemed to be made of some kind of pink fur. Their breasts, squat and upright on their chests, seemed too hard, water-filled. Their ribs were tight, their toes curled, their hair long and brown and waving and permed, their cheeks shining and plastic. It made them seem almost identical.

They were kneeling on a bed, facing each other. In between them, on all fours, was a man wearing a plastic dog mask, a dog's snout covering his whole face, cut-out holes for eyes – the sort you buy in fancy dress shops. Hal thought he was probably supposed to be an alsatian. Apart from the mask, the man was completely naked and his penis was erect. Each of the woman had a hand under his belly, and as the camera swung lower – no steadier than a home movie – it seemed that they were taking turns to masturbate him. The dog-man looked back at each of them occasionally and yelped and made panting sounds – Hal presumed this was to indicate that he was enjoying it. But he remained resolutely on all fours, never breaking from his role – Hal waited, but he played it for real. When the two women weren't touching the man, they were fondling each other, their arms stretching over the dog-man's back, touching each other's nipples, bellies, hair. They both wore painted smiles, heavy with red lipstick and the breathlessness of assumed pleasure. Occasionally their eyes slid sideways to check on the camera. The woman on the left then bent over, pushed her buttocks at the camera and pulled down her G-string. The camera swiftly moved in to close-up on her vulva – Hal was reminded of videotaped procedures she had watched as a student. Then the woman stretched her arms high above her head, arching her spine, and flopped down onto all fours. She was now alongside the dog-man. She turned her head back and looked to the other woman and barked – she made no attempt at a realistic sound: it was a child's version, an uninspired 'Woof Woof'. But this was a cue: the other woman then started to manoeuvre the dog-man so that he could mount the woman on all fours. She took his arms – again he behaved as if they were no more flexible than a dog's front legs – and lifted them up and round either side of the woman's back. The woman on all fours was yelling "Yes, Fido, yes, yes, Rover". Hal switched off the tape.

In the sudden silence she now heard the scramble of electric guitars that had been the film's soundtrack. Inaudible while she watched, now they filled her head clearly – the grind and aggression, the expression of the film's anger.

Hal looked down at Dimitri, still asleep. She picked up the brandy bottle, drank straight out of it.

She took another mouthful, running its bitterness round her mouth before swallowing.

The third mouthful she chewed, ran into the back of her throat and then spat out across Dimitri's body. He didn't wake up.

She walked over to the video recorder, found and pressed the eject button, wrenched the hinged flap off the cassette and started pulling the tape out. With each stretch of her arm, it spooled out and up and down onto Dimitri. She continued stretching and pulling the black ribbon – it spaghettied onto his body, forming a maze on and around his chest, his abdomen, his penis, his thighs, his ankles and back along his body. She was covering him with a shroud of tape, a scattering of filmic earth.

He looked as though someone had crossed him, out, scribbled over him in black marker pen.

Hal sat on the punched black metal bench. It was speckled with pigeon-droppings. On the next bench, two street alcoholics had laid out a tarpaulin to protect themselves, even though their clothes were already smeared with mud, grime, yesterday's vomit. They wore once-strong tweed suits, one still even had the waistcoat, now held together with string.

They passed a bottle of Thunderbird between them, leant forwards, elbows on knees, talking conspiratorially as though everyone passing wanted to eavesdrop on their most intimate secrets.

Hal tried to harness her thoughts but they kept sliding away, meshing with the mumblings of the two drinkers. Whenever she looked up, to focus and decide what to do, she saw the two women from the tape, walking along the street, shopping, on magazine covers in the newsagent, waiting for friends outside the tube station.

When Hal got home – about eight – she went straight up to Nicky's room, lay down.

After an hour, when she went downstairs, Dimitri was watching golf on the television in the kitchen. There was an open bottle of wine on the table. He asked if she'd like him to cook them something for supper. She said she'd do some pasta, put the kettle on, sat down at the table, opened the newspaper.

She knew it the moment she entered the ward. Ursula – probably warned by the nurses' network while Hal was still in the lift – swept across the lino in a cascade of starch: 'It's nothing to do with me. He just disappeared, during the night.' Her hands were outstretched, supplicating.

'How can he discharge himself? He can barely walk.' Hal knew Ursula was lying, could see her shoulders shrugging into it.

'I swear to you, you can talk to Sandra, she was on last night. One moment he was in his bed, looked completely asleep, Sandra got called away to—'

Hal wasn't going to wait to hear whatever she and Ridgeway had fabricated: 'Where the bloody hell has Ridgeway hidden him? Has he sent him somewhere? Some hostel or something?'

'Sandra got called away to the Sluice Room,' Sister Ursula was determined to finish. 'When she came back the bed was empty and his clothes and trainers were gone.'

'His fingers are still bandaged, he couldn't get shoes on.'

'God's honest truth. He walked out of here. It's the only thing could've happened.'

'How long was Sandra in Sluice?'

'About . . . at least ten minutes she said.'

'What the hell was she doing in there?'

'She does have a lot of responsibilities. She's left in sole charge of the ward for six hours.' Sister Ursula almost smiled. 'That's not my fault, it's the new shift pattern.'

'Did anyone see him go?'

'We're still waiting for the night staff to come back on. Sandra spoke to one security man, last night, said he might've seen him.'

'How could he miss him? Boy with skin peeling off him, bandaged fingers, no nails, bugger all hair.'

'He took the bandages off his hands. Sandra found the dressings all on the bed.'

'Why wasn't I called?'

'There was a doctor on call. And . . . and he's Doctor Ridgeway's patient.' Sister Ursula enjoyed this part of it.

'How could he walk out of this hospital unnoticed, looking like that?' Hal knew they were lying, needed them to be lying. 'Looking like . . . that?'

'Police or someone'll find him in a park or something. He won't be much the worse for it, when all's said and done, bit of fresh air.'

'You're right. Next thing we know Ridgeway'll be prescribing midnight walks round the park for all his critical patients.'

Hal walked back along the ward, back towards the lift, taking off her white coat, throwing it over the counter at the nurses' station, leaving behind her only stares. A nurse's voice said: 'Doctor, we've got someone we need you to look at. It's the lupus, she's taken a turn.'

But Hal walked down the aisle of beds, through the rubber-edged doors, past the crumbling Sluice Room door and through more swing doors into the stairwell.

She knew the police wouldn't bother to look for him. She knew no one would find him if she didn't.

Hal walked fast, almost breaking into a jog down Pancras Road, feeling the paving stones slide and tip under her feet. On either side, warehouses, windowless red brick and brown curved plastic, yards parked with rows of red vans.

She was running but she didn't know why she was running: Jem had left the Royal Cross five hours ago – if Ursula was to be believed – how could she hope to catch up? But then maybe she could – he was sick, he had lost toenails as well as fingernails, he could only move cautiously, on the sides of his feet. Hobbling round the ward a few days ago he had tried to laugh it off, saying he was a gorilla.

At the intersection – four roads curving round, lorries, taxis, diesel – he could have gone anywhere. But Hal knew: he would seek the darkness, the wall he could rub against, the parapet he could hide under, the shimmying edges of streetlight. A three-lane road swept up towards the north, another road led back down to the stations, another past mesh-covered shops led up to Camden High Street, and the last, the side turning, was a long-ignored street where people still lived. This was the one he would choose.

Against the flow of the traffic, Hal worked her way across. She held her hand up, forcing cars to slow and to acknowledge her.

To her right, a terrace of prefabs, a picket fence round each, roses and camellias, light green paint, aluminium funnel chimneys. Jem would not have dared stop here, he would have been intimidated, his city-child's loneliness too visible.

On the left-hand side, the solid hard wall of a disused engineering factory. Through the wrought-iron gate, Hal saw the abandoned yard – buddleias forcing through the concrete, almost trees, working round the armchairs and supermarket trolleys and rusting machine tools. Jem might choose this. But Hal tried shifting the gates – not even a rattle – and he wouldn't have had the strength to climb over.

The prefabs shot past the edge of Hal's eye as she ran to the bottom of this street, looked right and left. In front of her, up on a Victorian brick viaduct, the railway line to King's Cross cut across her path. Underneath, a seemingly endless row of empty arches, a row of tunnels that led deeper into the maze of terraces and wire fences that marked the edge of the estate.

Jem could be long gone in the opposite direction, picking up a lift on the North Circular. He might be sitting in the cab of a lorry as it drove him to Folkestone or Manchester, spinning one of his stories of street-fighting or of a family life he never knew, painting his life as it might have been. Or he might have collapsed, already be back in the hospital, speaking her name and waiting. But if he was still walking, he would have arrived here where Hal now stood, drawn to the tunnels, attracted to their honeycomb of possibilities.

She ran down the first tunnel. Though only about seventy, eighty yards long, the light barely penetrated to its centre. She looked up and down the gutter: for Jem, for a discarded bandage, any sign that he might have come down here. But there was only the damp-squashed cardboard takeaway boxes, a tyre, a dustbin lid.

She ran on, out at the far end, shocked by the sudden light, and, U-turning immediately to her right, ran straight back down the second tunnel. She called his name and heard it flung back at her. She called it again. The ground was wet and the oilslicked water kicked up her tights, her heel levered over scattered lumps of brick.

She reached the end, turning back and ran down the next. A train drummed overhead. She stopped in the darkness to let its vibrations fill the tunnel. She would find Jem, trying to stand, heaving himself up, using a scaffolding bar. He'd be trying to take the weight off his scarred feet, but, starting to cry tears of anger, tears of solitariness. She would walk gently up to him and begin the process.

She was running, as fast as she could, breathing the foetid air, knowing she had to hurry, that Jem could collapse at any moment, and then she tripped. Without warning, she found herself falling forwards, putting out her own hands to stem the coming pain. The shining ground spun towards her face. She took the impact on her palms then skidded sideways, rolling onto her shoulder, feeling damp shockwaves rippling into her. The air was knocked out of her lungs and something cold tore across her knees.

She lay silently for a moment, rolling onto her back, feeling her hair caught in the greasy wetness beneath her. She looked up at the tunnel roof, then she turned her head and saw that she had tripped on a car exhaust pipe, still spinning on its axis, rising and turning.

She rolled onto her hands and knees and then stood. Ignoring the stinging, the bruising in her breasts, she started to walk and then broke into a run. On into the next tunnel – the sixth or the seventh, whatever it was.

She felt something brush against her calf and saw the satin lining of her skirt was ripped and flapping. Her hands were wet and inflamed. She held them out on either side of her body as she ran, palms into the wind, forcing the air of her own movement to cool them. She shouted Jem's name louder. She was running through the tunnels, as fast as she could, burning the dampness out of her shoulder.

The last tunnel threw her out into a quadrangle of nettled ground, walled in by the estate and canal. In the middle of the pale grass stood a caravan. The towing arm had long since rusted and the wheels were missing, the axles propped on bricks. But it was not abandoned: someone had painted childlike circles and rings and starbursts all over it – primary blue and green and red. There were simple green sunshine sparkles spinning off the circles, snail-shells of rainbow colours turned round and round the windows and in the top corner, the words: GRIM DOG. From these words, a black arrow line pointed diagonally down to the bottom corner. A wheel had been replaced by breezeblocks and topped by a piece of hardboard – a makeshift kennel. A Yorkshire terrier lay half in and half out of its home, biting something out of its pads, wrenching with its jaw, and then looking up at her again.

She was still deciding whether to make her way into the estate, to look behind the wheelie bins, in the burnt-out cars, when, without warning, the shock arrived – the shock of the running, the fall, the solitude and echo of the tunnels. All she wanted was to sit and close her eyes. A nausea rose through her.

There was a garden chair in front of the caravan's main door – buckled plastic fabric in green and white stripes, greying aluminium tubing, white armrests.

Hal said to the side of the caravan 'Excuse me, I need to sit down,' and sat in the chair. As soon as she leant back, feeling herself slide over the plastic material, the waves of sleep moved up her body. She put the side of her head against her palm, shut her eyes.

'Make yourself comfortable.' The man was standing over her. He had made no sound as he emerged from the caravan and walked up to her. Or had she been asleep?

'Sorry, I . . .' Hal tried to lever herself up out of the chair.

He put out a hand to stop her. 'No, I meant it. You look

like you need a sit down. Someone had a go at you, have they?'

'I fell over. In the tunnel.' Hal could hear the slurring in her voice. 'Tripped on an exhaust pipe.'

'Did you?' The man clearly didn't believe her. 'Is that cold or are you scared or what?'

The man was pointing at her hands. They were trembling unstoppably, her knee banging against the side of the chair.

'You look like you could do with a drink.' And he went as silently as he had arrived. She watched him through the open door of the caravan as he found a mug and came back outside to a barrel. It was lashed to the side of the caravan and was fed by an open, upturned, black umbrella, spiked into the top of it. The man drew a cupful of water through the tap at the bottom of the barrel, rinsed out the mug, poured the waste water into a tub of thin herbs and went back up the steps into the caravan.

Just inside the door, he started to choose from a forest of bottles that filled the sink. He lifted one up, examined it, decided against, allowed it to slot back down. He selected another, read the hand-written label.

He was probably no more than thirty, but his sundried skin, his straggling beard, already greying in threads, made him look older. He was wearing overalls, a mechanic's blue suit – on the back, faded to pink, was a Kwikfit logo. The suit was open to the waist and underneath he was wearing a tie-dyed T-shirt. Round his head was a green handkerchief, tied pirate fashion. He was wearing no shoes. His toes were buckled and black. He came back down the stairs, holding a bottle and the mug.

'Nothing to be scared of. I've found the miracle cure. Take this.' He handed her the mug. Hal took it but had to place it on the armrest to stop it shaking.

'You've got it bad.' And he poured some of the clear

liquid into the mug. It smelled strongly alcoholic but pure and clean.

'What is it?' Hal said, except she could barely articulate, her lips trembling, her jaw shaking.

'One of my specials. It's good. Don't worry, strictly kosher.' He looked at her, waited for her to take a sip. 'Drink. It'll steady you up.'

Hal put the mug to her lips. As soon as it started to burn its hot path across her tongue she wanted it.

The man went across to the doorway of the caravan and picked up a chair, identical to the one Hal was sitting on, folded it out and sat down directly opposite her, their knees practically touching.

'I got two,' he indicated the chairs, 'for when I have guests. But then I don't get as many as I'd want. Usually just the pigs and when they come, they don't want to sit down. They just stand there, with their forms and notices. I say "Sit down, take the weight off your legs," but they never do. It's such a waste, I got two. I say "Come on, man, just sit down, we're all humans when we get in the bath." Instead they hand me the pieces of paper saying The Secretary of State for this or that requires you to do this or vacate that site by such and such. I say, why doesn't he come down here himself, this Secretary, and he could sit on my other chair, we could talk about it? They just say he's too busy. Of course he is, building all these roads – why does he want to build all these roads? Why does he? You work over at the hospital, don't you?'

Hal, calmed by the drink, whatever it was, was suddenly jolted: 'How do you know?'

'I live here. You're one of my locals. Not much I don't know. I've seen you coming to work. Going home to hubby.'

'I've never been down here before. The tube's the other way.'

'You think I just sit here all day and all night? I take a

look around. Me and Grim, we like a walk up round the Cross. Nice garden you've got next to your gaff. Isn't it, Grim?' he leaned sideways to look at the dog. The dog stood, expectant. 'Not much I don't know, see?'

'Do you know my name?'

'Of course I don't. I'm not a spy, I don't bug phones. Anyway, what's a name? A name's just some way of labelling you. I don't want to label people. I want to know them, inside, not out.'

He sat back and looked at her. Grim Dog came and jumped onto his lap. His chair creaked, metal on metal.

'So tell me what you want to know.'

Hal now felt more confident, stared back at him.

'What are you doing here? How about that?'

'I'd rather not say.'

'No sweat. What happened to you?'

'I was running down one of the tunnels, under the railway line; there was this old car exhaust, something like that. I didn't see it. I tripped.' She held up her hands to show her black-red, grazed palms.

'You want to get them cleaned up?'

Hal found a tissue in her pocket, was about to spit on it, when she asked: 'Do you mind?' She held the tissue over her mug.

'It's yours.'

She dipped the end of the tissue into the drink, started to dab it on her knee. It burned less than it did in her mouth.

'Useful stuff, isn't it?'

Hal looked up and saw the man smile. 'Tell me your name. Or what I should call you.'

'People on the estate call me Spider. Happy Spider. That's why Grim Dog's called Grim. So you can tell us apart.'

'He doesn't look too grim to me.'

'He has a dark side. Sees the skull under the skin. He broods. Don't get him going.'

Hal had got most of the blood and grime off her knee, revealing a skidding trench of missing skin. She wanted to start cleaning her hands, but the tissue was sodden. Spider was already up and handing her a toilet roll.

'Three-ply – feel how soft it is. I have to have the best.' He sat down again, sent Grim back to his kennel.

Hal cleaned her hands, picked out the splinters of tarmac, the oil from between her fingers. By the time she had finished, her hands had stopped trembling. She leant back. 'Any chance of another drink? I like it.'

'Sure. You need a clean mug and all.' And he was already shooting off to the caravan. 'I make it myself, you know.'

'I thought you might. What do you call it?'

'There you go with names again.' He seemed almost offended. 'Have I asked you yours?'

'You can if you want.'

'It's OK.' And he poured the nameless drink into her mug. And sat down again, just watching her.

'Aren't you going to join me?' Hal asked.

'I don't.'

'You don't drink at all?'

'Never a drop. Not for about five years now.'

'Why do you have all this drink then?'

'That's in case anyone comes round, like I told you. Got the chairs, got the drink.'

'It's very sociable of you.'

'You've got to be sociable, you're right. There should be more talking. People should sit and talk a whole lot more.'

But again they passed into silence, Hal sipping her drink, Spider sitting, enjoying her enjoyment.

Hal started to feel guilty: 'I need to get back to work, I suppose.'

'Is it that important?'

'Sometimes. It can be.'

'If it wasn't you, it'd be someone else, though, wouldn't it?'

'You're quite a philosopher.'

Spider was not to be deflected: 'It doesn't have to be you, does it? You can decide Not Me Today and there'll be someone else there.'

'But what if everyone thought that?'

'That's not the point. You've got to decide for yourself.'

'But sometimes, occasionally, not often, you think Only I would have done that, only me. My decision helped that patient. Only I would have managed that.'

'Looking like that you're not going to manage anything.'

Hal looked down at the frayed lining hanging from her skirt, her ragged tights, the oil on her shirt.

Spider was jumping up. 'Hold on, I'll get a safety pin. You pop in there, get those tights off, you're better without.' He ushered her towards the caravan steps. 'Go on, no dragons.'

She shut the door and rolled her tights down: the same circle painting from outside had been continued inside – except with a finer brush – but with the same lack of inhibition, the same happiness. Even the kitchen sink and draining board she had already seen, bristling with bottles, had been painted. Next to that, an armchair – 1930s brown, cream horsehair floating out of it like smoke.

When Hal opened the door again, feeling the Spring air on her legs, Spider was standing at the foot of the steps, a safety pin in his hand. 'Don't move, now,' and he knelt in front of her, bending back the front of her skirt, pinning up the torn lining. Why didn't she feel scared?

He finished and stood back, checking the straightness of the hem, 'It's the best I can do, I reckon.'

'Thanks.'

'Your white coat should cover the rest. Keep it buttoned up tight, no one'll ever know a thing.'

'How do you know I'm a doctor?'

'The boy told me.'

Hal's heart started to balk: 'What boy?'

'There you go asking me for a name again.' Spider was shaking his head in disbelief. 'You know who I mean. He said a doctor might come looking for him. That's you, isn't it?'

'Why didn't you tell me this before?'

'I wanted to be sure. Sure it was you. And that you were going to be alright for him.'

'Was he . . . How was he?'

'I've seen better. Not much hair on him. I gave him a hat, should keep him warm enough. And a coat, a donkey jacket.'

'How did he get here? Did he have someone with him?'

'Not till he met me.'

'But he can't see. He only sees shapes and colours, how did he get through those tunnels?'

'He sees more than he's letting on, if you ask me. Left eye specially.'

'What did he say, where's he gone?'

'He said he'd meet you. Said if you came, I should tell you where and when.'

CHAPTER SEVEN

It was gone eight when Hal arrived home – four hours until she was due to meet Jem. Spider had told her to be outside the post office on Kingsway – where Jem had originally been found – at midnight.

Back on the ward no one had said anything about her abrupt departure. No one said anything at all and it wasn't until she happened to glance in a mirror that she discovered the oil in her hair, the grime smeared round her temples. Leaning over the nurses' station, writing up notes, Hal saw Ursula smell the alcohol on her breath – but nothing was said. Jem's bed had been remade and late in the afternoon was reallocated to a chronic parapsoriasis.

Finishing the shift at seven, handing it all over to the House Officer, she wanted only to go home and shower and be ready.

Gareth was standing in the kitchen – her kitchen – wearing an apron, fish slices in his hand, frying sausages: 'Is that a fantastic smell or what? They're Balinese. Something like that. Smell brilliant, don't they?' he lifted the plastic wrapper and read: 'Lemon, marinated suckling pig with a satay style peanut and chilli garnish. Fantastic. I got enough for all of us. How are you? Had a good day?'

Hal stood in the kitchen doorway. 'Where's Dimitri?'

'Went to the pub to get us some wine. You're completely out of it, not a bottle in the house. Tut-tut.'

'Very funny.'

'What do you think, mustard or ketchup or relish or chutney?' When Hal said nothing: 'You're right. Let's have it all and damn the consequences.' Hal watched Gareth scoop the jars off the shelf, carry them cradled in his arms to the table. He left them where they settled and returned to the frying pan, shaking it.

'What are you doing here, Gareth?'

'That's not very nice, Henrietta. I saw these sausages. I was in Brewer Street. I thought Tonight I Shall Cook For My Friends. Sit. Let me serve you. Come on, sit down, everything's nearly ready. Wine's on its way. Would you prefer beer?'

'I told you to fuck off.' Hal remained unmoving in the doorway. 'Several times.'

'You told me you wanted the chance to redeem your shares in the business. I've got all the paperwork in my case.' He grinned at her and then looked down at the sausages. 'How do you stop these things burning? I mean, get them done all the way through without turning black on the outside. I really should learn to cook. You'll teach me.'

Hal felt exhausted already. 'For Christ's sake, Gareth, we don't want sausages.' She turned back towards the stairs and he caught up with her by the sitting-room door.

'Sorry, sorry, sorry.' But his voice had no tone of apology. 'We have got to sort this out, haven't we? I was being too flippant.'

'What's to sort out? We thought you were our friend, you turned out to be ripping us off. I thought you were my friend then you made a move on me. Basically you've shafted Dimitri twice over.'

'I'm making the best of things. And I don't want to rip you off. Not us, I mean. You and me, we can still share everything.'

'What do you want, Gareth? What's all this play-acting about? Time to come clean.'

Gareth held up his hands, all innocence: 'What did I say? Are you offended?'

'You just can't stop, can you?'

'I don't know what I've started, Hal. Tell me.'

'You want to shaft me as well? Is it all about that, a quick fuck, the final big one over on Dimitri?' Gareth looked shocked. 'Don't tell me, ladies shouldn't use that sort of language. Or just me, is it – I shouldn't? Am I on a pedestal, Gareth? Have you got me up there, so you can gaze up at me, look up my skirt when you fancy a bit?'

Hal turned and walked up the stairs, listening to Gareth's breath, his nails on the banister.

She stood in the middle of the bedroom, looking round at the heaped duvet, the empty bottle, the pile of books spilling out from the corner, the clothes pulled out of the wardrobe, the clothes pushed back in. She used to want to tidy a room like this.

She was about to lie down when she heard his breathing again. She turned and he was standing in the doorway. 'What now, Gareth?'

'What do you want?' he was now trying Little Boy Lost. 'What do you really want? Please tell me. Please, Hal, I don't know.'

'Spare me.' Hal wanted to lie down, to relieve the pressure on her ripped knee. 'You'd better go now. I think that's what I want.'

But instead Gareth moved forward, placed his hands on her shoulders, looked into her face: 'I know what you want, Hal, I know you know too.' He was pressing down on her shoulders until she was sitting on the edge of the mattress.

And Hal wanted to sit; she couldn't fight him. She waited for him to start talking again but instead he pushed her backwards, and Hal knew she wanted to lie back, wanted the softness of the duvet under her, to be absolved of the weight of her own body.

Suddenly Gareth was lowering himself onto her, laying his weight on top of her, his flat heaviness all over her, thinning her out. Was this really what he wanted, some false, forced intimacy? She didn't have the strength to struggle and he would stop soon. She allowed him to move his mouth against her face, mumbling words she couldn't make out. She decided she would lie inert, allow him to paw her and kiss her and he would soon realise she didn't want him at all. The wetness from his lips seeped down the side of her cheek, running into her ear. She would let him kiss a motionless woman and he would finally become aware of the humiliation; he would be shamed into stopping. His hands were running up and down her side, his palms and fingers pulling and rippling her clothes. Her inertia would force him to stop, to really listen to her, and then he would know once and for all. Then he was pulling her shirt out, floating his hand onto her belly, down again to squeeze her thigh. She didn't want this. She reached down and tried to take hold of his wrist but his hands were determined, his fingers digging into her flesh. Against her thigh, she could feel his penis hardening, his hips rotating. Then Hal felt his finger searching for a way past the elastic edge of her knickers. She brought her hands up and pushed his shoulders away but his weight was total – he barely seemed to notice, his head buried in her neck, his hands between her legs. She tried to lift her hips to tip him off but he only pushed harder against her. She said something like 'I want to stop, Gareth. Now, please stop.' He ignored her, his breathing quickening. Hal felt the panic rising in her chest, her blood beating. Suddenly the edge of her knickers was pulled harshly into her thigh and he forced two fingers against the edge of her vagina, searching, pinching, trying to push inside her. She hit him then, banging her fists against his back, driven by the wave of fear coming up into her throat. 'Stop that. For God's sake, Gareth, stop.' But it was as though she didn't exist – she was no longer Hal to him, she had become merely something. He took his weight onto one elbow, using the other hand to jerk her skirt up to her waist. He was no longer trying to look at her face.

Feeling the draft of air momentarily chill her stomach, Hal pushed harder at his chest. She had to get away, roll out from under, his hands were inside her, on her, his breath on her face, his erection pushing at her. She tried to get her hands up under his throat but he only knocked them to the side and said something like 'Take it easy, sweetie. Take it easy.'

'Get off me now, Gareth. Stop touching me; stop it.' She was pedalling her legs, swinging her shoulders from side to side, anything to dislodge him. Her whole body was urgently alive but every time she tried to move he held her more firmly, his weight on her shoulders and knees. 'I don't want this.'

'Yes, you do. That's it. Yes.' She felt the cold of his belt buckle on her belly, the bones of his fingers as he unbuttoned his trousers. He was still levered over her on his elbow. She felt his hips judder up as he pulled his trousers down, his shirt up. 'Like it rough, do you?'

She forced her heels against the edge of the mattress and tried to push out backwards. Gareth merely snatched her wrist and held it tight behind her head. She brought her leg up to knee him but he pushed his weight down harder and she could do nothing. He said 'We're going to do this, Hal.' Rolling his own legs sideways, he pulled her knickers down and pushed her knees back open. She was trying to keep moving constantly, it seemed the only way to prevent his prick from entering her. If she kept wriggling and jerking, he couldn't get it inside her – she could still stop him. Then she remembered the safety pin Spider had used to fasten her skirt hem. With her free hand, she felt down to where the lining was rucked up round her waist and started to work the pin out. He noticed she'd stopped fighting him and said 'That's it, you do want it, don't you? See, you've just got to let go.' His full weight was back on her chest and stomach and now she could feel his naked erection, his rough hair

103

against her belly, his balls against her thigh. He was grinding himself against her skin, pushing against her, his forearms running under her back, his abdomen bucking against hers. He was mumbling, gutturally, between gasps: 'Take me inside you, please, hold me, take me.' And then the pin was free of the lining. But it was hard to get a grip on it, impossible to get it out straight. She brought it down square into the middle of his back but it felt as though she had merely torn it across his skin. Gareth spasmed, arched his back and gasped. He said 'Fucking hell' and reached round behind his back and took her wrist. She dropped the pin – gone – and he looked down at her and said 'Don't be too rough' and let her wrist go free, raised his own hand and swept it down across her face. She felt the stinging rush of blood to her cheek, the bruising impact, the noise against her ear. Then she decided to feel nothing. He pushed a hand down between her legs. She was dry and, pulling her open with his fingers, he let his weight drop down, pushing and driving. She recoiled from the harshness, saw herself flinch from the sharpness inside but did not feel anything.

'Is that good?' he seemed to be shouting into her head, his lips bumbling against her ear, condensation dampening strands of her hair. 'Is that OK, is it OK, is it?' He wanted her to want it.

And he ignored her silence.

She felt him lift and sink. He pushed and slid his prick in and out of her. His body was straightened with the effort, a minute trembling tension across his shoulders each time he pulled back.

He was breathing faster now, his intakes of air chasing each other – he would come soon. His testicles were grinding against her and then, with a shout, he started to ejaculate. With each spray he shouted, perhaps five or six times, and then he became still, his chest rising and falling.

Hal opened her eyes and saw a black fog filling the room.

Thin streams of clouds were spinning round the lampshade, slowly propelled by unseen drafts. Greybrown pockets of smoke clustered in the corners, snaking in and out of the plaster cornice. The darkened ceiling seemed to be tilting and rolling and dropping down.

Gareth now started to lift his weight off her chest, up on to his elbows, opening his eyes, trying to smile. He followed her eyeline to the ceiling and after a second said 'Fuck. The sausages. Shit.'

He pulled out of her and bent to pull up his trousers. They had remained bunched round his feet while he had fucked her, now he just kicked out viciously, forcing them off his feet as he stumbled towards the door. 'I forgot to turn the fucking sausages off. Christ, sorry, shit.' Hal watched his erection, still almost hard, sticking out in front of him, glistening, bouncing each time he moved.

She lay back as he ran down the stairs. She heard him yelling in the kitchen, a hiss of steam and then it was quiet. Hal lay back, her knees still up, Gareth's liquid running between her buttocks down onto the sheet. She was already moving forwards, thinking of it in the past, thinking of Gareth's arrogance and her own weakness. For a handful of minutes she had been his property, now she was free again.

'Frying pan was on fire. Jesus.' Gareth's eyes were bright as he came back into the room. 'I had to use my shirt to put it out.' He stood uneasily, using a casually held hand to half-shield his penis. Then he turned and set about reclaiming his trousers from where he had kicked them into the corner. With his boxer shorts on, he came and sat next to her on the bed. 'OK?'

Hal didn't move, still watching the chains of smoke dance across the ceiling.

'Is everything alright? Hal? Hal?'

Hal thought she should have expected it, but she wouldn't give him the satisfaction of crying. The light pricked behind her eyes and she concentrated on the future. She ignored the filth running between her legs, the stench of his sweat on her skin. She remained motionless, removing herself inside.

'Can I borrow one of Dimitri's shirts? He'll never notice, will he?'

Why was he talking to her like this? What did he think had just happened?

'God, Hal, you really kept me waiting for that one. You've wasted just so many years on Dimitri. I should never have introduced you to him. We were always meant to be together.' He walked over to the window, opened it fully, 'Need to get this place aired out.'

Hal lifted her arm up off the bed, looked at her watch – still only ten past nine. Still two hours and fifty minutes to wait.

'She moves, thanks be to God.' Gareth stood watching her from the window. 'Come on, Hal, cover yourself up.' And he moved over, stood beside her, tried to pull the duvet over her, to cover the wet, tangled space between her legs. She saw him look away, not wanting to see her. 'Do you want to get into bed properly? Or have a shower? I've got to get dressed, in case . . . you know, in case he comes back.' He gestured towards the door. 'Sorry, I just think I should. Don't you?'

Hal lay, the duvet in a peak by her knee, seeing the smoke glide out of the room. Gareth went over to Dimitri's cupboard – 'Is this his stuff?' he asked, though she could hear he was already riffling through the shirts. He came back into her vision wearing one of Dimitri's polo shirts, sat down on the armchair and started to unknot his trousers, pushing his arms down the legs. 'Jesus, how did I manage this? Bloody sausages. Ridiculous, isn't it? Satay sausages. There were flames coming out of the frying pan, I didn't know what to do. Smothered it with my shirt in the end. It was a good shirt too. Oh well, it was worth it, wasn't it? Eh, Hal? God, we've got some serious thinking to do, haven't we?' She could hear Gareth doing up his laces, pulling them tight, each bow symmetrical.

'Do I pass muster?' The shirt was too small for him, squeezing up under his arms, forcing his shoulders high and his stomach out. 'Come on, Hal, you can't stay there like that. Come on, let's be a bit realistic here.' Again, he turned away from her open legs. 'We've got to keep control here, if we're going to get what we want.' He dropped down on his haunches, looked across the surface of the carpet: 'Was I wearing my tie? Can you remember?' He found it and stuffed it into his pocket. 'Come on now, Hal, this is getting beyond a joke. He could be back any minute. We don't want a scene, not this early on.'

He stood awkwardly, wondering where to put his hands. 'Look, I'll fix us a drink. I just don't think we should be found up here. You need to change and everything. Your make-up's all . . . your skirt – and the bed. Look at it. Please.'

And he was gone, padding down the stairs, humming.

Hal pulled her knickers back on, rolled her skirt down, buttoned up her shirt, found some new tights, squeezed her shoes back on.

At the Royal Cross, Kitty was on lates. Hal got the key to the Pathology Labs and Kitty took the samples for her, had them date-time stamped and then logged and locked them in the safe in Dermatology. Then she borrowed a key to Kitty's room at the Nurses' Hostel and had a shower.

She stood in the doorway of WH Smith's, warmed by the strip lights inside the display windows, watching the post office on the other side of Kingsway.

She had arrived there half an hour early, walked past the sleeping bodies in the post office porch, backwards and forwards four times, until she was sure none of them was Jem. On the corner of Sardinia Street she kicked through the white styrofoam and discarded crusts left by the soup and sandwich run and settled on the Smith's opposite as the place to wait. She mustn't scare him off.

It was now ten minutes past midnight.

She pressed her cheek against the plate glass, wondered if she was running a temperature, its coolness was so reassuring. She refused to think about what Gareth had done to her – if she did, if she let it dominate her, he would have succeeded in possessing her and she would not allow that.

Her eyes relaxed into a reverie, only to be broken by a sudden rush of noise as a group of people spilled out of the restaurant on the corner. They walked past her, down to the Aldwych, a man and a woman with their arms round each other's waists, two men walking behind talking about cricket, a last man cupping his hands against the wind, lighting a cigarette. He threw the match into the shop opening where Hal stood. Then he noticed her. They stared at each other for a count of five, then he walked on. She had become, as she hoped, invisible, one of the untouchables. It was quarter past.

The taxis nosed up and out of the underpass, levelling up onto Kingsway, drove towards Bloomsbury. Newspaper lorries came down from Euston and King's Cross, whined as they stopped at the traffic lights in front of Bush House. The sculpted figures over its porch looked down at them. Journalists emerged from the bright revolving door beneath, blinked, wrapped coats tighter and dispersed. It was twelve twenty.

Hal's eyes flicked to the post office every few seconds even though practically no one walked down that side of the street. She couldn't've missed him: she had got there early, absurdly early. Or had he seen her, watched her, decided she was too eager? Had it been a test and she had failed? He would have seen she was alone: no policemen or ambulancemen lurking to recapture him. He knew she was trying to help. But then he could barely see anyway.

So she crossed the road – maybe he had slipped in during one of those moments her attention was deflected and was now lying there feverish, without the strength to even call out for help.

She knew, as soon as she got near the porch, there was no way Jem had found a way in. There was hardly any floor left to sleep on. All the same, driven by disbelief, she stepped over one body and then another to check behind the pillars. Her foot stumbled on someone's arm and a hand flailed out. Instinctively she said 'Sorry' and heard her accent bounce back around the three walls.

Two careful steps took her to the back wall of the enclosed porch. She leaned against it, the hollow of a steel letter box against her shoulder blades. Four bodies lay curled in cocoons of brown and grey and maroon. Faces were covered, leaving only a slit of white skin. Hal leant back in the darkness.

After an hour, she stepped out between the bodies, walked down to the Strand and booked into a large, marble-clad hotel. In Room 437, impersonal and inhumane, she showered again, put on the fluffed bathrobe and in the hard armchair, her legs tucked under her, fell asleep.

CHAPTER EIGHT

Gareth rang at about nine the next morning, just as she was about to start a ward round.

'You haven't been home all night.' He was petulant. 'Where on earth did you get to? You just walked out of the house.'

She had taken the call at the nurses' station: 'What are you talking about?'

'I thought you were going out to get a pizza or something. When you didn't come back I started to get really worried. I almost called the police.'

Hal said nothing, limited her thoughts.

'Are you angry with me or something?'

Hal passed the phone to Sandra and watched it settle on the cradle. Ridgeway swept into the space.

'I want a cuddle. Move across. Come on.'

Hal inched backwards and Nicky settled into the curve of her body, pushed against her until he was filling every space. When she breathed in, she sucked in his hair.

'Couldn't I be a scientist during the day and a spy at night?'

'What?' Hal was barely waking up.

'I want to be a scientist during the day and then I could go to that building by the bridge and be a spy during the night.' She could feel his shoulders work as he organised the thought.

'When would you sleep?'

'In the afternoon.'

'You wouldn't get much science done.'

'It'd be enough. Science is all about thinking cleverly. Other people can do the experiments. Really great thinkers have great ideas, that's what Miss said.'

'I suppose that's true.'

'Could you come and have a look at the cellulitis, Doctor?' Ursula was leaning round the office door. 'She's asking for more pain relief.'

'I'll be right there.'

'Thanks.'

Ursula was gone and so was Nicky.

At about ten, Hal left the hotel, walked down to the river.

There were children sitting on the benches overlooking the river, homeless children trying to claim a stake of adulthood. Hal walked between the benches and the river – Jem might be sitting here, killing time before moving up to Kingsway.

Whenever their eyes met Hal's, they slid away, under baseball caps, into collars. They wore their street grime like war paint, something to remove and camouflage themselves. No one said anything to her – they continued their own dialogues or stared out at the hardening darkness over the river.

Jem wasn't there.

She climbed the stairs up onto Waterloo Bridge and looked left and right through London. Hal felt the enormity of the task pressing down on her. If Jem would not come to her, she had no chance of finding him, there were too many dark places.

Hal walked along the paved boulevard, past the people emerging warm from plays and films and recitals. She walked back over Hungerford Bridge.

It was about eleven when she got to the post office on Kingsway. The same people as last night seemed to be bedding down – the same blankets, the same woollen hats.

She walked up to Russell Square. She bought a cup of coffee at an all-night café. She was still untouchable – even the taxi drivers sitting in fours, smoking, eating fried food, barely glanced at her. She walked back down through Holborn, holding the polystyrene cup, occasionally sipping from it, waiting for midnight.

She was outside Smith's at about twenty to twelve. She watched the same traffic emerge and flow together; she watched the same figures arrive and disperse from restaurants and offices.

At about one thirty she returned to her room in the hotel.

At lunchtime the next day, she found a letter from Gareth waiting for her, delivered by courier. She glanced through it – he wondered if maybe he had offended her somehow – and slipped it into her pocket.

Kitty wanted them to have lunch in the canteen. Instead she worked her way back through the tunnels to Spider's caravan.

'Morning, Doc.' He didn't seem surprised to see her. She didn't know if she wanted him to be. His casualness undermined her urgency.

'He's really not well. If he doesn't get more treatment soon, he could die.' It seemed so clear, so necessary, yet Spider stared back, impassive, sitting on his haunches, watching over the campfire, the kettle balanced on a cast-iron tripod. 'We have to help him. Soon. Please, help me.'

'I've got some fennel I dried out, or vervain from a dealer, but it's good. What'll you have?'

'Spider, listen to me – do you think you're going to see him? He really needs to come in for treatment. I won't make him stay, if he doesn't want to; we should just check him out. Please, Spider, I beg you: tell me where he is.'

'What makes you think I've seen him?' Spider let his head fall to one side, ran fingers through the length of his beard.

'Do you want him to die?'

'There are other ways of healing. He'll be looked after. You don't need to worry.'

'Where?'

'If I knew . . .' And the kettle started to whistle. 'Fennel or vervain then? I've warmed the pot.'

Hal looked away, knew Spider was testing her. 'I don't mind.'

'Please.'

He was winding her up and she shouldn't let him. '. . . Fennel then.'

'Good choice.' Spider leaped inside the caravan, found a hessian pouch amidst the bottles, jumped back down, Grim Dog barking at his heels. 'Watch the fire, Grim.' He carefully poured the dried leaves into the billy can. With a rag taken from his back pocket, he gripped the kettle handle and poured the water. Then he looked up: 'He'll come to you when he's ready.'

'He needs treatment.'

'He'll meet you at the place, at the time, when you both need each other. You just have to wait.'

'I've spent two nights waiting already. It's bloody cold out there.'

'Maybe that's the point.'

'Christ, all this "It'll Happen" crap. If it doesn't happen, Spider, what then? He could fall over and die.'

'He's being looked after.'

'Who by? Tell me. Please.'

'Here.' Spider was holding out a cup, more of a bowl, of light green tea. Hal took it, drank a sip.

'Smile, please. It'll be OK.'

'If you see him, Spider, I only want to help.'

★

By the third night on Kingsway, Hal felt entitled to sit among the sleepers in the post office porch. She walked straight there from her hotel, forcing the so-carefully modulated air from her lungs, the scent of shampoo from her hair.

She squeezed into a space by the door, slid down until she was sitting on the cold tiles, her knees hugged tight against her chest. Teachers had told her not to sit on stone walls, it gave you piles.

'That's Jem's space.' The voice came from the sleeping bag on her left, hoarse and resonating, a growl from a shell.

'That's who I'm waiting for.'

'He won't like it if he finds you there.'

'Do you know where he is?'

And now the man rose up until he was sitting and facing Hal. But he wasn't a man – this man's voice belonged to a boy no more than seventeen. 'Who are you then?'

'I'm a friend.'

'Who are you?'

'I'm a doctor.'

'Why do you want Jem?'

'I was treating him in hospital. He's not ready to be out like this. He's very sick, he could relapse at any time. There's something called an electrolyte level, if that dips too low then he'll be in danger of going into a coma.' She had to tell him, tell someone, anyone. 'Then if he's not found soon enough—'

'Haven't you got enough other patients?'

'I want to find him.' Why did no one understand her? 'I just want to see him.'

'You can't find any of us. You've got to wait till it happens.'

'So people keep telling me. That's why I'm here. I'm waiting for him, waiting for it to happen here.'

'Why don't you wait over there, like you usually do?'

Hal realised her invisibility had existed only for some. 'I want to get in out of the wind.'

The silence grew. They both turned and watched the

hubcaps spinning past, watched the railings at the mouth of the underpass, the taxis moving past. Stillness, sudden movement, stillness.

When Hal woke up it was half past one. A policeman was standing over her.

'You alright, Madam?'

'Yes, thanks, I'm waiting for someone.'

'Are you sure you should be? Waiting here, I mean?'

'I'm fine. Please.'

His radio crackled and he walked away.

Once he was out of sight, Hal stood up, felt the cold through her bones, the squareness of her back. She limped back to the hotel. The receptionist asked if she was alright. She nodded, got into the lift and waited for the silence of her perfected room.

On the ward the next day, Dimitri rang twice, Gareth once. Hal did not ring back. When Gareth arrived at the ward, she stayed in her office and made sure the nurses got rid of him. They enjoyed the gossip of it, looked almost enviously across the ward at her. Gareth left another note – he wondered if maybe he had hurt her the other night.

Ridgeway asked Hal if she was feeling better. She said she was. He said she looked it, was glad her little episode was over, shame about the necrolysis boy running off like that. He hoped he'd got himself admitted to another hospital. Hal agreed.

Tonight she wouldn't just sit and wait, she'd go out looking for him, she'd walk circles round Kingsway, wider and wider until she found him.

The wind had found new strength and was whipping through the streets, biting into faces and forcing the trees to concede. Hal didn't prise herself out of the warmth of the taxi drivers' café until ten to twelve – arms crossed, tucking her hands into the opposite sleeves, head down. She took up her position over the road.

Smith's had changed the window display – there were happy young wives and happy would-be wives, baring their teeth in wide smiles as they proffered perfect chocolate cakes and dewy salads. Hal let their gloss warm her while she waited.

She saw him come round the corner of the block, edging out, cautious and wary. He was on her side of the road, nosing out from the street to her left, sliding through the pillars of the portico.

He was about eighty yards away. As soon as she saw it, Hal knew the woolly hat, the once-white trainers she had first seen on the floor of the Resus Room, and the donkey jacket Spider gave him. He scanned both ways along the street – he hadn't seen her, blurred by the neon brightness behind her.

She watched the figure leave the safety of the pillars and hobble to the edge of the road: his dropping shoulder, his head barely supported by the neck, his hands carried tense, each finger electrified.

He started to cross the road towards the post office and she remembered he could hardly see. And a lorry was swinging round the corner from the Aldwych, seizing the chance of empty lanes. Jem was moving into its path.

Hal wanted to shout but a black ball of liquid jammed her throat. The lorry ground on towards Jem who was isolated half-way across two lanes, limp-hobbling, presuming he was safe.

Hal should have run to the kerb and flagged down the lorry, but her legs were immobilised, weighted down.

Then Jem seemed to raise his head, hearing the lorry for the first time. And he stopped. And he took a few drunken, unbalanced steps backwards and let it pass in front of him. The slipstream blew across his face. He shrugged, letting his head loll from one side to the other as though shaking the grit out of his hair. He dodged over to the central island.

What he had done, how Hal had seen him react to the threat, seemed animalistic, nothing but instinctual. He had done only what was necessary, only when it became necessary. He had been invisible to the lorry and he had made sure it remained that way.

She called out his name. He turned round to look in her direction, raising his chin to smell her on the wind. Hal saw that his face was muffled by a scarf over his mouth, cheeks, ears, pulled tight round the bridge of his nose. Was he looking for her or at her?

He turned back and, letting a wave of cars pass in front of him, stumbled the rest of the way across the road. Hal called to him to wait, heard her voice dissolving into the rumble of city noises.

Hal was now hurrying along the kerb, waiting for a gap in the traffic, presuming he would wait there on the other side of the road. Instead he shrugged his too-big jacket up onto his shoulders and, without looking back, cut away down a side-street. Hal waited for a taxi to pass before sprinting across first one side of the road, and, after a posse of motorcycles, the other side.

Watching the traffic, she had taken her eye off Jem and the side-street was empty, the far end swallowed in the dark mouth of Lincoln's Inn Fields. Why was he doing this? He had asked her to be there, given Spider the time and place. And surely he couldn't move so fast, even limping and sliding and loping? Was it her shouting that had scared him off? It must be him: his jacket, his cap, his trainers – she didn't need to see his face to know for sure.

Hal ran into the darkness, shouted his name, her name,

stood and waited while the echo died and her eyes acclimatised. She checked each doorway of the old brown brick buildings, looking down into each basement area. On the other side of the road, on the flat front of the concrete office block, a metal shutter started to wind down. She ran across, dropping to her hands and knees to peer under before it snapped shut. She saw only her own reflection staring back from the polished windows of a reception foyer, leather sofa, pot plants behind.

She reached the railinged corner of the Fields and looked along one side of the rectangle, then the other. Inside the railings, the children's slide caught an edge of moonlight, the bronze of the statue glowed green. Jem could be moving along either side of the park, or could have levered himself over the railings and onto the grass – or could have hidden and then doubled back into Kingsway. All she could do was pick a direction and pursue it. She was about to move straight ahead down the edge of the railings when, about fifty yards to her left, she saw the black plastic on the shoulders on his donkey jacket slide in and out of the light. She ran down the pavement, saw him blink in and out of the next bell of street light and then cut to the right round the far corner. She ran, the gravel turning under her soles.

At the corner, Jem could have turned back onto Kingsway or gone right, further down, under the arch, and into the streets behind the Law Courts.

She stood trying to get her breath back – which way would he turn for safety, for invisibility? She felt the heat rising from her body, unbuttoned her coat, allowed the wind to slap it against her calves.

And he was there, under the archway that led into the maze of Victorian backstreets, his back against the shop window. It was almost as though he was making sure she saw him before he ducked away, forcing her to play catch-up. What did he want?

She jogged down to the arch, wishing she was wearing flatter shoes, wheeled left through it, found herself on a cramped street of crowded houses. Jem must tire soon, he could not possibly have the energy for this. Breathing in gasps, fast-walking, half-trotting, Hal checked each doorway, keeping an eye on the end of the street.

She saw him as he cut over the crossroads at the end, caught in the light from a silversmith's showroom, his back shining as he loped down. They were both running, the diesel of Fleet Street on their right, the bricks tight on their left. Hal saw him about three hundred yards ahead – he weaved past a row of traffic cones and slipped in under a scaffolding frame. Hal ran, determined to get there before he could fade away. She heard her heart hitting her ribs and her feet hitting the tarmac and when she reached the scaffolding cage he was gone.

She put her hands on her knees, feet apart, tried to fill her lungs. She shouted: 'Enough, Jem. This is far enough.' She waited. 'Come on, Jem, OK, you've proved it. Let's talk.' She waited again, heard a taxi pull up down a side-street, slowly U-turn and drive away.

The silence was restored. As loud as she could: 'Jem! Come on! Please!' She heard the anxiety in her voice. She was still gasping for breath, the sweat bursting onto her skin.

Nothing moved. Hal held on to the scaffolding upright, feeling its damp coldness, the grating rust. 'Jem, please! Now. Come on.'

He was there again, at the end of the street off to her right, sitting on the kerb, as exhausted as she was. Hal started walking towards him – not running this time, not even walking fast, just walking. He seemed to be allowing her – was he finally going to stop and let them talk? But when she was about thirty yards from him, he stood, quickly pushing himself first onto all fours and then up off his fisted hands. He just turned and started off at the same pace as

Hal, walking away from her, leading her quite knowingly. Hal refused to quicken her pace: if this was the game he wanted to play, she would play it, see where it led.

He turned left and right and she followed him. He turned right and she followed him. They were now level with Ludgate Circus, but he kept them twisting and shuffling through thin streets, only occasionally emerging onto main roads. They walked about a hundred yards apart, matching each other's pace perfectly, even though he rarely, if ever, turned to look back at her.

They walked for the next hour, Jem bowlegged, still taking the weight on the outside edges of his feet, Hal slowly lulled into the rhythm, unconcerned now, allowing him to make the decisions.

They had left the centre of the city, were now in the forgotten zones east of London. They walked past desolate rows of besieged shops, billboard advertisements ripped and flapping. The wind grew fiercer behind their backs, hurrying them forwards and cooling their path – Hal had rebuttoned her coat, wishing she had worn another jumper. They passed minicab offices – inside men sat reading exhausted tabloids, staring at nothing. Graffiti signed the buildings, the walls, the railway bridges. Occasionally a new brick building broke the smoothed-over greyness. Inside its reception, a uniformed security guard, counting time.

Jem led them through an estate, low-rise and crammed. She ran her hand along the pebbledash concrete that walled the walkways, looked at the abandoned cars, the grass bursting through cracks.

They kept walking. A police car slowed and the driver looked across at Hal, she stared resolutely forward and they accelerated away. She watched them do the same to Jem in front, and again drive on.

They were on the edge of London and she could hear a motorway roar in the distance. He turned left and she followed him down a terraced street, turned right and left and then she was inside a web. A huge spider's web of rope netting ran from one side of this street to the other, pinnacled on the chimney stacks and telegraph poles and gutters on one side, it looped into and out of the branches of trees on the other side – and sometimes these trees themselves contained houses, makeshift platforms. Hal saw two figures sitting in one of them, watching her.

Jem was standing in the middle of the street, stopped for the first time since they had started walking. He was facing her. He dropped down on his haunches, allowing her to approach closer. Had they finished the game? When she was only about fifty feet away, he darted in his lop-sided fashion into one of the houses. Hal followed. There were no lamps in this street, so it was only as she neared the front garden that she noticed how each house was painted, in patterns, in circles and starbursts, swirls of colour – the patterns she had last seen on Spider's caravan.

The front door was open. Hal pushed it open, saw a bareboard hall, a bare staircase that seemed to have been stripped of all its walls, isolated on two or three rough wooden stilts.

At the top of the stairway, on the landing, she could see Jem's trainers, his jeans. He spoke for the first time: 'Up here, Doc.' But it wasn't Jem's voice, it couldn't be Jem's voice, but still she went up the stairs. There was light coming from the room at the front of the house. She went along the landing and into the room and saw Jem standing in front of her. He still had the scarf wrapped round his face, the woolly hat on his head, except his posture was no longer twisted and dodging. He was pointing at the bed. Hal looked across: Jem was lying in the bed. Looking blindly round the room for her, Jem said: 'Is that you, Doc? You found us alright then?'

CHAPTER NINE

Hal was woken by the light. The air she was breathing was damp and icy and she could barely feel her toes.

She had spread three blankets over herself before falling asleep, by the morning they had heaped themselves into a mound, warming and weighing down on her middle, leaving her shoulders, her arms, her calves and especially her toes exposed to the cloying, misty cold. She felt sick.

Trying to move as little as possible, she brought one hand out of the blankets and swivelled her watch round her wrist – twenty to six. Greybright light was filling the room through the uncurtained, unglazed bay window.

Hal was on a mattress facing the corner of the room. When she rolled over, she saw that all the other mattresses were empty. Last night there had been about six or seven people sleeping in here.

She could hear talking in the street below. Grasping the blankets round her – for the cold, she was still fully dressed – she stumbled over to the window frame and looked out. In the road, thirty or forty people were standing round a trestle table, sitting on a battered sofa, squatting in the front garden, eating out of bowls, drinking out of mugs. They were dressed in baggy cotton trousers, layers of jumpers and beads and hats; some were holding guitars or mandolins or drums.

Pol looked up and saw her: 'They're coming soon. We heard an hour ago – we've got a mole at Town Hall.' His eyes were pulsing, enthralled. 'The Tower's seen the transits parking up on the other side of the heath, great line of them. Police, bailiffs, hundreds of them. Come and have some breakfast while it's still quiet. Danisha's made porridge – bit burnt, but some people prefer it like that.' And he turned away to deal with a woman who was tugging at his sleeve.

Hal looked out at the street for the first time in daylight. Opposite the row of terraced houses ran a railway line, shielded by a row of horse chestnuts. In front of them, a wall running the length of the terrace, painted as a panoramic mural – expressing all the hopes and dreams and angers of these last residents. In swirling, definite colours and thick brushstrokes, it merged from rural paradises into abstract patterns into teardrop angels into silver tigers jumping over green, leafy elephants.

Hal threw off the blankets and started to climb the ladder out of the window and down to the garden. Time to find out what Pol really expected of her.

It was Pol who had led her through the London streets the night before, masking his face, imitating Jem's bow-legged walk and crabbed fists.

'Why didn't you just tell me what you wanted?' Hal asked once the deception had been revealed to her. 'You could've explained and then let me come and see for myself. You didn't have to make me chase you all the way here.'

'Jem here didn't reckon you'd come. He said you'd want to get him back to hospital, duty first and all that. Said you wouldn't think about us while you had him to deal with.' Pol had the careful, cautious eyes of an urban outlaw. 'Said if you did come over here, you'd have to make it all official, call in an ambulance, things like that. We wanted you to see for yourself without having to answer to nobody.'

Hal turned on Jem, hurt: 'You know me better than that, Jem. I wouldn't do all that if you didn't want it.'

'Do I?' his voice was still distant, his tongue still barely moving. 'Since when?'

'There was nothing I could do about Doctor Ridgeway. He's my boss. I'm not allowed to argue.'

'You could've. You know you could've.' Jem's unseeing eyes faced up at her accusingly, nursing the memory of pain.

'He told me I wasn't to treat you. He told me I couldn't go anywhere near you.' Hal was remembering the frustration of her powerlessness. 'Do you think I liked it?'

'Didn't hurt you like it hurt me.' The skin on Jem's face and neck was still roaring red and he was totally bald – Hal wondered if the last few hairs had been shaved. 'Doesn't hurt you every time you move.' He was lying on the bed as straight as he always had, arms by his sides, head facing up.

The moment she had entered the room and realized that the real Jem was lying in bed, she had knelt down beside the blow-up mattress to start a full examination. Amazingly his condition had not seriously worsened. Pol – though she hadn't known his name then – said they had been bathing him in essential oils, lavender in particular, tea-tree for antisepsis. Pol leaned over her shoulder as Hal examined the blistering on the full length of Jem's skin. Pol told her they had been applying Balm of Gilead and Chinese herbs in the creases of his skin and burning menthol in the room to keep the air moist. That's when she had snapped and told him to shut up and let her concentrate. Pol said nothing, calmly took off Jem's jacket and scarf, laid them neatly in a pile on the floor and sat on an orange plastic beer crate in the corner. When Jem said he couldn't roll onto his side, Pol wordlessly came over to help her. Hal noticed how gentle Pol's touch was.

The welts on Jem's back had subsided more than she would have expected and new, harder skin was starting to grow in his nail-beds, the crusts beginning to fall away. The shaving of his head – though it emphasised the proud flesh – at least made him look somehow healthier, determined to be someone again.

As they helped him roll back onto his back, she asked: 'How's the vision?'

'Left eye's still like looking through a fog, but it's good out the other one. Getting better, I mean. Getting a lot better. I can see everything, except they're all just shapes. Can't get nothing to focus yet.' Jem had not lost his hopefulness. 'And colours are all a bit the same, you know, except really bright colours.'

'We've been using seaweed compresses,' Pol spoke quietly, 'Three times a day.'

'That'll help.' Hal could see that Jem had been cared for, whether these magic potions did any good or not. On the wall above his head someone had painted "You Can't Evict The Spirit".'

'He's a lot better than when he came here. Should've seen him then.'

'I did.'

'No, you didn't, not after he'd spent a day on the streets, walking round. Falling round, more like.' Pol looked at Jem to share the joke. 'Wasn't it, mate?'

'Don't ask me, can't remember a frigging thing.'

'Why did you leave the hospital, Jem? You were being looked after.'

'The fuck I was. I were sick of it. And I was alright that night I left. Just wanted a bit of peace.' Jem's clouded eyes seeking out the reassurance of Hal's face, the shape of her face. 'I put my gear on and I walked out of there. Well, kind of limped, you know me. It was good to have my clothes back on. Got in the lift and went down. No one even spoke to me, not even to try to stop me. If you ask me, they'd been told to let me go.

'It was so good to be out of that place – those nurses, what did I do to them? What did that one in charge want, what did I do to her, eh?

'I got over the road, the one right outside the hospital,

went down that street, with all the little old houses on it and then I got lost in all those fucking tunnels. Fuck, do they go on for ever or what? You go in and out and before you know it you don't know where you are. At last I stumbled out of there – my feet are fucking agony by then – and there's this hippy with a caravan. He's got this kind of campfire in front of it, and a stupid looking dog and candles all around him and he's sitting there and he's smoking a pipe, like he's some, you know, Apache. Shit, I think, I'm out of my head or something. But he just gets up, takes me over to sit next to him. Well, I had to lie down a bit, get my breath back. Then he passes me the pipe – don't know what was in it, but it was fucking strong gear, it was the right fucking bollocks. Took the pain away and all. Turned life fucking wonderful for the first time since I took those tabs. Think I must've slept for a bit, just there on the ground – he put a blanket over me.

'When I woke up, I knew I had to keep moving, I knew they'd be after me. He tied some rags round my feet, to soften them up, and I told him where you could find me if you wanted.

'London looks different through one eye. It goes all flat. Fucking cars come at you out of nowhere. You go across a road and suddenly they're right there, on their horns. Taxis are death – they don't give a shit, they want dead people.

'I was wandering around the place, I knew I was wasted. No, I was blasted. Totally blasted, Doc. After Spider's blow I thought everything was good, I didn't know I was falling all over the place. I was banging into people. One guy grabbed me, had me by the collar, up against the wall, going ape-shit – I laughed. I don't know – that's when Pol saw me. He brought me here. He's been looking after me – all the people here. The stuff he's been putting on my blisters – feels amazing, better than what that shit was you gave me in the hospital.'

Hal saw that Jem wanted to let her know how he had managed, telling her he could do without her and also telling her he couldn't. She turned to Pol: 'Where did you find him?'

'He'd wandered into this burger place. We were outside collecting signatures. We'd watched him go in. Poor lad, he knew he was hungry – thirsty more like. Jem here didn't know what was going on, he was only looking for something to drink and something deep inside him told him this was the place he was going to find it. Only problem was he looked like something out of a Hammer horror. They didn't want that in there, scaring the customers. Can't say I blame them. We got him back here and put him to bed. I've been treating him since. He's shaping up OK?'

'He's still in a very fragile condition. He could relapse at any time. He still needs monitoring in hospital.'

'I'm not going back.'

This time Hal didn't argue. She had no more to give. Hal felt the exhaustion seeping into her stomach. 'So what's this whole game been about tonight?' She looked at Pol, sitting assured, benign. 'If he won't come back to hospital anyway, why did you drag me out here?'

'They're moving in any day now to demolish this street. They want to build another motorway. More roads, more cars. It's all they want. We're here to stop them, well, slow them down, cost them. We're going to need a doctor, to help and to witness. Jem told us about you. We had to make sure you'd come.' Pol was smiling at her, that wouldn't-harm-a-fly look.

'What's wrong with ambulances, the local hospitals?'

'Our people won't want that, they'll want someone here, on the inside.' He seemed so reasonable, so prepared. 'If they go to hospital, they can't stay here. We have to stay here for as long as possible, as many people as possible.'

'Then perhaps you should have asked me to bring my

bag. I've got nothing with me.' Hal knew this was ridiculous. She couldn't stay here, it was crazy. 'I haven't even got a – I don't know, a packet of aspirin.'

Pol was unshaken. 'We've prepared bandages, and splints, and compresses. They're all sterile. We've got oils. It'll be enough.'

'You're talking like there's going to be some battle. They're only going to evict you, isn't that it?'

Pol smiled, maybe even patronisingly: 'We're barricaded in. Some people are going to bury themselves in bunkers under the houses. Each house can be cut off from the next. There won't be any staircase left up to this floor. Some people are going to harness themselves to the trees over there, to the chimneys up on top of us here. If all that's not a battle, what is?'

It was gone three in the morning and she had walked several miles across London – she still didn't know exactly where she was. Pol stood up and touched her lightly on the shoulders.

'We've saved a place for you to sleep. We wanted you fully rested for tomorrow.' He led her out of Jem's room and through a hole that had been smashed through the wall into the next house. They walked along a wooden plank balcony over the stairwell of that house – the staircase below them had been smashed away. Holding on to the rope handrail, she looked up – the roof had also been torn away and through what remained of the rafters and slates, she could see the netting covering the street and through that the stars.

Pol led her into the next house. There, in the front bedroom, was the 'dormitory', a large room packed with mattresses and sleeping people. There was one free mattress in the corner and Hal, barely aware, lay down on it and pulled the blankets over her shoulders.

Now Hal was standing in the street, this street in Leyton-stone, eating semi-burnt porridge out of a striped bowl, while Pol explained everything they had done to prepare for the eviction.

The street, Byron Grove, was the last street they needed to demolish – all around her, Hal constantly heard this 'They'. For weeks these protesters had been squatting in the empty street and preparing for the day when the contractors and police would move in to extract them.

'We can't stop them. But we can hold them up. We can make everyone notice what they're doing, covering the land in tarmac, destroying homes and places where people live.' Pol easily slipped into speech-making. 'We can fill up the police cells and prisons and each time they let us out we can come back here, waste more of their time, piss them off a bit more. That's why I changed my name.'

After his fifth arrest – he was a veteran of Twyford Down and Newbury and Manchester Runway – he had changed his name by deed poll to Police Are Fascist Thugs so that now, every time he got arrested and was forced to give his name . . . Everyone called him Pol for short. On the other side of the barricades – the police, the bailiffs, the contractors – he was known as Pol Pot; on the arrest forms, he was PAF Thugs.

The atmosphere around Hal was excited, hopeful, relieved and sad. A sympathiser on the Council had told them that the Under Sheriff would start moving in this morning. They had been working towards this moment for three months.

Hal looked down the length of the street: an ordinary, Edwardian terrace, not particularly outstanding even when pristine. Now it had been turned into a living barricade, a huge defensive wall protecting only itself, proving its point just by being there.

To get down from the dormitory she had had to walk

along what they called the rat-run – a passageway running from one end of the terrace to the other, smashed through the bricks at first-floor level. She had worked her way through each house until she came to a window with a ladder propped against its front window – nearly all the staircases had been removed – and climbed down.

Opposite the terrace, in the trees that had once shielded the inhabitants from the noise on the railway line, the branches were infested with houses and platforms and rope harnesses. Men and women were even now working at them, hammering and welding, sliding scaffolding poles into position, building ever more complex shapes. Pol explained that the object was to make it as hard as possible for anyone or anything to get near the trees – the real enemy was the hydraulic crane, the cherry-picker, which would manoeuvre its platform right up to the tree houses and allow bailiffs to start hauling the protesters out.

Creating a ceiling above the street was what Pol described as their Spiderman netting. An unbroken patch-work of nets covering the entire road, it looped over the branches halfway up the trees and sloped down to the chimneys on the other side of the road. Occasional support-ing ropes from higher up the trees ensured that it maintained an almost constant height above their heads. As people walked across it, it buckled like a huge trampoline. This was the web that Hal had seen last night.

Higher still than this, a huge scaffolding tower, over a hundred feet high, dominated the centre of the terrace. Its feet straddled one of the houses, braced against its walls, and then rose like a haphazard Eiffel, with platforms every twelve feet or so and finally rising to a cage-like box at least a hundred feet off the ground. Men, stripped to the waist, were welding on extra scaffolding spikes, the only defence against the cherry-picker.

From the top of the tower, sealed in the cage, a man with

binoculars was keeping a commentary on the police parked several streets away: 'They've all got thermoses. Sandwiches. And pies. They're having their breakfasts.' Then he picked up a megaphone, yelled in their direction: 'What's for breakfast, boys? Do pigs eat bacon?'

Pol shouted up: 'Rozzo, Rozzo, nothing offensive, mate. Keep it cool.'

'Are you in charge then?' Hal asked.

'No one's in charge. We all do what we want.' That benign smile again. 'As long as it's non-violent you can do what you want. We're all trained in non-violent protest techniques. And we're all volunteers. No one has to stay. Like you, Doc, you can stay here and help us, or you can go.'

'I'll stay if you think people are going to get hurt?'

'Is that your hypocritical oath, eh?'

'Something like that.'

Pol reached into his back pocket, handed her a mobile phone. 'Need to call in sick?'

When Hal raised her eyebrows at the phone, he shrugged and said 'A sympathiser's paying for it – we have to contact the journos somehow. PR's half the battle'

'You haven't answered my question. Are people going to get hurt? I thought you said it was all non-violent.'

'What do you think?' Pol stood, hands on his hips, 'We're costing them millions. If we cost them less than two million, we've failed. They know that. We're not popular. This is their big chance to let us know how they feel.'

'There'll be ambulances, surely?'

'We've got to handle what happens before the police let the ambulancemen in. They don't rush to call them. They like to let a bit of blood flow first. Easier too now they don't let television cameras anywhere near.'

'Then what about Jem?'

'He insisted on staying. That's his choice. He'll get stretchered out when they're ready to take him.'

'Are you going to leave the stairs up to his room?'

'All the staircases have to go. If we leave even one, the whole upper storey's vulnerable. But he'll be OK. None of us are going to occupy that house.'

Suddenly Rozzo was shouting down from the tower, his voice trembling like a sports commentator: 'They're all out of their transits . . . they're all lining up . . . They're all in their riot gear – lovely big blue romper suits.' The irony didn't hide the anticipation in all their voices, the adrenaline tremor.

Everyone in the street stood in silence while Rozzo watched for the next sign. 'They're coming down this way. They're coming. This is it, they're definitely coming.'

The people standing around Hal were scattering. Each person seemed to know what they had to do. Some ran towards the tree houses and started to climb up rope ladders which were then dropped to the ground once everyone was installed. Some ran towards the house which formed the base of the Tower – they climbed up out of a hole in the roof and onto the lower platforms, shinning up the scaffolding legs. Sparks arced down on them from the top cage as the three inside welded themselves in and then lowered the blowtorch down on a rope.

Hal was standing in the middle of the road watching the activity when Pol called from the doorway of the middle house. She ran over.

'We're about to demolish the staircase. You'll be better off watching from up on the first floor – if you're needed on the street, we can drop a rope ladder for you.'

Hal ran up the stairs and watched from the landing above as Pol used a sledgehammer to knock away the single supporting beam of wood. With a slow tear, the staircase collapsed. Then Pol moved over to a rope that went through a hook in the ceiling joists; he took the strain while someone else unknotted the rope from where it was secured to the landing. Together they took the weight and, telling everyone to mask their eyes, with a yell they let the rope run through their hands, whipping through the hook in the ceiling. Released, a door smashed downwards and out of the front room poured a mound of bricks and concrete. Dust rose into the stairwell, momentarily obscuring everything. Once it settled Pol said 'I warned you to cover your eyes.'

Hal looked down and saw that the front door was completely blocked with rubble, lumps of concrete, tyres. They were isolated.

Hal turned and went through the rat-run. The landing on every other house had been demolished and replaced with a simple plank walkway – this could also be removed at will, isolating each house in turn and preventing the police and bailiffs from seizing the length of the terrace at a stroke.

Jem was in the last house but one. He was lying in the same position, straight in the bed, eyes open, seeing and unseeing.

'Is that you, Doc?'

'Yes.'

'Was that the staircase going down?'

'Yes.'

'They're coming then?'

'You'll be sensible, won't you? Don't get into any fight. You're not strong enough.'

'I'm glad you stayed.'

'Make sure they take you back to the hospital. Tell them you're supposed to be at the Royal Cross?' Even though she would never go back there.

Outside a chant had started up – "No More Roads, No More Roads" – but it couldn't obscure the sound of bailiffs shouting their orders through megaphones, the heavy machinery coming up the side roads.

That low diesel rumble and Hal was again walking down the slope to school, the gloved hand in hers, the frost in the air. The noise was always behind her and there was never enough time, those same few seconds running again and again. If she had heard it sooner, she would instinctively have pulled Nicky tighter against her; if she had listened; if she had been walking on the outside. If the lorry had not been there. The lorry should not have been there, no one argued with that; none of the lorries should be there.

'I'd better go and see what's happening.'

'Sure, Doc. I'll be OK here.'

'You should have gone earlier, before all this.'

'You're needed. Go on.'

Hal went out on to the landing. She looked through the rat-run corridor: she could see practically to the other end of the terrace, the view randomly interrupted by people slipping out of one house into the next. She saw Pol running straight through the tunnel towards her. When he saw her, he shouted, called her towards him urgently.

Hal dodged through the archways in the brickwork, banging her shoulder on a piece of timber, kept running forwards. When she got to where Pol was waiting for her, he led her to the front window so that they could look out into the street. 'We need you to see this. Since Manchester and Exeter they keep all press out, no one gets close enough to film. So they'll believe you when you tell them, people trust doctors. They think people like us just make it up.'

'Is that why you really wanted me here?'

'Just look at it all. Please.'

Hal looked out on the street below. The bailiffs were moving in from both ends of the terrace. In solid lines, in uniformly bright blue riot suits, black helmets and grey visors, and black shields, they were climbing over the barricades at each end. They moved slowly over the tyres, the rubble, the supermarket trolleys filled with concrete, scaffolding tubes sticking out of them in all directions.

The ant-like bailiffs swarmed down the barricades and

started to lift away the sit-down protesters. Hal watched one of them struggle, a woman about sixty years old – she was turning out to be harder to remove than the bailiff had expected. Each time he put his arms round her chest, under her arms, she would let herself go limp and slip down. As she slid through for the third time, the bailiff punched her hard in the back. Hal watched the woman's body arch backwards. He lifted her up, his arms round her waist, clamped over her belly, and, walking backwards, started to manhandle her back up over the barricade. She was screaming, crying, begging, but did not have the strength to fight the bailiff as well as the pain. Hal turned to Pol: had he seen it? But he was gone. She turned to look at the other end of the street and saw a policeman push a sit-down protestor onto her back and force his knee into her breasts. She tried to push him away and roll sideways but he maintained the pressure, staring impassively down at her. When he pulled his knee back up and stood, she doubled over clutching herself, her mouth open for air. He and another policeman grabbed her under the arms and started to frog-march her, face down, out of the road. She was screaming, but not struggling. Hal wanted to try and remember it all, to try to memorise the numbers stencilled on the back of the policemen's helmets, but it was all happening too fast. Each time she seemed to have memorised one, she had to cram another in – all around her the blue suits seemed to be wielding their sticks, their blank visored faces moving passionlessly.

Suddenly, back at the other end of the terrace, she saw a huge bulldozer start to push its arm through the barricade; the sheer force of the metal claw moved smoothly through the timber and the cars filled with concrete and the bed-frames welded to the road. It was pushing through the wall of objects without even straining. But this meant that the smaller objects heaped on top of the barricade started to cascade down the inside of the ridge, a landslide of rubble and waste. The people sitting at the foot of the barricade quickly pulled back. The bulldozer moved forward, bright yellow; the claw was at the end of an arm that extended thirty feet in front of it, hinged twice, dangling and threatening. The two toothed scoops moved down and bit at the concrete slabs, lifting them up and tossing them aside.

Seeing it forging a pathway through the barrier, three people ran forwards and lay down in front of its tracks, the arm hanging out over their heads. It rumbled to a stop and bright blue bailiffs moved forward to remove them. One, a woman in a wasp-stripe jumper, didn't wait for the riot stick across the thighs, but jumped up as the bailiff approached and, climbing on her partner's shoulders, reached up and hauled herself up into the spiderman netting above. A cheer went up from the houses and trees as she established herself above all the bailiffs, free. She moved across, holding on with both hands and feet, swinging under the netting, hanging down monkeylike until she was right over the digger's claw. Then she let her feet slip out of the netting and she hung for a moment, straightened. Hal could see her jumper pull free and the taut muscles of her stomach as she took a couple more grips across the netting. Her toes touching the top claw of the digger, she dropped bodily down onto it, getting her arms round the width of it. She lay there, about twenty feet above the ground, hugging the top of the claw, her cheek flat against the steel, her feet gripping the sides, trying to find a better hold.

Everyone was watching her – police, protesters, bailiffs – half-admiring, half-fearful. It was a stand-off, an act of mad cunning. For the first time since the invasion had started there was silence, everyone stilled. It lasted for perhaps five, ten, fifteen seconds – Hal stood in the first floor bay window looking – then a flurry of shouts, from the police, from the men in yellow hard hats and long yellow anoraks. Some of them shouted at the woman, angry and appalled, some shouted at the digger driver. Hal saw the panic on his face and his bewilderment as he forced the gear levers in his cab and, looking behind him, started to reverse the digger.

But that first jolt of movement, sending a tremor down the arm, bounced the woman and Hal saw her try to glue herself to the metal. It wasn't enough and she was thrown to the side. She started to slide off the side. It seemed to happen so slowly. Hal watched as her fingertips looked for new holds and did not find them. As she slid past she grabbed at the lower scoop, cupped upwards, but it only ripped through the flesh she offered it. She was falling, her arms and legs uppermost, her head falling backwards, her throat exposed.

Did she scream? Or did anyone else? There was silence as she hit the ground, a clear crack as her rounded spine bounced on the road. She lay flat, thin and formless, nothing more than filled clothes. Her stomach was again visible, joining the two broken halves of her body.

Hal leant out of the window frame, looked along to find where the nearest ladder was – four houses away. She went back inside, turned and ran as fast as she could through the rat-run until she reckoned she had been through four houses. She cut left into the front room, pushed her way through the people standing shocked round the front window, practically slid down the ladder and ran across the pitted road surface. She pushed through the shouting bailiffs and knelt by the woman. A policeman was halfway through yelling Hal to get back when he noticed her practised movements. He returned to yelling for paramedics as Hal tried to find a pulse. There was blood seeping from the back of the woman's head and the twist of her legs meant that her spine was almost certainly broken. Hal was starting mouth-to-mouth as the ambulancemen arrived.

She helped until they started the shocks to restart the woman's heart and then Hal walked slowly towards the tree platforms, newly inviolate. Around her bailiffs continued to march away most of the protesters who had gathered round the woman. Most of them were too shocked to struggle – a few realised and slipped out of the bailiffs' grasp and ran past Hal, back up ladders.

Hal started to hear the chants of "Killers . . . Killers . . . Killers . . ." growing until it was in full flood around her. Everyone – in the trees, out of windows, on the roofs, on the tower – was pointing down at the police, at the bailiffs, while they tried to carry on consolidating the ground they had won. Hal saw a yellow anorak talking to the digger driver – was he talking him into going on, asking him to withdraw? The driver jumped down out of the cab and went off, gesturing angrily, walking down the slope of the barricade on which the digger was now angled. He had his head down and was ushered into a police coach. Hal saw his fist beat on the inside of the window.

Hal climbed the ladder into a tree as a man wearing a yellow plastic jacket came into the now-empty No Man's Land between the two sides, a megaphone in his hand. Hands helped Hal climb back up into the first-floor room while they listened to the man's amplified voice: 'Quiet, please, let me speak, please. Please. Please.'

Hal was sitting slumped on the floor, her back against the cool of the wall. She heard the man say 'This land has been nominated for development. Let's have no more accidents, please. Everyone should come down now, please. No one will be arrested if they come forward peaceably. This site must be vacated by order of the Secretary of State.' This aroused an angry, disgusted cheer. 'If you all come out, immediately, there'll be no more arrests. No one else will get hurt. You've made your point. If we have to do this by force, there are bound to be more accidents. We don't want that.'

Hal sat listening. The monotone became soothing. People jogged incessantly in and out of the rat-run next to her, some in and out of this front room, all knowing what they were doing, where they were going. Occasionally someone stopped, stood over her, thanked her for what she had tried to do for the woman in the wasp jumper – apparently her name was Megan. Her daughter was somewhere in one of the trees, had seen it all happen.

Hal realised that the megaphone man had finished, the shouting of encouragement and orders had resumed, even the diesel motor of the bulldozer was again thumping in the background. The digger was again moving forward, starting to push obstacles out of its path as it drove towards the first house. There was a new driver in the cab.

Hal watched a team of bailiffs start to sledgehammer their way into the front door of the house on the end of the terrace. Each blow threw a shock wave through the line of prancing unicorns painted up the side of its porch and over the front bay. Another team of bailiffs lifted a ladder to the first-floor window of that house and one of them climbed up and shouted something into the room. Immediately hands pushed out of the room and a wrist handcuffed itself to the top end of the ladder. The bailiff on the ladder, who had been trying to talk to the protesters inside the room, started to climb down again, shouting for a bolt-cutter. As he did this, others started to climb out of the window and up on to the roof the house. They jumped up, caught onto the spider netting and started the slow swing across the road. Holding themselves thirty foot above the ground, they arm-walked across the road to the trees, some hanging under the netting, others crawling over the top of it. Each was cheered as they arrived on a tree platform, an arm raised in triumphant salute to the audience all around.

But everyone turned when they heard the rumble of a motor at the other end of the terrace. It was the hydraulic crane, the cherry-picker. The basket had been brought to the height of the netting and the two men inside were armed with bolt-cutters. They started to cut their way through the rope squares, snapping the loops one by one – those caught climbing across scrambled back to the safety of a roof or a tree. Everyone screamed at the bailiffs in the cherry-picker that they had to stop, that they were going to kill someone. The bailiffs continued their cutting.

Once a path was cut through the first section of netting, it sagged away towards the ground and the basket manoeuvred until it was alongside the first tree platform. Hands desperately tried to push it away, only to be grabbed themselves. A girl was pulled off the tree platform and headfirst into the basket. Hal saw her legs scissoring as she disappeared into the yellow metal box. The basket started to lower, only her feet visible, the bailiffs' hands shielding their faces, protecting themselves from her wild kicks. One of them sank down out of sight into the basket to deal with her.

When the basket reached the ground, two bailiffs ran to haul her out. They took her under each arm and hustled her away, but just as they started climbing the barricade with her, she slipped back out of their grasp and ran back towards the houses. There was blood running from a gash in her forehead. A bailiff turned and catching her up, threw himself on top of her. The two of them fell to the ground, entwined like lovers, until more bailiffs ran up and the girl was removed.

Now all the ground belonged to the police and anyone emerging at ground level was instantly hustled away behind the barricades, handcuffed, videotaped, put in a van.

Hal watched the police enter the second house of the terrace, the one where Jem was lying. She saw the bailiff climb the ladder to the first-floor window, his surprise as he discovered a boy, lying in a bed with sheets and blankets. He looked back, clearly confused by this moment of respectability. He climbed into the room, followed by two more bailiffs.

The next thing Hal saw, about half a minute later, was these men pulling Jem's body – at this distance he looked barely more than a stuffed rag-doll – pulling and wrenching him towards the window opening. The bailiffs had taken Jem's docility for another passive protest, were irritated by his unwillingness to move. They were pulling at him ineptly, roughly, dangerously.

She watched his body being sat on the window sill, a bailiff yelling at him, Jem's hands fluttering for a clue to place himself. At any moment, he could tip back and fall out of the window – the bailiffs hadn't realised he was all but blind. Hal saw Jem's hands fumbling behind him, feeling the outside of the wall.

Before she knew it, Hal was jumping forward off the tree platform onto the netting. She felt it give under her, bounce and rebound. She clung viciously to the rope squares and started to climb diagonally across the road to Jem's house, hauling herself on all fours on top of the netting. As she dragged herself over, the rope burning her skin, she saw the cherry-picker crane off to her right, cutting its indiscriminate way through the middle of the net. She seemed to catch the eye of one of the bailiffs just as he severed one of the high supporting ropes and Hal felt the netting suddenly slide away beneath her. She rolled with it, hanging on with her hands, and found herself hanging head-first downwards, her feet way above her, swinging ten feet above the ground. She tried to heave with all her strength, to climb back up onto where the netting still had tension. But the section was starting to unravel: she swung round and climbed a couple of feet higher, but could get no further. The next rung was too far above her, she could not haul herself up the sheer, vertical ropes that connected her island of ropework to the remaining netting. Seeing the cherry-picker basket moving towards her, to scoop her up, easy meat dangling above the middle of the road, she started to allow herself to slide down the rope. Her palms burned and then, about five feet above the ground, there was no more rope to climb down. With a breath in, remembering PE lessons, she bent her knees and allowed herself to drop.

The ground jolted up at her and she tumbled onto her side, forced to remember the hip she had bruised in the tunnel. Two policemen on the barricades had been watching her, waiting to see if she would jump. They ran towards her. She had about fifty feet on them and she set off at a breathless sprint towards the house.

The bailiffs were pushing Jem head down, out of the window. One bailiff had hold of each of his feet and another bailiff was waiting halfway up the ladder to take hold of his shoulders. His head was bumping on each rung as they lowered him and his hands were weakly flailing for some security, some clue as to what was happening to him. The bailiffs were yelling at him to help himself as Hal ran up. She shouted:

'He's ill. His skin is very delicate. Get a stretcher for God's sake.' She could hear the fear in her voice. 'He can't see.'

The bailiff on the ladder turned to her: 'Leave this to us, can't you?'

Hal put her foot on the rung of the ladder and hauled herself up behind the man. He turned, was just starting to shout, when Hal pulled on his belt. She pulled as hard as she could. The man, surprised, found himself falling backwards. He scuffled down the side of the ladder and ended up on all fours on the ground next to the two policemen who had been chasing her . . .

Hal climbed up to where Jem's head was now resting against the ladder. 'It's alright, Jem, it's Hal. I'll see you're alright now.' She cradled his skull in her arm, ran her palm over his cheek.

'Where am I, Doc?' his voice croaked. 'What are they doing?' He wanted to hide his own fear. He couldn't.

Hal looked up to shout to the bailiffs holding Jem's legs,

when she felt the hands pulling her down. The policemen had each grabbed one of her legs and she felt herself pulled backwards, almost flying, until she was sitting on the ground at the foot of the ladder. She heard Jem's head bang free of her grasp. The policemen reached out to pull her up and march her away. She had to stay, she had to look after Jem.

'I'm a doctor. Get off me.' She knew she was yelling, would not sound like a doctor. She knew they were probably not listening. 'This is my patient. I have to make sure he's looked after.'

'You're under arrest for obstruction.' The voice was lifting her as well, forcing her to stand. 'Come with us now.'

Hal felt the hard hands clench round her upper arms and she punched out. Her knuckle bounced over the hard buttons of his riot suit. She kicked her foot up and her ankle caught the softness of his groin. The policeman in front of her doubled up. But still the other policeman was pulling her backwards, gripping her arms. She turned round to push him away and she saw his still, round eyes through the grey visor as he brought up his riot stick and brought it down at an angle on her head.

All the noise stopped. The stick had caught her on the temple. She only thought that because instantly that side of her head was numb. There was no pain, only a hot nothingness. She slumped down to her knees. The liquid was sliding down her cheek, over her eye, into her neck – a sudden rush of heat after the coolness of the impact, the frozen point where the hardness had broken against her. She remained looking up at the policeman, his riot stick drawn back ready to strike again. She knew she should get up and start helping Jem again, but she was in church, kneeling, praying, her head completely still, her vision blurred with the intensity of the light around her, all her feelings suddenly pinpointed clearly on the future. She reached up to the policeman with her hands, pushing out towards him, begging him, supplicating. She heard the other man behind her – she knew he was there, she remembered him falling away from her – she heard him move close behind her and say 'fucking bitch'. Something like that. Then she felt the ridged rubber sole of his boot against the back of her head and she was seeing the ground move quickly upwards.

part two

CHAPTER TEN

Sometimes, when Hal's standing on the pavement in Louth or Alford or Mablethorpe – dodging pushchairs or delivery trolleys – her mind slips away. No one notices: she goes on holding out the clipboard, asking and smiling and shrugging and thanking, while inside she's alert.

What she's doing is watching. She's been shown a way through and she is watching Nicky grow up: he's almost six months older now, almost seven, has new toys and new words and new friends. Toys she didn't buy him and friends she's never met. He's a little taller and starting to fill out; he's developing his father's physique and his hair is getting darker and curly.

Some things haven't changed: the splaying twist of his right foot as he runs – as though he's dancing a furious Charleston. Folding his arms too tightly across his chest when he thinks he's being unfairly denied and tipping his head back like a baying wolf. The smile turning the edge of his mouth or the yellow plastic strap of the 101 Dalmatians watch. The freckles emerging on the ridge of his cheek, the puckered ring of flesh where the elastic of his shorts tightens round his waist. The almost unbroken collage of bruises and grazes on his sins.

He's growing up without her. She knows now that the day he was killed was merely a single event on a single day. For a while, for all those hazy months, she couldn't see it like that, didn't realise that's how things happen. She thought his death was the end of everything and as a result she couldn't see him. Now she knows he's living his life, still playing, still working his way through the Famous Five – probably well into the Secret Seven.

And thinking about this, seeing how he lives, Hal is sustained. No, it's better than that. She can feel a purpose to her life and Nicky's. She's smiling again. She's still angry but she's found a way to smile as well.

And all she's waiting for now is the day when Jem joins Nicky there. Sometimes she can see him in the bushes on the edge of the park where Nicky is playing; she sees him watching, not daring to step out into the open. Hal thinks he'll find the courage soon enough.

'Would you like to sign our petition it's about the BonChem factory we're trying to do something about the discharge they're putting into the estuary they've got pipes just pumping toxic waste into the marshes and deforming babies?' The approach has to be made in one unbroken plunge. Most of them don't want to sign, they just keep walking. 'OK, no problem thanks would you like a leaflet then read about it see what you think OK?' Breath in. 'Excuse me, would you like to sign our petition?'

She was lying on her back, and probably on a bed, but she couldn't move her head. All she could see was the shiny yellow ceiling.

She felt as though she was encased in foam, with still more foam pumped inside her head, disconnecting and isolating her brain.

She slowly lifted a hand and discovered her head was bandaged, thoroughly swaddled. Some of her hair had been shaved.

She could remember climbing the ladder, being pulled backwards, the kicks from behind, the hardness of the gravel and bricks and concrete shards, and then a few seconds of cold pain before she lost consciousness.

Her hand continued to move and found the metal bedframe. Definitely a hospital bed. The foam inside her head was probably anaesthetic after-effect. Her head was strapped to prevent her moving.

The nurses saw her hand move and were suddenly all around her.

A face manoeuvred itself into her eyeline and explained: an emergency operation to remove a blood clot on the brain, and get her broken nose reset – but everything was going to be alright now, everything was on the mend, would she like some water? And if she just told them her name and who to get in touch with, they can call her family? They looked at her, waiting to be told, and Hal realised that she must keep utterly silent.

They asked her again for her name and she still said nothing, blinking at the nurse's face. They asked her if she could remember anything and she said 'Everything.'

'Now come on, now, we're just trying to help.'

Hal said nothing.

'It's nothing to do with the police or anything. It's just . . . your family and everything. What's your name?'

Hal said nothing.

The nurses fussed around, said she'd had a nasty crack on the head, sometimes it makes you come over a bit strange – as soon as she saw her family everything would come good, they'd seen it all before.

Hal asked what hospital she was in and when they told her a name that wasn't the Royal Cross she knew she was safe. She shut her eyes.

The next day, Spider arrived. He didn't explain how he found her. He was sitting there beside the bed when she woke.

'I tried to bring you one of my special brews. They told me it wasn't right. Put it in their office. I don't think they trust me.'

'What happened, Spider?'

'To you?'

'To the street.'

'Great big field of mud now. Men in their yellow tin hats, their machines all over it. It'll be concrete soon.'

'What about Jem?'

'They hurt his back. Really fucked it over. He's in intensive care.'

'Have you been to see him?'

'They won't let me. Apparently he's mostly machines, you know, keeping him alive.'

Hal isn't surprised. But it doesn't mean she isn't angry.

'You haven't told them who I am, have you?'

'I don't know who you are, do I?'

'Thanks, Spider.'

After three days the straps were removed and she was allowed to sit propped up in bed. She then observed this ward, the process that had been her working life for fifteen years, the battles and the misunderstanding and disdain. She watched the pain and loneliness and knew nothing would ever change.

Each day, the nurses asked for her name and each day she walled herself in, remained this new, unnamed person, free to choose a new life, whatever she wants this time, whatever sort of life takes her fancy. She was going to start again.

Her right arm is stretched straight out from her body and Tom lies across it, his back to her. She starts to feel numbness in her palm and then the pins and needles and she strains to slide it out without waking him.

'You only have to ask,' he says and lifts his torso to allow her to pull free.

'Thought you were asleep.'

'Not yet.'

'You're not normally so quiet, that's all.'

'I'm thinking.'

'What about?'

'Women I've known.'

'Charming.'

'And why they weren't like you. I mean, why did it take so long before I met you?'

'That's better. Keep going. Tell me how beautiful I am next.'

'Don't push your luck.'

Hal looks at the thin buttons of Tom's spine pushing against the whiteness of his skin, the corners of his shoulder blades, blackbrown moles peppering the surface. She feels so suddenly buoyant, almost disjointed by happiness – no, it's not happiness, it's a sense of control and opportunity, the opportunity to do whatever she wants. 'Can I play join the dots with your moles?'

'No.'

'I'm sure it's a rabbit.'

'No.'

'Koala bear?'

'I'm falling asleep here.'

It's about five in the morning. They woke an hour ago, the faintest light creeping round the door frame, and started making love without saying a word. More asleep than awake, Tom's morning erection rubbed between her buttocks and she pushed back against him. His hands came round and squeezed her nipples and the shock ran down the length of her skin. Their fingers fumbled and nudged against the other's body. She rolled comfortably onto her back and drew him inside and held him tight against her. Their lips met but were too dry to kiss. His thrusts were quick and simple and she didn't want to come – his satisfaction was enough and then feeling him softening inside her, the warmth and the wet. They both fell back to sleep like that – dark, intense, mobile sleep – and then had woken almost immediately feeling drugged and sore.

Hal turns to look out of the caravan window. In the blue dawn light she can see the tops of the fir trees opposite, the crows nesting in the highest branches, one perched, ready to swoop. She sees it launch itself into the air, a black explosion as it spreads its wings and then soars down and out of her sight.

She stands and rests her fingertips on the thin aluminium strip round the window and looks out across the marshlands, the bulrushes parted and combed by the wind, the water in the trenches blown into peaks like icing on a cake. It's early June, but the winds are still cold and the ground leafy and moist. When the sun breaks through, the earth sweats and a strong smell of peat fills the caravan, permeates everything they eat.

Looking out from this side of the Circle, none of the other vans are visible and it feels like there's nothing and no one between her and the black North Sea.

Spider visited her in hospital nearly every day, sometimes alone, sometimes with friends. They tended to have names like Phoenix or Dingo or Yag, except for the one called Tom.

'Pol's in Brixton otherwise he'd've come. His case comes up in two weeks and he was refused bail – he told them he'd go straight back and protest again. Too honest for his own good is Pol. He says he's like those blokes in Colditz, you know, their duty to disrupt the enemy as much as possible. I might go and see him next week – you're allowed as many visits as you like when you're on remand.'

Hal was sitting up fully now, allowed an occasional walk round the ward – but the bandage across her nose and under her chin made talking difficult and Spider knew his job was to keep up a stream of noise. More often than not, Tom sat next to him, though hardly ever speaking. Hal wanted to know what he was thinking – he was different from Spider's other friends, more reserved, more anxious. He was tall and thin, pale brown hair flat across his head, still a gangly schoolboy in many of his movements. His eyes, a pale bluegreen, looked out naively from a cream skin breaking out in summer freckles; the hair on the back of his hands was almost blond, the nails bitten. He saw her looking at him and turned away, drumming his fingers lightly on the metal end of her bed.

And whenever she was left on her own, Hal thought about Nicky – though she hadn't yet learned to see him then. And she thought about Dimitri. On her first walk, she had made her way to the phone in the dayroom. She rang (what she used to call) home and it was answered by Dimitri's sister – she must have come over from America, she'd sort everything. Now Hal knew there was nothing left for her to worry about, all the remains of her past life would be parcelled away. She hung up without saying a word – if she started, if she even began to talk, to tell them she was somewhere, that would finish everything. This was her chance to disappear completely.

After a week, the nurses had given up nagging for her name, had even given up trying to prise it out of Spider, and spent their time making up nicknames for her. Hal answered politely to them all.

When they finally agreed to discharge her – after three weeks on the ward – Spider offered to make room for her: mid-April and the weather was warming up, he preferred to sleep outside, he said.

Hal, dressed for the first time in a month, drew back the curtains from round her bed and said she wanted to go and see Jem. Which is when Spider told her how his doctors had decided to turn the machines off about a week before. They'd tried to find his parents and somebody thought his mother was in prison (for killing his father). But when they couldn't trace her, they took the decision themselves. Spider had thought about telling her all this at the time but decided it was best if she didn't have any choice, didn't have the chance to jeopardise her own health. Spider said he was worry he lied to her.

Tom drove them to Spider's place in his van, his eyes constantly flitting across at Hal, anxious, but also wanting to know more. She looked out through the grimy windscreen at a completely different city.

When they first arrived here on this spit of land on the edge of the Lincolnshire coast, the vehicles had spontaneously parked themselves into a circle and hadn't moved since. Only Tom's transit, used for market runs, is parked outside the ring, its snub-nosed bonnet pointing down the track.

The rest of the Circle is made up of the charabanc – a single-decker 1950s coach, still with its original tartan seats, reminding Hal of trips to Roman villas and dreary Shakespeare at the local rep. No one sleeps in the charabanc – except Chip and South when they stay over – they just use it as a place to sit when it's too cold. They arrived here at the tail end of April and the rain was still sheeting in from the east, the surrounding firs offering little protection.

In front of the charabanc is Zippy's pick-up truck – when he lived in the city, he'd got into scrap metal, totting anything you can sell. He says he's given that up now, totally sick of money. Now he wants to go back to the land, he says, live by hunting and trapping: eat the flesh, clothe in the skin, knit the wool. He says that, but he's more often hunched over some bit of rusty metal, twisting it back into shape, his thin spine arching through his singlet, his bluewhite mohawk falling forwards, his boots planted firmly on the ground. He keeps his dogs kennelled on the flatbed of the pick-up, a kestrel in a cage on top of the cabin. Every day he takes the bird out hunting, but he says he's still training it, hasn't caught anything yet. In front of him is Lizzie's van – they had to tow it the last thirty miles from London and it won't ever move from here. And in front of that, Phoenix's dormobile – painted in multicoloured chevron stripes running front to back. And then Tom's caravan. Looking at it again now, it isn't a circle, though everyone calls it that – it's a gap-toothed pentagon.

On their second day there, Lizzie had done her best to make it into a genuine circle – she thinks circles have the Power of Healing and Safety – and she collected about a hundred stones off the beach, set to work planting them in a ring just in from the vehicles. She had painted the stones, each one a shade further on in the spectrum so that the colours gradually work their way through the rainbow in a constant chain. Which is why she's now called Rainbow Lizzie – though she had always banged on about rainbows and the 'perfect colours of life'.

The tops of most of the stones have been scuffed away by now – she had planted them like teeth, pointing upwards, a barbed, defensive circle – but their colours remain as strong, lime green and recurrant red and Devonware blue. Everything about Lizzie is strong – she has what she calls 'her plan' and it's only a matter of time before it reaches fulfilment. And she has the energy – she's always the one on market runs who looks harder, who bothers to check behind the last pallet and finds the forgotten bunch of grapes or she gets the council cleaners to let her go first and finds a bag of mostly-good potatoes. She's a small, round, solidly built woman with round, high cheeks, waving black hair and always smiling, shrugging, jostling from one foot to another. She wears the long green army surplus anorak and jeans but every part of her is festooned with ribbons – a multitude of different colours, naturally – round her arms and legs, in her hair and round her wrists, looped through the shoulder straps and in place of laces. Each time she moves, there's a small explosion of colour.

Right now, she's poking at the fire, bending forwards to blow air into its roots, then twisting back and selecting exactly the right stick to slip into the flames next. She slides it in, sits back on her haunches as though she expects to see a sudden surge of heat and flame, and looks almost instantly disappointed. As always, there's a cauldron balanced over the fire.

'What's tonight?' Hal asks as she steps inside the circle of stones.

Lizzie doesn't look up; she's not taking her eyes off this fire: 'Chilli stew. Found some brilliant jalapeños – bloke hadn't sold hardly a single one, not much call for them round here, so he let me have a pound for fifty p.' And she pushes another branch into the crumbling red heart. 'I've put it up on bricks, can you see? We needed air under this fire, no one listened to me.'

'Seems like it's been working fine to me.' Hal says deliberately, knowing Lizzie wants to explain.

'Aren't you sick of lukewarm tea? Half-cooked chow?' Lizzie's parents, war-traumatised drop-outs, brought her up with pure green ideals, but also filled her with the language of that long dead war. Lizzie now phrases the struggle against concrete and pesticides in the slang of Spitfire pilots and quietly stoical resistance fighters. She hears no contradiction in her use of the words. 'Aren't you sick of it?'

'I hadn't noticed, I suppose.'

'Well, I noticed. Can't even get a decent cup of soup. And we should be able to. This should be the most efficient form of cooking there is. My Mum used nothing else all summer, every single summer.'

Lizzie likes to remind them all that she's the real thing, a second generation green. Her mother had brought her up on tea made from weeds torn from her own wild garden and all her childhood toys were either cardboard or wood. She has never worn new clothes, she likes to boast – one of many boasts.

'About May, we'd set up the fire in the garden, on bricks like this, and we wouldn't cook off anything else till September. October once. Apparently I always used to ask my Mum if we could keep going until Guy Fawkes, but that's when she was getting her rheumo and said enough was enough.' Lizzie's down on all fours now, trying to peer into the fire, the space under the bricks, not talking to anyone in particular, just talking. 'It's collapsed, can you see? We really need something like a grate, balanced across the bricks, the fire chocked up on top of that.' And she sits back up on her heels, looks around as though expecting to see a cast-iron grate casually lying on the grass, hanging in the trees, among the reeds that surround the Circle.

When Tom's uncle had first offered them the site, it was going to be nothing more than a chance to get out of the city, to escape the eviction notices. His uncle was sympathetic to Tom's new way of life and he had half-mentioned this desolate land of his before – he had once owned the adjoining farm but had been unable to sell this plot and had kept it as a romantic memento. Now it was theirs for the summer, longer if it worked.

Tom gathered the others – mostly evictees from Byron Grove – but at the last moment, Spider refused to leave London.

'Where are you going to live?' He had three days left to leave the site near the Royal Cross.

'I clocked a bit of land over by Battersea Power Station, just beneath the scrap metal yard – perfect for me and Grim.'

'Why not come with us?'

'I'm just not built for country living, Hal. Tom'll look after you. You'll look after him. You'll be good for each other. You don't need me any more.'

Hal wanted him to be right.

And it seemed as though he was. There was the excitement of making the Circle encampment come alive – Lizzie painting and planting her protective stones while she argued with Zippy but eventually agreed to cook his meat for him, unable to watch him 'ruin her fire'; Phoenix would drive the van into Skegness and within hours would be back, having found the best dealers and traded (something – no one ever seemed to know what) for half an ounce. He's a thick-set man who is betrayed by an almost high-pitched, whining South London voice. He's the oldest of them, in his early forties probably. From the hints he's let slip, Hal pictures his life before: he's worked as a building labourer or a security guard (he's built for heavy work, a man of patient stamina and no aggression), he's spent years at a time without work, he's resorted to nicking stuff and he's done time. He had a marriage and, like most things in his life, it failed. Hal doesn't know why he's called Phoenix and doesn't ask – for him, like her, travelling is an escape, a refuge not a choice.

But the Circle wasn't many days old before they noticed too many dead animals around the reedbeds, and then Zippy – out on a hunting trip – had found the outlet pipes and the closer he moved towards the pipes, the more sick and dying animals, the withered reeds. If the animal wasn't dead yet – a stoat or an otter, say – it would be shaking uncontrollably, twitching, a thin white line round its lips, its eyes weeping clear white tears. Within hours it would be dead. The vet in Alford said he'd seen plenty like that, and everyone presumed it was the BonChem factory but nobody had ever been able to prove anything and there weren't that many interested anyway. Since the US Air Force bases had gone and the fishing quotas came in, BonChem (real name Bonneville and Loudon Chemical Factors Limited but nobody called them that) was one of the few places offering steady jobs.

Then Lizzie made contact with the handful of people round about who were trying to get something done about BonChem. Chip and Del came out to visit the Circle but it was their daughter, South, who forced them all to realise there was no turning back. Del had carried the child in his arms round the Circle and they had all watched her face become slowly illuminated by Lizzie's coloured stones, the stripy painting of Phoenix's van, Zippy's kestrel stretching its wings. Her eyes would stare, trying to read the patterns as Del manoeuvred her to see everything – she can't hold her head straight and her chin hangs loosely down. When she really wants to, she has just enough muscle control to smile and then it seems as though, just for a moment, the imprisoned child escapes, tunnelling out through the light in her eyes. Her arms are foreshortened – people in the street presume she is a thalidomide victim – and her fingers are stubby. She is nearly always clutching an orange plastic clown, unwilling to be parted from it awake or asleep, its once-smooth surfaces now chewed and pitted. Her mother, Chip, swam in the river when she was pregnant – she and Del lived then in a fisherman's shack on the edge of the estuary. It was supposed to be their escape: they lived almost entirely self-sufficiently and she swam every day of the pregnancy. When South was born and diagnosed with cerebral palsy and other unnamed malformations, they had no choice but to move back into the town – without the benefits of electricity and running water, South would have been taken into care. Six months ago Chip found a specialist who agreed that effluent from the pipes was a possible cause – no one could offer a better explanation for South's disfigurement. Then Chip started the campaign against BonChem. For a long time, she had been on her own.

So it was South who had really forced them to take action – 'direct action' was what they all talked about, but Tom had said they must start with a petition, see how that went, go from there, maybe there was a groundswell of support just waiting to be tapped. Phoenix drew the pictures for the leaflet and they had started collecting signatures.

But those first few weeks before they started campaigning – it was probably only ten days, a fortnight at the most, before they had met South – Hal remembers those as the best days. When they were just camping there, even before the giros came through, surviving on market cast-offs, sitting round the fire, breathing the air. Tom as well had seemed so relaxed. Now his frame is taut and stringy again, but then he had lain contentedly across her stomach, his fingers playing in her hair while they dozed. They had made love and talked.

Tom told her about his time in software, as a teacher, how his depression had grown and grown until it was a ball rolling through the snow, collecting up all his stray fears until he was as good as suicidal. He never attempted it, just spent much of the time thinking about it. One day he took his class on a guided tour of a new ringroad site, got to talking to some of the protesters instead, and a week later packed a backpack and left. His parents – comfortable, well-organised *Daily Mail* readers – were confused and embarrassed and only his uncle saw the sense in it, finally offering Tom this unwanted outreach of land.

She and Tom walked through the reedbeds, alone, watching the egrets landing on the marshes, the gannets nesting out on the offshore islands. To Hal, it was a part of England she had forgotten existed – the brownblack bulrushes and the fields of green reeds, falling left and right in the wind, and the unkempt grey sea and redbrown watercourses of the estuary. She and Tom spent whole days out there, drinking the silence, eating the patience of nature. And then she and Tom would return to the Circle for sleep, such peaceful sleep. It had been a chance to rest her body – suddenly exhausted, she presumed it was the shock of the operation, though she also felt her body was changing – and it was a chance to nurse her anger, at what had been done to her, at what had happened at Byron Grove, at what had been done to Jem. And to Nicky – most of all, Nicky, she refused to forget Nicky and everything that had been wasted.

CHAPTER ELEVEN

She pulls off her sweater, throws it at Tom, and jumps into the watercourse. She feels the hardness of the water as it moulds round her feet, her knees, her thighs, the coldness as it slides up the legs of her jeans. The current pulls at her knees and she steadies herself on the muddy bed. Tom is saying 'What the hell are you doing now?'

They were walking back from the beach, through the reedbeds. She didn't even think about it: she was hot and she wanted to cool off – she jumped into the water.

She strides into the middle of the stream. She cups a handful of muddy water, allowing it to spill down through her fingers. She scoops up another handful and this time throws it up into the air, a fountaining arc. She does it again and again – she admires the water's infinite change.

'What the bloody hell are you doing, Hal?' Tom's looking down at her, hands on hips.

'I felt like a swim. Come on in.'

'Don't drink any, whatever you do.'

'I wasn't planning to.' She throws more water into the air and feels it run down her arms, into her hair, down onto her neck. 'Feels OK. Come on in.'

'I don't want to wear soggy clothes for the rest of the day.'

'Alright, alright. Give me a hand, Tom.' And she reaches up for him to haul her out. She jumps up and down on the mudbank, willing the water out of her trainers. 'I don't suppose you've got a towel or anything?'

Tom slips off his jacket, moves to wrap it round her shoulders. She stops him: 'No point in us both being cold.'

'I think I'll jog back to the Circle. Let the wind dry me out.'

He's saying she's crazy, she'll catch her death as she's already running past him down the path. It's only three, four miles back to the Circle and she wants to run.

To start with she keeps her eyes down on the path – it's barely wider than her, nothing more than the flattened top of the earth ridge, sloping down to trenches on each side. She watches her feet hitting the earth with each pace, feels the shock wave move up her calves. The soil is brown, almost red, thick and wet and crumbling like dough.

The mound starts to flatten down into the lane – she turns sharply away into the reedbeds, following a path snaking through the heads. She lets her arms float out beside her, brushing the tops of the rushes, the air forced up inside her T-shirt, pushing out the damp.

When she gets back to the Circle, she heats a large kettle of water, strips off her clothes, sponges herself down until the water in the bucket is dirtier than her and then falls asleep.

The security guards are shuffling their feet, watching carefully but working hard not to show it. Their names are embroidered on the pocket of their shirts just below the company name. They cross their arms and the tattoos on their forearms flex.

Tom and Phoenix and Rainbow Lizzie and Chip stand by the reception desk, South is in her buggy. Tom is holding the petition – a hundred scruffy pages of signatures in a plain green cardboard folder. The photographer from the local paper is back by the revolving doors, not wanting to be there, checking his light meter. Hal stands next to him – she can't take the chance of being photographed, to the photographer she pleads shyness.

They've been waiting about fifteen minutes – they fixed an appointment to hand the petition to the Leader of the County Council in person but he's been 'delayed'. At least the marble foyer of the Town Hall is cool – outside it is suddenly hot, suddenly bright.

Now the photographer looks at his watch and suggests a shot of the four of them without waiting for the man from the Council. He asks them to group close together by the statue in the centre of the hall, to smile, to look positive at the lens (Phoenix grumbles but Hal's put them all on best behaviour). But then he lowers his camera, says 'It's no good, won't work.'

'What's wrong?' Tom moves across the reflective marble squares, the thumb of each hand tapping against fingertips. 'Is there something we're doing wrong?'

'Have you got anything like a dead fish?' The photographer seems pained, grimacing as though he's caught tight in a mantrap and only the perfect photo opportunity will release him. 'Or a bird, that's be even better. Covered in oil, you know the sort of thing, looking kind of pathetic and sad, feathers all clogged up, little red eye blinking. I can do colour if we need it – the centre pages are colour-run.'

'It's not oil that comes out of the pipes.' Tom's explained this to the man several times already, with diagrams.

'Well, covered in whatever does. We've got to sell this. The picture has to speak as much as the words.'

'That's why we thought you'd like one of us handing over the petition to the council,' Tom says. 'It's over a thousand signatures of protest.'

'It's been done, petitions, know what I mean? We need an angle on this one.'

'It's a chemical effluent, you see.' Hal takes over. 'It's slightly green, but it's barely coloured. It doesn't leave any obvious trace.'

'Except it kills animals, right?'

'And deforms babies in the womb,' Tom can't resist adding. 'And lots of other people have developed respiratory diseases.'

'We know we can't get into all that, don't we now?' The photographer's eyes flick over to South in her buggy. His face frosts over as he reminds himself of South's foreshortened arms, her over-large head, the unfocused eyes. 'And anyway that link hasn't been proved, has it?'

'Hasn't been disproved either.'

'Well, anyways, let's keep the baby out of it, shall we?'

'She's four actually.'

Hal catches Tom's eye, telling him not to lose his cool: this publicity's important. Tom draws breath: 'But slowly, you see, it kills the animals slowly. It's not like oil that stops them moving, suffocates them, or a chemical that burns them, or anything. This effluent is a cocktail of chemicals that builds up and finally destroys the nervous system. The animals crawl into a hole and die, sometimes unable to breathe, sometimes from heart failure.'

'We're here for a photo-op, aren't we, or what? This isn't some David Attenborough number, is it?' The photographer stands with his hands on his hips, cameras on straps pulling his shoulders forward.

'What about Zippy's kestrel?' Phoenix's tentative voice echoes off the hard floor. 'Could we get him to bring the kestrel over, get her to settle, like lie down in his hands, like she's dead?'

The photographer likes it. 'Could we cover it in gunk? I mean, not real stuff just, say, golden syrup, or something like that? Wash it off afterwards.'

'That's ridiculous. Just ridiculous.' Tom stares at the ground, not wanting to face the man, sadness curving over his features. Hal has already learned that when confronted, when forced down, Tom retreats into this morose self – it's a silent, eye-blinking depression that refuses to argue.

Hal says to the photographer: 'You'd do this shot if we were the Women's Institute.'

The photographer's unabashed: 'I'm sorry, yeah, I want to give it a go, but I just know the Editor'll spike it. Most people – you know what they call you, what they say about you – people like you, I mean. BonChem provides a lot of work. I'm putting myself on the line really.'

But suddenly the Leader of the Council is striding down the stairs, a bag-man on either side, a half-pace behind. He skirts carefully round South, doing his best to ignore her. He walks over to Tom:

'Are you in charge here?'

'Are you?' Lizzie has crossed the floor and is facing him, front on, hands deep in her jacket pockets.

'Look, I haven't got long. Who do I talk to here?'

'That's not how we work. You can talk to all of us.'

'Right, I see, typical.' The man is pointing at the folder in Tom's hand. 'Is that it?'

'Do you mind if we do a shot, sir?' The photographer is bobbing at his side, trying to steer the moment back to the statue. 'As they hand it over?'

'Yes, I do mind.' A bag-man moves towards him and the photographer shrinks back. 'Now listen to me, all of you.' He breathes in like a headmaster, fastens the last button of his double-breasted suit. 'We don't want this kind of thing here. You move in, you New Age people, you camp on our land, you make a mess, ruin the countryside and then you start telling us how to treat our local businesses. We're not interested. Understand?'

For a moment, none of them can find anything to say. Hal senses South's eyes staring at the action on this side of the hall, trying to read the patterns.

'Do any of you pay your Council Tax here? Do any of you invest in this county? Do any of you have anything to lose, like your job? Do any of you work, for that matter?'

And now Hal feels the anger rising: 'All the people who signed this petition, they live here, pay taxes here.'

'If they actually exist.' He talks dismissively, as though irritated. 'Give it to me then.' He holds out an apathetic hand.

Hal looks across at the photographer to ready him for this moment, but he's already dismembering the camera, slotting it back into its case.

The Leader takes the folder from Tom and, without even opening it, walks over to the litter basket by the revolving doors and drops it in. 'That's what I think of that. Not even worth recycling, the paper's too low grade.'

'People agree with what we're saying,' Tom is almost crying. 'Don't you respect democracy?'

'I respect it a darn sight more than you. I give the people who live here what they want. We'd like you to leave now.'

'Why should we?' Suddenly this is Chip, South in her arms. She holds her child out to the man: 'This happened because I swam in the water polluted by those pipes. I was pregnant and this is what the BonChem muck did to my child.'

'That's nonsense,' he says and tries to push the child away, out of his eyeline. Lizzie moves behind Chip and holds her shoulders so that she can remain firmly in front of the man, South staring impassively into his eyes.

Phoenix has slipped round the side and retrieved the folder from the bin. He now hands it to Hal. She slaps it against the man's chest. 'It's your job to take this and read it.' When he doesn't react, she does it again, probably harder.

He turns to her: 'I think that was an assault. I won't press charges this time, if you leave. I'm asking you for the last time.'

'Take the petition.'

The man turns and indicates with a thumb to the security guards. They've been waiting for this. They move forwards trying to look menacing like they've seen it done in the movies. One of them says 'Can you go now, please?'

The Leader is already back at the foot of the wide, crimson-carpeted stairs. Hal runs over with the folder and throws it at him as he goes up. It catches the back of his ankle but he doesn't even turn. The sheets spill out down the stair carpet. Hal feels hands on her shoulders steering her back towards the doors.

'We'd like you to leave now or we'll have to call the police.'

'This is a public building. We have every right to be here.' Lizzie is pushing her chest back at the guard in front of her.

'We also have the right to clear the building. In a public order situation. Thank you.' One of the guards has unlocked the single door next to the revolving doors and now holds it open for them.

'We're not leaving until we've handed over the petition officially.' This is Lizzie, her voice shrill.

'That won't be possible.'

Phoenix, less certainly: 'We've every right.'

Hal says 'Let's not bother.' The others turn to her and in that moment they all decide to go.

They walk out into the sunshine. The photographer goes past them without saying a word.

She had told no one where she was going. She stood outside her house, in the phone booth on the corner. It was about eleven in the morning. No one answered the phone but the machine wasn't on either. There was drizzle blowing along the street and blossom in drifts in the gutters. She stood and watched the house for another half an hour. The curtains were drawn and only the porch light was on. She was wearing a beret to cover the side where her hair had been shaved, she felt the scar tissue pull against the wool. She wrapped a thick scarf round her throat and pulled it up over her chin and lower lip. She put dark glasses on and felt ridiculous and took them off again.

They were leaving for Lincolnshire the next day. Before she could leave London, before she could change her life – maybe forever – she had to visit Nicky's room once more.

She rang the doorbell. There was silence. She rang it again, just to be sure, listening hard – the hall was tiled and as soon as she heard footsteps she could turn and run. She could probably get to the corner before anyone opened the door. She bent down and looked through the letter box and half-expected to see the face of Dimitri's sister there on the other side. But the hall was dark and empty and she thought she saw dust. She rang the bell one more time and – though it didn't mean there wasn't anyone there – she put her key in the lock and the door was open.

There was a rush of damp, stale air and then everything was the same. She had expected it all to be different, as different as things had become in the rest of her life – she wanted to see the rooms convulsed, wrecked. But this house that had once been hers was no different, her absence the only marker.

She didn't want to stop and look at anything else. She knew it exerted a force to suck her down, to smother the anger that now fuelled her. She almost ran up the stairs – there was dust on the banister rail – past the room where Gareth had raped her and up to Nicky's room. She pushed the door open.

The bed had been slept in. The room had been used as though it was just a room, a bedroom in a house, a spare bedroom. Was it Gareth, or Dimitri himself, Dimitri's mother, someone she had never met? What did it matter?

She stood, trying to decide. Should she remake the bed, restore the room? But that would show someone had been there. Then again, it might not be noticed and at least she would leave the room how she needed to see it.

She walked in and sat on the bed. The give of the mattress rang a note through her body. She looked up and saw his baseball cap on the shelf and realised how stupid it would be to try and do anything. What could she change by making the bed, tidying the room? She had decided to leave this house and this life – the room was part of everything she had abandoned; she had no rights any more, that's what she had chosen, she had chosen to forget.

She ran back down the stairs and banged out of the door. She ran down the street. She didn't look back.

When she got back to Spider's caravan – she had forced her mind to sleep for the duration of the tube journey – she had wept deep sobs that came out of her like consumptive coughs, tremors working up and down her body until the sweat was cold on her spine and her ribs felt glassy.

Tom sat himself down next to her – she was perched on the sagging edge of the cot in Spider's caravan – and he seemed to be trembling as much as her. He put an arm around her shoulders, said nothing, offered her the comfort of a fellow refugee. He had also needed to flee and find a new way to cope with his sadness. It was then she realised that she must somehow yield to Tom's softnesses, she must allow herself to be enclosed. Tom's kisses were balm on her face and his body on top of hers was hard and soft. Later he explained how she must see that Nicky had merely moved forward, into a new type of life, he was growing up, continuing to change but in a new place. A few days later she had seen Nicky for the first time.

And when they arrived here, a few miles north of the Wash, made their camp amidst the bulrushes, Hal had shaken everything clear. She could see everything and felt secure in the flatness all around, punctuated only by windburnt huddles of fir trees and a cluster of silos about a mile down the lane. They looked like matchsticks from here.

Within hours of the vehicles forming their circle, the encampment had taken on its rhythms, echoing the pulse of each of its members, allowing her anonymity and time. Apart from Tom, no one here knew about Dimitri or Nicky or the hospital or the plaited twist of fear and revenge she carried in her heart every moment of every day.

Hal, Zippy, Phoenix, Lizzie and Vicki – a new arrival – are sitting in the centre of the Circle, watching the flames, watching Lizzie stir her vat of chillies. Tom has cycled to the village to get the evening paper, just in case there's anything about what happened at the Town Hall. The evening is warm but thick with damp and the smell of the grass.

Occasionally someone speaks, but they barely need to – what they all feel is shared, all of them experiencing the same despair, the same black desire to vent the disappointment. They need to find a purpose for the hours spent cajoling signatures, for the sore feet and boredom, for their wasted weeks assembling a petition which was so easily discarded.

'It's like they just line you up and shit on you.' This is Phoenix – for him, it always seems personal. 'They really, like, enjoyed themselves.'

No one replied. No one disagrees. Phoenix scuffs the earth in front of him with the heel of his boot, scraping it forwards and backwards. Vicki squeezes his arm.

The air in the Circle is electric with shared rage.

Leaving the Town Hall, they split up, each making a solitary way back to the Circle, each too disjointed to share feelings. Hal felt breathless, unable to speak, needing to walk – through the town, past supermarkets, through the country roads, down the lane, needing movement to bring her to a steadier place. She thought about how they had been treated and at least now she knew they were armed, armed with the right to act.

By the time they were all back at the Circle, most of the frustration was gone, though none of the anger. They all had different ideas for what to do next. Tom wanted to wait and see if the incident did attract any publicity; Phoenix said there was no point trying to help these people, there were plenty of other good things they could do. Hal listened to the others, her body knowing precisely what she was feeling, merely waiting for the words to speak it.

Lizzie is the angriest, practically hitting the cauldron with her spoon: 'If we haven't reached the point of direct action, when will we?' She looks around at them daring anyone to gainsay her. 'We've offered a democratic, peaceful way. Hundreds of signatures. They don't care. You have to make them care. You have to put it somewhere they can't ignore it.'

'If there's something in the paper—'

'That paper's crap. My parents read it, think it's all true.' This is the first thing Vicki's said. 'They don't care what they trash, what gets thrown away, they just want more money, more things. You know, things, just things. They want to own more and more things.' Vicki's a local girl, full of small-town irritation and claustrophobia, staring up at them from under hooded eyes, almost snarling, though Hal presumes this is just habit. Hal wonders if she is too young – she seems about twenty, but her near-shaven head and thick blue eye shadow make it hard to tell – she could be fifteen, she could be twenty-five. She sits close in against Phoenix, sometimes leaning her head against his shoulder – a kittenishness at odds with her aggressive skull, her hanging-lipped, bared-teeth way of speaking, her sharp shoulders.

Apparently Phoenix hitched a ride down to the sea-front after the Town Hall and met her there – she'd been squatting one of the beach huts and then the owners had arrived to open it up for the summer. Phoenix found her sitting on the wet sand, well below the tide mark, waiting for the sea to move up and cover her. Said she couldn't be bothered. Phoenix felt much the same but by the time the water was swilling round their boots, Phoenix had talked her into a drink in the pub. Now her rucksack sits in the doorway of Phoenix's dormobile.

Tom rides up on his bike. He's got the paper furled in his jacket pocket but he's looking bashful. Hal stands, trying to interpret his disappointed sheepishness: 'There's nothing in it, is there?'

For a moment, Tom says nothing, leans his bike against the side of the van. Hal knows this silence: he doesn't know how to start, he's looking for the best first word. She sees the frowning corner of his mouth, the freckles coming out across his cheeks. 'No, it's . . . it's worse than that.' With infinite weariness, he reaches back to pull the paper out of his pocket.

'Come on, what's the big secret?' Lizzie is striding to the front. 'Let's see it then.'

Lizzie snatches the paper out of Tom's hands – it's already folded back to the right page. The others come and stand behind and beside her, craning, nudging. Hal exchanges a look with Tom before she moves forward to look. His face says ' Sorry,' then he turns away to fiddle with the chain on the bike.

It's a small paragraph:

Police have decided not to prosecute a group of New Age travellers who staged a sit-in at the Town Hall earlier today. A BonChem spokesman said 'Something needs to be done about these people, they are standing in the way of the economic recovery of the East Coast.'

'Fucking hell. I can't believe this.' Lizzie wants to fling the paper away, but the other hands round her hold it still, looking for more words, words or pictures that aren't there. 'It's like the petition never existed. Phe's right – they shit on you, these people, from a height.'

Hal pulls back from the huddle round the paper, trying to find a way of reading something good into the piece, something that might do some good. 'At least people'll look at it,' she finally says, limply. 'They'll know something's happening.' But even as she speaks, she wonders why, she knows it's not what she really feels.

Lizzie turns and looks at her and then plods back to the cauldron, pushes the spoon brusquely from side to side.

'It's clear, they're never going to listen to us. Not the way we want them to.' Tom has finally found the words he wanted to say. 'We're not popular, the factory is.'

'Do they really want jobs more than they want the land, the world?' To Lizzie it's incomprehensible. 'It makes me sick, some of these people.'

She would go on, filling the evening with words, but Zippy isn't going to give her the space: 'Let's just think about this, Liz. Just give us a moment to think about this. Just a moment, OK?' Zippy says everything at least twice – before going on the road, he was a salesman: kitchens, windows, anything. He says he was good – that was the whole problem, too good.

By now they're all wandering back to their places round the fire, some sitting, some remaining standing; Vicki hasn't moved throughout – Hal's not sure she understands, but she's making sure she looks as though she does – and now Phoenix comes back and squats next to her.

Made to stop and think by Zippy, no one says anything for a few seconds. Then:

'So what are we going to do about it?' Lizzie is looking at each of them in turn. 'We really thought this might get some attention. It's obviously going to be harder than we thought.

We're going to have to be more imaginative.'

'Like what?' Phoenix is half-dismissive, half-curious.

Lizzie doesn't bother to answer this. 'Or are we going to let them go on pumping their shit into this paradise? Is that the best thing after all?' Lizzie is prone to smugness at moments like this, the certainty of her own rightness over-whelming her, becoming the most important part of her.

'I don't see what we can do. We've tried a petition. Friends of the Earth told us to try the local paper, start getting support that way – they're obviously not going to. I don't know how to do this.' Tom seems suddenly limp with the effort – Hal wants to put out a hand and hold him. But he remains standing, leaning against the transit van. It would be too meaningful to move across to him now, she knows he wouldn't want it.

'We step up the protest.' Lizzie's cheeks are shining. 'We've got to get into direct action.'

'Anything we do, they just shrug it off.' Zippy's experi-ence of the world of commerce carries weight. 'Corporations are too powerful.'

'Seems simple to me.' Lizzie is aflame now. 'We occupy the plant, their factory. Lock ourselves in. Shut it down good and proper.'

Everyone stops and thinks about this. Inside each of them it germinates and grows and they know it is right. Hal is glad she has waited, allowed Lizzie to be the one to speak the idea – now she can follow and watch and wait.

CHAPTER TWELVE

Only Zippy seems to be really enjoying himself. He's bent over the railway tracks, the rounded visor and heavy gauntlets making him look like a medieval knight kneeling to pray before the crusade to come. Hal wonders if maybe they shouldn't all kneel and pray.

Zippy picks up his welding torch and straightens his back, hinging the visor up from his face. He looks up at Hal from under the black curved metal overhang: 'Want me to start?'

The first haze of light is pumping into the clouds at the eastern end of the tracks. Hal turns and checks the embankments once more – she's been watching them for the last few minutes and hasn't seen a trace of movement, not even a cat weaving amongst garden fences. 'Clear as it'll ever be.'

Zippy lowers the visor, ignites the torch and bends to his work. What was a small, hissing, controlled jet of flame becomes a sudden arc of orange filaments as he starts welding. It's a clear, bright target – and it can't go unnoticed for long. They'll have five, ten minutes maximum. Then everything begins, one way or the other.

Vicki and Lizzie jog over, attracted by the magnetic ferocity of the flame. The three women stand looking down at him, allowing their eyes to be filled with the heat and light. It's barely rained for the last two weeks and the ground around them is reflecting dry heat.

He stops to take a breather and before he's turned off the jet, Lizzie asks: 'How long do you reckon this'll take?'

Zippy doesn't rush to answer. He doesn't even look up, just tilting the visor and wiping his forehead with the sleeve of his camouflage jacket. 'As long as it takes.' Even in this early morning cool, he's sweating while the rest of them shiver and stomp their feet. 'Do you want it done proper or not?'

'Sure, proper. Just we haven't got long, know what I mean?'

Of them all, Lizzie seems the most nervous. Not that anyone asked her to take charge, no one pushed her to the front. It was just that she always seems to make the most noise – noise Hal finds it hard to argue with.

The day after she suggested occupying the works, Lizzie, Tom and Hal cycled over to BonChem. Lizzie called it a recce. The three of them cycled up the new black strip that cut through the flat fields, purpose-built to connect the BonChem factory with the coastal A-road. Arriving in front of the wasp-striped barrier, the security guard's box, the three of them turned to circle the perimeter. High wire fences went uniformly round, broken only by one other entrance, the loading bay that met the single-track railway line.

The three of them stayed all day, sitting a couple of hundred yards away under a tree on the edge of the estuary. They watched staff arrive at the double gate. They watched the birds combing through the reedbeds, plucking worms out of the mud. Twice, a goods train pulling cylindrical tankers like ants' eggs, made the run down the line, was admitted inside the compound, the gates locked behind it. Occasionally lorries were let in or out of the front gate – guards checked papers and waved drivers through.

But it wasn't the security which discouraged them, it was the isolation. They had never noticed it before – either on their first, polite visit or later when they were petitioning the staff themselves (one signature).

No, it was utterly isolated – a wilderness punctuated by this single industrial adventure. The plant's aluminium chimneys burst spontaneously out of the ground, unexpected and unwanted. The staff arrived by car or bicycle or mostly in the chartered buses from the town; at four or five or six, they left the same way. No one lived in sight of the works and the area was silent within minutes of the end of the shift. If they occupied the factory, no one would see, no one would know. Even if they broke into the compound, they would be summarily removed and no one would be there to bear witness.

By the end of the day even Lizzie admitted there was no point in an occupation, however symbolic.

Hal and Tom cycled back to the Circle. Tom sat in front of the caravan, bashing out another press release on the typewriter balanced on his lap. Hal lay inside, enjoying the steady rhythm of the hammers and watching Nicky – he was playing French cricket in the park with boys she had never met.

But Lizzie went into town on her own, bumping her bike along the railway track, saying she wanted to know where it went. Three hours later, after dark, she returned to the Circle with the plan to occupy the railway station.

Apparently she followed the line, found it went right into Alford Station, Platform Five, out on the edge. She got one of the station staff talking, he confirmed it: most of the chemicals shipped into the plant went along that line, straight through the station. Here was a target no one could miss, she said, and they had every right to hit it.

After two weeks of careful watching and measuring, dull days spent putting together the factory train's weekly routine, early mornings and late nights monitoring the station staff, here they are, at half past five in the morning, standing round the deserted station while Zippy welds scaffolding tubes onto the railway line.

'We've only got half an hour until the first staff clock on.' Lizzie is still fretting. 'Is that going to be enough time? Zip, is it?'

This time Zippy just carries on welding – or he intends to. What stops him and makes them all look back along the track is the sound of a train. To begin with they don't want to believe it's on their line or if it is, it'll soon branch away. But they know this line, they've checked it: there isn't a branch, this is the end of the line – any train on these tracks has got to come through the station, probably using this section of track.

Zippy is instantly furious. He flings down the torch, turning on Lizzie: 'I thought you fucking said the first train didn't come through until eleven?'

'That's right.' Lizzie is shocked but defensive. 'I mean, that's what happened on the days I watched. I mean, Thursdays must be different or something. Don't blame me.' Her voice is rising to a pitch.

'Maybe it's late, or early, or something.' Hal tries to soothe things.

'Great. I mean, just great.' Zippy looks down at his work. 'This just isn't ready, I need a whole lot more time.' Zippy's already shifting his tools out of the way, making sure they're safe, his mind already set on going.

'We've got to stop the train?'

'You want to stop the train?' In the middle of this near panic, Vicki's voice is frighteningly calm – she doesn't seem hurried, let alone scared the way the rest of them are. 'There's no problem. I can't see the problem.'

'We need to block the tracks.' Lizzie looks up and down the line, trying to think, trying to have a better plan.

'Oh.' And Vicki steps onto the railway line and starts walking towards the approaching dot of the train. For her first ten or so paces, none of them manages to say anything – it's too unexpected, too weird. Or maybe they're confused by the way she moves: it's surprisingly graceful – she's wearing light plimsolls and her toes arch forwards with each careful step she takes. It's balletic. By the time Hal is shouting after her – 'Vicki, for God's sake, come back here' – she is into her stride, pacing along the sleepers, throwing a hand nonchalantly over her shoulder back at them. The train is still moving down towards her – not fast, but not slow – and she doesn't slacken her pace either.

Lizzie yells: 'Come back here, Vicki, don't be so bloody damn fool stupid.'

Vicki just turns around and starts walking backwards, shouting at them: 'Get on with it then. I'll stop the train.'

Hal can't help noticing that Vicki, though walking backwards, assuredly places each foot on the middle of each sleeper behind her. There isn't the faintest hesitation about how she moves. Hal watches her running towards it, bouncing up off the wooden sleepers, kicking up the gravel behind her. It is beautiful. It has an athletic ease, a rhythm.

'She'll jump out of the way at the last moment.' Lizzie is trying to sound certain. 'She will, won't she?'

But the train can't be more than about six, seven hundred yards in front of her now, twenty seconds apart. And Vicki's dressed entirely in black – maybe the driver won't see her: the only paleness is her shaven head, harshly greywhite. Hal sees Vicki's heels pushing back at them, the soles of her shoes, the elbows pumping. She's not slowing her pace. Nor is the train, flat-fronted, the slit of the cab window dirty black, a blind face. They won't see her, Hal is thinking, it's not possible, they won't be looking for her, they won't see her.

'Was that the brakes?' Hal doesn't know she's saying it until she is and she's listening for the first, faint squeal.

'Was it?' Lizzie's leaning forwards, they all are.

Hal tries not to fool herself, but then she thinks she hears the train's brakes starting to catch. She looks closer, and yes, it's slowing, even if Vicki isn't. She's still running headfirst towards it, if anything even faster.

By the time the train has stopped, she's not more than a

road's width in front of it. She keeps running and almost seems to run up the front of the train, landing a heavy boot on the nose of the fender and turning round as she does so, back squarely onto the tracks. There's a moment of stillness as Vicki stands there, probably smiling, then she just stops and sits down on the track, cross-legged, cross-armed.

She remains sitting, immobile like an Indian chief, until the driver flings open the side door of the cab and starts to climb down – at this distance, Hal is watching stick-like figures moving against a giant backdrop. She sees Vicki quickly reach into her pocket, get out the handcuffs (it had been her job to find the Adult shop in Skegness and buy them each a pair) and cuff herself to one of the ring bolts on a sleeper.

All they can see from the station is the driver's wild arm movements, the fury as his limbs are thrown around, kicking out – either at her or the track, they can't tell at this distance. Vicki seems to turn back and look at them and they know what she's saying.

'She's got balls, hasn't she?' Zippy's packing up his welding gear. 'You don't need me now.'

'OK, let's tell the others we haven't got long.' Lizzie doesn't look at Hal, just expects her to follow. Hal lifts herself up onto the platform – why does she feel so much heavier? – and then jumps down onto the next pair of tracks. All the while, she's wondering why she resents Lizzie's so easy assumption of authority, wondering why it releases a wave of exhaustion through her body.

Tom and Del, South's father, are standing outside the locked doors of the building, the placards stacked up against the wall, a box of leaflets, petition clipboards. All Lizzie cares about is: 'Haven't you got through that window yet?'

'It's locked.' Del has his usual expression of innocence confounded.

'Then smash it.' Lizzie's answer is simple. 'We've got to get in there.'

'Hold on here, we can't show evidence of a break-in.' Tom is reverting to his I've-said-this-a-million-times-before voice – it's always Lizzie who brings this out in him. Suddenly Hal is overwhelmed by a feeling of sickness, a dread of what is to come hollows her out inside. She can't stand up for one moment longer and she sinks onto the bench in front of the snack-bar window.

She drops her head into her hands, feels the sweat suddenly on her forehead, hears Tom continuing 'If we do, that's criminal, that's burglary, they can arrest us.' But the voices seem brittle, Hal feels as though she is becoming detached from everything around her, the nausea a barrier.

'They're going to arrest us anyway, Tom.'

'Not necessarily. They often don't press charges.'

'They're going to throw the book at us, Tom. That's the point.' Lizzie's eyes are burning. 'If they don't, we've done something wrong, haven't we? We're here to piss them about. We want to get in the way, don't we?'

'They often decide not to press civil actions if it's just going to give more chance for protest and publicity. If we break in, they have to bring a criminal charge, we're not offering them any choice. These things don't work if we paint them into a corner, you have to give them a chance to save face.'

Hal looks up and sees Lizzie looking down at the ground. She seems to be listening to Tom, thinking about what he says. But no, she's looking down at a flowerpot – trailing blue lobelia and white geraniums – and now she picks it up and heaves it through the glass panel. Hal hears it the dull thump as the pottery implodes on the floor inside the booking hall. Tom doesn't know what to say; Del starts giggling, a sweet, toddler's giggle, bringing his crabbed hand up in front of his mouth, half-embarrassed, but enjoying it.

'You've fucked it now, Liz.' Tom finally manages to get out, exasperation nearly silencing him. 'Seriously fucked us all.'

'They can't prove it was me.' And Lizzie holds up her gloved hands. 'See? No fingerprints. I'll say it was like this when we found it.' And she leans carefully through the gashed opening and turns the Yale on the inside. Lizzie strides onto the tiled floor, Tom follows, still petulant, Del follows sheepishly. Hal hears their feet echoing in the cold space. She hasn't got the will to get up and follow. Has she come this far only to unearth her own fear?

She looks back along the tracks. Vicki's still sitting there, calm and straight as a statue – the train driver's a few hundred yards away, speaking into some kind of phone attached to a telegraph pole. He keeps looking back at Vicki, gesturing as he talks.

Hal drops her head down between her knees, wills herself to vomit, anything to clear the haze that's fogging her. She must stand up.

Exhausted, shattered, last night, sitting round the fire, she had lain back while the others went on talking about the new law of trespass, the importance of non-violence, the cult of protest. The noise and the talk had merged into a single buzz and Hal had floated away.

He was kissing her. That's how she woke, still lying on her back, one side of her body warmed by the fire, the other stiffening with the marsh damp. Tom's lips were touching hers, barely kissing, just floating and trembling against hers, the warmth of his breath.

'What's happening?' Hal was still lost in the fog of sleep.

'Everyone's gone to bed.' Tom's fierce eyes stared down at her, his head at right angles to hers. 'Lizzie gave strict orders: early night for all, got to be ready for tomorrow, ship shape and Bristol fashion, upper lips stiff and you know the sort of thing. I'm supposed to wake you up so you can go to bed.' Tom's smile was wide, honest, anxious.

'How long was I asleep?'

'I don't know. Things got kind of intense. They just won't understand – if we smash our way into the buildings, they can do us for—'

'Don't, Tom, not now, I believe you.' Hal had pulled his head down again, repaying the kisses she had taken from him while she emerged from sleep. She reached her hands up to stop him drawing back, to save him from his too-easy embarrassment. His hair was thick, slightly curling, black. Hal forced her fingers through the roots, wanting to hold his head tight, wanting to squeeze all of him down towards her. She felt his resistance, his wish to pull away from her intensity, to be under cover of darkness and privacy before he could be safely immersed in her.

Tom straightened up, pulled away from her. 'Let's get some rest. What do you say?'

'Tom, are you happy?'

'Happiness is a funny concept.' Tom did his eccentric professor face, using it as a mask to hide real feelings. 'Linguistically speaking, it's a slippery fish.'

'OK. Would you rather be somewhere else, doing something else?'

'No. Alright, probably not.'

'That's a start, isn't it?'

'Sure. Can we go to bed?' Hal had loosened her grip and he stood up, took a step back from her. 'We're getting up at four, remember?'

'I've never been happier. Did you know that?' She looked into the darkness for his face, his chin, his white skin caught by the flames of the fire. 'Each day is a wonderful thing, isn't it? I never knew that before. We waste so much time, don't we? Thinking we've got to do this and do that.

And we haven't. You can just do what you want, when you want.'

'Except we've got to get up in about three hours. It's Lizzie's D-Day.'

Hal rolled over the ground, reaching out for his ankles. He jumped back out of her reach. 'Cheat. Come back, you snake in the grass.'

She watched him disappear through the door and then stood, brushed herself down. Lizzie had added to her circle of painted stones – at the four points of the compass there was now a wind-vane of turning mirrors. She walked over to East, caught one of the oval mirrors, and looked carefully at herself in the moonlight. She saw her hair, bleached a lighter brown by the sun, hanging down each side of her face – what her mother would call rats' tails, uncombed, unkempt, muddled – she hated going to the public baths in the town and relied on the sea. She felt she had put on weight as well, her cheekbones less prominent, her chin somehow rounded, less sharp, or maybe that was just the dulling effect of the dust smeared on her face? She saw her eyes, brown fading to blue, thick eyebrows, her forehead uncreased. For weeks now she hadn't touched make-up and she felt cleaner and purer. And she hadn't had a period since her operation – a godsend, really: they had no running water and only a latrine they'd dug on the edge of the woods. But amenor-rhoea was perfectly normal following that kind of trauma and the medication she was given – her body would emerge into a new cycle when her new life was finally established.

Just hearing the textbook words in her head summoned her former life. She knew what they would all say: she had swapped one restriction for another, Dimitri into Tom, Royal Cross into New Age, a terraced house in Battersea into a caravan on the edge of a circle of painted stones. Was she any freer? they would ask, Was the really? She could see their accusing faces, contorted with righteousness, flushed with normality. But she was free, freer – she could see it in her eyes, in the weightlessness she felt as she rolled over the ground trying to grab the ankles of a man she had found less than three months ago and would probably lose in as many.

How they would all laugh and howl – those people who had buttressed her life before. How they would reel in shock and accuse her of irresponsibility, fecklessness, carelessness – those great crimes of Middle England, the greatest of all crimes she had been brought up to believe. But none of them knew the beauty she had found in this wilderness, in the whispering silence of the reedbeds, swinging through the waist-high grass. This was something to fight for, something to protect, whatever they said.

In the caravan, she found Tom lying on the bunk, searching through his law books, his direct action manuals, checking and cross-checking. She sat next to him and stroked the back of his neck, his thin shoulders.

'See? I knew I was right. Here, look.' He's holding the pamphlet up for her. 'If there's a sign of forced entry – it's not even criminal trespass, it's burglary – trespass with intent. They'll throw away the bloody key.'

She won't mention it, not tonight, it would spoil the time they still had together – and it wasn't like there was anything she wanted to do about it, whatever Tom said. She would just roll and roll and roll across this new ground, this undiscovered country, and find the new life that was promised at the end of it.

By the time the police vans arrive, Hal and Lizzie have chained themselves across the main doors of the station building, Phoenix has locked himself onto the tracks by Platform One and Del is up on the roof, sitting calmly on the ridge like a Punch and Judy puppet, legs over the edge of the stage. They've put their banners up in front of the door, the largest draped over the roof tiles. Tom decided not to chain himself up – this way he and Chip can go on handing out leaflets – he says they can't stop them doing that.

The policemen who clamber out of the van are blood-shot but early-morning excited, shaken from the dull hours of the shift. Hal recognises the Sergeant walking towards them – he's hassled her when she's been collecting signatures on the High Street. He recognises all of them too, sighs, looks down at his thick rubber soled boots, thinks he can shame these hippies away, make them into naughty children. Tom walks straight up to him, offers him a leaflet: 'This is a non-violent protest, Sergeant. Against chemical dumping in the estuary. Here. Read this, please.' Suddenly Tom's lisp sounds prominent, at the front of his mouth, weakening him.

The Sergeant takes the leaflet and hands it, without looking at it, to a constable at his side: 'Bag this. It's evidence.' Then he turns to Tom: 'You in charge here, sonny?'

It takes Tom a moment to mouth the words, his lips working silently until: 'We don't have anyone in charge.'

'How am I going to get you out of here then? Who do I talk to?'

'All of us,' Lizzie comes in. 'We make decisions collectively.'

The Sergeant gives his most histrionic, disbelieving sigh, leans back, pushing his hat back on his head. Only then does he notice Del on the roof. 'That's all we bloody need.' Del waves back down at him.

He looks at the three on the ground. 'And I hear we got another of you chained up out on the tracks.' He looks around, waiting for a response. When none comes, he focuses in on Hal: he's noticed that she has so far said nothing, reckons she's the weak link. 'You going to unlock yourself now, sweetheart?'

'Not a chance.' Hal hears the words come out of her mouth, disembodied from her own actions. Something else is moving her forward now, a part of her she's glad to be discovering.

'Come on now.' The Sergeant moves towards her, pulling on the chain that runs round her waist and through the looped door handles. 'Give us the key then, love. We've got people needing to get to work, you know. You're not being fair to them.' Hal narrows her eyes on where the brass of the door handles has been worn away, the history of a hundred years. The Sergeant is trying to find the padlock, saying 'We don't do things this way round here.'

Hal backs off, pulling hard on the chain, watching it go taut, whiplashing, trapping his fingers momentarily. He pulls his hand back, licks the knuckle of his index finger. He looks her straight in the eyes. 'I'll be looking out for you.'

'Fuck you. Just fuck you.' The bile is rising in Hal. And she's letting it come. 'Fuck you sideways.' She's heard these things, on the street, in Casualty, from patients in pain and anger. Now she's saying them out loud to a policeman.

'Careful now, Missy.' More than anything, he looks disappointed – had he wanted to flirt with her?

'Why? Why should I?'

The Sergeant doesn't bother to answer. He goes back to the transit van, talks to the other policemen standing round. One of them drops his chin like a violinist and talks into his radio.

Lizzie turns to Hal: 'He didn't like that.'

'I hope not.'

'It'll start to get nasty now. They'll call in the heavies, the tactical support group.'

'Good.' Hal feels something changing, a fearlessness, a lightness in her muscles – it doesn't matter any more. The sickness and the dread has done and nothing matters any more – does it? – As long as you're saying No.

And she's not alone. The loneliness she's known all her life is gone.

The police have found some wire cutters and the commuters are swilling around the road in front, watching, shrugging, looking for a café. Hal had expected jeering, anger, hostility – but what they get is silence, one or two acquaintances daring to whisper. A man in a suit is yelling at a guard, blaming him. The people look up at the banners, read the words about BonChem, about the damage they're doing, but it's like they can't take them in – they have their opinion, they're not ready for another. Chip stands at the front, with South in her buggy, handing out leaflets. They try not to look at her.

Tom is moving among them, looking bashfully downwards as he hands out leaflets, smiling his gentlest smile. He's embarrassed, seemingly regretful to be doing what he's doing. When the coach drives past, taking BonChem staff out to the plant, the faces turn in unison to look down on Hal and Lizzie, up at Del on the roof. The faces are blank.

Hal wonders if Vicki is still sitting in front of the train, staring at its monolithic eye. If she's sensible, she'll make a run for it before she's arrested – she's done everything she can by now. Phoenix too.

Now they're coming towards her with the bolt-cutters.

When Lizzie's chain is cut, Hal watches her go limp, forcing the police to take her under the arms and drag her heels across the tarmac to their transports. As they're inviting her to step into the van, she slips under and out of their grasp and runs back towards the station. She dodges past one policeman but then, standing in front of the doors, the Sergeant calmly puts out a hand as she passes, and locks his arm round her neck, brings his other hand up to secure the hold. Her hands go to her throat as she is suddenly deprived of air. He doesn't loosen his grip until he has walked her backwards to the van and handcuffed her to another police-man.

When Hal's turn comes and the maintenance man snaps through the chain link, she wants to just lie down and be a rag-doll as well. But she can't. She has to let them know she is here. Her hands fly out at the uniforms, she pulls at the brass buttons, the epaulettes, the helmets. She feels hands grasping her shoulders, an arm around her waist, an elbow pushes the air out of her stomach, another tugs on her hair, forcing her head back, her throat exposed like a sacrificial calf. She pushes out her limbs in a crazy dance and she is lifted off the ground on a trampoline of hands. She shakes her head, trying to get free of the hand ripping at her hair but all she feels is still more of it coming out at the roots. She kicks with each foot, kicking into space, flexing and jerking her knees until she feels her trainer connect with the softness of a stomach, she hears the intake of breath and the anger that follows it. Her eyes are spinning, the sky turning and rotating; she sees clouds and the roof, the upper storeys of buildings and someone's sudden red face. Then she sees the roof of the van and she's inside it, floating for a moment, before the metal floor lifts up and slams against her back. Her wrists jerk upwards as her arms hit the row of seats along each side of the van. The pain starts along the bones of her spine, the back of her skull.

Lizzie looks down at her, holding out a hand to pull her up – she's smiling down at Hal: 'Better than sex, isn't it?'

CHAPTER THIRTEEN

Hal dreams about when she was pregnant. She's lying in water: maybe a bath, maybe a swimming pool, maybe a lagoon. She hears the word 'lagoon' and so that's what it is. She's on her back, her head propped up on something solid, her body floating away from her, just below the surface. She's looking down at the straining pulse of her child, filling out her belly, stretching her skin impossibly, the veins writing a map across the vulnerable whiteness. This is her new map of the world.

But it's too big, whatever's inside there has grown too large – it must be born soon.

The current of the water catches and gently ripples away from her navel. The water is green, reedy, there are particles of something suspended in it – she presumes it's mud, strands of red soil. Then she sees they're moving, tiny brown eels are what they look like. When she tries to touch them, tries to lift up a handful, she can't. They float away, untouchable. She pushes her hand through the water and can't even feel them. She wonders if they're actually there. No, they're not. Or maybe she is just numb, numbed all over. She rubs her eyes and it stings – she hadn't expected the water to be salt.

Nicky is standing next to her, talking. She wants to turn her head, see what he's standing on, make sure he's safe: he mustn't fall into the water – he can't swim; she's sure he can't swim. He doesn't seem to realise he's in any kind of danger, just goes on talking to her about the island he's discovered.

She wants to talk to him about the baby. She explains everything to him: that it's him inside her, how he started by growing inside her and then he does some more growing on the outside of her and then he has to finish it all on his own.

He's saying he doesn't want to ever finish when Hal wakes for a moment, her head jerking. She's immediately back to the grey plastic cover on the foam mattress beneath her, wet with puddles of her sweat, the shiny blue ceiling above. The bulb in the ceiling leaves a yellow trail on her retina. Almost immediately she drifts back into sleep.

She's climbing up out of the water now, up onto a kind of mud bank, but the weight in her stomach is so draining, so ponderous, she can't stand, she can only move forwards on all fours like a low-slung animal. She hears someone say 'She's like a beast of the field' and wonders if that's her saying it or just someone else thinking it. She moves slowly, she can feel the gritty mud rubbing against her knees, her palms, she feels the fronds of the weeds pulling against her calves, pulling her back into the water, wanting to tie her down. She knows she can only move forward if she uproots the plants that are lashed around her ankles. She strains, putting all her energy into her legs, and with a sudden pull, her knee slides forward and she hears the earth tearing and suddenly she can move forward again. She worries that the effort may have dislodged the baby, that it may come sliding out of her now. She smoothes a hand round her womb, pacifying, reassuring for both of them.

She lies down on her side, on the mud, seeing herself like a cow, and goes on explaining to Nicky about growing up. She's got to make him understand, she's got to make him realise that it'll be better this way, they all will, he just has to understand. It's crucial he sees the truth of it – if she does nothing else, if she never moves from this mud bank ever again, this is what she must achieve. She must go through it all, make him listen to the very end.

But she can't see Nicky any more: he's behind her back and he's speaking in Dimitri's voice. He's talking about her, how beautiful she is, how beautiful her back is – she can feel his hands running down her spine, sliding over her buttocks, running a finger into the crack between. She tells Nicky to stop. He says – it's still Dimitri speaking, even though it's Nicky – it's alright, it'll be alright, she's so beautiful. She can feel him pushing his erection between her legs, forcing for a space. She says he mustn't, he really mustn't, tries to put a hand down to stop him. He says 'It's fine, it's really fine, it'll help me understand.' The pain of his pressure starts to run up her spine, starting as a dull ache in her coccyx which swarms up and out, filling the muscles of her back, using spine and ribs and shoulder blades as a pathway, running down the nerves into her arms. More than anything she feels it in her wrists: they've become unbearable pinpoints of sensation.

She wakes. The first thing she remembers is how Dimitri hated making love to her when she was pregnant. How he thought it was wrong, somehow unholy.

Then she hears keys outside. The levers of the lock turn deep inside the door. The cell door opens and a policeman is standing there, not one she's seen before. He's older, fatter. He leans against the doorframe, almost out of breath.

'Have a good sleep, love?'

'I need a doctor. I'm in pain.' She's not going to cry, she's definitely not going to cry. She'll use her anger to push her tears aside. 'From when you threw me in the van. You've probably broken my wrists.'

'Don't get aerated now. Won't do no one any good, will it?' The policeman, under his condescending tone, seems sympathetic, seems as though he wants to be sympathetic. 'She's here, the Doc. That's what we've all been waiting for, isn't it?'

'Thank God.' Hal turns to look up at the ceiling, waits for the Doctor to come in.

'Sorry, love, she doesn't do house calls. Her room's along

here.' The policeman stands back to allow her to pass out of the cell. She raises herself up off the mattress, pain in every movement, swivels and stands.

As she walks past him, she notices that the man is shorter than her.

The Doctor is a large matronly woman, late forties, set, greying hair. She listens to Hal's story, nodding and tutting, neither agreeing nor disagreeing, approving nor disapproving.

She examines Hal thoroughly, with gentle fingers, testing for broken bones, for torn muscles and ripped ligaments. She takes photographs of the bruising and measures each, dodging between her clipboard on the filing cabinet and Hal lying inert on the couch. She apologises each time she presses a bruise, says she has to be sure how tender they are. 'Ridiculous, isn't it?' she says. 'I have to hurt you so that I can write down that it hurts. Sorry. I expect you'd rather I didn't bother. All things considered.' Hal likes her in spite of herself.

When she starts to examine Hal's stomach, her testing fingers become careful, determinedly exact, her eyes flicking towards Hal's face, smiling when they make eye contact but quickly looking away. She asks Hal a few questions – about marital status and accommodation – and when Hal says 'No' or nothing, the doctor's movements become more studied.

When the Doctor is finished, she makes Hal dress again and then gives her a chair while she stands by the couch, looking down at her notes. She says she must speak to her before the Sergeant comes back. She says: 'I'm sorry to have to ask this. Did you know that you are pregnant?'

'Yes.' Hal's voice is flat, determined to appear unconcerned. 'Of course.'

'Who's your doctor?'

'No one, I haven't registered.'

'You'd better get on with it then.'

'Is it alright? The baby?'

'I should think. You're probably due a scan anyway soon, aren't you? They can check everything for you.'

'I'm only two months.'

'No, you're not, you're nearer four – over four, I'd say. I'm surprised you're not showing yet.'

Hal remembers how late she showed with Nicky. 'I think you're wrong. It can only be two months.'

'I do know a thing or two about this, you know. I might be out by about a month, but not more. You're somewhere between three and four. Certainly in your second trimester.' The doctor has become breezy, certain of her knowledge, unaware of Hal's. 'This isn't your first, is it?'

'No.' Hal mustn't talk about Nicky.

'How old is the other one?'

'He's almost seven.' And he is. His birthday is in a couple of weeks.

'Lovely. I'll give you a note for the hospital and they'll fit you in with a scan this week. That'll make it certain.'

'It's not possible. I wasn't having sex four months ago.' But even as she is saying it, Hal knows what this doctor will say. They all do.

'It's amazing what people forget, forget what was happening when. You know how it is. And you do only have to do it once, you know.' The Doctor tries to smile. 'Now you have a good hard think and everything'll fall into place. Either that or the age of miracles is come again. If you want counselling, I'm sure the GP'll line you up with someone.'

Hal doesn't bother to argue any more.

'Here's the letter. Go to the hospital as soon as you can. In Lincoln, or Grantham if that's easier. No bones broken so I'm going to certificate you fit to be interviewed – so that's it as far as I'm concerned, I'm afraid. Good luck.'

CHAPTER FOURTEEN

'Any more of this ridiculous behaviour and you'll be asked to pay up to one hundred pounds. You made life very inconvenient for a large number of people trying to go about their daily business. It's quite unacceptable in a democracy like this. Do you understand? There are channels for this sort of thing. This kind of protest is simply unnecessary. Is that quite understood?' The Magistrate looks down at her, turning the outsize sheets of paper on his table, waiting for her compliance. Hal just looks away, looks at the people sitting at the side of the court. 'Are you willing to be bound over to keep the peace?' The people along the side of the court, awaiting their turn, remind her of the faces at the Out-Patients' from her old life – the same fearful faces, the same willingness to sit, listen, take and then go.

Hal is able to combine her trip to the Ante-Natal Unit with the summons to the Magistrates' Court.

'Alright, I take it that's a Yes,' the Magistrate says, 'That's all. You're bound over in the sum of one hundred pounds. You can go. The usher has a piece of paper for you to sign.'

The Radiologist puffs out his professional chest, moves his cursor over the length and breadth of her foetus. 'There's a leg. You'll feel that kicking soon. That'll be fun for you,' he says, as though the child only exists thanks to his efforts in making it appear.

She is bound over to keep the peace for a year; the Radiologist tells her to come back in two months. 'We like to keep a close check on mums like you.'

'Don't worry about me, I'm keeping the peace.' The

Radiologist smiles, narrows one eye at her, decides he won't try to find out what she means.

At least the conducting gel is cool on her stomach, the ultrasound sensor sliding through it, pushing it around like jam on a slice of toast, no, on the skin of a pear, rolling and spilling down the sides. Outside a July heatwave has silenced the middle of the town, few cars are moving, the gulls are silent.

When she emerges back onto the grey concrete hospital steps, she is alone – she told the others to go back to the Circle without her and how she wishes she could keep it that way. But even her body has been invaded now, splitting again into two, filling out with new necessity.

Zippy says they're going about this all the wrong way. He wants to plug the pipes. Apparently it's no good protesting, making noise, getting up a petition. 'People don't care – real people, people in power, they're all the same, they can't none of them think about the future. We have to do it for them. So if there's something wrong, you shut it down. You don't wait for 'People' to vote for it. Democracy's such a fucking sham. It's all about selling the most things, now, here, all the time, sell, sell, sell.' This is Zippy's regular speech – he hates money. 'You can't get past all the advertising, all that shit, you have to strike them in the heart.' Hal agrees with much of this, if not the plan Zippy is proposing.

When Lizzie pushes him to practicalities, he reckons he could make a giant plug, more a kind of metal sheet, like a beer bottle top which he'd weld over the mouth of each pipe, blocking it completely. 'Then we just sit and watch the gunk feed all the way back up the tube into their own back yard. That'll wake them up.' If they come and remove the bottle top, he'll do it again. Until they're having to guard the outlets full-time. And then, when it's costing them too much, they might be willing to talk about it. 'You have to make it cost,' he grins. 'You have to make it hurt the budget so much it's worth talking to us.'

While he's talking, Lizzie gets more and more excited, kneeling forwards to prod the fire, sitting down again, playing with her beads, nodding her head. She reckons this is the best idea yet. She likes the mixture of skill (the design, the welding) and strategy (the best time, the best way to get at the pipes for long enough to fix them on without getting arrested). She starts devising their first raid. She needs to work out how many people it will take to keep look-out, how many to carry the welding equipment. She's getting a scrap of pencil and paper and asking Zippy to estimate how long it will take, as Hal walks away down to the edge of the reeds.

She wants to strike back too, she wants to make BonChem squirm but this isn't the way, carrying on this guerrilla war, pinpricks in the hide of the beast. And soon she won't have the energy for these physical protests. Anyway, they'll be brushed away each time, a barely noticeable mosquito, at best a scratch. They will always lose, will always be more vulnerable.

It had already been spelt out. They returned after the arrest, after the weak tea in smoky interview rooms, to find the Circle vandalised, the vehicles attacked, the painted stones upended. Lizzie wanted someone to get the police but Chip, who'd been there the whole time, was shouting at them that it was the police who had done it. Tom, who'd also seen it all, just sat in the middle of what had been the Circle, weeping, not because of the casual wreckage, but because of his own powerlessness.

While the others salvaged the overturned baggage of their lives, Hal slid down beside Tom, put her arms round his shoulders, hugged him as tight as she could, attempted to still the juddering in his shoulders. She shared his anger, was burning inside with the same hates, the same shouting despair. Around them, the others grumbled and kicked, threatened to sue the Chief Constable. She just kept hugging Tom, rocking with him, backwards and forwards, backwards and forwards, not letting him slip away. They would win this battle together.

Chip relished explaining what had happened: how the CID had arrived, looking like cheap nightclub bouncers in elbowed suits. 'They didn't even have a search warrant, said they didn't need one if someone had been arrested.' The policemen, ties loosened, had gone through everything, ripping open drawers, emptying cases, pulling down ceilings, letting down tyres, kicking down exhaust pipes. When Chip had asked what they were looking for, they said not to be so stupid. When she asked them why they were kicking over Lizzie's stone circles – there couldn't be anything to find under there – they didn't even answer. Tom had known not to speak, every interruption would only prolong their anger. They left after half an hour, dusting off their hands, climbing into their fresh, upholstered cars. They were smiling, Chip said, they really got off doing this kind of damage. The last man to leave had come up to Tom who was sitting by the cold fire, determined not to show them his desperation, and said: 'Anything you can do, alright? Got it now?' When Tom didn't even look up at him, he had grabbed Tom's hair, pulled his head back, and repeated it: 'Alright?' Tom had said 'OK' and the man let go and walked away to the open door of the car.

Now, two days later, the court appearances over, the camp just about restored, the stone circle re-laid, her pregnancy charted and filed, they're planning their next wave of protests – capping the pipes. Hal knows she should be arguing, putting her own ideas forward, whatever they are – she doesn't know herself yet – and instead she's down here, kicking at the reeds. She wants to do so much more, to really win this battle, to really prove this point, and instead she's looking out at the sea, waiting for God knows what. There's so much violent energy in her she doesn't know how to even start to channel it – if they let her, she'd run to that factory now and start clawing at the fences, pull them down with her hands if she could. Only by forcing herself to do nothing, say nothing, practically think nothing, can she keep herself from frenzy.

Now she can hear Tom's footsteps approaching behind her. It could only be him walking so steadily, so wary of disturbance. Any of the others would be yelling out to her, running down to her, cajoling and wheedling, singing or chanting, expecting something before they had even arrived. Tom moves up on her slowly, knowing it is the quiet that is precious to her and what they share best together.

She knows she must tell him now. Maybe he already knows and has kept it tactfully to himself – it seems amazing he hasn't noticed the rounding swell of her belly, the weight of her breasts, the heaviness of her thighs. Of course, she realises, he has never known her not pregnant – this is simply the body he takes to be Hal's, the shape that is her. Now he will discover that it belongs to someone else as well. Hal worries what that will do to him, will he run from it or accept it?

If she tells him now, something will come to an end. Of course, it's not a secret she can keep forever, but what she and Tom have is something she wants to last as long as possible.

But she wants to tell him everything, she wants him on her side in the battle to come – and yet she knows it will dig a ditch between them.

She tells herself again and again that it is impossible to tell him everything, that knowledge of this kind is a festering wound.

But she knows that if she does not tell him everything it will always be a deception and that's something she thought she had left behind.

Since the scan yesterday afternoon she has pushed it around her mind, hoping to find a crack, an opening that will allow her a sane way out. Maybe she should tell him merely that she is pregnant and leave him to presume the rest. But that's an even greater deception – he will only presume that it is his. But is contentment, a false contentment, a carapace, such a dangerous thing?

What is she thinking? That she'll stay with Tom forever and he will bring up this child? She knows she had never planned anything like that and now her brain is running wild, creating some future paradise home. She knows it is madness and yet something inside pushes her to play with these ideas, to form a future that makes this baby safe. She is its prisoner already.

'Don't you get sick of all the arguing?' Tom's behind her now, talking softly, looking out over her shoulder.

'They like it. People like Lizzie, that's what they're in it for. The action, the actually doing it, that's the boring bit for them. They get it over with fast, so they can get back to arguing.'

'I suppose we do have to decide what to do next.' Tom can't not defend anyone being criticised – even when he threw the first stone. As soon as someone else adds to the attack, he must start backpedalling – finding the middle way, he would call it.

'Tom, you know it's all garbage. It's all talk. BonChem's too powerful, too rich, they're just going to walk over and over and over us until we give up.'

'What about Brent Spar?'

Hal felt she might kill if she heard those two words ever again: 'That was Greenpeace. It cost them millions. Even then it was a lucky break. Whole governments were against Shell as well. And Shell have a big, public profile they needed to keep. BonChem don't give a flying fuck what anyone says about them, no one's ever heard of them and no one ever will.'

Tom's holding up his hands in mock-surrender: 'Hey, sorry, I concede. You're right, I'm wrong.'

'Sorry, Tom,' Hal hears herself now, 'It's just so bloody stupid.'

'So what should we do?'

'Something that gets them where it hurts. It seems to me you've got to go for the managers, the directors, the boss. I haven't worked it out yet, but you've got to hassle them – at home, on the way to work. Make life uncomfortable for them, real life. At the moment we're giving them problems to deal with at the office – it probably makes their life more interesting. We've got to give them something so irritating, it's not worth fighting us any longer.'

'That's a good idea. Come back up and tell everyone. Put it to the group.'

'I don't know.'

'No, come on. Don't be shy.'

'That's rich.'

'Come on, Hal. Please.'

'I don't want to. Not now.'

But Tom's already pushing her up the slope, encouraging her forward. 'I'll back you up. It's much better than these things Zip wants to make – which almost certainly won't work anyway.'

'Tom, let me go, we need to talk about something.' They're already cresting the slope up onto the edge of the clearing, passing through the line of conifers.

'No, come on, we've got to get them to listen while there's still time.' And his arm locks round her waist.

'Tom, I'm pregnant.'

And he stops. 'You're not serious, are you?"

'I am. Police doctor told me. Then I went for a scan after the court thing. That's where I was. Sorry, I needed to be alone.'

'You're pregnant.' Tom's saying the words, weighing

them up. 'You're having a baby?'

'Well, yes.' And Hal's watching him carefully, seeing which way he jumps – will it be into fear or joy?

'That is fucking brilliant. Absolutely bloody fucking brilliant.' Tom is plunged deep into the joy of it. He doesn't even ask whether it's his or anything. He just presumes. Or maybe he presumes not to ask. Either way, all her self-questioning has been pointless. Tom's dancing round her, swinging them round and round. 'It's so wonderful, so wonderfuuuuul. When's it due? How long do I have to wait?'

'Tom, I don't want anyone else to know, not yet.'

Instantly serious, stopping himself in mid-twirl: 'No, sure, I understand.' And he looks across, sees how close they are to the Circle, starts to wheel her back towards the reeds. Everyone inside the circle's arguing so fiercely, they haven't heard a word – only Vicki looks across and scans the shadow language between Hal and Tom, then looks back to the gesturing figures around her.

Tom singing now, whisper-singing: 'Hal's gonna have a baby, Hal's gonna have a baby.' He's prancing, arms above his head, kicking in and out of the clumps of reeds, clapping his hands above his head, released, freed into himself. For as long as it lasts, Hal feels it's worth it for this moment alone.

By dawn, Hal has refined her plan. She's going to go to London, to Companies House, get a full list of the shareholders, the directors, all the names they'll give her. They'll bring the struggle to these people's homes as the police brought it to their circle of stones.

She gets up without waking Tom. From the moment she told him, he hasn't stopped smiling – even though Hal had insisted they keep it a secret from everyone else – and even now, he seems to be grinning in his sleep.

Hal dresses and into a rucksack she stuffs some old clothes – the clothes of her former life. Today she needs to pass unnoticed, to be the respectable researcher with a perfect right to this information.

Zippy is watching through the flap of his tent as she slips out of the Circle on one of the bikes and before long she is anonymous among the commuters. No one recognises her as one of those who closed the station a week ago.

CHAPTER FIFTEEN

She drives northwards through the villages, keeping along the coast road, looking for the perfect house. But it's summer, almost the school holidays, and every last holiday home is booked out. She begins to wonder if they wouldn't be better off in the anonymity of the city, but then starts to imagine them there – out of place, constricted – and continues driving.

The house is the most important thing – there's no way they could hide him at the Circle, it'll be the first place they come looking. So each day she goes out in Tom's van – he wants to come with her (he's changing in just some of the ways she feared, becoming squelchy, fixing cow eyes on her) – so she tells him she wants some time on her own, wants to 'think about the baby', that it's 'important for her'. He looks disappointed but can't argue. A part of her feels guilty, but she knows if Tom knew now about her plan, he would drag her down, talk her out of it.

Hal is hugging her idea until it's ready. Silhouetted by the bright, clear light it sheds, everything they've done until now – and everything else they are planning to do – is futile. She watched Zippy furiously hammering at the sheet metal, welding together his giant patchwork bottle top. Lizzie stands over him, checking his work against the measurements she's taken of the outlet pipe. Hal's not interested and even Tom privately admits he can't see it working. The Circle is silently divided: those who believe in Zippy's scheme (Lizzie, Chip, Del, Phoenix) and those who are already thinking beyond it (Hal, Tom – not that he dares admit it – and Vicki).

It wasn't surprising that David Elliot turned out to be a director of BonChem: she remembered Gareth boasting how his father 'collects directorships like other people collect stamps'. From that point on the plan seemed obvious, but Hal decides to get everything straight in her head before she tells them what they're going to do. She copes with all the problems her idea will confront – her mind is buzzing with checklists, imagined eventualities, timetables of how each day will progress. She knows things like this go wrong just because people don't plan enough first, they get too excited about the 'great blow' they're going to strike, and not excited enough about the practical details. She's seen them on the news, read about their trials in Sunday newspapers: they've rushed into it, forgotten a crucial fact that ends up letting them down. She's not going to make that kind of mistake. It's the practical details that are all important – the Great Blow bit comes later, only comes if everything else works according to an unstoppable plan.

She finds the house she wants about twelve miles up the coast beyond Mablethorpe. When Hal finally manages to force a window at the back, the house has stopped in time. The movement of years is visible only in the mildew, the damp curling up the walls, the desiccated ice-cream yellow wasps' nest hanging from a rafter in the corner. On the mantelpiece, there's a snow globe and a pair of crimson jelly shoes – they look about the right size for a ten-year-old. Next to the fireplace, the alcove bookshelf has a stack of paperbacks, book-ended by a Monopoly set, the red of the logo faded to palest orange. The shelf below has nothing but a deck of playing cards in a rubber band – Hal runs a finger through the dust. The cowling round the gas fire is grey and spotted with brown blebs. The sofa and armchair, never new, have been eaten away in patches by moths and visible springs are rusted. Tucked into the corner of the large room, the kitchen looks almost brand new – were it not for the half-used bottle of Sunlight washing-up liquid by the tap, the scouring cloth, the tin of Ajax. On the back of the door, there's a green, hooded anorak on a wire hanger.

Once it was a holiday bungalow but it's been forgotten long since. She imagines the family using it every summer, the Morris parked outside, the two children allowed to sleep in their tent in the garden when the weather's warm, fish and chips round the gas fire when it isn't. Then she sees the parents dead – maybe a car crash when the children were teenagers – and they're grown up now and in new continents, in marriages that allow them to obliterate the bungalow on the coast from their memories. After the crash, neither of them wanted to sell it or even empty it of the few things they kept there, and it's remained shuttered up ever since.

Hal moves through into the bedrooms, finds the beds have been neatly squared up, the blankets mothballed and folded in step pyramids on the end of the mattresses. There's a third, small bedroom off the main room, a zedbed folded in the corner – that'll be perfect. The bathroom, at the other end of the main room, was left spotless, ready for the next summer: just another tin of Ajax, the scouring cloth, a dried soap-on-a-rope hanging from the shower rail, a bottle of Vosene on its side in the soap rack, mouse droppings in the basin.

This is the house. There's a long thin garden, run to seed, sloping fiercely down to the sea, but sheltered on both sides by uncontested conifers. At the bottom, a chainlink fence before the ground falls suddenly away into a sandy cliff. The sea is a greybrown treadmill – a solid rectangle of movement framed by the channel of trees.

There isn't another house within half a mile but it will still be important to look right from the outside, do it right. Hal's already decided they'll call themselves an art group, rent it for the summer. It can't take longer than that – she hasn't got longer anyway.

She closes up the house, masks any sign of her visit, and drives into the nearest village, Saltfleet. There's a pub, a shop, and a garage. She tells them she's an artist and she wants to rent the bungalow by the cliffs for the summer. It's the man at the garage who knows about it: a long time ago, he says, he was asked to keep the number of the people who handle it. Hal doesn't ask him who owns it.

The man rummages in a desk drawer and finally hands her an oil-grubby card, holding on to it three seconds too long while he looks her up and down. He insists she uses the phone on his desk and she rings the number of an estate agents' in Louth. Her interest surprises them – the house hasn't been let for years, they're anxious about damp. She says she's looked in through the window, she'll take it as it is. But they can't find the file and Hal has to stand in the perspex-walled office longer than she wants, the garage man's eyes on her breasts, his hands winding and unwinding a spanner. Then they find the paperwork: fifty pounds a week, though they have many other, more attractive properties on their books which they're sure she'd be more interested in. No, it's the views from this one, they're unique, she's an artist, she says again, she wants to sit in the garden and paint those views. They offer to send her the documents, or meet her at the house, but she says she can come in person, she can be with them in an hour.

Now Hal waits until Lizzie's first attempt on the outlet pipe has failed. She lies on the bed in the caravan, her hands on her belly, watching Nicky and waiting for a chance to tell him about this child to come.

Lizzie and Zippy and Tom had gone off that morning – Tom said he couldn't not help, he just shrugged and climbed onto the back of Zippy's pick-up. Hal watched him bouncing in the back, gripping the side rail as Zippy gunned it down the lane. There was a sudden gap in the Circle.

They came back two hours later. Apparently, the end of the pipe was too corroded, making it almost impossible for Zippy to get a good purchase. But after an hour's welding, with Tom and Lizzie on look-out, convinced the boiler suits were going to show up at any moment, Zippy said he'd managed it. The three of them had sat alongside and waited for the next discharge to flood down the pipe. They heard the liquid coming down, Tom said, and heard it slam against the obstruction. It swilled around in the pipe, nowhere else to go, and started to back up. For a moment – five, six, ten seconds – they had all felt the surging excitement of success. It was working, they'd plugged it up, BonChem was in for a nasty shock. Thirty, forty seconds. So simple, why hadn't they done this earlier? Fifty, sixty seconds. A tiny slit had opened up in the welding, a few drops sweating through a crack. Then the covering had started to tear away from its join at the top and quickly ran right around, releasing the flood of effluent into the watercourse. The covering was still just attached, hanging limply off the bottom.

Apparently, they had stood and watched until the last of the liquid was gone and then Zippy had gone over and kicked at the covering until it dropped down into the water. Tom reckoned he was more embarrassed than angry. Lizzie had tried to say things about what they had now learned and that they knew how to make it work next time. Zippy said it couldn't be reused, but Tom had helped Lizzie load it into the pick-up. Zippy said he didn't want to drive back to the Circle yet, so the two of them had had to walk back. Tom shrugged, said a walk was a good idea, and Lizzie talked about Zippy being too immature for protest work, unable to take a knock-back, which, frankly, is what it's all about.

And Zippy still hasn't reappeared when Hal suggests her plan that night, round the unlit fire – it's a genuinely hot evening.

'You're fucking crazy, Hal. What are you on?' is Lizzie's first reaction.

'I'm not sure, I'm really not,' is Tom's.

Vicki says 'I like it. It gets right to heart of it. It'll make them sit up and think.'

'I thought we were supposed to be non-violent?' says Phoenix.

'It will be non-violent,' Hal insists.

'Come off it, Hal,' says Lizzie, 'he's going to come voluntarily?'

'I know him, he might, that's what I'm hoping, that's the brilliance of it. There won't be any need for some big scene. He's a friend. He'll think I'm just saying Come For A Drive. He'll get into the car.'

'And when he realises it isn't just a drive, he's going to stay in the car, stay in this house of yours voluntarily?' Lizzie's voice is self-righteous, prim. 'Of course not. At some point you're going to have to use violence.'

'And Hal, I mean, right now, you can't—' Tom starts and is silenced by Hal's sudden stare. He remembers his promise and looks away into the night, frustrated but loyal – no one has noticed her growing shape.

'Or the threat of violence.' Lizzie continues. 'There's no such thing as a non-violent kidnapping.'

'All I mean,' and Hal knows this is the crucial moment, 'is that we're not going to do willing violence; it's not going to be gratuitous; we're not going to actually hurt him. If it doesn't work, at the end, we'll just let him go.'

'Even though he knows exactly who we all are?' Tom's voice is fearful.

'He doesn't have to see anyone else but me. You can all stay out of sight or wear masks. It's perfectly easy.'

'Fucking hell, this is out of control. I don't want to get into no kidnapping.' Phoenix gets up, walks around the circle, jerking his arms outward. 'I mean, that's prison. Have

you been in prison? Have you? I have. It's fucking terrifying. I'm not going back. Not for a few poxy reeds, I'm not.'
Vicki moves over to him, runs soothing hands over his
shoulders. He slides against her; she makes sure he goes on
listening.

Over his shoulder, Vicki says 'Nothing else has worked,
has it?' And Hal has her first ally. Her hands still on
Phoenix, Vicki turns to everyone else. 'We've tried demos,
publicity, the capping the pipe idea won't ever work. This is
what'll make them notice. It'll get in the papers too.'

'That's because it's a major crime, Hal.' Tom's voice is
wavering, scared underneath. 'We have to remember that.
I'm not saying that's everything, just something we should
remember. We really should, seriously.'

'And I've got a child,' Del says. 'I'm responsible for her. I
can't. I just can't. I've got to help Chip.' Chip's at home,
putting South to bed. Del stands up. 'I'm going to pretend I
didn't hear any of this. You guys do what you want, just
count me out.' They watch him as he walks away and climbs
on his bike and cycles down the lane. They use the moment
to think their thoughts in silence.

Tom says 'And this sort of thing, it costs money.'

'When I was in London I used a hole in the wall
machine: I took plenty out of my account. I've got about two
thousand in cash – less what I've put down for the house.'

'What I don't understand,' Lizzie is back on the attack,
'is what we're going to try and force them to do. You can't
kidnap someone without a demand.'

Hal's ready for this: 'Demolish the pipes. Donate money
to clean up the reedbeds.'

'Well, they can just build the pipes again when it's all
over.' Lizzie is so certain of herself. 'Ask for the money
back.'

'They'd look pretty stupid if they did. They'd look mean.'
Vicki is practically trembling with the excitement of the idea

now. 'By then the whole world'd know the pipes were bad.'

'And all the publicity would be running against them by then. They couldn't go back on it.'

'The publicity'll be against us. You know how the press are.' Tom wants to find it in himself, Hal can see, wants to make this leap. 'Once you step out of line. Once you threaten the way of the world. They hate it. They fight you.'

'For a while, yes, we'll be hate-figures, sure. I know. But aren't we already?' Hal looks around and no one denies her. 'The big thing is, when we release him, and he says he's been well-treated, and well-fed, and that we're nice guys, things like that, and he's not been hurt or anything, people'll realise there's something worth caring about, that we're only trying to help before it's too late. They'll know we're not crazies or the PLO or something. I mean, no one is actually going to get hurt.' To Hal it makes such easy sense. 'Maybe we have to do the odd drastic thing, but sometimes it works and no one's much worse off and the factory's been stopped.'

'So you want to kidnap this man, threaten violence, maybe even threaten to kill him—'

'We'll only be pretending.' Why can't they understand this? 'No one's going to get hurt.'

'But it has to be good pretending, doesn't it? Otherwise it's not going to work, they do have to believe it. They have to believe you'll kill this man unless they demolish the pipe.'

'Yes. That's right.' Hal holds herself quite still. It's the first time she's heard someone else describe it. It sounds good.

'Kill? Fuck, fuck, fuck.' Phoenix is shaking his head, walking round. 'How did we get into this? This is scary. This is too fucking scary.'

'We're not into anything yet, Phe,' says Lizzie. 'We're still just talking about it.'

Hal looks at Lizzie, who meets her gaze. Hal sees Lizzie's fear of losing her supremacy, her unspoken right to lead.

'Why this man, Hal?' says Tom.

'His father, Sir David Elliot, owns a large chunk of BonChem shares. He's a non-executive director. He can make them do things.'

'Then why don't we kidnap him?' asks Tom.

Just to hear Tom say this, to accept the kidnapping idea, however hypothetically, fills Hal up – she can feel him moving her way. 'Because he's just the sort who'd've told everyone never to pay a ransom for him. He's probably even got insurance for it – you know, for when he goes to Russia and places. But if we get his son, he can't say . . . the father can't say they shouldn't pay the ransom, he's responsible for him. He'll have to get it done. Don't you see? You have to hit their weak points, where they can't just shrug it off.'

There's a moment's silence. Her thinking is paying off, they can't argue against it.

'And anyway, I know the son, he's a . . . an old friend. He'll be easy to get. No one'll suspect anything. Not when we actually get him. I mean.'

'But . . . hang on, Hal, that means, if he knows exactly who you are, you're bound to get caught.'

'He won't. I just know he won't.'

Hal knows Lizzie is looking at her, wondering what there is between her and this man. So is Tom.

'Like I said, I've taken out a lease on this house up the coast. I've told them we're an art group. Painting the views. There aren't any neighbours nearby though. So we can do what we want. It's perfect.'

'Except we have to leave the Circle.' Maybe for Lizzie this is the hardest thing.

'We couldn't keep him here. This is the first place the police'll look.'

'But if we move off, and then this bloke is kidnapped and the demand is that BonChem demolishes its pipes, they're bound to know it's us, all of us.' Tom says this slowly, painfully.

'That's why we're going to demand a news blackout. We'll say that we'll go through with it if they go public.' Hal is strong; she has an answer for everything.

'But they'll still know it's us. They'll be looking for us.'

'Which is why we're going to stay nearby. They'll think we're in the city or something. We're going to give them things that look like clues. Except they'll be wrong. And we'll be just a few miles away.'

'They'll still know it must be us.'

'They won't be able to prove it. There'll be no evidence. I've worked all this out. I'm the only one he'll ever see. Yes, they'll suspect all of us. But they won't ever be able to prove it against any of you.'

'It's a hell of a risk.'

'Do we want to do something or not?' Hal knows this is the last question; this is the one question they all have to face – now that she has offered them the choice.

Tom decides to mediate: 'Why don't we all sleep on it? Think about it. There's no rush. It's a big step. We can decide slowly, can't we?'

Tom spent the night trying to talk her out of it. Now, as Hal watches the light filter into the clouds, he is asleep on her shoulder, having divided the last six hours moving between the Pregnancy Argument, the It Simply Can't Be Done Argument and You'll See Sense In The Morning. By five o'clock, half-drunk with sleeplessness, knowing he would not stop otherwise, Hal used her body to silence him, taking him inside her and soothing him into silence. She remained awake, charting the mauve light moving across the window, thinking of all the moments to come.

As a result, she is the first to hear the engine noises creeping up the lane. She eases Tom off her shoulder and slips out of the bed – the air is cool and unhurried except for the distant rumbling. Every day she feels more weight in her belly but knows that the others must not realise until her plan is under way and they are safely in the house by the sea.

She pulls on yesterday's clothes and steps down onto the mist-damp ground. The cold, surface wetness is a shock, but she forces herself to run towards the noise.

As soon as she rounds the corner of the charabanc, she sees them, in convoy, coming up the lane. There's a shiny car at the front – a Ford or a Vauxhall or something, two men in it – behind that a transit van, just as shiny, a slick, aggressive logo painted down the side, and behind that, which is what she heard first, the bulldozer, the noise she won't ever forget. They're moving forward at a pace to suit the slowest, the bulldozer, so it'll be another minute at least before they reach the edge of the Circle.

Hal needs to wake everyone instantly. She sees the poker for the fire, sitting on the dirt in the middle and, picking it up, runs around the Circle, banging on each caravan door, the edge of Zippy's pick-up, the charabanc's wheel hubs. Whatever makes the most noise. At the same time, she's shouting.

So most of them are staggering out in the light, pulling on trousers and shirts as the two men in suits get out of the car – the convoy has drawn up in front of Tom's van. Hal waits, standing inside the Circle, making them come to her. And they cross over, unafraid, towards her: they're carrying clipboards and large manilla envelopes, wearing as good as identical pin-striped suits and carved, thin-soled shoes which tread gingerly into the dirt. One is older, plump flesh in a tyre round his neck, wearing a club tie, looks uncomfortable in his suit; the younger and thinner one, a parrot flash of colour on his silk tie, is narrowing his eyes, focusing on Hal.

'We're looking for someone in charge.' This is the older of them, Club Tie. He speaks like a Sergeant Major. Maybe it's a Regimental Tie.

'This is private land,' Hal says. 'You're trespassing.'

'Are you in charge?' the younger one, Silk Tie, asks. He's quieter, willing to enjoy his authority. He sweeps his hair back off his forehead with a flat hand. To his colleague he says: 'She'll do.'

So Regimental Tie starts: 'Under the powers vested in me by the Town and Country Planning Act 1947 I am serving you with an injunction on these dwellings. They must be removed immediately.'

'What's happening here?' Tom is still buttoning his shirt, blinking.

'Are you in charge?' Regimental Tie brightens at the sight of a man to talk to.

'Will you please stop asking us that?' says Lizzie, coming up behind the Ties, forcing them to swing round, change their angle – they don't want anyone behind them.

Silk Tie is smooth and certain: 'You have consistently ignored the notices to evict. We have thus secured an immediate ex parte injunction in the County Court. This is the paperwork.' Silk Tie hands Hal the envelope. Tom snatches it, takes a few steps away so he can concentrate on its tight words.

'We haven't received any eviction notices.' Hal watches Lizzie talking to them as though they are creatures of reason.

Silk Tie reaches and takes the clipboard from Regimental Tie and reads: 'Two weeks ago, July the third, an eviction notice giving you twenty-four hours to quit. A week before that, June the twenty-sixth, giving you forty-eight hours. A week before that, June the nineteenth, again a twenty-four-hour notice.' He hands the clipboard back to Regimental Tie, a snake's smile on his lips.

'This is private land,' Lizzie is continuing, determined to prove the system wrong to itself. 'You can't evict us from private land which has been lent to us. Get out of here.'

'This is agricultural land. There is no permission for dwellings on this land. It is in breach of the Town and Country Planning Act. You've had your chance to object, you haven't taken it.'

'We never got any of these notices.' Lizzie's anger causes Regimental Tie's chest to swell, to move half a pace forward. 'This is the first we've heard of it.'

'It's not my concern if you choose to ignore the documentation issued by the court.' Silk Tie loves this, his administrative sanctity.

Lizzie's saying 'Who got these notices? Who were they served on?' as Hal notices, over the Ties' shoulders, the men getting out of the transit van. They wear the uniform – the day-glo plastic waistcoats, the yellow hard hats, the jeans, the thick-soled boots. They're rubbing their hands together – for warmth or in glee at the mayhem to come – milling around the open back doors of their van. The bulldozer driver is still in his cab, reading a newspaper, a white sandwich in his left hand.

Tom re-joins the cluster that now includes Vicki and Phoenix, saying: 'Don't you see? We haven't had a single eviction notice, this is all complete rubbish. We'll make an appointment, come and see you in the Town Hall, sort this out.'

'I have a signed affidavit,' says Silk Tie, 'From the Process Server. You received Notices to Quit on July the third, June the twenty-sixth, and June the nineteenth. You have chosen to ignore them all.'

'This is a put-up job.' Tom is adamant, as he moves back into the group, having read the paperwork. He's gesturing at the men, getting close to them – closer than they like.

Silk Tie turns to the day-glo waistcoats round the van, catches an eye, waves them forward. Then he turns back to Tom: 'We now have an injunction to remove you. It's quite permissible to give you an hour or so, then we clear the site, regardless.'

'Look at these vehicles, some of them are several days' work from roadworthy.'

'That's not my problem. You ignored the notices, not me. You should have realised the consequences would be serious.'

'This is private land. It's private property.' Lizzie turns into the classic Englishwoman at moments like this, standing on her dignity, her centuries of democracy, her rights against the state.

It does no good, of course: Silk Tie repeats his chant. 'Under the powers vested in me by the Town and Country Planning Act 1947 I have served you with an injunction on these dwellings. They must be removed immediately. I have the right to demolish if you refuse to comply with the court order.'

By now the posse of waistcoats is standing a few feet behind the Ties, arms crossed, their foreman slightly in front, awaiting orders.

'I don't have to give you an hour. I can tell that bulldozer to push this little lot into the marsh, if I want. Just like that.' As Silk Tie says this, the Waistcoats tense their shoulders.

'We both know this is nonsense.' Hal can see Tom is trying to hold the gall rising in his throat. 'We both know you've faked these eviction notices. They never existed. You're just pushing this through because you don't like the way we live, the things we say.'

'Those are serious accusations, sir, and they wouldn't stand up in court.' Regimental Tie steps forward to protect his master.

Hal doesn't even know she's still holding the fire poker until one of the Waistcoats moves over and quietly takes it out of her hand. He's a young man, with a beard and condescending smile – he slides the poker out of her hand and drops it down onto the ashes of the last fire. 'Thanks,' he says, looking back into her eyes. 'Best you keep out of the way. Just in case, pretty girl like you.'

And he's made Hal see herself. She has been standing back, watching these men on their hind legs, their air-blown chests butting at each other until one gives ground. She knows there is nothing more that she can do, that any of them can do – play it their way and the Ridgeways and Sergeants and Gareths always win the day. Today the Ties will win, thanks to their manilla paperwork or their men in waistcoats. She will not waste her energy on this struggle – there are better ways to fight this kind of man. She watches.

She watches as the gesticulating between Tom and the Ties becomes more furious. She watches as Lizzie comes closer and closer to the centre of the action, first as a chorus to Tom's words, then pushing in to speak for herself. All the others are now watching from their doorways, from the cabs of vehicles, even Zippy is back, his head just visible in the slit of his bender.

Lizzie's face is stretched wide, an animalistic flare in her eyes. There's noise coming out of her mouth and Hal can hear the words but she isn't listening. Lizzie's hands shoot forward in the eternal, finger-stretched plea, and the Chief Waistcoat moves forward to stand between her and Silk Tie. This only further inflames Lizzie – as does Tom's calm hand on her shoulder. She shrugs the hand off and it's almost as though she is craning forwards to take a bite out of the Waistcoat. She isn't able to, because he brings up his knee, fast and suddenly and straight, into Lizzie's abdomen. She folds over instantly, down onto the ground, doubled over, bent in two, clutching herself. Tom drops beside her, not knowing where to put his hands; Vicki pushes past him, draping herself over Lizzie, wanting to bring her some healing comfort. There is complete silence, everyone's eyes moving between the Waistcoat and Lizzie's prone, compacted body.

'Sorry, sir,' says the Waistcoat, 'I thought she was about to hit you.'

'Of course,' says Silk Tie, determinedly unbothered. 'Thank you.'

Vicki is tending to Lizzie, who's taking in long, fearful, desperate breaths, breathing out staccato whimpers. Her face is buried in her knees as she hugs herself, holding herself in. Vicki cannot do more than run her hands up and down Lizzie's back, put her cheek against hers. Tom stands, shocked into silence, the papers hanging limply by his side.

Silk Tie looks at his watch. 'You have fifty minutes left to clear the site.' He forces a route back to his car, followed by Regimental Tie and then the Waistcoats. He sits in the passenger seat of the car, the door open, typing into a laptop computer. Regimental Tie brings him a cup of coffee from his thermos.

CHAPTER SIXTEEN

'Come on, Gareth, just get in.'

'What's going on here?'

'Get in, please.' Her voice is wavering. 'I want to talk.
That's all.' She mustn't sound too defensive, it has to look
natural, spontaneous.

'What is this? I mean, where did you get this van?' he
leans back, looks along the sides, the wheels. 'It's . . . completely disgusting.'

'It's a friend's, alright? You don't have to worry about the
van. Forget the van, Gareth.'

She had seen him walking along the street, just like
always: a clutch of papers under one arm, ostentatiously
attempting to read a newspaper pivoted in the other. She
thought about the rehearsal yesterday in the back streets of
Great Yarmouth, she remembered how far ahead she had to
get, how to do it without attracting attention. She accelerated into the left-hand lane and then pulled up fifty yards in
front of him, two tyres on the pavement. It was perfect. She
could feel the sweat along the back of her arms as she leaned
over, threw open the passenger door, shouted out as he came
level. He was reading the sports pages, she could make out
the lip-stretched photo of a footballer, gesticulating at the
referee, the points of his hair flying away from his face.

Now Gareth seems almost as histrionic: 'I can't believe
this. I just can't. You disappear off the face of the—'

'I want to talk, Gareth, don't you?' Come on, come on.
The engine's running, and people are walking past all the
time, looking across at them. She's got her beret pulled low,
making sure no one gets much of a look at her.

'Please just get in. I'll take us for a drive. I want to talk.'

'Then you just show up here, like nothing's happened, nothing at all, and suggest we go for a drive.' His voice is so rounded, so aware of itself, she'd forgotten. 'You're unreal, Hal.'

'That's right. Absolutely right.' Christ, please, please, why's he got to be like this? Her pulse is drumming in her ears. Why can't he just get in? She wants to just pull the door, slam it shut, drive off, forget the whole thing.

'Is that what you've been doing? Is this where you've been?' He flicks the seat, dislodging a slip of mud. 'Are you a hippy now?'

'Don't you want to talk, Gareth? Don't we have a lot to talk about?'

Now she's almost sure he's enjoying this, standing there on the pavement, right hand nonchalantly up on the door-frame, leaning slightly in, looking her up and down, his eyebrows commenting on her clothes, her hair. Not noticing her bump – she wears baggy jumpers or smocks all the time now.

'What about Dimitri? Do you have any idea what he's going through?'

'That's what I want to talk about, I want to talk about him, please get in. Just for a talk.' She's said it so many times now, that word – 'talk' – it starts to rebound in her head, lose its meaning and become a mere sound. She hears herself turning into a machine, robotically repeating the lines she rehearsed back at the bungalow, never expecting it to take this long. Why won't he just get in the fucking van?

'What's the big rush?'

'Gareth, please don't be such a prick.' No, no, no, this is a mistake, she mustn't push him into a corner. She feels her throat closing, something rising, gorging. 'Please, Gareth, this is difficult for me. It really is. You're the only one I can still trust, you know, not to talk to the others. I want to have a talk with you. I need to talk.' She hadn't expected all this. She had seen herself pulling up alongside, Gareth slipping in, her pulling back out into the traffic, the simple ease of it, like a movie, fast guitar music playing.

There's a moment's silence as they look across at each other. She softens her face, weakens herself: 'I don't want anyone to see me, not yet, I need to do things in my own time. That's why I need you to help me.'

'Don't worry, darling, I don't think anyone's going to recognise you in that get-up.'

'I can't wait much longer, Gareth. This is your last chance: I'll drive off and none of you'll ever see me again.' She's turning the tables and suddenly it's almost exciting as well as terrifying. 'Do you want to get in or not? This is it. If not, I'm gone and you've got to tell Dimitri you let me disappear again.'

This is dangerous, but it's half true. If she stays here much longer she'll be fixing herself in too many memories, too many witnesses. This is her last chance to bluff him in.

'You're a shit, Hal.' But he climbs in, making a show of his distaste for the seat, the muddied floor, the dayglo dashboard.

'Where did you get this thing?'

'Shut the door, Gareth.'

And she's hauling down on the steering wheel, looking over her shoulder, joining the traffic.

He's turned his torso sideways, loosened his tie, his elbow up on the back of the seat – not before checking it for stains or worse – looking at the side of her head.

'Where are we going?'

'I want to get into the countryside. It's got to be somewhere green.' She dares to look across at him. 'Wouldn't that be best?'

'I'm supposed to be at work. Has that occurred to you? I can't be gone forever.'

Hal has prepared this conversation. 'Since when did you care about that kind of thing?'

'We've got something big on. I was there till two last night.'

'You'll tell them something. You'll think of something.'

'That's not the point.'

'What is then?'

'The point is to find out why you're so desperate to take me into the countryside. "Got to be green." What is this, Hal? What countryside anyway?'

'I can't stand all this concrete. Sets me on edge. Doesn't it depress you?'

'What is this bollocks? Concrete? Have you gone completely crazy, Hal?'

'How about Cambridge, near there? Somewhere like that, I thought.'

'What do I get out of this?'

'You get . . . the whole story, how about that?'

'Is that all?'

'You want to know, don't you?'

'You had this all planned, didn't you?'

'Kind of.' Hal enjoys this irony, enjoys knowing far more than Gareth for once.

Hal's staring ahead, driving smoothly, volleying back each of his conversational attempts, no longer turning her head to look at him looking at her. This is a three-hour drive and she's got to pace it, keep his confidence, reveal herself gradually, keep cards to play, make him want more, make him stay in the van, not try to escape, not that he'd even know he was escaping.

'You're a weird one, Hal.'

'You always knew that.'

The next twenty miles go past in silence. She's driven

through the M25, over concrete ramps, over mudflats, past factories and empty lots.

'This is crazy. What am I letting you do to me?'

'It's an adventure. You always pretend to like adventures.'

'Like your last few months – where the hell have you been?'

'Sorting myself out. Things like that.'

'Living like a hippy?'

'Kind of.'

'Kind of.' Gareth snorts, shakes his head. 'Want to know about Dimitri? That's your husband, by the way. He's called Dimitri.'

'You're going to tell me, aren't you?'

'Fucking hell, Hal. You've got a husband, and a job, and you just walk away.' He's alrighteousness now. 'Christ, some people think you're dead.'

'Like you?'

'I never – it's a cliché – but I never gave up hope.'

'Sweet.'

'I don't get you. What are you so angry about?'

'What have you got?'

'So bloody glib.' Naughty words come out of his mouth strangely, like a headmaster caught in a brothel. 'You're right, let's play games. Let's not actually talk, like you said you wanted to. No, you're right, let's just laugh about it all.'

'You're the one who seems angry.'

'You've let everyone down, Hal, me included.'

'Maybe they let me down first. Maybe they could have thought about me a bit. Maybe they can get along just fine without me. Maybe it was all a fucking waste of time, everything up to now was a fucking waste of time.'

'Christ. You are so uptight. Where do you get it all?'

'Same place as ever. I'm just letting it out now. I think it's what's made me happier.'

'Dimitri is in a clinic.'

'Drying out?'

'He was in shock. His wife disappeared. No note, no nothing, could be dead.'

'And his friend and so-called business partner had shafted him.'

'He understands business necessity. I bought him out for a good price. He knew it wasn't the right time.'

'So he solved it all by diving headfirst into the bottle?'

'I would've. On top of everything else. Yes. When are we stopping, I'm getting sick of this van?'

'Sorry it's not a BMW.'

'Wasn't that a sign for – that was the turn-off for Cambridge? You said we were going to Cambridge.'

'I want to go a bit further.'

'Fine. Great, rubbish my whole day.'

Gareth opts to sulk and miles pass in silence, both allowing the movement of the fields, the road, the clouds, to fill the emptiness. Then, a smaller voice than before:

'You said you wanted to talk. That's what you said this was about. Come on, then, you're not doing much.'

'It's difficult. To know where to start.'

'Then why don't you stop this bloody bone-shaker so you can concentrate, give it everything you've got?'

'Just a bit further, please, Gareth, there's a spot, where it's peaceful. I can think there. It'll help me.'

He crosses his arms, turns to face front. 'The day's a write-off anyway, I suppose.'

'It's all in a good cause.'

'You're still as self-centred as ever.'

Thirty miles in silence, Gareth staring at the road ahead, appearing to humour her by suffering in silence. She doesn't mind. She just has to get him there.

'I lied, Gareth.'

'Uh-huh?'

'I had this all planned. I wanted to bring you here, there never was a place near Cambridge.' This is thrilling – almost admitting the truth, toying with him, it's a kind of flirting.

'That's been pretty obvious for the last fifty miles.'

'Yeah. I just want us to have some time together, you know.' Delicious, she's a cat with a mouse.

'Why's it got to be out here in the middle of nowhere?'

And now she's just turning down the lane to the bunga-low, it's in sight, the light on in the front window.

'This is where I'm living.'

'Ever heard of hotels? We didn't have to come all the way here.'

'I want you to see where I'm living.' It's so easy, the near-truthfulness providing the lines, fuelling her forward. 'I want you to see how I'm living. It's going to be important.'

'You could have taken some polaroids, brought them along. Shown them to me while we sat in the jacuzzi somewhere decent.'

She stops the van in front of the house. She brushes the horn with her elbow and there's a quick, plump noise. She turns to Gareth: 'Sorry. Accident. I think I'm a bit nervous. Wow.' She is and she isn't, she can feel the blood pushing up through her chest, closing her windpipe; she mustn't think about what is to come, she must just act, just obey the rehearsed impulses. Except she wants to call it off – they could call it off now. She really could just talk to him, they could forget this lunatic idea, keep up the leafleting and the picketing and the demonstrations. But would it ever end? Would they ever have any effect like that? No, they have to go through with this, they have to go for the big one. And they're nearly there now – the next few minutes are the riskiest, they all agreed on that, but after that it would all be in place, the winning cards in their hand.

'What is this place?' Gareth's stretching his shoulders, peering through the rash of burst insects on the windscreen.

'Just a holiday bungalow. I've rented it. D'you like it? Pretty, isn't it?' She sees the light go off inside, the answering signal to her horn.

'No one could say you'd spoiled yourself, Hal.'

'Do you want to come in then?' She giggles, a dumb-blonde giggle, enticing, masking her own anxiety.

'Might as well, now I'm here. Even if I am enjoying sitting still at last – it's quite a rattle this van puts up.'

'Plenty of time for sitting still later.' Hal turns and smiles at him.

She jumps out, runs round the bonnet and, playing at mock chauffeur, opens Gareth's door. No kidnap victim has ever been treated with such courtesy, but she has to make sure he's first through the front door, standing straight, expecting nothing.

He steps gingerly down onto the cinder path, flexing the stiffness in his knees. 'I'm still rattling.' He shows her his hand, shaking it exaggeratedly. 'DTs or what?'

'Come on, you old softie.' And Hal strides to the front door, turns the key and throws it open, seeing the flowery back of the sofa, lined up, hard and ready. She steps aside and indicates for Gareth to go ahead, to go first into the house, into the room, into the apparently empty room.

He shrugs and, stooping slightly through the low porch, walks in. She sees Tom and Phoenix spring forward from each side, from where they were hidden. Each of them takes an arm, firmly squeezing the shirt cotton tight in their fists. They run him forward so that he tips over the sofa back, his head thrust down into the pile of cushions on the seat. His arse sticking up into the air, his black brogues still firmly on the floor. She thinks she hears him shout out – what's going on? – but Hal's already moving to the mantelpiece, picking up the syringe, tapping it. She concentrates on clearing air as she hears Vicki – she presumes it's Vicki – click the handcuffs on Gareth's wrists. By now he's yelling loudly – Hal doesn't hear the words, she's upending the spirit bottle onto the swab – but Lizzie has shut the door and once she's got the pillowcase over his head, the noise is muffled. Hal walks over to where Tom has pulled Gareth's shirt sleeve up. He's wriggling fiercely now, but Lizzie's holding him like a wrestler round the neck and the two men have him spread-eagled over the sofa back. Vicki moves forward and clamps her hands at either end of the upper arm, forcing it down on the top of the sofa back, forcing it to be still. Hal dabs the spirit on the vein and injects in a single movement. The wriggling intensifies, reacting to the needle's entry, and as it pulls out, fiercer still. The noise from inside the pillowcase, Gareth's noise, moves from puzzlement to anguish. Then the noise, the wriggling, the sweaty fear – they all subside, slowing in motion, and Gareth starts to slide, to slip off the sofa back into a heap on the floor. Tom supports his shoulders until Gareth's lying flat back on the rug, a sleeping man in a blue and white striped hood.

Hal bends, pulls the pillowcase back, checks his eyelids and his breathing, turns his head to the side: 'He's asleep.'

'Sure?' Tom's breathing hard. 'Absolutely sure?'

'Absolutely.'

The five of them stand looking down at Gareth, his face now revealed. They watch him intensely, their chests rising and falling, seemingly in sync.

Tom sighs and slowly starts to unfurl the stocking from his head. This releases the others, breaking their shared focus: Phoenix yanks the stocking off his head in a single pull, the two women sliding their fingers up their cheeks, easing the stockings away from their faces, shaking their hair free.

But they all remain standing, looking down at Gareth, clutching their loops of brown nylon. Hal, still holding the syringe, feels the sweat drip down her spine, the clamminess on her cheeks, the weight in her belly.

'Fuck. I mean, fuck. Look. I mean, look what . . . fuck.'

Phoenix slides to the floor, sitting with his back against the sofa, next to Gareth's head, drops his face into hands, shaking. 'What a fucking mess.'

'We must stick to what we rehearsed.' Hal knows this is the most important moment, the moment to be strong. She looks over at Tom. 'The sooner it's done.'

'Right.' Vicki bends to unlock the handcuffs, leaving them dangling from one wrist, and Tom takes the other hand. 'Phoenix, we've got to get him moved. Come on, like we've practised. We agreed.'

Vicki keeps hold of the loose handcuff, Gareth's hand lolling beneath. Lizzie reaches to lift Gareth's foot. Phoenix doesn't move. He doesn't even lift his head.

'I'll do it,' Hal bends to Gareth's other foot.

'Sure?' Tom looks concerned.

'Come on.'

'OK. Just be careful. On three, everyone. One, two, three.' And they just manage to lift Gareth free of the ground – he's heavier than any of them expected. They shuffle across the room, pulling, breathing, and into the boxroom in the corner. No one says anything, until they allow him to sink back onto the floor beside the bed.

'OK. On three, a huge lift and we'll swing him onto the bed. One, two, three.' Hal feels her spine stretching and Gareth's body bounces on the put-you-up mattress. Vicki drops to her knees and refastens the loose handcuff to the corner of the bedframe.

The four of them stop again, looking down at his body, his arm stretched up behind his head as though he's waiting to ask a question, his shirt sleeve rolled almost into his armpit where he took the injection.

They're all four of them scared to break the silence and begin the waiting. Vicki kneels and refastens the shirt sleeve, delicately buttoning it round the wrist. Lizzie says: 'How long will he sleep for?'

'At least till tomorrow morning. And he won't wake up easily. This stuff usually leaves you with a pretty terrible hangover.'

'Poor bastard.' Vicki has already appointed herself his nurse. 'Plenty of water when he wakes up.'

'Sure.' And Hal moves to the door, to usher them out, to lock it behind them.

Back in the sitting room, without a word, Vicki and Tom swing the sofa round into its normal position facing the fireplace and both drop onto it at opposite ends. Tom lets his head loll back, Vicki remains alert. Phoenix is still cross-legged on the floor, staring at the carpet pattern, running a finger idly round the edge of a rose. Lizzie looks out of the front window. Hal says 'We must move the van as soon as possible.' No one replies.

CHAPTER SEVENTEEN

It feels as though everyone is awake and they're all just pretending to be asleep, Phoenix and Vicki in the room at the other end of the sitting room, Lizzie in Tom's caravan outside. Zippy drove away the day they were evicted from the Circle, said he was going over to Holland, said he'd keep his mouth shut about what he'd heard, which wasn't much.

Hal treads through into the sitting room. She glances across at the locked boxroom door. Why should it look any different? Maybe they should start calling it Gareth's Room now.

It is not yet six.

She goes into the kitchen and flicks the kettle on. She did it yesterday and the day before but it should feel different today. Why doesn't it? They're outlaws now and yet it's the same kettle in the same kitchen.

What she wants to do is run out the front door, run down the lane, never reappear, spend the rest of her life as a nothing, a speck, a fly, anything so she won't have to face the next few days and weeks.

She stares at the doctor's case in the corner, black plastic leather, silver clasps, square. Vicki suggested they sedate him and stole it the next day – she said it was easy, they're always leaving them in their cars. It seems to be the only sign that anything is different. They must hide it today. If anyone comes to the door – the estate agents have already 'popped round' once – there will be nothing to notice.

The kettle boils and she pours it onto two tea bags she doesn't remember placing in the mugs. She doesn't remember taking the mugs off the tree. She's testing the floorboard beneath her, checking it's been screwed down properly, and then she realises she's poured in the milk, is stirring it, putting sugar in Gareth's. She is detached from herself, unable to mesh thought and action. The only clear impulse is the baby growing inside her, the need to keep it secret and the need to keep it hers.

She stops outside Gareth's door, puts the mugs on the floor, listens for breathing. She checked him three hours ago and he was sound asleep. She takes the key off the hook on the wall and turns it in the lock. Then she turns the handle, bends down, picks up the mugs and goes in.

Gareth's lying on his back, his arm still cuffed to the bed leg, his eyes open. Hal puts the mugs on the chair and locks the door behind her.

'What. The fuck's. Going on?' It's a whisper, a bass drone, a semi-drugged mumble.

'I brought you some tea.'

'I can't. Move.'

'I'm sorry, I can't unlock you.'

'I don't mean. I mean my arm is. My arm is . . . I can't move my arm. And when I move my head it's like this drum banging.'

'That's the sedative. I'm sorry. That's why you need liquid. There's sugar in it to give you energy, you won't like it, but it'll pay off. Try and sit up. Here, I'll help.' Hal moves across to pull him up.

'Get fucking away from me. Just get right away.' He kicks a foot out in her direction. Hal sees real anger in Gareth's eyes. She backs off and watches as he hauls himself up on his unchained arm, up onto the elbow, then to sitting. He tries to hold his head straight, as though his ears are too heavy and they're dragging the weight of his head first to this side, then to that. His eyes are wincing.

She goes back and hands him the mug of tea. He looks up at her and says 'What have you put in this?'

'Strychnine.' Hal sits on the wooden chair, sips hers.

'I'm serious. How do I know there isn't something else in this?'

Hal goes over to him, takes his mug, leaves him hers. 'Alright?'

'Alright.'

'Do you want me to get you a pain-killer or something?' He doesn't answer and they both go on sipping in silence. This lasts for about five minutes while Hal watches Gareth slowly shake off the hangover. Then he puts his mug down.

'Right, thanks for the tea, I'm feeling a bit better now.' He's talking like a blood donor, rolling down his sleeve ready to go, but then his face hardens: 'OK, what the fuck's going on here, Hal? This is totally and utterly out of order.'

'Where do you want me to start?'

'OK, fine, first you unlock these handcuffs and then I'd like to go home. You can try talking your way out of it on the way.'

'That isn't going to be possible.'

'Just get on with it, you silly little girl.' His nostrils are flaring, widening in anger. 'I've had enough of this . . . this – whatever mad game you think you're playing.'

'It's not a game. It's very serious.'

'It certainly is. If you think I'm just going to shrug this off, you've got another thing coming.'

'No, you probably won't, I agree.' Hal is enjoying the calm she can bring to the situation, that she knows everything and Gareth knows nothing. If he discovers anything, it is entirely up to her.

He's continuing to rant at her: 'I'll be telling the police about this. If they want to press charges, they can.'

'Sure. All in good time.'

'Now. Henrietta. Do it, unlock this bloody handcuff.' He's pulling at it, trying to force it loose, but the bed has been bolted to the floor – there's no way anything will give.

'Do it. Before things get worse.'

'It's not up to either of us any more.'

'What is this nonsense?' His face darkens. 'You're not in one of those cults or something, are you? Moonies or scientologists or whatever you're called?'

She wants to laugh. 'No, you're safe from religious interferences. Nobody here believes in any kind of god.'

'Then what the fuck are you playing at? What's the bloody fucking point of all this. It hurts, you know, Hal. My head feels like bloody awful and my arm is aching and I want to go home.'

'I hope it won't last long. Then you'll be back home. None the worse.'

'What is it? What's happened to you, Hal? I mean, what is all this? This is so fucking serious.' He's flailing around in a sleep-fuddled mind, looking for words extreme enough. Now, when they come, there's a wave in his voice, a revelation of genuine panic. 'OK, let's get a few things straight. Have I been kidnapped?'

'Yes.'

'Who by?'

'By me.'

'Who else, Hal? I remember some men holding me down.'

'I'm not going to tell you about anyone else.'

'Who . . . I mean, what are you after, money?'

'Get real.'

'What then?'

'We want to get things done. We want to get things changed. The way the world is run.'

'By kidnapping me? I mean, me? Where do I fit in here?'

'We've opened negotiations with your father. He is in a position to change things. We want him to do it.'

'This makes no sense, Hal.'

'It's very simple. We want your father to use his power

and influence and directorships on various boards to change various practices.'

'What practices?'

'Various ecological things. He's a director of a company that's destroying part of the environment.'

'You're doing all this for a few trees?'

'If you want to put it like that.'

Gareth stops for a moment. She knows what he's thinking. 'You're pathetic, this is just pathetic. What's to stop him changing everything back as soon as you release me?'

'Nothing.'

'So what's the point of all this?'

'I don't think he will change everything back. I don't think those companies will.'

'You're crazy. And anyway what's to stop me turning you in afterwards?'

'Nothing.'

'You need help. You're not well.'

'I'm glad to see the colour's coming back into your cheeks.'

'Don't patronise me.'

'It's a one-way street, is it?'

'Look, I tell you what. Let me out of here now. Drive me to the nearest railway station. I'll forget all about it. Say it was just something stupid. Then we'll get you some help.'

'Too late. Your father gets the letter this morning. I posted it yesterday. It'll probably only be the first of many – we're expecting them to drag it out. That's the technique. You're the only one who loses if they do.'

'Fuck. This is just crazy. This is just not acceptable, there are laws, you know.'

'We think it's very sensible.' And Hal's standing, easing the mug out of Gareth's hand. 'I need to take the mug back, you're not allowed china. We'll get some plastic cups soon so I won't have to rush you.'

'I've had enough of this. I've got it now, this is all just some silly prank of yours, Hal, and it's about to end. Undo these handcuffs, now.'

'Haven't you understood anything?' Hal looks down at him, almost mystified. 'This is happening.'

'There are laws.'

'That's right, and we've stepped outside them. They're not going to protect you until this is all over.'

Suddenly meek, Gareth allows her to take the cup. He doesn't say anything until she is unlocking the door, ready to go out. 'Hal?'

'Yes?'

'I don't . . . what are you going to do if my father won't do what you want?'

'Kill you.'

Typed on the typewriter that Tom bought in a junk shop in Diss which is now safely under the floorboard in the kitchen:

Dear Sir David Elliot,
To save you unnecessary anxiety, your son is quite safe. He is our prisoner. Enclosed is a polaroid photo by way of proof.

He will be released on the following terms:

1. BonChem Plc will cease pumping effluent into the natural environment at all three of its plants in the UK. In future, arrangements will be made to contain-erise the waste and have it dealt with responsibly.

2. BonChem Plc will call a press conference and make a public commitment to the above.

3. BonChem Plc will establish the Bonneville Charitable Trust with an initial donation of £50,000 towards the cleaning-up of the sites of the previous

effluent and a further £200,000 for environmental causes. The trust will be governed by independent trustees.

4. A news blackout will be total throughout.

5. We can be contacted through the personal columns of the *Daily Telegraph* newspaper. Messages should be addressed to THE FRIENDS.

Any failure to meet any or all of these terms will make it impossible for your son to be released.

Signed, Some Friends of the Planet.

Tom goes into the village and buys the *Daily Telegraph* the next morning. There's nothing, no message, no sign. They hadn't expected anything about the kidnapping – they all know that the police would want a news blackout as much as them – but they had expected some announcement from BonChem, some slight shifting of ground.

'It's too early.' Tom sounds steady, reasonable. 'It'll take a couple of days, then we'll see some movement.'

The four of them are waiting when Tom comes back from the village shop the following day. But there's nothing in the paper. Nor the next day. By the fourth morning, only Hal is up and waiting for Tom when he cycles in through the front gate. He throws the paper on the kitchen table and leaves it there, unopened.

Hal's ready for this, she knew there'd be a slump after the first optimism. It's bound to take time – to assemble the BonChem Board, contact lawyers, things like that. They've all got to realise this is several weeks' work they're looking at.

Vicki tells her she knows she's pregnant.

'Do the others know?'

'Of course, but we realise you don't want to talk about it. It's not a problem.'

Vicki promises she'll look out for her. Hal wonders what

this means but Vicki's already skidding down the slope to the beach.

'This has all happened because you're not well, hasn't it? You weren't well before you disappeared. Everyone said you were behaving strangely. We all know why, it's not your fault. So we've got to help you, haven't we?'

Gareth's sitting on the edge of the bed, his left arm twisted behind him, straining. He hasn't been allowed more than a flannel wash since he arrived – five days now – and he stinks. He's been using a bucket next to the bed for piss and shit, but they haven't been emptying it often enough, let alone rinsing it properly, and it's adding to the foetid smell in the room. They're going to have to work out a way of letting him wash properly – they can air the room at the same time – they could blindfold him and lead him to the shower, something like that. His eyes are red-rimmed, his blond hair grease-flecked, his shirt collar blackened, his socks matted and wedged down between his toes. He looks up at Hal, reminding her of how junkies look when they're a couple of hours overdue on their next methadone scrip. 'I'll get you into a really good hospital, Hal, I promise. We'll pay – somewhere they'll make you better, you'll be OK.'

That's a nice touch, Hal thinks, she likes that, offering to pay. For a moment it even sounds attractive – the chance for a rest, to lie down, to let someone else make all the decisions, to do nothing and not care.

But Hal isn't alone this time – they have discussed this, they knew some sort of approach would come from him and things would be safer if there were always two of them in there together. Today it's Vicki, a blue-woollen balaclava loosely over her head. Her mouth is covered, so her words are muffled, made somehow more resonant: 'This is totally serious, Gareth. It's not a prank. I'm sorry if you're in discomfort, we'll see what we can do about it.'

'Shut up, you silly tart, I'm talking to Hal,' he snaps at her and turns back to Hal. 'Come on, Hal, undo the lock. Then just drive me to the nearest railway station. That's the last you'll hear of it.' He spent the first two days yelling about the police and prison and 'the authorities' – even when there was no one in the room with him, his voice booming out through the locked door. Vicki wanted to go in and gag him, and the constant noise was putting Phoenix on edge, but they all agreed minimum violence was essential from now on. So they put a mattress up against the outside of his door. He stopped his threats on the third day and since then he has been using (what he must have thought was) a subtler approach, trying to tempt Hal, offering her this no-consequence solution. She enjoys watching him thinking he's being so clever when they had expected it all along.

Vicki puts the tray down on the floor by the head of the bed – a bowl of tinned soup and a roll and a piece of cheese, plastic plate and cutlery – and goes over to the tall, two-door wardrobe standing in the corner at the end of the bed. It's brown mock-teak, flimsy G-plan. 'Shall I show you what we've got in here?'

'Go on, then, amaze me.' Gareth's trying to muster some bravado but there's a shake in his voice. He's recognised the fearlessness in Vicki.

She unlocks the thin, veneered plywood door. 'It's a kind of padded cell. Just for you.' Gareth swivels his head round, sticks his chin out like a sea bird and sees that the wardrobe has been entirely lined in foam rubber, insipid pale blue sandwiches coating the back and sides and even the inside of the doors. Hal and Tom did it the last afternoon before the lift, spreading copydex over the coarse grain, slotting the sheets of foam into place like a brick wall. 'If you decide to make too much noise, we just put you in here. We drilled holes in the back for a little air.'

'I'm really terrified.' Hal quite admires Gareth's sarcasm. 'When you let me out I could whistle "Colonel Bogie", like in *Bridge Over the River Kwai.*'

'Or we could just keep you in there the whole time. If that's the way you want to play it.' There's no tremor in Vicki's voice, she has such control, such anger. 'Do you understand? We could do that if we wanted to.'

'Where did you find her, Hal? She is something.'

Hal says nothing, this is Vicki's call.

'We could put a gag round your mouth, strap your wrists and ankles with packing tape and lie you in there twenty-three hours a day. If you wanted it that way.'

'Shoot the women first, that's what they say, isn't it?' He's still looking at Hal, but now he turns to Vicki: 'Are you a dyke? Is that it? Is this some great anti-men thing? All the dykes together?'

Vicki locks the wardrobe door and walks over to Gareth. Gareth draws in his legs under the bed, stiffens his shoulders. He's expecting something but he doesn't know what. He's determined to find the nerve to take what's coming.

'No, I like fucking men.' Then she brings the edge of her hand down hard on the bridge of his nose.

It's like an electric shock. He bounces backwards, bringing his free hand up to his nose, to try and touch the flash of agony. Hal begins to move forward in a gesture of comfort and stops herself. Gareth yelps, like a puppy that's been trodden on – more shocked than hurt – though he's clearly in pain as well. He draws his hand away from his nose and looks to see if there's any blood on it. There isn't. There's a circle of piss in the crotch of his trousers.

'Jesus. You . . .' Gareth wants to say more, to insult her, to make noise. But he doesn't dare.

'Just remember who's in charge now. If you want some-thing, ask for it nicely. OK?'

Gareth says nothing.

Vicki asks again, with easy menace: 'OK?'

'OK.'

Vicki slides the tray towards him with her foot. 'Your food's going cold.' She's almost out the door when she stops again. 'So what do you say?'

It takes Gareth a moment to think it through. 'Thank you?'

'Good boy.'

When he can hear Vicki's out of earshot: 'I just don't believe this, Hal. What have you got yourself into?'

'You heard her. If you want something, ask nicely. Otherwise shut up.' And she follows Vicki out, locking the door.

After six days they still haven't heard anything. Tom now goes to several different newsagents, buys all the news-papers, even the *Financial Times*, forces himself to go through them for a sign of concession to their demands, just some-thing saying there's been an emergency board meeting at BonChem, something like that. But it's as though absolutely nothing has happened.

Of course it'll take time, Hal thinks, and in the end they will crack.

She pulls on the surgical gloves and starts typing, her fingertips squeaking against the keys.

Dear Sir David,
It has always been our intention that this would be a non-violent operation throughout. But a successful outcome has always been dependent on your co-operation and understanding.

Please start to implement the proposals in our previous letter, otherwise our choices will become narrowed.

Yours,

The Friends of the Planet.

She slips the sealed envelope into a plastic bag.

She hitches a ride to the M1 and then over to the M6 and posts the letter where the lorry driver drops her in Ashton-under-Lyne. It's a hot August night and the city seems violent. She finds a cash machine, draws out her maximum and gets a lift straight back.

'They're not doing anything; they're just ignoring us.' Phoenix is running the handle of his spoon up and down the grooves in the pine table. Vicki snatches it out of his hand, puts it back down next to the placemat – it seems like a long time since she was the runaway seeking his protection. 'Maybe it's just not going to work.'

Lizzie's frying eggs: 'What did you expect? The entire capitalist system to collapse overnight?'

'I just don't see how we can win. If they don't do anything, we can't make them.'

'There's a clock running, Phoenix.'

'They don't seem to know that.'

'Any day now, you wait and see.'

Phoenix looks ready to cry.

'He's going to start telling us about prison again, aren't you?' Vicki's voice is hard with sarcasm.

'You haven't been there.'

'Haven't I?'

And everyone realises how little they know about Vicki, about where this buried fury of hers might have come from and how it might explode next.

Lizzie serves the eggs. Hal takes some in to Gareth, Tom lurking by the door, the stocking over his head hiding the stillness in his eyes.

They're all sitting on the sloping lawn, painting pictures of the sea, trying to think about nothing, when Spider walks through the side gate, stands there by the French windows.

Tom doesn't say anything. He barely moves; he's frozen. Hal jumps up off her picnic stool and, all smiles, trying to smile, concentrating hard on smiling, runs over and hugs him.

'I went to the Circle. The filth's all over it. I mean, what have you people done? They are seriously pissed off.'

'We left. They chucked us off.'

'They've got a whole office set up down there, the filth. One of those mobile ones. What's it about?'

'Did anyone see you there?'

'I hung back. D'you think I'd be standing here if they'd seen me?'

'Right.'

'What's happening, Hal?'

'Look, Spider, it'd be a whole lot better if you left right now. You'll thank me in the end.' Hal can feel everyone else watching her, paralysed, waiting for her to get rid of him. But also to find out how he found them.

'They wrecked my caravan, Hal. Why do you think I went looking for you at the Circle?'

'Who wrecked your caravan?'

'The filth, the fucking filth. What have you fucking done, they're going crazy out there?'

'What happened to your caravan?'

'Yesterday morning, day before, crack of dawn, there's this sledgehammer coming in through my door. I'd of opened it if they'd asked. Next thing I know there's these freaks, with these guns and baseball caps, pointing them at my nose. I spent all day yesterday at Paddington Green nick. Them asking me questions, about you, about Tom, about Liz. I didn't know the answers. They wouldn't even say what it was about. Then they let me go. They'd ripped everything out of the caravan, looking for I don't know what. It's fucking decimated – that's my home, it's a fucking ruin. And I still don't know why any of it happened. Except I know it's serious, it's not just roads. Is it, Hal?'

'How did you find us here?'

'I ran into Zippy in Norwich. He was out collecting scrap in his pick-up.'

'Fucking hell,' Phoenix's anxious whine floats up over Hal's shoulder. 'If Zip's shooting his mouth off.'

Vicki silences him: 'Cool it, Phe.'

'But I mean, if he's fucking telling everyone he meets, if he's . . .'

'He's not.' Spider looks over Hal's shoulder, reaches out a calming hand towards Phoenix. 'He's not. I had to squeeze it out of him – all he said was you were at some holiday place up round here. I hit lucky.'

'See?' Phoenix isn't reassured. 'Anyone can find us.' Phoenix stomps down the slope towards the beach.

Spider hasn't been diverted: 'Now tell me what's going on. I've come a long way and I want some answers.'

'You'd be better off leaving, Spider. Go now.' Hal tries to steer him back up towards the road. 'Please just go.'

'No way.'

'Go in peace.'

'Whatever you guys are doing, I'm in. I've had it with the filth. I've got nothing left, Hal, they smashed everything, every single bottle. They even took Grim.'

'Last chance. Please go, Spider. Don't make me tell you.'

'Just tell me.'

Hal breathes in. Leads him inside.

Now the six of them sit on the sloping lawn, watching the sea.

Tom has almost completely stopped speaking to Hal. With the others, he makes an effort, but when they're alone he stares out of the window, or reads the same page of a book over and again. When she asks him a question, he answers her flatly, as briefly as he can. They haven't had sex since Gareth arrived.

Hal types out another letter; Lizzie takes the train to London and posts it.

'My ankle's getting raw. You've got to get me some padding or something.'

'You said you'd prefer a chain round the leg.'

'I couldn't take that handcuff any more. You ought to try it, having your hand tied down all day and all night.'

Hal doesn't know why she bothers to talk to him. It's not what they agreed on – especially not alone. They all know you weaken if you start to like him. Hal reckons she's immunised.

'Any chance of a bit more variety in the food?'

'You eat what we eat.'

'You're putting on weight. You're looking quite plump.'

'Thanks. It's all this sitting around waiting for them to get on with their part of the bargain.'

'Any news?'

'What about? Inflation, unemployment, Northern Ireland, Hong Kong?'

Two weeks now and they've settled into a routine of it. Gareth's no longer whining, no longer trying to wheedle his way out. Everyone's waiting for it to be over, killing time however they can, marking through each day.

'Come on, is there any news about me, about this . . . thing?' What's happening, what they're all doing to each other, it still doesn't have a name.

'There's a total news blackout. It's what we expected.'

'So how do you know . . . I mean, are you getting what you want?'

'They're putting it together. It's a package of things.'

'So not much longer?'

'It's hard to say.'

'Shit. This is so boring.'

'How do you think we feel?'

'Is this going to work, Hal?'

'They'll fold, there's no problem. My guess is the end of the week. Maybe even tomorrow. I can sense it.'

'I meant . . . this.'

Tom's lying on his back and Hal's running her fingers through his pubic hair, stroking him, touching him. 'No reason why it shouldn't.' Hal says. 'I want you.'

'This turns you on, doesn't it?'

'Come on, please, none of this O-level psychology stuff.'

'I've never seen you look so alive.'

'I've never felt so alive.' Hal hasn't admitted this before, but it's like she's arrived.

'Right, it turns you on.' Tom has moved her hand off his prick, twisted round to face away from her.

'Aren't you . . . aren't you excited? Isn't it the most demanding thing you've ever done? To be doing something at last, I mean really doing. Making a difference.'

But she knows Tom's answer before she hears it: 'It's like, half the time it's boring, and half the time I'm just so worried.' She can hear the flatness of depression in his voice, the sadness that has grown over him since they started.

'What's to worry about?'

'Spider turning up like that. I mean, he found us, just like that. Christ!'

'He knows the right people. The police don't.'

'Then they'll pay, they'll pay people to find the people and they'll pay them to tell them. They're going to find out, I know it.'

'So what can we do?'

'Move again, where nobody can know we are.'

'If we move they'll clock us immediately. We're settled here. If we hit the road, we'll be visible, we'll stick out a mile.' Hal's been reading, she knows this would be fatal. Tom knows it too. 'Like Spider said, he got lucky.'

'Christ, let me go to sleep.'

Hal doesn't stop him this time – she just wishes Tom would seize his moment, seize his chance to live and burn like her.

Most mornings they try to make sure someone is out on the lawn, painting, keeping up the fiction. By the end of the second week, no one wanted to do it and a rota was established. They agree on two people at all times. Everyone else lies inside, on the sofa, on beds, trying to read, to listen to the radio, hoping for a glimmer of movement, or a chance to forget who is sleeping in the boxroom. Even when they're together, there is practically no conversation.

The six of them move around the empty space, coming together only to cook, the arrange shopping expeditions, to slop out the bucket from the boxroom. No one calls it Gareth's room.

They're into the third week, they've sent three letters and nothing has happened. Tom wants to go down to the BonChem plant and see if anything's going on there.

'They're bound to be watching it.' Hal knows they will be waiting for them to make this mistake. 'Waiting for us.'

'What if they have actually shut down the pipes?' of all of them, Lizzie is the one who most needs to be doing something.

'Then we would have heard. They would have announced it. Put it in the *Telegraph*. They wouldn't do something and not tell us.'

'Not necessarily.' Lizzie's not letting go. 'They might be willing to do it, but embarrassed, doing it on the sly, so it doesn't look like they're backing down.'

'That's what worried me.' Tom looks at the floor when he says this. 'Exactly that.'

'If they were doing it as part of the ransom,' Hal hears herself say this word and there's a moment's pause as everyone else hears it. 'If they were, they'd make damn sure we knew, there'd be no point otherwise.'

'And we said it had to be a public thing, anyway.' Vicki's lying on the sofa, peeling an orange. 'If it's not public, no deal.'

'Come on now. It'd do.' And now Hal knows for sure that Tom wants this over, would accept anything to be released from the waiting. She can no longer rely on him.

'It'd be madness to go down to BonChem – it's the one lead they've got; they'll be waiting for us to walk into the trap.'

'So we just sit here, painting pictures of the sea?'

'Dead right. Hey, who's supposed to be out there with Spider?'

'Me,' says Phoenix, coming out of the bathroom. 'Had to have a slash.' But he looks pale, lethargic, distant. He looks like he's been vomiting. Vicki's told Hal his nerves have got so bad he's hardly keeping anything down.

Lizzie stands up: 'I'll take over if you want, Phe.'

'Sure, thanks, great, I need to get some air.'

Lizzie stomps out of the room and Hal watches her anchor herself down next to Spider and start to talk to him, presumably telling him how Hal is such a cow and won't let anyone else have their say.

Hal's back is aching and nothing seems to make it stop. She walks down to the beach and lies on her side on the sand, allowing the heat to soak into her. It rained lightly during the night – the autumn is coming – and the beach is a moonscape of miniature craters of rain-pitted sand. She crumbles them between her fingers and thinks about how much longer. She thinks about where her child might be born and then what she will have to tell it, everything that will have to be explained eventually. But that's in the future.

Hal finds Phoenix at the end of the lane, where it meets the main road. He's looking up and down the road, his knees hugged tight to his chest. She knows he's waiting for the convoy of police cars to appear – he doesn't know whether they'll come from south or north or both at once, so he keeps a constant check in both directions. Is he hoping to get a head start, a chance to cut away across the yellow fields, to lose himself among the trees in the hollow? Or is he willing the police closer, to put an end to his uncertainty?

'I'm fucking terrified, Hal.'

'What can happen? Nothing that terrible can happen.'

'Can't it? Fuck, you haven't got a clue.'

'What's a little pain?'

'Was that supposed to be a joke?'

'Not really.'

'It's not pain I'm scared of. It's . . . you don't know what she's capable of. I don't want to be part of what she might be, what she might do.'

Hal knows he means Vicki.

'You brought her to us, you introduced her.'

'I'm not sure I did. I think she found me. I think she's made all this happen. I think she's kind of weird. Be careful of her, will you? I mean, keep watching her, alright?'

On the eighteenth day, Vicki comes back from Grimsby with a gun. Hal's sitting by the edge of the cliff path, looking down at the beach below and Vicki comes and sits next to her, putting the oily rag bundle on the grass between them. Hal can see it's heavy – she unwraps it.

'I thought this might help,' she says. It's heavy and oiled and cold and real. Hal picks it up, allows it to weigh her hand down.

'You mustn't tell the others. They'll go crazy.'

'I know. That's why I want you to have it. If you say you've got it, they'll trust you.'

'I'll hang on to it for a bit. Till the time's right.'

'Sure.' And Vicki's already getting up, moving back up towards the house.

'Where did you get it?'

Vicki stands in the middle of the lawn, looks down at Hal. 'You can get anything you want. You just have to know where to ask, and you have to know what price you're willing to pay.'

CHAPTER EIGHTEEN

The third week ends when Phoenix leaves and Lizzie calls a conference. They sit in the kitchen after supper, four of them round the table, Spider in the corner rolling up. Phoenix had left a note: 'I won't tell anyone. I swear. And you won't tell anyone about me. Sorry. Don't look for me. Phoenix.' Vicki hadn't commented on it.

Now Lizzie sits, her palms flat to the table: 'We've got to do something. Formulate a plan of action. This isn't working.'

'Who needs plans?'

'Shut up, Vicki. Look, Hal, you know things are getting serious.'

'Too right they are.' Hal stares her down.

'I'm glad you agree.'

'Come on, please,' Tom gets control. 'Lizzie you asked us all to sit down and listen. So what do you want to say?'

'Right. OK.' Lizzie pulls herself up to her full height. It's unimpressive. 'We're not making any progress here, that's the problem isn't it? I knew, you know, we all knew, it wouldn't be an overnight success. They have to learn to take you seriously. It's a slow process.'

Hal finds herself thinking about Phoenix. About how hard he'd tried. About his gangling frame moving across the lawn, trying to control his almost constant nausea, the jiggling anxiety. And now Vicki is still here, totally confident, totally in place, staring across at Lizzie.

Lizzie finishes her speech. She wants to call it off.

'I can't see the problem,' Spider talks slowly, still concentrating on the roll-up. 'The only danger about the time it's taking is it's adding to the chances of getting nabbed. But they haven't got us yet, so I don't see they're going to.'

'It could go on forever.' Lizzie sounds even more like a schoolmistress. 'And we're not achieving anything!'

'They're scared, I know they're scared.' There's an almost messianic fervour in Vicki's eyes. 'We've got them where it really scares them. If we let go now, they'll never be scared again.'

'We're trying to save the environment, Vicki, not ruin people's lives.' Lizzie says. Though it makes Hal wonder if that is what Vicki is about.

'If this is the only way,' Vicki shrugs, unworried, 'I haven't got a problem with it.'

'What about you, Hal?' Tom is sitting next to Hal, he rests a hand lightly on her wrist.

'We can't give up now.'

Vicki chooses this moment: 'I've got a way of speeding things up.'

'Yes?' says Lizzie.

Vicki's hand goes round behind her back and then carefully reappears, holding a knife. A large, hunting knife. When she slips it out of the leather sheath, the blade must be about five or six inches long. It's brand new, the metal shining. 'I'll cut his ear off, then we'll see something happen. I read about it: it's what they did to that Getty boy. It worked. It freaks them when they open a letter and an ear falls out.'

Lizzie laughs sarcastically, Tom tries to, Hal looks hard at Vicki. Yes, she means it, she quite clearly means every word of it. Tom knows she means it too; he looks down.

'No way, I mean, no way,' Spider's standing up. 'I'm not even going to talk about this. It's sick. Saving the planet's one thing, stopping roads, stopping chemicals, but I'm not going to be part of any violence.'

Vicki speaks quietly, with strength: 'No one asked you to

be part of it in the first place, Spider. Hal asked you to leave before you found out.'

'You got me involved. The filth got me involved. They reckoned I was one of you. They trashed my home. I've got to be here. I've got nowhere else.'

Vicki turns away from him, back to the others: 'Are we going to cut his ear off or not?' Vicki remains clear, focused. 'It's a Yes–No question, isn't it?'

'Of course we're not,' Lizzie is trying to be as clear.

'Why not?'

'It's barbaric, how about that for a start?'

'I thought you wanted something to happen. Nothing's happening because they don't believe us. We're not threatening. These things rely on threat. You all said they'd feel threatened – they clearly don't.'

'It's not on, Vicki.' Tom says, 'I'm not going to be part of anything like that.' He speaks quietly, fearful.

'Hal, what about you?'

'We've got to do something.'

'Hal! You're not serious, are you?' Tom is aghast.

'All I'm saying is we seem to be stalled. Lizzie started this, she's probably right. We've got to make them believe us.'

'Not by cutting off an ear! Jesus, I can't believe I'm even having to say it. Hal!'

They go on talking for another hour and of course, agree to do nothing, but everyone's thought about it now, the idea's sunk into everyone. Hal knows it's only a matter of time.

Hal enters Gareth's room alone and locks the door behind her. By now he spends most of every day in half-sleep, a cat lying on a bed, waking to be fed, falling quickly back into a doze. But she sees him notice that she is alone.

'What time is it?' Without a window in the room, his

body-clock is faltering, reliant on the crack of light under the door but often misled by it.

'It's the middle of the night.' Hal tells him. 'About three.'

This scares him. 'What's going on?' He's not experienced this before, this break of the rhythm. 'Is something happening?'

'Kind of.' Hal sits on the end of his bed, puts a reassuring hand on his leg.

'What? What is it?' He's very worried now, Hal can feel the tremble running through the muscles of his thigh, the wasting muscles. 'Is it finished?'

'Not yet. Sorry. I thought we'd have a little talk, that's all, you and I.'

'In the middle of the night?'

'I want us to have some privacy.' He lets his head fall back into the pillow, the centre of it a circle darkened by the grease of his hair. He's shut his eyes, may even be holding back tears. 'Cry if you want to.'

'I don't want to.'

Hal leans over and runs a finger down his cheek. He reaches up with his unshackled hand and holds her wrist, tight, manacle-tight, feeling her pulse, her warmth. 'Oh Hal, why?'

'Why not?' And she moves to lie down beside him. 'Move over.'

Gareth shifts his shoulders then his hips, shimmying himself across the narrow width of the bed until Hal is squeezed between him and the wall, her head close to his. She can smell him strongly – no longer rancid, he has moved through smelling bad into a pure animal smell. She rests her head on his upstretched arm, chained to the wall. When he moves his leg, she hears the chain flex.

Hal rolls onto her left side so that she is facing him and reaches out her hand so that it rests lightly on his chest.

'What are you doing now?' Gareth is tight and wary.

'I've missed you.'

'What?' His voice is more sleep-laden than surprised. He can't work it out, he can't order the ideas in his head.

'I've missed you. I've realised. Since we last . . . you know.' And Hal slides her hand down the buttons of his shirt until her fingers are lacing themselves through his belt buckle.

'Is this some new form of torture?' Gareth's still not moving, unwilling to commit himself.

'Look, no one's going to know.'

'Hal, what are you doing? What the hell are you doing?'

Hal's fingers are now working through the flies of his boxer shorts. She can't feel anything, she can't feel what she's touching, she's remembering instead, just remembering his penis when he forced her back on the bed remembering the rough force, the tightened skin. She starts making the necessary noises: 'Come on, Gareth, have me, come on, take me, please, I want you.' And her hands, without sensation, finger the roll of his penis. 'Please, please, please, I must have it.' She's climbing astride him now, both hands pulling down his shorts, working up and down his penis, his soft neck of gristle.

'Please stop, Hal, please.'

'I must have you. I must.'

And his penis refuses to harden, refuses to yield to her touching, even though she's rubbing furiously, keeping his one free hand at bay, using the other to rub the skin, to pump him. She thinks he's lengthening and so she pulls her body up over his, settling her weight hard on his stomach and then she lowers herself onto it, trying to force his penis inside her. She licks her hand and wets herself, trying to find a way to slide him in, but he's too soft.

She doesn't stop trying until she realises that he is no longer using his free hand to stop her, but is instead covering his own eyes, his chin shaking, stuttering, the sobs breaking through his hand.

Hal stands then, stepping onto the floor and lowering her skirt. She reaches down and wipes a tear off his chin with the flat of her thumb. He pushes her hand away.

When all her clothing is straight again, she asks: 'How was that?'

He's using the crook of his elbow now to cover his face, the snot running down into his mouth, sobbing in near-choking, unstoppable gasps that lift his chest off the mattress and down again with each breath in and out. Then, between each breath: 'Please. Let. Me. Go.'

'Why?' Hal asks and leaves the room. 'Why the fuck should we? Why should we do anything we're told ever again?'

All of them – except Lizzie who's beachcombing – are sitting outside on the lawn when Tom returns from his tour of newsagents that morning, the morning of the twenty-fourth day. His shoulders semaphore his disappointment. He flings the *Times* down on the grass, open at the business pages, the name "BonChem" clearly headlined.

'What's it say?' Vicki can't wait to read it through herself. Anyway Hal has snatched it, is scanning it eagerly.

'They've had an AGM.' Tom's voice is flat. 'Perfectly normal meeting. Nothing special done.'

Hal's shooting through the paragraphs: 'Apparently there were some protesters there. Asked about their disposal arrangements. They said they had no plans to change anything.'

'Probably Chip.'

'Fucking hell. I mean, fucking hell.' Vicki's arms flail around her. She needs to touch something, hit something. Hal grabs her hand, clenches the fingers between her own, forces the arm's movement to still.

'They don't know nothing about us.' As ever, Spider

sums it up. 'Management hasn't even been told, and if they have, they're set against it.'

'But if nothing's ever going to happen?' says Vicki. 'I mean, if they're just going to sit there for ever and ever and ever?'

'It means we have to do more.' Hal tightens her grip on Vicki's fingers, enthusing her, but controlling her. 'We have to find a way of pushing them harder.'

'There's nothing else we can do.' Tom is equally adamant. 'We've gone as far as we can. Probably further.'

'It's a case of perceived threats,' Hal is saying as Vicki wrenches her hand free and stomps inside, saying nothing.

'Angry girl,' is Spider's comment. 'She's one angry girl.'

'Aren't we all angry?'

'Sure. Crazy. But she likes it, she likes being angry.'

'What are we going to do?' Tom asks, practical. 'This is a real slap in the face, it's deliberate. They knew we'd see it.' Hal can see the lifelessness in his eyes – he just wants it over.

'Those protesters must've been hauled in, given the serious third degree.'

'What arc we going to do?' Tom asks her again.

'We have to decide now?'

'Of course not: I just want to know what you think.'

'I think they're taking a big risk,' Hal crosses her arms, she can be as practical as him. 'I think they're pushing us to the limit, I think we've got to do some hard thinking and we've got to have a really good idea and force them back to doing what we want. OK?'

'I'd like to know what that is.'

'Stop nagging me, Tom, what's wrong with you?'

'I'm disappointed, I suppose.'

'We all are. Doesn't mean you have to lay it all on me. Doesn't mean I have to sort it out here and now.'

'You're always the one with the big ideas.'

'Do you want to pull out? Is this you pulling out, Tom, have you had enough?'

There's a barely-existent silence before he says 'No way.'

'Then it doesn't matter whose idea it was, we're all in it now, we all solve the problems together.'

'I just can't see there is a—'

And then comes the noise. It's a cry, a howl like Hal's never heard before. It's the noise of an animal's fear and pain, shaping and splintering the air. It's about terror and exposure.

It's coming from the house.

They all immediately run towards the back door. Tom first, they charge in through the kitchen – it's empty – but they look across and the door to the boxroom is open and another howl is already flowing out.

Hal gets to the doorway first, but Tom's right behind her, Spider behind him. At first it seems as though Vicki is strangling him – Gareth's on his back and she's kneeling on top of him, his chest caught between her knees, her weight on his sternum, a stocking over her head. She's used the extra handcuffs to lock his other wrist to the bedstead, so both his hands are forced up, stretching him, leaving him defenceless. Even so, he's bucking his body up and down, trying to lever his hips off the mattress, trying to throw her off him, but she's tucked her knees right under his shoulders, she can't be shifted.

Hal takes a step inside the room.

Hal's first thought is that Vicki's strangling him, but the howls are too clear, and almost before Hal's got to the side of the bed, she knows what's happening. Vicki's right hand holds her hunting knife, its blade clear silver, her left hand is flat against the side of Gareth's head, her palm pushing down against Gareth's cheek, and pinched between her thumb and index finger is the flap of Gareth's ear. She's squeezing the lobe clear of blood, making it white, muscular, vulnerable. She rests the point of the knife against his scalp.

'How's that, sir, how's that, eh?' She bends down, yelling straight into his face. 'Or do you want it a bit closer? A bit closer, is that better?'

Gareth can't answer, can't make his mouth speak – all that emerges is the animalistic howl, the grind of fear. Hal sees the black redness inside his mouth as he opens it wide.

And when Vicki sits up again, Hal sees the blood running down the side of Gareth's neck in droplets, like rain collecting on a window pane. Vicki's cut a gash sideways into the ear, forcing a V-shape opening above the lobe. For a second this silences Gareth and Vicki, they're both shocked. Then his breathing speeds up, into quick panting gasps, not daring to take deep breaths, urgently taking in oxygen, trying to understand the pain. Then Vicki wipes her hand across the wound, wrenching a groan from Gareth, and smearing the blood across his face. 'Like that, do you? Can you smell it? Can you smell your own shitty blood?'

'Stop! stop it!' This is Tom. Hal realises they have all been stilled, all been silent in the doorway. 'For God's sake.'

And only now does Vicki turn and notice them. 'Hi,' she says. 'I could use a hand.'

'Just stop it, Vicki.' Tom moves cautiously forward. 'Put the knife down.'

'You try and stop me and the whole ear comes off.' Vicki points the knife back at them, the blade smeared and purple. Then she quickly puts the knife back against Gareth's head.

'OK, OK, I'm not going to do anything.' Tom holds out a placatory hand. His other hand reaches out to protect Hal's womb. She pushes him away.

'Come any closer and I'll cut his throat.'

'OK, OK.' Tom draws back to the doorway. We'll just stand here. But stop hurting him. Please.'

'Why?'

'I've got to get to that wound, Vicki.' Hal's caught

between Tom and Vicki, wanting to move forward and wanting to move back. She tries to think about how much blood Gareth is losing, about how long she's got. 'I need to get some stitches in. He'll be losing a lot of blood.'

'That's right.' Vicki's voice is blurred by the stocking on her head. 'He'll need serious stitches when I've finished.'

Gareth howls again, now more tearful. Gulping breaths in, desperate breaths out. He tries to speak but it's just a high-pitched sigh.

'Don't be crazy, Vic,' Spider shouts from behind Tom, beyond the doorway.

'I want to do some more.' Vicki now sounds calm, dangerously determined. 'We talked about cutting his ear off. Now the time's come. It'll work. We'll be out of here by the end of the week.'

'Please.' Gareth's voice finally emerges from the depths of his throat, unable to bring the sound to his mouth, begging them to stop her. His eyes find Hal's – she looks away, focuses on Vicki.

'Please don't, Vicki.' Hal is asking her and then she sees Vicki strain the muscles in her forearm and she knows what is about to happen. She watches Vicki grip the knife handle tighter as she places the middle of the blade against the wound, into the red opening. Gareth jerks, winces, tries to buck her off him, but can do nothing about it. Vicki grips his ear in her left hand. And then, quickly, in a hard movement, pulling from the shoulder, forcing her arm to work, she pulls upwards, through the sinew. Hal hears it cutting, fast, like paper tearing, like sand under your heel, and as the sound ends, the knife comes through the other side of the ear. The lobe falls onto Gareth's shoulder and down onto the sheet beside his head – a purplewhite half-moon, red-edges, unhuman. The blood pours down out of the truncated ear, down his neck. Gareth's voice is a single note of natural terror.

Vicki leans back and holds the knife up, her elbow on her

hip, her hand cocked, almost admiring her handiwork. Tom jumps forward and grasps her wrist and snatches the knife out of her hand. He thinks he's outwitted her, caught her off-guard, but Vicki doesn't care any more: she's finished, her job is done, and now she can leave it to them. Tom flings the knife into the corner of the room and Vicki falls back into Tom's arms, limp, almost somnolent. He drags her out of the room, drops her on the floor outside.

Hal bundles up Gareth's sheet, presses it against the wound, trying to staunch the blood flow. She tells Spider to get the doctor's case from the hall, tells Tom to get some ice. She places the earlobe on top of the cupboard.

And it isn't until Gareth's ear has been stitched and he's been sedated and they are all again sitting at the kitchen table that Tom realises he wasn't wearing his mask.

CHAPTER NINETEEN

When Lizzie returns, the earlobe – not more than the bottom part of his ear – is sitting in the middle of the table. It's wrapped in a cloth, bundled inside a tea towel. It's there inside the blue and white folds and they know it's there and Hal looks at the clock and they've been talking for at least two hours.

Not surprisingly, Vicki wants to send it off to BonChem: 'It's the whole fucking point. Scare the shit out of them – one look at that and they'll move like blue-arsed flies. And then we can get out of this hell-hole.' Vicki never talks about beliefs, about principles, about the long term – she's living the moment and anything she knows is everything she knows, right there and then, good or bad. Hal envies her.

Tom is talking, murmuring, saying over and over again: if they do anything with the ear, it'll backfire, it'll make them look worse, and it'll turn people against them. 'This has to be like Swampy or Brent Spar or Manchester Runway: we have to have popular support, it has to be romantic somehow. This will kill any support we might get.' He looks up and across at Spider, hoping for support. 'We have to keep this disaster secret for as long as possible.'

Spider's shaking his head, refusing to say what he thinks.

When Lizzie walks through the door, the conversation ends. Tom looks relieved to have a chance to relate it all to someone new, to blow it all off. Lizzie listens, biting her lower lip. Hal had expected her to explode, to throw her arms around, to stomp through the room accusing them of a million betrayals. Now Hal realises she is in fact calculating, playing the moment and its possibilities, waiting. Lizzie finally speaks, quiet and hard: 'If we don't get rid of that, I'm gone. And we need to talk about Vicki. It's against every principle of the group to go and do something like that on your own. She cannot be allowed to carry on like this.'

'Don't talk about me like I'm not here.' Vicki narrows her eyes and looks up at Lizzie. 'I am in the room, Liz.'

'Are you? Are you really?' Lizzie places her hands on her hips, a deliberately sarcastic pose. 'I don't think you're on this planet, actually, Vicki, I think you're out of your head and you're a danger to the whole lot of us.'

'I'm making something happen in case you haven't noticed.'

'You've cut a man's ear off. You've performed an act of extreme violence.'

'This whole thing is an act of violence.' Vicki's still sitting at the table, her torso twisted, her head thrown back to look up at Lizzie standing above her. 'Haven't you seen, so-called Rainbow Lizzie? This isn't a rainbow any more, it's a bloodbath.' And Vicki points at the blood smears on her jacket, on the knee of her jeans.

'You're out of your head. This girl has got to go.' Lizzie turns to the rest of them. 'She's bad spirit.'

Which is when Vicki reaches into her coat pocket and pulls out the revolver and points it straight at Lizzie's face. She doesn't even stand up, she just stays sitting there on the kitchen chair, her arm stretched up, a diagonal bursting out of the purple blackness of her jacket, and at the end of it a white hand clenched round the black steel tube, pointing at Lizzie like an overlong finger. 'How crazy am I? Go on, tell me. I want to know. Tell me, tell me, Elizabeth.'

Lizzie's hand grips the chair back in front of her, otherwise she doesn't move, she doesn't speak. Everyone looks at Vicki – her skin is translucent and her green eyes are suddenly almost orange, almost on fire, and her short, spiky hair seems alive with static, standing out from her head. She is beautiful.

Hal is the only one who has seen the gun before, the only one who isn't completely surprised: 'OK, Vic, that's enough.'

But Vicki ignores her: 'I cut some of his ear off, why shouldn't I shoot your head off, you wonderful rainbow girl? Make a rainbow out of your brains? Why shouldn't I?'

Hal doesn't know if it's the child kicking or her heart thumping. She sees the blood drain from Lizzie's knuckles. They are all watching Vicki, she is the centre, sending waves through the air to the rest of them, satellites drawn to her magnetic field, victims of her will. Hal feels Lizzie's fear pushing at her skin, rubbing against her face, tightening the skin across her belly.

Tom flicks his wet eyes at Hal, wanting to be told what he should do. She ignores him, keeps her eyes on Vicki.

Spider watches, his fingers still moving backwards and forwards on the cigarette he was rolling.

'Why shouldn't I shoot a hole straight through your empty head?'

Hal sees all Lizzie's calculations reduced to dust. Lizzie had so hoped to outmanoeuvre Vicki, force her out, take control of the group, return to her dominance. She hadn't thought about Vicki's gun.

Vicki drops her arm, puts the gun back in her pocket, shrugs, smiles at them all and says 'Give us that cig then, Spide.'

Lizzie breathes. Spider smiles, runs the cigarette paper along his lips, hands it to her. Tom drops his face into his hands, probably cries. Lizzie walks out of the room.

Vicki turns and looks at Hal. They both acknowledge the power that is now theirs. Hal can't remember a feeling like it.

An hour later, Lizzie has left. There are just four of them

now. Vicki hangs the gun on a nail by the kitchen door: 'For when we need it.' Hal feels ready for that moment.

Hal sits in the room with Gareth, reading; he lies on the bed refusing or unable to talk, staring at the ceiling. Occasionally she sees a tear well out of his eye and slide down his cheek, or she sees his hands start to shake tremulously and then stop. She doesn't say anything, she tries not to notice. She'll just be there when he is ready to emerge.

The next day she sits for a couple of hours before Gareth is prepared to speak. She sits on the floor, her back against the door, he lies motionless on the bed. She talks to him. She tells him about all their leaflets, the demos, the sit-in at the station. She tells him how none of it worked. How they had to do something big, just had to. If they didn't, their anger would boil over, something terrible would happen, really terrible. Finally he interrupts:

'Is that man your lover?' His voice is hoarse but surprisingly clear.

'Which one?' Hal replies.

'The one who stopped the girl.' The word seems to hurt him. 'Not the one with the beard. The one who got the knife off that mad girl.'

'She really doesn't like being called a girl.'

'Answer my question.'

'Yes, no, we sleep together. It's just an arrangement really.' She doesn't tell him that the 'arrangement' has unravelled, that, without either saying a word, she and Tom have withdrawn from each other, they hardly even touch, Tom's silence standing like a wall between them.

'That's how you like things, isn't it, Hal? Use people. Arrange them. Fuck them up. Walk away.'

'Look, I've told you, you must've heard. What happened wasn't supposed to happen.'

'I saw his face. I can remember it quite clearly. I could identify him.'

'He was trying to help you.'

'A bit late for that.'

'He tried.'

'It's not going to give me my ear back.'

'No.'

'She cut my ear off.' Gareth can only say it, say the simple sentence. It's all he can and needs do, to state and restate the simple fact. 'She cut my ear off, Hal.'

'The lower lobe.'

'Great. Thanks. Fuck. I thought you were going to get me a mirror?'

'I can't take the dressing off yet. Maybe tomorrow. I'll bring one then.'

'Is this worth it, Hal? Is this really worth it?'

'We won't know till it's all over. Then we'll all see what's been lost, what's been gained.'

'Then you'll just walk away and do something else?'

'I think this is what I like doing. I think it's what I'm good at.'

'Being a terrorist?'

'Is that what I am?'

'Don't play silly games, Hal. We've gone way past that.' It helps that Gareth is lying on his back, staring at the ceiling, refusing to look at her. Hal can hide the surprise on her face, the joy and shock when he calls her a terrorist. She genuinely hasn't thought of herself as one. The word has such power.

He fingers the wrap of bandages that circle his head, looping down under his ear and up over the opposite temple. The ear itself is padded, a huge lump of cotton wool pushing out the gauze, making it look as though his ear has grown, tumorous. He's slipping a fingernail between the overlap of the bandages as he says 'You'll have to go to jail for this, Hal.'

'If they don't catch us, you'll have to tell them it was me.'

'What makes you think I'm not going to? Especially now. I mean, look at me. Just look at what your harpy has done to me.'

'It was a mistake.'

'Give me one good reason not to see you rot in jail for the rest of your life.' There's such anger in his voice.

'Because our child will be born in prison if you do.'

A moment of breath, then: 'Say again?'

'I'm carrying your child.'

He says nothing. Then he whispers: 'Christ alive.'

'Don't you believe me?'

'I don't know. It could be another of your mind-fucks. Should I believe you?'

'It's true. I am.' And Hal stands, and for the first time, pulls her jumper up, forces someone to notice the swelling of her belly. 'Look.'

Gareth flicks his eyes across as though he's squeamish, about to witness something horrific. Instead it is just the rounded whiteness of a woman bearing child.

'What does that prove?'

'I'm pregnant with your child. Look at your child. Look at it, Gareth.'

'How do you know it's mine?'

'Why do men always ask that?'

'You've just told me you're sleeping with someone else already. Didn't waste much time finding a new man to screw, did you? How do I know you haven't been putting it around for years?'

'This baby started when you raped me.'

'Don't talk like that.'

'That's what it was.'

'For Christ's sake. You wanted it. Cutting my ear off, that was a rape. That was a real rape.'

'So now you know what it's like.'

Gareth's up on his elbows, looking at her full in the face. She's looking back. He asks 'Can you be sure it's mine?'

'It's six months almost. That's when I was still living with Dimitri. But he hadn't got it up, not for months. Not for me at least.' And she remembers the video, the man in the dog mask, the room, Dimitri on the bed, his penis in his hand. But this image in her mind: it is as though she is walking through a museum, stopping to look at this room, a special display. It doesn't come from something she can call her own life. It is someone else's. Someone who used to live Hal's life but no longer does, someone who refused to listen to what she really wanted, listened too much to what other people expected her to be.

'What about that doctor in the hospital? The one I found out about.'

'I wish. You think I want it to be yours?'

'It could still be his.'

'Do your sums: too long ago.'

'There was really no one else?' Gareth asks again, except this time she can hear that part of him wants it to be true.

'No one else. It's yours, and I'm having it.'

'You're clever, Hal, I'll give you that.'

'And you're a father now.'

'And at least you're enjoying all this. At least someone's getting something out of all this.'

With Gareth something more like normal, Hal stands, starts to unlock the door.

'You can't just go. Hal!' She stops turning the key. 'You can't just tell me we've having a baby and then walk out.'

'What do you want me to say? What do you want to say?'

'Well, the baby. What are we going to do?'

'One thing at a time, Gareth.' She closes the door behind her.

★

And the next morning Tom is breathless when he bangs through the door with the newspaper: 'This is really serious.' On the front cover of *The Times* is Hal's photograph, Tom's, and the headline that apparently someone has been arrested, a woman. The police aren't releasing the name, have applied to a judge to extend custody.

'It must be Lizzie.'

'She won't tell them anything.' Hal says.

'Don't bank on it. She drops us in it and she gets off lightly herself.' Tom is practically shaking.

'It may not even be Lizzie. It could be straws in the wind. They do that kind of thing. Get us scared, make us panic, show ourselves.'

'There's supposed to be a news blackout. They're breaking the terms.' Tom sounds hurt.

'What do you suggest we do about it?' Vicki asks, not needing to say any more.

But what the article doesn't mention is the kidnapping. Not a word. 'God, they still won't admit it's happening.' Apparently Hal and Tom and two others are 'wanted in connection with the Prevention of Terrorism Act'; people are warned to be on the lookout but not to approach. 'We're dangerous, it says here.' Vicki's smiling, her shoulders moving lightly, she's bouncing on the balls of her feet. 'Probably armed.'

Tom turns and punches the wall, the plaster flaking onto his knuckles. It's fear more than anger. 'I told you we should have pulled out while we still had the time. Now, look, they're watching all the stations and airports and things.'

'There's still time if you're turning chickenshit,' says Vicki.

'They know my name!' Tom is shouting, the first time in a long time. He kicks out at the skirting board. 'They know who I am. We're completely fucked. It's alright for you. Your photo isn't all over the front of the newspapers.' It's one blown up from a school class photo, his teacher's jacket pulled tight across his shoulders, tension in his smile.

'I'll ring up and tell them my name as well if it'd make you feel better.' Vicki leans over the table, pushing her shoulders at Tom. 'Send them a few holiday snaps if you don't want me left out.'

When Spider walks in, even he is forced to react: 'Plenty of places you can go underground. They'll never find you. Time to disappear, dump the man on the road somewhere and go.'

'We don't want to go underground, Spider: we want to see this through.' Vicki's strength is a beacon. 'If we let him go now, they'll laugh at us. They'll have won. There'll never be another chance, never a better edge.'

'They? Who's "They", Vicki?'

'The ones who wrecked your caravan, Spider. The ones who wrecked my life, dumped me in that shitty town with nothing to live for. The ones who wrecked Tom's job. The ones who are pumping that shit into the reedbeds. The ones who ruin everyone's lives. They're all the same.'

They've heard this from Vicki many times before, they're not listening, not even Vicki. The four of them are standing round the table, looking down at the photos in the newspaper. There are so many things they could do, should do, must do. But no one can suggest anything – some things are too frightening, some are too pitiful. Finally Hal realises:

'Spider, they don't know you're involved. They couldn't. You've got to go. Go underground. Like you said, they'll never associate you with any of it. We'd never tell anyone.'

Spider shrugs.

Vicki's just come back from giving Gareth his evening food. He didn't eat his lunch and the congealed stew and curling bread sits on its paper plate on the side of the sink. They've spent the last day and a half talking: just three of them now, sitting and talking.

'If we back off now, they'll walk over us every time. They'll say to themselves: they block roads, they dig tunnels, but at the end of the day it just costs money to chuck them out. We have to make them pay a higher price.' Vicki's skin is burnished by an afternoon painting in the garden, her cheeks bright with windburn. Hal insisted they keep up the front – this is the worst time to start changing the routine, drawing attention to themselves. 'They've rejected all our offers, they haven't moved one inch towards us. I told you we should have sent the ear.'

Almost inaudibly Tom says 'We agreed about that.' He burned the ear and threw the ashes into the sea.

'We wouldn't be in this mess now. They'd be scared of us instead. We'd be getting somewhere.'

'Still doesn't mean we have to go all the way,' Tom says. As they've talked and talked, 'going all the way' is how they've come to describe it. No one has used the word and no one has discussed who will actually do it. If it has to be done. If they have to go all the way.

Tom continues: 'We have tried to twist their arm, we've twisted it and we've threatened to break it – it doesn't mean we have to. Break it, I mean, we don't have to. That's how I see it.'

'I do understand, Tom. I do understand your position.' Hal feels she must speak clearly, decisively. They have dithered about this too long – hours of talk and they haven't moved one step forward.

But Vicki is no longer interested: 'Tom, don't you get it? If we don't carry it out, do what we've threatened, the movement'll be set back years.'

Tom looks at her and says nothing – is this the moment when he has no more energy to fight? Vicki leans back, folds her arms, pursing her lips – probably to prevent a larger smile breaking across her face.

Hal watches Vicki force the matter home – 'You know I'm right, don't you? We have to go all the way.' Hal sees Vicki forcing the decision but says nothing.

Tom is still silent.

'You must answer us, Tom.' Hal hears Vicki say 'us' but says nothing.

Vicki waits and Hal watches both of them. Something is happening. Tom forces it out, a word at a time. 'Do. What. You. Think.'

Vicki picks up the beer bottle in front of her, drinks a long mouthful, puts it back on the table. 'Great.' Tom stands and walks through into the bedroom. She hears the mattress creak as he sits.

Three hours later. Maybe four. It's probably about midnight. Tom is still lying on the bed in their room, Hal and Vicki are still at the table in the kitchen.

'Well, what did you expect?' Vicki asks, the foam still tracing a line round her upper lip. 'It was always going to be just us.'

Hal reaches across the table and takes the bottle. There are several already empty on the table, whisky as well. She drinks a mouthful, feels the warmth in her throat, the confidence. The house is quieter than it has ever been. They have reached a point of simplicity.

Vicki stands, takes the gun off the hook and puts it on the table in front of them. 'It's up to you now, isn't it?' she says, her face untroubled, pure.

This is the moment it crystallises: that they all expect her to be the one and that she has always expected herself to be the one. Even Vicki pulls back now to allow Hal the freedom she needs. From the day Hal walked out of the Royal Cross, out of the house in Battersea, walked out on Dimitri and the entire life she was bred for – since that day, she has been walking towards this moment. There must be a consummation. She will be letting herself down if she does not move forwards now. This is what she told herself she wanted. A final chance to communicate, to shout over the bedlam, to halt the noise and be heard.

And do it quickly is all Hal can think. Go straight in there and do it. Best for both of them if there's no thinking, no talking, no romantic talk. It's a sordid, red, slippery moment – always will be – and there's no point in trying to pretend it isn't.

She knows that if she can just stand up and start, if she can pick it up, feel the greased metal in her hand, then she can do it, all of it.

'Another drink?' Vicki tips a bottle towards her. 'There's plenty more in the fridge.' They're talking about beer and Gareth is lying next door, waiting, waiting until.

'No, thanks.' And deciding this, just deciding whether or not to have another mouthful of beer, gives Hal the strength to stand and pick up the gun. Each time she has touched it, she has been shocked again by its weight, the amount of solid metal involved, the intricacy of the masculine workmanship, the coldness it can preserve even in the hottest air. Because suddenly the room is absurdly hot, she can feel the droplets of sweat bursting out of her cheeks.

'It's fully loaded.' Vicki says without turning round. 'Just make sure you slip the safety catch.'

Hal's wearing her long overcoat but now she's too cold to take it off. She drops the revolver into the low, deep pocket. Her arm is straight, her hand still on the handle, her finger flexing against the trigger, she unlocks the door to Gareth's room and pivots inside. The air inside is muggy, thick. She must do it fast. Gareth's lying on the bed. He's asleep – she allowed him two valium earlier. She looks at him: his eyelids are fluttering, he's dreaming, almost awake.

Except now she can't walk forward, can't make herself step any closer to the bed, her knees won't bend, there's an unwilling stillness in her thighs, a trembling in her knee – is it the cold or the unevenness of the floor? She realises she's not wearing any shoes; she feels a knot in the pine beneath her toe, she feels the smoothness surrounded by the ridged grain of the plank.

Hal wants to speak to him – even though he's apart from her, even though he won't hear. But she can't think of any words, no words will form. Her mind shuffles, speeds, races through empty corridors, tumbles down dark tunnels. What do you say? There are no words in her head.

Hal concentrates on her elbow. If she can just bend it, make it lift the gun out the pocket. She concentrates everything on her elbow, tensing the muscles, forcing them into action. Nothing else matters, nothing else to be thought of, nothing else to worry about. She thinks of anatomy lectures, she pictures the network of muscle and sinew in her arm, the tendons and bones, the fragile skin over it.

She remembers how Vicki taught her to tighten her thumb on the hammer, pull it back slowly, slip the safety off.

She feels the hammer snag on the lining of the coat pocket as she lifts it out. She flicks her wrist and it's clear.

She remembers Jem's face staring at her from the hospital bed, Nicky's on the pavement.

She looks at the gun but suddenly it's inert, unthreatening, pointless metal.

And she knows now she is not going to use it. She can feel the child kicking her inside; right now it is stretching against her ribs, feeding from her, making itself important. And even though it is this man's child, arrogantly forced upon her, she realises she will have to find a new culmination for her life, not the one she has been imagining. She thought she wanted a chance to scream back at them all but there is only one thing she can do now, one thing which will make sense of everything, make sense of everything she has ever tried to do and everything she will do in the future. The child she will bear and name. Gareth will have to be released, justice will have to be done some other way.

She sits carefully on the mattress next to him and looks down at his head, his head cushioned in a halo of pillow. And she knows she can and never will be able to reach the end of this journey – after this child inside her will come another, and another, after them, another. The violence done to Nicky and Jem and South and all of them at the Circle, at Byron Grove, on the streets of the city – she cannot add to it.

Her finger rests on the suddenly-safe steel of the gun. She is liberated now, able to see it for the first time, to be immune from its pull. She feels the channelling round the chamber, the moulding of the handle, the curve of the trigger.

And then she hears the noise.

part three

CHAPTER TWENTY

Vicki's mouth is falling away to one side, saliva swilling in the corner of her gum, snailtrailing down onto the pillow. I've been expecting this – people keep telling me they've seen her – and I remember what she looked like when I last saw her. But now I have to look at her for myself. And it seems so unfair, her shining certainty blunted and shaven, her anger wrapped and bandaged. Her lips are coming together and blowing out, a kissing circle, a fish breathing.

From the back of her throat, a round, squashed, tongue-less noise. Except she wants the noise to become words. I don't know if they're words she cannot say or just cannot remember. But she is trying to speak to me, eagerly forming sounds that will not come. She knows she hasn't got long, this is only accident allowing us to be together – me sitting up here in bed, her abandoned alongside, double-parked on her gurney.

I lift Zoe and hold her up for Vicki to see. I hold her out for Vicki's one clear eye. For a moment, Vicki's mouth stills, the lips coming together in a final, noiseless plop. She is seeing Zoe and knowing exactly what she means. There's a moment of stillness between the three of us.

The porters return and Vicki is wheeled away, through the flapping, rubber double doors.

I remain sitting on the end of my bed, Zoe's easy weight along my forearm, Vicki's after-image on the doors, the rest of the week ahead of me. After that, I'll be going back to my cell. After that, another week.

★

'It's Greek,' he says. 'It means life, living thing, something like that.'

'I suppose it is. I hadn't thought of that.' I had thought of it. I don't let it bother me, it's just chance.

'You're telling me that means nothing?' says Dimitri, looking at me so hopefully, so needfully.

'Sorry. No. Nothing. I just liked the name. Plenty of people like the name. People who've got nothing to do with Greece.'

'I think you're trying to tell me something.'

'Come on, Dimitri, think of the maths, do the sums. Think how long I was out of your life. Think about how long before that we ever made love. Zoe was born last week.'

'I can't remember. I really can't remember what happened during that time.'

'Take it from me, it's simply not possible.'

Dimitri shrugs and says something but I don't hear it, the noise from the play area along the corridor is suddenly deafening. I can hear Sheila clapping her hands, trying to calm things down, saying she'll have to ask some people to leave if they can't keep things a bit quieter. From her chair in the corridor, Daphne keeps her eyes on us – a visitor in the cell is a very special privilege and you have to be watched all the time. Daphne keeps her hands folded neatly in her lap, straightening the cuffs of her white shirt, making sure we don't get too close. It's not a problem.

When I look back at Dimitri, his hand is running up and down his green silk tie, compulsively smoothing down, riding up, smoothing down. The fingers of his other hand tap on his knee. He looks around at the posters on the walls, the photos torn from newspapers.

'They're all Dora's.' I tell him. 'My cellmate.'

'They told me they'd put you in a cell on your own.'

'No.'

'They said it was something to do with security. You're

Category A, high risk. Had to be on your own.'

'I wish.'

He nods. Looks at the photos on the wall more closely. Then he looks at me: 'What's she like?'

'Just like the rest of them.' Except she isn't. To start with, Dora's a lot older. Or I think she is – some days she looks far too old to be here in the Mother and Baby. She's just had a girl – her first ever, she said. Said she'd been having boys all her life. But she didn't explain. Waiting for me to ask, I suppose. She killed her husband apparently.

'Are you living at home now?' I ask Dimitri.

'Yup. They've let me out. They reckon I can hack it on my own.'

'Can you?'

'So far. Not at all bad.'

'Good.'

'Except I miss you.' It's his hangdog face again. 'I really miss you.'

'Better get used to it.'

'Don't.'

'It was over anyway, Dimitri.'

'Maybe. Maybe not.'

Zoe's arm punches the air, stretching out in her sleep, looking for the hard walls of the womb, finds they're no longer there, and the absence jolts her awake. I wait to see if she falls back to sleep. She already is. Dimitri leans forward to grasp her hand. His stubby fingers drown hers.

Daphne stands, catches my eye round the back of Dimitri's head, taps her watch, lets me know we should be saying our goodbyes. She doesn't realise we've barely got as far as hello.

It took a while before I bothered with Dora's pictures – the ones stuck on the cell wall.

The other girls – we're all 'girls' here – stick up posters of kittens, or babies, or parents, or men with steroid-pumped muscles crushing coke cans. But Dora's pictures, they're torn from history books, from greygrainy newspapers, from Sunday magazines. They're all pictures of men, but not with muscles, these are men with real power: prime ministers and dictators, lieutenants and inspectors, men with guns and men driving tanks, men wielding truncheons, men telling people what to do and being listened to. These men are all shouting or shooting or posturing or evading or telling. The pictures are all raggedly torn out of the papers – not cut in neat nail-scissor crescents like other girl's pin-ups – and they're not neatly blu-tacked in the corners, each is glued to the wall with a single splodge, a muted grey-coloured mass barely different from the rest of the wall.

But it wasn't until that day I came back in here from the infirmary, with Zoe slotted into my side, when I was just falling asleep, that I started focusing on the wall of photos and I realised what they were telling me.

For a few seconds – God knows how long it really was – I thought I had pulled the trigger. I simply presumed that the cannonade filling my ears had come from the revolver in my hand.

I opened my eyes – without knowing it, I had squeezed them shut when the noise started – and saw Gareth, a tightly clenched ball on the edge of his bed, forcing himself into the corner, his knees up to his face, his hands over the back of his head. I noticed how grubby the webbing between his fingers was, I saw the grime round the signet ring on his little finger, there were wet patches under his arms and it smelt as though he'd soiled himself. And he was alive and breathing and the gun in my hands was still cold.

There was another loud bang, an explosive pop followed

by a soft reverberation through the house, glass breaking, wood splintering, men shouting. There seemed to be shouting coming from all the rooms around me and more from outside the house: it was hoarse and male and angry. And there was a smell coming from under the door, acid and thick, catching at the back of my throat.

I wanted to open the door, to allow the noise and smoke into this room, to merge myself with the chaos. But my body remained fixed, too confused to move. I was the still centre and I was bewildered and unknowing. I wanted to apologise to Gareth.

But the decision was made for me. The door was thrown open. I expected a heavy uniform, blue or green or black – a policeman, a soldier, a paid assassin – but it was Vicki. She had a handkerchief over her mouth and was coughing – she was followed by a cloud of smoke, hanging in the air in translucent white droplets. Vicki looked at me, at Gareth on the bed, saw that he was still alive and then she looked again at me. Only her eyes were visible above the handkerchief – I still don't know if she was angry or relieved.

I was no longer thinking, I no longer knew anything, I was merely sensing, falling back into the relief of inaction, knowing that soon, very very soon, I would no longer have to do anything, everything would be taken out of my hands and people would start telling me exactly what to do. They would tell me where, when and not to bother with why. I knew there would be pain before I got there, I knew there would be hostility and violence while I crossed over, but that in itself would be a sort of freedom: I would be asked only to feel what was inflicted, only to listen to taunts and anger and yells. I was not going to be allowed to respond even if I wanted.

Vicki wrenched the pistol out of my hand. Freed from the gun's weight, my arm seemed to float away. I remember thinking: Is she going to finish him off? But I didn't move.

She took the revolver and charged back into the main room.

By now the shouts had turned themselves into words, if not yet complete sentences. The sounds were curiously warped, all the harshness of the consonants smoothed out: there was "Armed Police" and "Lie Down On The Floor" and "Keep Still". But over and over again, like a chant, like a confused cry for mercy. And maybe I only know now what they were shouting, since they've all told me what happened.

I turned my back on Gareth and moved towards the noise, following Vicki. She had run straight into the main room and now she was standing in front of the two men. Tom was on the floor at the far end of the room, beyond the sofa, on all fours. I remember thinking, just for a second: he's lost something, what's he looking for now? There was a policeman standing over him. I know now he was a police-man – during those moments, smears of gas between us, he looked like something from a science fiction movie: he had a gas mask on, a thick black bullet-proof jacket and a short, stubby, black gun pointing down at the back of Tom's neck, a few inches from the collar of his shirt. He was yelling down at Tom in his muffled way "Lie down, lie down. Stretch your arms out on the floor. Lie down. Lie down." I could see Tom was too terrified to move. He was begging the policeman "Stop. Please stop. Please stop," but the policeman couldn't or wouldn't hear. Tom had lost the ability to move, the policeman had lost the ability to do anything but shout. The gun moved closer to Tom's neck. He was about to execute Tom.

Only Vicki – I now recognise – had decided to play them at their own game. She had the revolver in two hands out in front of her, pointing it directly at another policeman. She was yelling at him, long, sharp strings of words – I couldn't make them out. Maybe they weren't even words, just screams. Caught suddenly by her charge out of the box-room, the policeman could only point his stubby gun and yell back. Over Vicki's shoulder I could see the fear in his eyes, visible even through the portholes of his gas mask. He was unable to move out of her way, unable to move forwards. They went on yelling at each other, Vicki waving the revolver in his face, he holding out one hand, levelling his gun in the other. It probably only lasted three, four seconds, but it seemed to solidify what was happening, forcing everything else to fall away on either side. Then there was a burst of noise, three fast slappings like the jaw of a Punch and Judy crocodile. At the same time my face and shoulder felt pinpricks of wetness and then, almost immediately afterwards, there was the shock, the sudden, soft battering as Vicki's body was thrown back into mine.

We fell together, backwards. I heard the clatter as her wrist hit the floor and the revolver bounced away. Winded, gasping, I smelt the fumes from the policeman's gun. I felt my spine flatten against the floor, Vicki's wet weight on top of me, crushing my belly, her legs tangling with mine, a numbing pain in my knee where she'd probably kicked me as she'd flown backwards. She had put herself between the bullets and my child. I reached round and hugged her. I felt for where the bullets had struck her. Her right shoulder was punctured, I could feel the entry wound where it had singed the skin, pushing it in like a thumb through plasticine, and I could feel the exit wound in her back bleeding down onto my shoulder. It had missed the spine. But when my hands moved up to her face, I could find only sticky wet fibre and dislocated flesh, splinters of bone and her ear pooling with blood.

And then the policemen's hands were all over us, dragging Vicki off me, roughly allowing her head to bounce back on the floor, but giving me a chance to look across and see that the bullet had probably entered just below the eye-socket, shattering the cheekbone. Another policeman now knelt on my chest, one leg across my throat, forcing out the little breath left in me. I wanted to scream but no sound came; I wanted to bite but couldn't move my head. His hands roughly, quickly ransacked my body and then, easing his weight off me, his fingers tightly clenched on my shoulders and he spun me round so that I was facing down into the floor and I felt my hands handcuffed behind my back. I tried to bring my knees up, I had to ease my belly up off the floor, to take the weight off my womb, but he forced his knee into the small of my back, not allowing even the slightest movement. I concentrated on pulling my baby further inside me, taking short, sipping breaths. I started to feel the pain in my knee and blood seeping down out of it. My toes refused to move. I waited, tried not to breathe the gas.

There was more shouting. The policemen were searching each room, kicking doors, throwing the beds over, shouting words like "Clear" and "Support Here" and "Support Needed". After a minute or so, the activity started to slow, fewer feet moving past me, less shouting, the air clearing.

Still lying manacled on the floor, my head on one side, I saw Gareth being ushered out, a brown blanket dangling from his shoulder, the smell of his bowels clinging to his legs. I didn't see his face and I don't know if he looked down at mine. He was stumbling and the policemen on either side of him were supporting his shoulders, calling for a wheelchair – their gas masks were off by now. They walked him out the door, I heard the ambulance siren and he was gone.

A few feet away, I could just see Vicki, her eyes glazed but her throat rising and falling, her pulse moving weakly. They hadn't cuffed her, just left her lying on her back, the blood puddling on the floor. I tried to raise my head, to shout to someone that she was the one who needed an ambulance. But as soon as I even began to move my head, a gloved hand pushed it down, twisting it away so that I was no longer facing her, smearing my cheek into the floor. I could feel the stickiness of Vicki's blood where it had splashed over my face. I shut my eyes and began counting slowly.

At about seventy, I heard the paramedics come for Vicki. They were quick and she seemed to be gone soon, almost noiselessly onto a stretcher. I heard them tell a policeman to hold a compression pad to her shoulder, against her face.

At about three hundred, I felt hands under my arms, working up to my shoulders and I was being pulled backwards and up. There was a moustached face close to mine and it was saying the magic last words for this phase of my life, the words I had waited to hear: he was telling me I didn't have to say anything.

They walked me through what remained of the room – one man holding each of my arms – I couldn't put any weight on my leg anyway. When I tried to look across to see if Tom was still there crouched on the floor, my head was again twisted away.

They floated me through where the front door had been and along what had once been the deserted lane. Now there were police vans and cars and another ambulance and there was a van with the doors waiting open at the back. They marched me straight in, my shin cannoning off the step, and I was allowed to slump to the floor. The ridged metal floor of the van, the white enamel scuffed and smelling of vomit. I remember I felt very tired.

'I lost my first in the big flu after the War.'

It's a lock-in (Hazel found a sharpened screwdriver in somebody's cell) and Dora is sitting in the plastic leather chair feeding her baby, so the only place left for me is my bed. Zoe lies on her back on the quilt, staring back up at me. Her soft nails, perfect pink rounds, catch and soften the light of the bare bulb in the ceiling. 'It took them so fast. First day, bit of a cold, bit sick, sneezing. Second day, fever, throwing up, exhaustion. Third day they were gone. Just gone, burnt up.'

Dora is a large woman, her body capacious and giving, a straightforward mother figure. But her age is indecipherable – some days she looks thirty, other days she looks eighty. I suppose we all go up and down in here, feeling bad, feeling better, looking older, looking younger. But some days Dora's hair is grey and tired, other days it seems blond, shining blond and young again. Only her eyes remain the same – purest blue.

I've asked the others about her but they won't tell me anything. They tell me to stop going on, stop my stupid talk.

She's talking about Liverpool: 'We were living down by the docks. Me, my man, little boy. Plenty of work as long as you don't fall out with the gang masters. They had the nod and that nod decided whether you got work that day or not. You fall out with them, you were going to starve. And that's what he did, my man. Got into some silly argument with a ganger.'

I stare into Zoe's eyes, seeing her staring back at me. Dora always chooses these moments of quiet – when we're locked in or when everyone else is at association – to sit and talk to me. I've never seen her talking to anyone else.

'Everyone knew the gangers took their cut from the bosses, the ship owners, and my man, he didn't like that. Decided to stand up about it, said they should organise themselves, a rota of work, not just one man's say-so. You can imagine how that went down.'

Everyone in here's got a story: a slow, melodramatic unfolding that blames everyone but the teller.

'All day he stood there and every day the gangers picked everyone but him, even the blacks. Him and the boys too young to lift a bale left standing there, hooks hanging on their shoulders, waiting. Everyone else got the nod and the gangers just walked past him grinning. Still, he went down there all the same every morning. Stood with the others. Let them know he wasn't cowed, telling them silently he wasn't going to come crawling back, lick their boots. Even if I wanted him to for the sake of the little one.'

And, reminded of her first child, she shifts her baby up, burps her, allows her to settle to the other breast. Hearing the cry, Zoe's eyes suddenly widen. She pulls hard on my finger and then relaxes. Dora's talking becomes a humming noise in the back of my head.

'He was in the Party, of course. It was probably the Party that told him to get into the argument in the first place. They all used to keep secret about it – not supposed to tell a soul, not anyone. I wasn't even meant to know. But he left one of his pamphlets in his after-work trousers, something about a meeting. Not that I ever told him I knew. He would have been too embarrassed that he'd let me find out, all careless like that. It was just the sort of thing you were supposed to check on, make sure didn't happen. They were more strung out on that conspiring stuff, keeping their blessed secrets, than actually getting anything done. It's one of those men's games, isn't it? Isn't it, love?'

I know she's looking over at me, wanting a reply, but I allow Zoe to fill my vision, bending my head lower and allowing her to pull at the hair of my fringe.

'Feeding you, that's another thing the Party wasn't inter-ested in. You lose your job for their sakes and they just carry on like nothing's any different. For me and the child, plenty's different. We were all too weak to go without. He'd come back from the War, gas in his lungs, the things he'd seen still at the back of his eyes. And it was in the child too. Don't ask me how, something in his seed I suppose. But the boy had the same greenness, the same confusion, and the same far-away stare.

'Now I see them again, they were both slipping away into the dark even then. So there wasn't much chance for them when the flu came. Some people said it was Spanish. Some people called it the Asiatic. What did it matter? Everyone was getting it and doctors couldn't do nothing about it. I kept the boy inside, he was about eighteen months by now, kept him in practically one room. They said you got it off other people's breath. Not that we knew anything. It was all just suspicion, and the people who really knew, the men who knew what to do, they weren't going to tell us. Whole world was getting the influenza and they weren't saying anything, weren't doing nothing.

'It was the end of July when the boy got it. Hot, very hot, that June and July. And I don't know, I thought, let him go in the garden. Thought the danger was gone down the road. He got caught in the rain. I dried him off but we couldn't afford the coal for the stove to heat the water. My man went down to the Party Secretary. Begged sixpence for a few bits of coal. Got down on his knees, he said, said he'd do anything. Course this secretary reckoned my man was a hot-head, thought he was after his job, wanted to squeeze him out of the Party, told him it'd look suspicious, sent him away empty-handed. My boy died the next day. Spent the first day in a sweat, emptying himself till he was hollow. The next day, he lay still. I held his hand, it was so hot, the fingers flexing, a gentle shake in the knuckles. And then it was cold.

'He went crazy, my man. The baby was all we had left and even he was gone now. He blamed them all but it was just the flu epidemic and the weakness and what he'd been through in the War. Then it was the funeral – couldn't afford much – and it wasn't till we went out into the street that we heard. The police were on strike, suddenly Liverpool didn't have any police force. It was more than most people could resist, especially down the docks.

'But my man, he knew what it meant. He was certain – it was the beginning of the Revolution. For a week he'd been

at home, crying and just sitting thinking and refusing everything. Suddenly it's all different again – the British Revolution is here. The old order's coming down and maybe now
the death of our little boy was going to mean something, it
was going to be worth it, it was going to be the first shot
fired in the big struggle, the first martyr. Another of men's
games, isn't it, martyrs and all that?

'And when he went out onto Scotland Road, ready to
lead the march on the barricades, to storm the Town Hall, to
march on London, what did he find? They were thieving.
They were just standing in the street, working out which
traders had the best gear and they were smashing their way
into their shops. There were kids, standing down on the
corners, selling bottles of beer for a penny each, bottles
they'd hauled out of the off-licence two blocks away. Someone had pulled a huge roll of damask out of a draper's but
they'd lost control of it and this huge strip of crimson was
rolling itself out down the cobbles. Someone said "Is the
Queen coming, and all?" And there was a huge shop,
Finnegan's Grocery Emporium, looking like a bomb had
gone off but now suddenly white, everything coated finely in
white from the burst bags of flour, the cloud rolling along the
ground and out into the street.

Maybe it was the cloud that tipped him, reminding him
of the mustard over No Man's Land, but he started shouting
at them all, shouting at them to stop. 'Course they didn't take
a blind bit of notice – they had handcarts pushed up along
the smashed shop-windows, wheelbarrows, sheets laid out
on the paving stones.

'But he wanted them all to get on with the Revolution
instead. He raced up to them, tried to pull the looted stuff
out of their hands, put it back inside the shop fronts. They
just pushed him out the way. He was stopping the barrows
that were off down the tenement rows – they were shimmying around his outstretched arms or just happy to knock him

straight down. He kept getting up – he was shouting. But he didn't get angry, it was like he expected this to happen and any moment now they were going to realise he was right. If they just followed him, if they just forgot about food and coal and sewing machines and tables and chairs and best Irish linen. If they forgot about all that, if they fought now, for their independence, they'd have everything soon enough. The British Revolution would bring it to them.

'I tried to drag him home, drag him out of there: there was going to be trouble soon, anyone could see that. But he shook me off his sleeve, told me that this was the most important day of his life. Told me I was a typical woman. Told me to go home. So I did.

'I walked down Scotland Road. I could hear him still shouting out to people, saying the Revolution was starting. I could hear them jeering back, tipping the stolen beer down their throats, smashing bottles against brick walls.

'Just before I turned down our row, I stopped and looked back. He was standing in the middle of the street, arms waving, meaning nothing.

'The next day I got myself on a boat, a banana boat going back via Boston, nothing but emigrants and fine Wedgwood china.'

'They've already granted you a three-month adjournment because of the baby, I can't see them going any longer.'

'I'm finding it hard to concentrate. My leg's only just starting to heal.'

'Three months is a pretty standard maternity-leave period.' This solicitor chews the corner of his half-moon glasses, grips his biro tighter, doodles a curlicued corner on the edge of the committal notice. 'You'd be expected to go back to work, say, on the outside.'

'I'm not on maternity leave here. I've got to defend

myself against a life sentence.'

'I can ask for leave to make an application to a higher court for leave to adjourn but I honestly wouldn't hold out much hope.'

'Whose side are you on?'

For a moment, he looks aghast. But I realise it's practised, he'll have sat in Holloway (or Brixton or Belmarsh or Wandsworth) and been asked this question so many times by outraged clients, demanding his support for their assumed innocence. 'I'm here to advise you on how the courts are likely to behave. We can't live in cloud-cuckoo land, Hal. We have to start preparing your defence. If I waste two weeks trying to get an adjournment and don't get one, we'll be even further behind.'

'I haven't got much defence anyway, have I?'

'We'll have to see. I'm still waiting for instructions from you. Even in outline.'

'I'm still thinking.'

'Couldn't we make a start? Just start to let me know how you're feeling about the charges? About what you say happened.'

He arrived that evening in the police station, just the duty solicitor on call for drunks and careless burglars. And he found himself dealing with a terrorist, a kidnapper, or just a confused woman. I liked the way he didn't see a difference, just did the paperwork, did the talking, told me not to talk, made them take me to a hospital, X-ray my leg.

'If they don't grant an adjournment then we do have to have something to go into court with. I need something to brief counsel with.'

'Tell him the truth.'

'Which is?'

'I have to feed Zoe. I'm sorry.' The need is tugging down on my breasts, I must be with her again. 'We'll have to finish.'

CHAPTER TWENTY-ONE

'I shall be taking her as soon as I can. I thought you had a right to know my intentions—'

'Who?'

'Zoe, of course. I want to bring her up.'

I can feel the hard beating of my arteries, the pulse closing up my throat, a sudden panicking lightness at the back of my brain. 'What do you mean, taking her? Taking her where? How?' I'm pretending this is a shock when it is an axe I knew would fall, had to fall, would inevitably fall.

'To live with me. Six months the Governor said you had the right to keep her. After that I intend to adopt her.'

'Nine months if I can get a transfer to Styal.'

'What difference does it make?' Gareth lets the smile play round his lips. He knows the power of his words, he always has. Today he feels especially powerful. 'You're going to be here for quite a while, let's face it.'

'That's not the point.'

'Isn't it? Who's going to look after the child?'

'Not you.'

'I'm the natural father. A quick DNA test'll ratify that. I don't think there's a court in the land that'll stand between me and the child. I'll have my solicitor send you our counsel's opinion. It was incontrovertible.'

'I'm sure it was.' I'm trying to hide behind this sarcasm, to stay ironic and aloof, disengaged and uncaring, but inside I can feel something tearing. There's a rope already unravelling itself, the coir slowly turning and unthreading and pulling apart. My breasts start to ache – I want to feed her, to remind her of me, to fill her every second before she is gone.

When I look up again, Gareth is still sitting there on the other side of the table, his arms, his chalk-stripe suited arms still folded, paperwork spread across the table in front of him. You'd have thought he'd never want to see me again, and, though he's unwilling to look me straight in the eyes, here he is, the same man. In the corner, his solicitor sits watching, the Detective Inspector next to him, looking down, rubbing the edge of his shoes along the join of the lino. He knows me well, we spent whole days shut in those rooms together, talking or not talking.

'Is it normal for the chief prosecution witness to insist on a meeting with the accused?' I'm turning back to ask my own solicitor, sitting symmetrically opposite theirs.

'We explained the special circumstances, I believe Miss Dowson.' This is Gareth's solicitor. I don't even need to turn around, I know his petulant bark.

'We did agree to the meeting,' my solicitor says to me, adding a despairing shrug of the shoulders and a half-smile.

'Alright.' I turn back to face them all. 'Is there anything else you want then?'

'We need to know if you intend to contest it. It goes without saying it'll be much better for Zoe if you don't.'

I can feel the walls moving closer, the tunnel of the next ten, fifteen years shutting me off from my daughter. I'll see her every few months, visits like this, overlooked, watched, cold, pointless.

'I've got nothing more to say.'

Gareth stands. 'As you wish.'

In my cell, I'm alone but for Zoe's breathing next to me. I listen to the slamming of doors further down the Unit – someone's throwing a wobbly and Daphne's trying to calm her. None of us can really cope with coming back on the Unit after a visit, leaving behind that sniff of the world outside.

And it's going to be like this for years to come. Years in here on my own, without Zoe, knowing she is changing, being taken further and further away from me, sliding down that road to a country where she becomes a person who doesn't know me or want to know me.

I know now I cannot let this happen. I will fight them in every way they've left me.

There's not much in the prison library, but I'm reading whatever I can – mostly history, mostly twentieth-century. I'm reading about women and I'm reading about how things change. I'm starting to realise I'm not alone, that everything I've done is just part of something that's taking a whole lot longer. Vicki and Tom and Gareth have all existed before – and Jem and South, for that matter. We're just the ones who got caught in the vortex this year. It's a process.

What I want to know, what I want the books to tell me, is why does it have to be this way? Who makes it like this? Dora keeps telling me it's men.

Yesterday they came and complained about a photo of the Nuremberg trials missing from the *Radio Times*, apparently the issue's still current and there's something about football on the back. I couldn't deny it, the picture was there on the wall, part of the collage – the smirking man, the headphones, the judges. I told them to talk to Dora; I told them it was nothing to do with me. They said to stop mucking about, said that I'd done it, that it's part of this project of mine – they don't like people using the library too much, it scares them. I told them it's my cellmate who cuts out the pictures. They said I ought to have an appointment with counselling. And Zoe and I were confined to our cell for the rest of the day.

I've tried to write to Tom but they won't let me, not even censored. My solicitor is allowed to speak to his solicitor. He says Tom doesn't want to have any contact with me.

My solicitor tells me he's made a full statement, admitted his part in everything. But without naming anyone else.

The policeman's third bullet scraped Vicki's ear – the faintest graze, the doctors said. It hit the doorframe behind us – missing me completely – but a fragment, a large blunt splinter, ricocheted back off the frame, curving downwards and into the muscle above the back of my left knee. At the time, I thought Vicki had kicked me – only later, when my solicitor insisted on the X-ray, did they find the metal. It partially severed the tendon and my knee was still in plaster when I went into labour.

I'd been transferred here by then. There was talk that I was too dangerous to be let out to have the baby in a normal hospital, that my 'terrorist friends' would launch a raid on the maternity ward, blow it up, attack with submachine guns. The newspaper campaign was at its height, that security camera picture of Patty Hearst was being printed almost every day, people were saying I'm worse than the girl from the IRA. The Governor wasn't worried, said I'd be going to the Royal Cross when the time came, it wasn't possible to arrange a different hospital, they were used to that one. I was almost looking forward to seeing it again.

They took me in through the goods entrance in the basement – large cardboard boxes and porters leaning next to packing crates, smoking. I was having regular, spaced-out contractions but I was still aware of the armed policemen checking the doors ahead of us, standing above and around me in the lift – they'd decided to shackle my ankles, so I was in a wheelchair.

When we got to the ward there were more armed policemen sitting inert on metal frame chairs by the nurses' station. They all knew there was no armed gang out there waiting to 'bust me out' (*Express*), no 'New Age Desperados' (*Sunday Telegraph*) prowling the building for a chance to hustle me away. Even if there had been, I wouldn't've wanted them: I was too busy thinking about Zoe and the effort that would bring her into this world. But the newspapers had put pressure on the Governor and the Governor had put pressure on the police and the result was this armed posse surrounding me.

It wasn't until Kitty turned up that anyone thought to remove the shackles. She told me later that the news had gone round the hospital grapevine in minutes and she came up to the Delivery Suite. She was in uniform, full ID badge, so no one thought to stop her. She was intending only to stand by the wall and wait until she could let me know she was there if I wanted. But as soon as she saw the shackles, she lost it. She went down to the Sister and before long the Consultant was called and he insisted on them being removed. Which was the first I knew that she was there.

She stood alongside the bed as the Warder unlocked it and, I think, asked if that felt better. Of course, I was somewhere else, finding the strength to breathe, looking for a darkness that was somehow lighter than the rest of the darkness I was in. For what seemed like an eternity I had been concentrating on myself – from the outside world, I felt only hands on my shoulders and elbows and the sound of my own gasping. Now I recognised Kitty's voice, if not what she was saying – it was good to know that she was with me. I think I remember the weight lifting from my ankle when the shackle was removed but with the plaster round my knee it didn't make much difference.

Kitty was kneeling by the bed, her lips whispering in my ear between screams. I do remember words that only she could have said to me but the blackness in the air around me was too intense. She squeezed my hand and she tells me I squeezed hers back, but it may have been my only way to express the pain and the impossible squeezing happening inside me, turning me inside out.

And I thought about Nicky. I was quite clear-headed that it was Zoe I was waiting for, but my thoughts – whenever they took on enough shape to be called that – roamed through Nicky's short life, through the pain I had seen him endure and the happiness he had missed out on. I saw his newborn face at my breast, compacted and scrunched and desperate; I saw his heels kicking behind him as he ran towards a bouncing ball, the soles of his shoes forming a pattern in the air behind him; I saw his laugh, the wincing slant in his eyes when he knew he shouldn't find it so funny. These were momentary visions, thrown into my head like old photographs each time the contractions lessened, each time the graph of pain dipped and forced me to take a breath and remember who I was. It seemed as though I was doing this for Nicky, that the only good reason was him. I know none of this quite makes sense, but it did then, with a clarity that was the only possibility.

But as the contractions increased, I even started to lose touch with Nicky and the sense of purpose he had given me. Now there was only one need: to stop the pain, to surrender to the panic if that would make it end. And when my body seemed to be imploding, there's a sudden, bright emptiness and a sudden fullness and the midwife is handing her to me and she is at my breast. I haven't the strength to do more than let her settle there and let the joy flow down through me.

Apparently I asked 'It is Zoe, isn't it?'

And she said it was a girl.

And Kitty said something like 'She's beautiful.' I turned my head on the pillow and looked at her for the first time. Apparently I said 'Thank you.' Kitty's fingers swept the hair back from my eyes, dabbed sweat from my forehead.

And I remember looking back down at the matted head of this new woman called Zoe, bloody and smeary hair, strongly black, her stub of a nose, her high, puckered cheeks, her clenched mittens of hands, and her bluebrown eyes looking up towards me, all sensation and no thought. I thought of how this moment would never return for either of us – her day of perfect unsullied existence, my chance to be insulated from everyone else's determination to change me.

Dora's been inside for years – done a stint in all the women's prisons she says. She won't tell me how she got pregnant – just said something about a weekend pass. She was transferred here to have the baby and she'll be sent back somewhere else when the child is taken into care. She says this one's staying with her, she's preparing an appeal.

But she never talks about the murder, about why she's here. On purpose, I'm pretty sure. It's like she takes it for granted. She'll change the subject, usually to one of her stories. She'll start telling me about America during Prohibition, as though she was there, or the Spanish Civil War, as though she was in one of the brigades. I don't argue with her, I think she believes it herself.

'My lawyer says that as we are married, man and wife, were married at the time of conception, I am the child's legal father. I have every right to bring it up. Everything's on my side.'

I've asked for this meeting to be in the visiting room, surrounded by the anonymous formica tables, our eyes focused on the crimson, pleated foil ashtray in the centre. Dimitri feels uncomfortable, feels as though he is being watched. Which he is.

'Suddenly everybody's got lawyers.'

'I have to be sure of the facts. If we have to go to court.'

'Won't the court ask if you were capable of such an act at the time?'

'How are we to know?'

'I might tell them.'

'It'll be your word against mine.' His voice takes on the practised humility of the Twelve Step Programme. 'Anyway, even if I have to officially adopt, my lawyer says I've got a good chance.'

'Why does everyone want my baby?'

'She can't stay here forever, Hal.'

'I don't intend her to.'

'Then we have to make plans.'

'I am.'

'We have to ensure her future. If we just put our heads in the sand, there'll be a disaster.'

'Gareth intends to start adoption proceedings.'

'He'll have a job.'

'He can prove the child is his, not yours. Says he'll get a DNA test.'

'Let him. I'm the legal father, married in law makes me the father. There's plenty of precedent for it staying with me.'

'And he can probably prove you have depraved tastes in porn videos.'

'Please. Don't. Not again.'

'And there's your medical history. Your history of addictive behaviour.'

'Do you want Gareth to bring up this child? You want that?'

'I can't think of anything worse.'

'So who else is there?' Dimitri looks baffled.

'She's staying with me.'

'You know that's not possible.'

'Anything is possible. That's what I've learned.'

And so we go round, our words creating circular paths along which we chase each other, neither of us knowing who is fleeing and who is pursuing.

I haven't seen Nicky since the day Zoe was born. It's not surprising really. She needs me more.

I lie on my bed – most of our time is spent sitting or lying on our beds – and talk to Zoe about her brother. I'm telling her all about him.

She points her fingers in the air, telling me to look up, to stare up into the open spaces beyond her, beyond her eyesight. She moves in jerks, as though suddenly feeling a surge of electricity which is gone as soon as it arrives. I talk to her about how she arrived in this world, how I carried her through that time, how she was with me, giving me the conviction to carry on, even when it seemed so stupid or at best unreasonably optimistic.

And we both know the time has come for me to get tough, that there's no more time for pretending to be uninvolved.

She tells me she wants to stay with me and I must do whatever I can to achieve it. She doesn't mind how much it might hurt her in the future. We both agree this is the only way.

CHAPTER TWENTY-TWO

This time I am chauffeured to the police station, my first time out of here since Zoe arrived. Suddenly I have become a victim. I am still a risk, an unexploded bomb – but I'm a risk who must now be treated with grudging respect. The two CID men and one woman sent to collect me (all new, I've not had any of these before) are wearing heavy suits, cladding flesh that already seems to have grown an extra layer. They arrive at the Mother And Baby and block the doorway with their confident bulk.

They move me swiftly down the stairs into the yard and one sits on each side of me in the back of the car. The driver accelerates up to the sliding gates, guns the engine up the sliproad and we turn sharply into Parkhurst Road and up Seven Sisters.

And then we're dawdling through the North London traffic and I see that the city is still grey, angry and impatient. Inside Holloway, a world of bare concrete corridors echoing with shouts and slamming doors and trolley wheels, it's hard to imagine that normal life continues anywhere. Occasionally you have a visitor and they come in, wearing their outside clothes, reminding us of the possibility of bright colours – any brightness inside gets wiped out as soon as your clothes enter the prison laundry. Visitors have a sheen which make us seem muddied.

So it's a relief to be reminded of everything I am fighting to regain, that Zoe must be allowed to know this world. So this glimpse of North London is reassuring – it tells me I am doing the right thing.

Inside the dull, hessian-covered walls of the interview

room, I lay out the details of my allegation. They've given me a new Detective Superintendent, a woman this time, a rape specialist apparently, and she listens hard while the other one, the woman from the car, makes the notes. I concentrate on the red flashing light of the tape recorder and recite everything I remember. I am aware of the Superintendent nodding sympathetically, shutting her eyes occasionally, sometimes checking to see that her assistant has made a note of something she considers important.

When I get to the end of my story – now so long ago, it seems just like a story, one of Dora's stories – the policewoman puts down her pen and the Superintendent lets her head fall to one side and starts looking considerably less sympathetic. 'You realise that his brief, everyone for that matter, will say this is just a counter-charge to get you off the hook in the other matter?'

'Nothing I can do about that.' I'm aware I'm sounding hard. 'Am I supposed to just pretend it didn't happen?'

'Then why did you wait for so long? Why has it taken you until now to make the allegations?' The Superintendent leans forward, interlocks her fingers on the table between us, waits with studied patience.

'I decided to take matters into my hands. Well, you know all about that.' And my solicitor, until now sitting so quietly next to me, is instantly forward, his shoulders electric with tension, and whispering in my ear. He's reminding me that anything I say here, even though I'm here as victim, can still be used in my own trial. I tell him that's unimportant and he leans back, almost offended that I'm unwilling to play his game of concealment. I turn back to the Superintendent: 'Isn't that good enough? I mean, I'm not saying anything about what happened to Gareth and all that, but that's why I didn't rely on you first time round. Now I realise I should have and here I am.'

'Rape allegations are notoriously hard to make stick.

Like this, I mean, when it's just your word against his.'

'There's Zoe. She exists. She proves something, doesn't she?'

'DNA tests for parentage are rarely accepted by the court. Not in criminal cases. They're just too unreliable, apparently there are too many variables. What we need is proof. Proof that it was against consent, proof that there was some violence maybe, proof of his intercourse on that day, in the violent way you have described. The hard truth is that we rarely get a conviction unless the victim is examined by a doctor within twenty-four hours.'

'I was.'

Her eyes light up: 'What's this? Who examined you?'

'Me.'

Her shoulders slump. 'I mean a proper, full examination. Samples taken. Things like that. You know what I'm talking about.'

'It's in the Pathology safe at the Royal Cross. I gave instructions, Staff Nurse Hamilton took a sample. Took two I think. You'll find it dated and logged at the Pathology lab. It was signed in and sealed that night.' I watch the Superintendent's eyes open. 'Staff Nurse Hamilton took photographs on a timed and dated camera, the film is in the safe. Also signed and dated in. I suffered extensive bruising to the upper thighs and a bruise under my left eye. That's all recorded.'

I stop. There's a delicious silence in the room, moving out from me like ripples across a pond.

'OK. Sounds good, sounds terrific, well done. That proves that intercourse took place that evening, as you allege. But it doesn't prove it wasn't consensual. The event happened, but it's still your word against his as to whether it was rape.'

'He wrote to me afterwards. Twice.' And I hand them the notes Gareth sent me that week. I watch the Superintendent as she reads phrases like 'Did I hurt you?', 'I thought you wanted us to,' 'We must talk about this, I presume you're angry with me, I never meant to go against your wishes.'

Then the Superintendent looks at me. 'You were wise to keep these.'

'Thank you.'

'Just one question. Why the hell didn't you tell us all this earlier? Why have you kept it all secretly locked up?'

'The BonChem Corporation is a powerful animal. That evidence is precious. They would have destroyed it if they knew it was there. This conversation had to be on tape, with witnesses; the investigation had to be underway.'

'You could have arranged it earlier.'

'I also had to decide if this was the right way to proceed. Whether it was right for my child to grow up knowing this, knowing all the circumstances of her . . . creation. Finally, I realised there was no alternative.'

'It's a shame you didn't come to us straight away, after it happened I mean. Let us sort it out.'

'I got interested in other solutions.'

'But they don't work, do they? You proved that.'

'Did we?'

And my solicitor, feeling more indiscretions are imminent, leans forward, distracts the Superintendent with technicalities, talks to her about witnessed statements, forensic tests, samples from the suspect.

So things are happening. I listen to the jargon and just hope I can manage to keep some kind of control.

'It was a long valley, more a hollow, dead-ended and narrow, cutting straight into the flank of the West Virginia ranges. Those valley sides were steep, covered in trees, magnolia, scarlet vine – in the heat of summer you need a machete to cut through. In the Spring, the children'd hide out up there, pretend they were someone else. And the air, even down in the river-bed, it was always thick with sap, thick with green. It could have been a real good place.'

Dora's stories have become a balm. We lie on our beds, the noises from the corridors exploding beyond the door, metal and concrete clashing, shouts corkscrewing down the stairwells. But inside our room, with the stories – telling them as though they happened to her – we build walls round our private world. Dora talks to me alone, explaining, making real everything I just read about. I never see her with anyone else. She belongs to me.

'The man I got in with, he was born there, met up out East and he took me back when we got married. He got a job in the mine, alongside his Pa and his brothers, his sisters were wed to miners. Since the day the company arrived, mining was all anyone there knew. Before, they'd been trappers, now they were miners. Except no one wanted coal anymores – later we learned to call it the Depression, but right then it was just the owners trying to cut us.

'Arriving there, coming down that road into the hollow, all I saw were these houses like chicken coops up on stilts, a rusting railway line, a pitted road, children running round barefoot and rickety.

'Some of the houses were painted – yellow or green, whatever was in the company store that year – and some weren't even painted, the weather pasting its own colour onto the clapboard. Either way the company owned them all. The company owned the houses and owned the road running through the old river bed and it owned the mines – the one there in Stopes and the one in Mammoth in the next valley along.

'A man earned about three dollars a day for it, whatever it was. But we didn't ever get to see US dollars. We got paid in company scrip. Raggedy, thin aluminium things, run through with holes, you could only use them at the company store. Except prices there were fixed so it came out worth about sixty cents – at least, when you went to the movie house in Charleston, that's all they gave you for it. And you couldn't ever save, you were always in hock to the store. They weren't making money out of coal, they were making it out of the store.

'The kids never had enough. We had three by then, three boys, and my man was a cutter down at the face. You got a bit more money but his work was the hardest. Everyone knew if you got injured, they didn't want you no more, just took the next man. That's if they didn't bring in some machine. Those days we lived off potatoes, beans and sow belly.

'And then the company decides on a wage cut. It was '31. Says they can't pay even pay the lousy three dollars. Except the owners are sitting there in Washington in comfortable suits and their mansions up on Dupont Circle and we're living in shotgun shacks, five of us in two rooms, not even shoes for to go to school. And they want us to drop twenty cents a day.

'So we went on this march, up to the state capital. Governor came out wearing a white suit and told us a hard-luck story, said he was doing everything he could. But when we got back to Stopes, the company started evicting anyone who'd done any talking up there in the capital. Whole families left sitting in the road by the telegraph pole, just an umbrella for shade, their bed and chairs stacked alongside.

'Except there was trouble, these were people's homes. They'd decorated them, possum skins on the doors, grown vines up the stilts. They'd planted trees in the yards and they'd sat swinging on the porches and they'd walked along the river edge in their best Sunday dresses like anyone else. They were girls and boys like anywhere else, except here a company man in Washington could tell them to get out of the home they grew up in. Men who tried to stop the evictions got thrown in jail. And more people got angry. And we had this meeting, called it a Speaking, down on land at the end of the hollow – company wouldn't let us hold a meeting on their land, but there was this rail stockyard down there, about the only thing the company didn't own. And my man insisted on standing up and saying his bit and there were stoolpigeons there and I knew from then on there was going to be trouble for us too.

'They sent organisers down from the East, the union, telling us about how we had rights and we could do what we wanted, even stop working if we wanted. We were the ones with power. Some of these organisers were workers, men who'd taken to working for the union full time, and some were boys and girls, Ivy League types, straight hair, straight dresses. They told us about how in Russia the workers owned it all anyways and that sounded pretty good. And they got us singing and suddenly the strike was on. The union sent us down lorries of food from the East, sometimes even fresh food from nearer by. We were eating better than we ever had – and we were on strike.

'And there was one girl, dark black hair, bobbed, from one of those East Coast colleges, wearing trousers tucked into boots and talking about world revolution and Trotsky. And my man thought she was pretty well something. Thought everything she said came straight down from the mountain. And she needed someone – she wasn't union, she was just filling in time before she went back to her New England life – she needed someone to do her bidding and she saw my man sitting there at the front of the hall, a little puppy dog, and he was going to be her one. Gave him books and things, told him he should get educated, be an organiser – all he had to do was everything she told him to do. That wasn't going to be a problem – he'd bought the package the moment she smiled at him. He came back to the house full of it all, but I knew it wasn't just politics that was getting inside him.

'Course the company sent in breakers. They was mostly blacks. And you couldn't blame them, they was near-starving down there in Atlanta and these white folk come along and offer them jobs for pay. But you had to stop them all the same. There was some name calling and then shooting and other kinds of trouble.

'She gave my man a gun. Told him the company had his name down on a piece of paper somewheres. What did he know what to do with a gun? Gentlest man you ever met – he was a dreamer looking for something to believe in; he couldn't say no to her, not about anything. People told me they were together up on the slopes, but I knew it didn't matter. Somebody else told me she'd seen them kissing. I thought, maybe that'll make things better afterwards, after she's gone. We were all waiting for some great change that was going to make the valley into the Garden of Eden. We were all dreaming, I reckon.

'My man was out there every night, out with her and I knew we were riding for a fall. I told him he was falling in deep with something he didn't understand and he just looked at me like I was dirt. I decided to stay back, look after my boys, and wait till it was all over.

'And then we heard the company was going to agree terms. We could go back on the higher wages and no more company scrip, real US dollars. There was dancing down that night. Except there was a note on my table. Said he was going back East with her, going to work for the union full-time, go round making speeches for the workers. Said he was Sorry But. He left a dollar bill, everything he'd ever saved. Said his brothers'd see us right, he'd spoken to them.

'Except the company twisted everyone. The miners all went back to work, waiting for pay day, still two weeks behind. And what do they get? Company scrip. Rate was up but still in company scrip – and when we got to the store, the prices were up. We'd been through that whole strike for nothing, got nothing, but wasn't anybody in that valley had the heart to start again. Men walked to work thinking they were somewhere else.

'So that wasn't a good moment for him to come back to the valley. She'd dumped him at St Louis. Just left him there on the track and jumped on to a Pullman going North. Left him a note, tied to his cardboard suitcase. She said Sorry too. Said she'd made a big mistake but it was never going to work outside the valley. Sorry But.

'So when he stood there at the door I took him in. I was the only person he could tell. But it wasn't good for him. The company knew he'd been a union organiser and they'd taken his job and everyone in the valley knew he'd agreed the deal which the company had gone back on. They knew he'd run out on me and come back like a sick dog. They weren't good days but I reckoned he'd stick it.

'He was awake most nights. So it got how he'd be the one to take the baby out back to change the diaper – the youngest was still in a crib by our bed. Then he'd bring him back changed, lie back down in the bed, try and sleep, usually just lie there. So I didn't even wake when the baby cried that night and he got up like always. The Constable reckoned he wrapped a blanket round the muzzle – it was the gun she'd given him.

'There wasn't a note this time. But he didn't need to. He'd read the books and listened to all the ideas and reckoned he'd found what he'd been looking for and ended up with nothing. And he was leaving us with nothing and he reckoned that was his fault and it was better to make it like it had never happened. Except those communist books of hers, the ones that started all this, they were still sitting there on the window sill.

'As soon as they took the bodies away – him and the boys

– I sat down and started reading them. Looked to me like they made some kind of sense.'

Apparently the Deputy Governor has agreed it. Apparently Vicki has been distressed since we met, agitated, and she's only just been given a computer screen and finger-operated alphabet cursor to spell out a letter at a time. Once they realised it was me she wanted to see, the doctors had to convince the Governor it would be therapeutic and he had to decide if it was worth the overtime for the warders to escort me over there: Vicki's now in a special unit on the other side of London, in a hospital which specialises in her kind of brain trauma.

I'm learning all this in the car over there. Hazel and Jane got the job – these car rides are getting to be a habit with me, Hazel says, they've never had a prisoner ferried around all the time like me, I must be something special. Jane stares out front, unamused. Hazel even managed to borrow a baby car seat from her sister-in-law and Zoe's strapped in the front, watching the roofs go past. Hazel sits next to me in the back. She unlocked my shackles as soon as we were in the traffic.

The hospital is in West London, beyond the flyover, beyond the Victorian terraces, in a hinterland of concrete and indecision. It's a low, terraced building, built in the Sixties, with a wide stretch of green in front, snaked with rose beds and wide-spreading azaleas. There are the standard park benches dotted about the lawn where, as we pull up on the gravel drive, patients are sitting with family members trying to find a way to communicate or nurses smiling and thinking of other things. All the patients here have suffered some kind of brain trauma and they all sit with those glassy eyes staring out from their in-body captivity.

We find Vicki in her wheelchair next to a new bench, the

pine still bright yellow. Hazel stands next to me while Jane goes and drags another bench over so that they can sit directly opposite and watch. Jane wants to shackle me to my bench but Hazel makes it clear she's not prepared to be part of that and goes and sits on their bench, opening up the newspaper she brought. Jane sits with her hands in her lap, primly watching me. 'Half an hour, remember, that's what the Governor said.' I smile to let her know how much I appreciate his generosity.

Vicki is already fighting to move the cursor along the screen towards the first letter of the first word. To move it one letter along, she need only lift her little finger to which the electronic contact is strapped – but each movement up and down seems a labour. Eventually: G.

Her arm is tense again, setting the cursor off towards the other side and I can hear how forced her breathing is. Her head is clamped in a brace attached to the back of the chair and she has to force her eyes down to watch the flashing square move across the screen. U.

And the cursor is moving back along the line of letters now. I want to guess but know I shouldn't forestall her. But I look at my watch and realise we have already used up over ten minutes. Jane is watching us carefully but she cannot see the screen and I turn my head away whenever I speak to Vicki – in case Jane thinks she can lip-read. Jane's a high-flyer, bored with the drudgery of routine work on the Unit, waiting for her promotion to High Security or Central Planning or the Home Office. N.

And Vicki looks across towards me, her eyes alight with achievement and sweat breaking her brow. I try to share her delight but I have no idea what she is trying to tell me. She wants a gun? She has a gun? Something about the gun we had? 'Keep going,' I say, but I can see she is exhausted.

Her finger moves on the button again. N.

I squeeze her hand as she moves the cursor. I wait. O.

'You can't go on? That's alright.'

But Vicki's eyes are angry and I realise she's already moving the cursor on again. P.

'Nop?'

Even angrier eyes. The cursor is going back down the alphabet now. Twenty-five minutes have been used up. I.

'Right. N-O-P-I. Keep at it.' I can see she is flagging. The effort it demands from her is new and she is determined to master it, break out of its restrictions. I look at my watch because Jane is looking so resolutely at hers – twenty-nine minutes. N.

'Nopin?'

Vicki's eyes are saying, That's right, Understand me. But I don't. I can't.

'Time's up.' Jane is looming over my shoulder.

'Can't be.'

'The Governor said half an hour. You've had more. We must go back to the car.'

'Please, just five minutes, we're almost there.'

'Hazel comes alongside. 'The traffic was a doddle over here, we can say it was bad. It usually is.'

'That's not the point.' Jane likes points. 'The Deputy Governor said thirty minutes. That's what she's allowed. That's what we've given her. More.'

I can see Vicki desperately begging me to understand. But I can't say it out loud, not with both of them standing next to me, not if it's something to do with a gun. 'No pin, is that it?'

And Vicki's face is suddenly full of light. Her facial movement is limited, but what she gives me now is translucent joy. She slumps back into the brace supporting her. I lean down to squeeze her hand. 'I'll try and get back soon, soon as they'll let me. All right?'

Vicki's eyes tell me to hurry back.

And anyway, I have to come back. I haven't a clue what she's trying to tell me.

CHAPTER TWENTY-THREE

'He can hardly come and see you, can he? He only just got bail. Dimitri's hands work overtime on the table in front of me, fingers tangling like snakes in a pit. 'And he had to go to the High Court for that.'

'But getting you to do it, to come here. You agreeing to do it. It's sickening.'

'He's explained a lot of things to me.' He flips the foil ashtray over and is surprised when remnants of ash slew across the formica. He tries to wipe the surface clean and ends up with a black smear down the edge of his hand. 'Also I have to accept that I wasn't behaving . . . you know, before . . . normally, like I should have been. He had to do various things for my own good. I know at the time I didn't quite realise. I do now.'

'Gareth does what he wants. Right now he wants you again and you've fallen for it. When he doesn't need you any more, he'll drop you again.'

'You mustn't be so cynical.'

'You haven't got religion, have you?'

'I've met some people who've taken comfort from it. But I came here to talk about Gareth. To try and find a solution for both of you.'

'I thought you were fighting for Zoe? The two of you thwacking it out like Tweedledum and Tweedledee?'

'We've talked about that. He's helped me a lot. I'm not ready, I mean this wouldn't be the right time for me to try bringing up a child. I still haven't got over Nicky.'

'Why do you always give in to him, give him what he wants on a plate?' I want to lean over and slap Dimitri's face.

Except that would end the visit immediately. Maybe that's not such a bad idea.

'He's the natural father, you have to admit that has a certain power. I hadn't seen it that way before.'

'He raped me. He doesn't deserve the name Father.'

'That's exactly it. He didn't. He knows you're just doing this to spoil his court action for Zoe.'

'Get real, Dimitri. This isn't some dream of mine – I took samples at the time, he admitted it in a letter, they're prosecuting him. It's serious – like you said he only just got bail.'

'He says you wanted it.'

'No, really?'

And suddenly Dimitri is ashamed when he says: 'There is some evidence for that.'

'Why are you here, Dimitri?'

'Gareth wants to know what he has to do for you to drop all this? It's no solution, taking him to court, it can't change what happens to you, where Zoe ends up.'

'He wants to deal.'

'No. I've got strict orders: No Deals, No Compromises. He just wants to try and understand and make things better for you so you don't have to go all the way with this silly rape thing.'

I can't believe that's what he said. 'Go all the way?'

'I mean it really doesn't have to get to court, does it?'

'Out of my hands, sorry.'

'Don't be ridiculous, it all hangs on whether you give evidence against Gareth. You can pull out.'

'So can Gareth.'

'He had half his ear cut off!' For the first time Dimitri's face comes alive.

'I was raped. I was vaginally penetrated by a man's penis against my will. My body was invaded and a seed left growing inside me. Maybe all in all I'd rather lose an earlobe.'

'You're talking nonsense.'

'You're talking like a man.'

And we find we're both sitting back, lips flushed with anger, his fingers now tightly clenched, my arms tightly folded. This is a row we had many million times and are both shocked to find we are having again.

'Anything more to say?' I know I am doing this to irritate him.

'Look, the point is, can we sort this out, before it gets to court?'

'Gareth knows what I want.'

'He's not dropping the kidnapping thing. He can't. He'd be a laughing stock.'

'He can hack it.'

'He won't. I know he won't.'

'Then he'll have to face the consequences for once.'

Whenever I return to my cell, she's always waiting there for me with another story. I look forward to them, I want the music. They lock me in and there she is, sitting on the armchair. What is she telling me?

After America, she says, after reading the East Coast woman's books, she went to the Soviet Union, because she'd been told that's where the workers owned everything. She says it was the best time of her life, in the tractor factory, in the electrification platoon, in the Party. Somehow she avoided the purges, Stalin's massacres, never even knew about them at the time – she heard rumours, but Russia's always swimming in rumour, she says. Believe just half of them and you're certifiable.

And when the War came, she was in Leningrad and decided to stay. 'I had another boy. But he went off to a Pioneer Corps.'

'How many have you had, Dora?'

'Who knows? What does it matter – none of them live. It's all men and their arguments eating up my children.'

'And all boys?'

'Till this one.' Her baby girl sits on her lap, staring back at me. 'Something's finally coming to an end. Maybe it's all coming to an end.' For a moment, she seems to lose the thread, submerged inside her own thoughts. Then she snaps back: 'Do you want to hear about Leningrad or not?' She asks petulantly as though this is a treat I have been begging for. I want to say No. I want to tell her these stories are wearing me down, rubbing away at my skin and leaving me exposed and defenceless.

'My man was in a protected occupation, in electrification, that's where we met. But once the Nazis got close to the city he joined up. Was sent almost straight to the front. But it was only fifteen miles away, getting closer every day. We used to go and visit him – get on the tram at Nevsky Prospect and get off when you could hear the guns. The trains were still getting into the city and there was plenty of fuel – none of us knew what was going to happen later. When he was sent back from the front for a rest, he could telephone through and we'd take him some food. All the wives did it, even if it wasn't their own husbands.

'He was killed the day the Nazis pushed into the suburbs and captured Schlusselburg on the shores of the lake. My man's unit found themselves facing panzers and all they had was rifles from the Civil War.

'Which left me alone, pregnant. That was the day I found out I was expecting. The day the city was cut off, the day my husband died and the day Leningrad discovered it was fighting for the history of Europe. There were three million of us trapped inside that city and every one of us knew that if our city fell, Moscow would fall and Russia would fall and Hitler would rule Europe. It was so simple. For weeks we had been working, every hour – concrete blocks, barbed wire, gun emplacements, road blocks – miles and miles of it round the city. You worked ten hours each day and a rest day every seven, two if you were working outside the city limits. I was just like you, I didn't tell any person I was pregnant.

'That was September. On the eighth, the Badayev warehouses were hit by incendiaries. The air in the city was raw with the smell of roasting wheat and melting sugar and we were getting three hundred and fifty grammes of bread a day. Then the electricity had to be rationed. In October, the Germans captured Tikhvin and cut off the rail link and we were down to two hundred and sixty grammes and less than half of that was flour, mostly wood and cellulose. People were taking up floorboards to find food that had been dropped, flour under bakery floors, malt under breweries.

'By January, even though the ice road was open across the lake, a thousand people were dying every day. Two thousand maybe. Three thousand. How do you tell the difference? Can you imagine a thousand and then two thousand? How different do they look? What does it matter as long as it's not you?

'I couldn't tell them I was pregnant. They would have evacuated me. I didn't want that. I wanted to be there. I ate my ration and thought about my babies – by now I knew it was twins.

'The Spring was good for the cold but it meant the ice road across the lake was gone and it meant that when the snows melted, you found what was under it. Rubbish and bodies. People who had dropped down in the street, unable to go on, covered with snow and ice. Can you imagine a thousand? Can you imagine two thousand?

'By now it was clear I was pregnant. But my twins belonged in this city, however long it took for us to be rescued. They were born in July and I wasn't surprised they were both boys. By then I knew how my life was going to be. They were healthy, fresh with new life. But I knew everything would change with the coming winter. And it came soon too, harsh winds as early as September and blizzards by October. The ration just wasn't enough for the three of us, I wasn't making enough milk. By November the choice was clear. Some people in the apartment block said it was a crime. Some said it was brave. But no one stopped me, no one could suggest any other way, and worse things got done during those days. He screamed a lot on the first day, he was so terrified, so confused. I lay with a pillow over my ears and the other one in my arms, rocking him, squeezing him, believing in him. By the evening, he was dropping in and out of sleep. He'd wake suddenly and start crying, hoarser now, his energy seeping out of him. By the next morning, he was comatose and started to move away from us. I watched my milk flow into the other one, I could see him getting stronger already. While I watched that, the other one went.

'It meant the two of us would survive – twins was a luxury Leningrad could not support. And he did survive that much longer – thin, spindly, sad-looking but alive. He lived until the week after the siege was lifted, he was eighteen months old. They sent in trucks loaded with food and I watched them from the window, holding him as he went cool in my arms.'

CHAPTER TWENTY-FOUR

'There is no possibility of the prosecution against you being dropped.' For the first time, DI Nichols' face shows anger. All we've been through, dissecting the events in that house by the cliffs, talking through each moment, and he never once lost his cool – he sat and asked me questions as though it was a history test and even though I wasn't getting any of the answers right, he barely ever raised his voice. But now he's angry. 'We intend to proceed with all matters.'

'Without Gareth Elliot's evidence?' This is my solicitor, hovering as ever at my shoulder, his voice a definition of incredulity.

'I will say it again: Mr Elliot has become a victim of blackmail. We do not intend to see him lose his rights as a result.'

'That's an outrageous charge. If this meeting was being taped—'

Nichols sets his face: 'You threatened him with a rape charge. Of course he had to back down. I'd probably do the same myself.'

'Both your colleagues in the police force and the Crown Prosecution Service decided there was a charge to answer. The samples were fully verified and accepted. The letters were effective admissions of non-consensual intercourse.'

'He's been scared off and we all know it. Why wasn't the matter brought up earlier? You only brought it up to use it against the chief prosecution witness. Which is why we'll be looking into a charge of perverting the course of justice. There's also the firearms charges at the very least, even if we can't proceed with the actual kidnapping.'

'Your only witnesses will be police officers, who were too busy shooting defenceless women to notice the actual circumstances.'

'Defenceless!' Now Nichols is shaking his head, disbelieving. 'She was armed to the nines. Attempted murder is what she'll be facing when she's well again.' It seems as though we all want Vicki to recover, but for different reasons. Not that there's any hope of recovery.

'This whole thing is going to end up looking like a fabrication. No jury'll stand for it – hounding people who were just trying to make a new life, bringing various environmental concerns to public notice.'

'I think the jury will see the truth of the matter.'

'It won't be admissible to mention the rape matter in court. They won't know why Mr Elliot isn't giving evidence. It's a collapsing house of cards.'

'The jury'll draw their own conclusions. Any sane man would see the poor man has been blackmailed.

'But there are no witnesses to show what he is scared of: why on earth should he be scared of these people?'

'The ransom note. Don't forget that.'

'No prints. There's nothing to link that note with my client.'

'Apart from her known history with BonChem. She was on bail for terrorist offences against them already.'

'Terrorist? What's happened to the right to protest?' These two men sit on either side of the table, butting at each other, chests out, rebounding backwards from each collision, staggering, not quite losing their balance, moving forwards again.

'Peaceful protest, yes.'

'If you were going to fit someone up for this, obviously it's going to be one of the existing protesters.'

'This'll never get through committal.'

Nichols stands. 'You'll be hearing from the CPS when

they've reassessed the situation.' And he walks out of the room. My solicitor indicates to the warder that we need another five minutes. The door is shut and locked again.

'I'm not really surprised,' says my solicitor. 'The police hate it when this happens.'

'I thought I'd be walking out of here.'

'They're going to keep after you. The firearms charge is the tricky one. You were definitely found in possession of it – as a group, with common purpose. That can carry a hefty penalty – years in prison, as many as the judge fancies really. Even without the kidnapping matter, they can still strongly imply it, everything that goes with it. They can use the sentence for the firearms to allow for everything else.'

'We can't let them.'

'I just don't see how.' He's slipping files back into his case. 'You were lucky with the rape matter.'

'That wasn't luck.'

'No, of course not. That's not the sort of thing I meant. Not that. I meant, it's turned out, you know, well, to be in our favour.'

'It's a case of justice. Balancing the scales.'

'I suppose it is. Yes. Then we'd better deal with this matter of the gun for you, hadn't we?'

'We need to speak to Vicki. She's the one who bought it, got it.'

'But she's . . . can she?'

'You need to speak to her.'

Dora's stories guide me through my own life. She is my own voice: she tells me everything I know, making me listen, making it real.

In the Sixties she came back to Britain and found it throwing off its colourlessness, willing at last to embrace itself. It seemed like a golden age, she said. And she avoided men and the sons they would give her – she was learning the lessons fate wanted to teach her.

By 1974 she'd met a man. She smiles 'I know, I know.' Soon there were more sons. She was living in the Park Hill flats in Sheffield and her man was a steel worker. The last son, Jeremy, was born the day her husband was laid off. The new world order was starting to bite and it bit straight into Dora's home, chewed it up and spat it out.

'My man's father had been in the steel mills and his father. It's what my man expected to do. All of them in Sheffield expected it. It was the same year as the Falklands thing so it was no good telling him the Koreans were making it cheaper. He didn't care about Koreans. He was a Sheffield man who made steel, he'd never thought about them that was buying it or not buying it. That's not how it works, is it? You can't tell a man there's no point in wasting time on book-learning because there's plenty jobs down the foundry and then tell him there isn't going to be any more work and he should've got himself some qualifications. You can't tell him it's his fault when it isn't.

'There were three boys and soon he couldn't stand the sight of them, always there, always looking at him sitting there in his armchair, drinking up the redundancy and not even thinking about finding some other work. He didn't know about any other kind – he only knew about the foundry, been going down and visiting it since he were a nipper. He didn't ever think about how else to earn money – didn't want to work in a shop or factory, it was not what he was, I mean, not as a man. You can't blame him.

'He did a few weeks as a security guard and packed it in. Come to think of it, he packed the Foreman in with an uppercut and that was that. He wanted to use his skill, what he could do with steel, not just walk around a chainlink fence and put a tick in a book and feed a dog. Every night he put on that stupid blue uniform with those stupid blue epaulettes he felt like a tosser, he said. He looked like one too – not that I told him. I tried to keep him going, but we both knew we were fooling none but ourselves.

'The eldest was ten. Starting to need a Dad – you could see it in his eyes. He looked up at his father and saw a man who was drunk from giro day until it ran out. His Dad hit him – there was no other way he could talk to him, no other way for them to speak. He reached out his meaty fist and struck the boy and the boy howled and that was it, they were talking. There was no other way for them.

'Before long he was at the other one as well. The eight-year-old looked at his brother taking a pasting and he wanted to know why, wanted to hear the talk they had between them. He looked at his father and the look was enough.

'I didn't ever leave him alone with the youngest, my little Jem, five years old, he was too breakable, too vulnerable, looking up at the world around him and not knowing why. I kept him by me all the time my man was around. Most of the time he was in the boozer with all the other steel men who'd lost their lives.

'But I fell asleep one night before he got back. I was that tired. I woke hearing this strangled cry, this gargling noise. I ran into the kids' room and he was at his throat, my eldest's, squeezing the life out of him, the poor thing didn't stand much of a chance. The other two were on his back, like monkeys, trying to pull their father off.

'By the time the police had arrived, my eldest . . . he was still alive but his brain had done without too much air, they said. He lay there in the hospital, drips and things, not moving nothing. Until we switched him off.

'I went back home. He was sitting there in that chair, watching Doncaster or Chepstow or whatever. The police had said there wasn't enough to prove what happened, not enough to take him to court. I got the bread knife from the kitchen, came up behind the chair and, hard as I could, I pulled it across his throat, pushing and sawing for everything I was worth. I didn't look, I shut my eyes and sawed. It wasn't sharp enough though – it cut him, but didn't slice him open like I'd imagined. He fell forwards onto the carpet, yowling, and I waited to see this blood waterfalling down his chest but it didn't. So I lifted the knife up high above my head and brought it down into his back, into the kidney they said. And I pulled it out, watching the serrated edge ripping up his skin, and I pushed it in again and again and again. There was plenty of blood now.'

'How long ago was this?' I ask, almost scared to hear the answer.

'About ten years ago, twelve.'

'And what about your sons?'

'They went into care. The middle one, eldest now, he was fostered. The little one—'

'Jem?'

'That's right. He went into a home.'

'Your son was called Jem?'

'You know he was.'

'Where is he now?'

'I don't know. They wrote me a little while back, last year, he'd run away. They were still trying to trace him.'

'Do they know where he went?'

'They all go to London, don't they? Nothing good ever comes of it.'

'I met him. I tried to help him.'

'I know.'

But then the door is suddenly open and Jane is standing there with a tray and Dora is gone again.

This time it's raining and Vicki is parked in the day-room – green paint and a herd of pilled, tweedy chairs and a television. She's in the corner when we arrive, already fixed on her computer screen, forcing it to do her work. On the monitor so far: 'N.O. – F.I.R.'

I kiss her on the top of the head, it smells of purity. 'What's this?'

She goes on driving the cursor across the screen.

'I.'

We all – solicitor, Hazel and Jane again – sit around her, watching as she slowly picks off the letters.

'N.

G.

–

P.

I.

N.' And she leans back, gasping for air.

'No firing pin in the gun: is that what you mean?' Suddenly my solicitor is eager, alive. 'In the revolver you were found with?'

Vicki smiles at him.

'Why not? What use was that?'

She continues.

'I.

–

C.

O.

U.

L.

D.

N.

T.

–

A.

F.

F.

O.

R.
D.
–
A.
–
R.
E.
A.
L.
–
O.
N.
E.'
'Why did you get it then?'
'F.
O.
R.
–
A.
–
L.
A.
U.
G.
H.
–
W.
O.
U.
L.
D.
N.
T.
–
Y.

O.

U.

?'

'You mean, when I thought I was going to have it, it didn't have one? Was never a real weapon?'

'It was never much more than a replica. This is incredible.' My solicitor looks like a man who wants to dance round the room. 'It means you were never threatening violence. They can't say attempted murder. They can't say attempted anything. The most they can go for is Threatening Behaviour, maybe Possession of a Firearm.'

'But why haven't they told us? About the gun being useless?'

'They probably don't even realise themselves. Or if they do, they want us to admit to something before they reveal it, then it won't matter.'

I squeeze Vicki's hand and touch her cheek. She had allowed her head to sink back into the headrest, sweat in droplets on her skin. She surges forward again.

'W.

E.

–

D.

O.

N.

T.

–

K.

I.

L.

L.'

'Of course not.' Except Vicki's eyes know that I went into that room to see if I could pull the trigger.

'Their case is in ruins. Utter ruins. I'm going to ring the Crown Prosecutor now, demand to see the gun, have it

339

examined by an expert. They'll know I'm on to them. Then I'm going to get you bail, probably have to go to the High Court. You'll be out of that prison tonight, latest.' And he's rushing off across the ward: 'Where's a pay-phone?' he's shouting at one of the nurses. 'I need to make an urgent call.'

I realise we've been here two hours, while Vicki slowly scraped across the alphabet. She's fallen asleep now, exhausted, her eyelids pulsing and jerking, dreaming of easy movement. A nurse comes and wheels her away.

Hazel nods her head towards the car park and I follow her and Jane down the corridor.

Back in the cell, Dora has folded her sheets and blankets on her bed and now she's packing everything she owns into a carrier bag. 'I'm going,' she says simply.

For a moment I'm crushed. I realise how much she has become a part of my life, I expect her voice, her stories. And I need to ask her more about Jem. 'You've been . . . I mean, where are they sending you?'

'No one's sending me anywhere. That's not how it is. I've decided to leave. Thought I'd tidy up before I go, take a few necessaries with me.'

'I don't understand. You can't just decide.' I'm panicking – that she's going, that she thinks she's going. I've always known she could go whenever she wanted.

'You can come with me if you want.' She's picking her daughter up, lowering her into the sling round her neck.

'They won't let you just go.'

'She's something special, isn't she?' Dora's looking into her daughter's eyes. 'My first daughter. Somebody that's made it all worthwhile. All those years, all those boys of mine. This little one's obviously special.'

'They're not going to let you just walk out of here, Dora.'

'I'll find a way. You must come with me, after what you did for Jem.'

'What do you mean?'

'I know about everything you did for him. I know about all my sons. I forget none of them. They're all in my stories.' Her voice is still calm, still unhurried, unafraid. I watch her stuff the last few things into the bag, knot the top. She turns back to me. 'Come on then. Time to go.'

Zoe is sitting on my lap and Dora takes me lightly by the shoulders and I find I'm standing up and the Deputy Governor is hovering in the doorway. Just him and me in this cold, single room. I'll never see Dora again.

'Ready then?' he asks, his voice calm and sounding kind.

'I think so,' I say, but I'm confused.

'What about all your books?' He gestures at the piles on the windowsill, the books I've had sent in.

'I'm leaving them. The library can have them.'

'Are you sure? There's quite a few there. Must be worth a few bob.'

'They've served their purpose.'

'Well, thank you. I'm sure the Education Department'll be overjoyed, they can start a whole new history section.'

The Deputy Governor smiles at me, everything forgotten: it's as though we have always been friends and nothing ever happened.

'What about all your collages?' He points at all the photos on the wall. 'Want to take any of them?'

'They belong here as well.'

'You're probably right.' He bends and picks up my holdall. 'I'll take this. You've got your hands full. Ready?'

He leads me past the play area – Hazel's clearing up the toy pen and Jane is sitting in the control office watching through the perspex. Everyone else is locked in. Hazel waves at me as we go through the pass door and down the corridor.

We pass through all the look points, waiting between gates, Zoe alert and watching the metal plates slide, until finally we are by the open door, the reception desk, the evening light beyond. We walk outside and he drops my holdall at my feet.

I think he asks me if anyone is meeting me and I say I hope so. He hands me my bail form, says Good Luck Then and turns to go back inside.

I'm standing there in front of the huge green concertina door, Zoe cradled in my arms, the traffic of the city moving past. We are alone in this city for the first time.

Nicky and Jem cross Parkhurst Road and start walking towards me down the sliproad. I watch them as they cross in front of me, unaware of me, talking about something I can't hear. The skin of Jem's face and arms is pure and new, his eyes shining.

When they're almost out of sight, I lift Zoe up onto my hip, pick up the holdall and set off down Seven Sisters Road.